HOLDFAST IMPERIUM

Christopher Mitchell is the author of the epic fantasy series The Magelands. He studied in Edinburgh before living for several years in the Middle East and Greece, where he taught English. He returned to study classics and Greek tragedy and lives in Fife, Scotland with his wife and their four children.

City Ascendant
Dragon Eyre Badblood
Dragon Eyre Ashfall
Dragon Eyre Blackrose
Dreams of Kell
God Restrainer
Holdfast Imperium
World's End

Brigdomin Books Ltd
First Edition, January 2023
ISBN 978-1-912879-70-0

For my father

ACKNOWLEDGEMENTS

I would like to thank the following for all their support during the writing of the Magelands Eternal Siege - my wife, Lisa Mitchell, who read every chapter as soon as it was drafted and kept me going in the right direction; my parents for their unstinting support; Vicky Williams and Marilyn Hopwood for reading the books in their early stages; James Aitken for his encouragement; and Grant and Gordon of the Film Club for their support.

Thanks also to my Advance Reader team, for all your help during the last few weeks before publication.

THE PEOPLES OF THE STAR CONTINENT

There are five distinct peoples inhabiting the Star Continent. Three are descended from apes, one from reptiles, and one from amphibians. Their evolutionary trajectories have converged, and all five are clearly 'humanoid', though physical differences remain.

I. **The Holdings** – the closest to our own world's *Homo sapiens*. Excepting the one in ten of the population with mage powers, they are completely human. The Holdings sub-continent drifted south from the equator, and the people that inhabit the Realm are dark-skinned as a consequence. They are shorter than the Kellach Brigdomin, but taller than the Rakanese.

2. **The Rakanese** – descended from amphibians, but appear human, except for the fact that they have slightly larger eyes, and are generally shorter than Holdings people. They are descendants of a far larger population that once covered a vast area, and consequently their skin-colour ranges from pale to dark. Mothers gestate their young for only four months, before giving birth in warm spawn-pools, where the infants swim and feed for a further five months. A dozen are born in an average spawning.

3. **The Rahain** – descended from reptiles. Appear human, except for two differences. Firstly, their eyes have vertical pupils, and are often coloured yellow or green, and, secondly, their tongues have a vestigial fork or cleft at their tip. Their heights are comparable to the Holdings and the Sanang. Skin-colour tends to be pale, as the majority are cavern-dwellers. Their skin retains a slight appearance of scales, and they have no fingerprints. They are the furthest from our world's humans.

4. **The Kellach Brigdomin** – descended from apes, and very similar to the Holdings, they are the second closest to our world's humans. Their distinguishing traits are height (they are the tallest of the five peoples), pale skin (their sub-continent drifted north from a much colder region), and immunity to most diseases, toxins and illnesses. They are also marked by the fact that mothers give birth to twins in the majority of cases.

5. **The Sanang** – descended from apes, but evolved in the forest, rather than on the open plains that produced the Holdings. As a consequence, their upper arms and shoulders are wider and stronger than those of people from the Holdings or Rahain. They are pale-skinned, their sub-continent having arrived from colder climates in the south, and they occupy the same range of heights as the Holdings and Rahain. The males bear some traits of earlier *Homo sapiens*, such as a sloping forehead and a strong jaw-line, but the brains of the Sanang are as advanced as those of the other four peoples of the continent.

DRAMATIS PERSONAE

Colsbury

Karalyn Holdfast, Dream Mage

Kyra Holdfast, Karalyn's Daughter (8 years old)

Cael Holdfast, Karalyn's Son (8 years old)

Sable Holdfast, Mage

Belinda, Third Ascendant

Silva, Faithful Servant of Belinda

Shellakanawara, Custodian of Colsbury

Kelsey Holdfast, Blocker of Powers

Frostback, Kelsey's Silver Dragon

Halfclaw, Frostback's Mate

Agang Garo, Sanang Retiree

Van Logos, Banner Commander

Lucius Cardova, Banner Officer

Alara'osso (Lara), Captain of the *Giddy Gull*

Travelling to Colsbury

Daphne Holdfast, First Holder of the Republic

Thorn Holdfast, Soulwitch, Empress-in-Waiting

Caelius Logos, Banner Sergeant

Olo'osso, Dragon Eyre Pirate

Pechtang, Matriarch of Sanang's Brother

T'Lang, Matriarch of Sanang's Brother

Plateau City

Bryce, Bridget's Son and Emperor-in-Waiting

Keir Holdfast, Storm Mage

Daimon, Imperial Mage

Brogan, Bridget's Eldest Daughter

Bedig, Bridget's Son from Triplets

Berra, Bridget's Daughter from Triplets

Bethal, Bridget's Daughter from Triplets

Tabor, Holdings Vision Mage

Tabitha, Holdfast Housekeeper

Tilda Holdwain, Young Aristocrat

Ravibattanara, Rakanese Clay Mage

Nadia, Rahain Stone Mage

Dean, Kellach Fire Mage

Broadwater, Sanang

The Matriarch, Ruler of Sanang

Aberfeld of Hold Terras, Holdings Vision Mage

Holdings

Weir, Deputy First Holder

Celine Holdfast, Hold Fast Estate Manager

Jemma Holdfast, Celine's Apprentice

Cole Holdfast, Keir and Jemma's Son (9 years old)

Marchside, Kell

Corthie Holdfast, Convicted Felon

Aila Holdfast, Demigod from City

Killop Holdfast, Corthie and Aila's Son (2 years old)

Konna Holdfast, Corthie and Aila's Daughter (2 thirds old)

Kallie, Chief of the Kell

Ulna, Dragon Eyre

Blackrose, Queen of Ulna

Maddie, Blackrose's Rider

Ashfall, Dragon from Lostwell

Austin, Rescued Demigod

Shadowblaze, Blackrose's Mate

Greysteel, Blackrose's Uncle

Oto'pazzi (Topaz), Master of the *Giddy Gull*

Atili'osso (Tilly), Captain of the *Sow's Revenge*

Vizzini (Vitz), Master of the *Sow's Revenge*

Ari'anos (Ryan), Carpenter's Mate

City of Salve

Emily, Queen of the City

Daniel, King of the City

Lady Aurelian, Daniel's Mother

Lady Omertia, Emily's Mother

Elspeth, Emily and Daniel's Daughter (1 year old)

Naxor, Released Demigod

Lydia, Surviving Demigod

Doria, Surviving Demigod

Jade, Guardian of the Salve Mine

Dawnflame, Guardian of the Salve Mine

Implacatus

Edmond, Blessed Second Ascendant

Bastion, Edmond's Lieutenant

The Magelands
The Unknowable Ocean
Realm of the Holdings
Shield Mountains
Royston
Holdings City
Blackwater
River Holdings
Barrier Mountains
Plateau City
Inner Sea
Arakhanah
Sanang
Twinth
Broadwater
Mya
Beechwoods
Tritos
Black Mountains
The Plateau
Rainsby
Forbidden Mountains
Basalt Desert
Grey Mountains
Akhanawarah
Tahrana City
Jade Falls
Rahain Capital
Calcite City
Brig
Domm
Fire Mountain
Kell
Lach
Rahain Republic
N

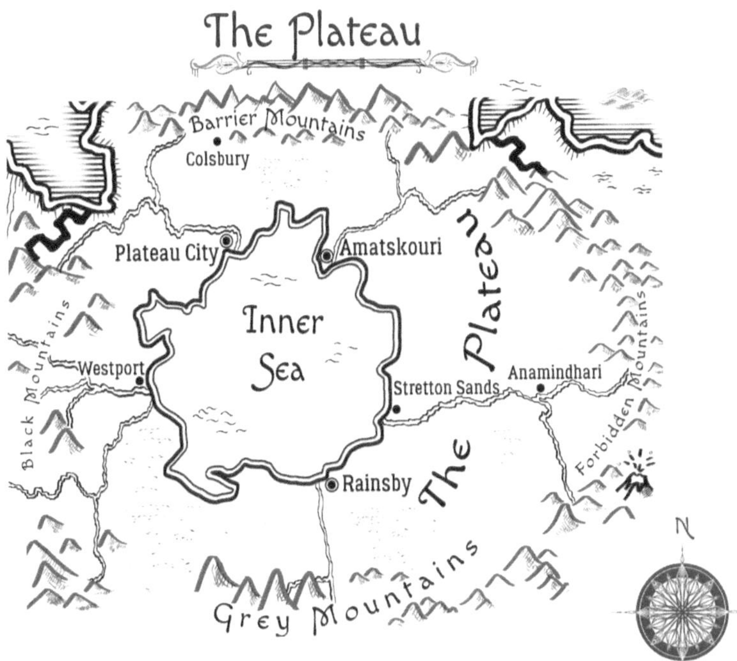

The Plateau
Barrier Mountains
Colsbury
Plateau City
Amatskouri
Inner Sea
The Plateau
Black Mountains
Westport
Stretton Sands
Anamindhari
Forbidden Mountains
Rainsby
The
Grey Mountains
N

Kellach Brigdomin

CHAPTER 1
WAKING FROM THE NIGHTMARE

C olsbury Castle, Republic of the Holdings – 17th Day, First Third
Autumn 534

Belinda screamed in the darkness.

She lifted a hand from the sweat-drenched sheets, and her fingers brushed her eyes. No mask was covering her face. She shuddered, her breath ragged and hoarse.

'Everything's all right, my Queen,' said Silva. 'You are safe.'

Belinda glanced to her right, and saw the demigod crouching in the shadows by the bed. Silva had barely left her side since they had returned from Implacatus; first staying with her in Dragon Eyre, then moving into the room that had been assigned to the Third Ascendant within the walls of Colsbury's Great Keep.

'Was it the same dream, my Queen?' Silva said.

'It's always the same dream,' said Belinda. 'It's always the mask. Light a lamp; I hate the dark.'

Silva rose to her feet, and lit one of the chamber's wall lamps, dispelling the thick shadows.

'It will soon be dawn, my Queen,' the demigod said.

Belinda sat up. 'Stop calling me that. I am the queen of nothing.'

She looked down at her hands. 'I should have died when Lostwell was destroyed.'

Silva sat on a chair by the side of the bed. 'Please don't say that, your Majesty. You are the most precious being in all the worlds.'

Belinda shivered. 'I hate this place; I hate Colsbury.'

'I know, my Queen. I hate it, too.'

'I've never belonged here.'

Silva said nothing.

'And I hate the Holdfasts.'

'I hate them, too, your Majesty,' said Silva; 'but, at the same time, I have to acknowledge that, without them, it would have been impossible to rescue you. After we were chased out of Cumulus the first time, it would have been easy for the mortals to have given up; but they didn't. Karalyn, Sable, and Kelsey – they risked their short lives to save you.'

Belinda kept her gaze lowered.

'What about Corthie, your Majesty?' Silva went on. 'You used to say he was like a brother.'

'Then, where is he?'

'Karalyn explained that; don't you remember? Corthie is in prison, somewhere far away.'

Belinda stared at the bed sheets. Her memories were confused and unreliable; her dreams mixing with reality. At times, it seemed that all she could remember was being locked within the agony of the restrainer mask; everything else seemed vague and fleeting.

'How long was I in the mask, Silva?'

'I don't know, my Queen. When I arrived in the Palace of the Almighty, you were wearing the spiked crown. At some point, Edmond or Bastion must have removed the mask and placed the crown upon your head in its place. If you were put into the mask as soon as you were captured on Lostwell, then I would guess that you remained in it for at least two years, but I cannot be more precise.'

'Two years?'

'Yes, your Majesty. You will recover. Do you remember Princess

Yendra? You met her in the City of Salve. She was in a restrainer mask for three centuries, and she recovered.'

Belinda felt sick trying to imagine what three centuries in the mask would be like. To her, two years had been an unceasing, living nightmare that dominated her every waking thought. Two years had been enough to break her; to shatter her sense of self.

'I am not as strong as Yendra,' she whispered.

'You are an Ascendant, my Queen. Compared to you, Yendra was a child.'

'You don't understand, Silva. It's been ten years since Karalyn scoured my mind; six, if we exclude the four years that vanished when Karalyn took Sable and me to Lostwell. That means I spent a third of my waking life in that mask. The crown was a blessing after that – I can't remember anything from the time I wore the crown. I wish I was still wearing it.'

'The crown made you no better than poor Theodora, your Majesty. Unlike the First Ascendant, you were still breathing, but your mind was a void.'

'But I could feel nothing,' said Belinda. 'And now? All I feel is pain and shame. I want to die, Silva. I don't want to be immortal.'

'You will feel differently in a hundred years or so, your Majesty. Trust me. You sound like a young god; someone struggling with the concept of living forever. It will wear off.'

Belinda pulled the sheet from the bed, and placed her bare feet onto the cold floorboards.

'Edmond once told me the same thing,' she said. 'In Alea Tanton. He told me that I cared about mortals because I was acting like a young god. Then he destroyed my world, while I watched. If the price of immortality means hardening my heart until I am just as cold and ruthless as other gods, then I don't wish to pay it.' She glanced at Silva. 'Leave me. I need to wash and dress for another meaningless day.'

Silva stood and bowed her head. 'Shall I fetch hot water for you, my Queen?'

'Cold is fine. Go.'

The demigod bowed again, then left the room. Belinda gazed around at the small bed chamber. Of all the places to have ended up, why did it have to be Colsbury? She remembered opening the gates to Agatha and her army. It was the worst act of her life that she could recall – Colsbury was the scene of her great betrayal, and it felt like a punishment to live once more within its walls. She walked over to a table, upon which sat a basin and a jug of water. There were no mirrors in the room, and that made her glad. The last thing she wanted was to be confronted by her own reflection. She washed, then pulled on fresh clothes, selecting the dress that sat on top of the neat pile of garments. She wondered who the clothes had belonged to. Kelsey, perhaps, or maybe Sable. No, not Sable. Sable didn't wear flowery gowns. She always dressed for battle, even within the peaceful confines of Colsbury. Belinda glanced at the bedroom door. Beyond it lay the rooms of the other occupants of the Great Keep, including Kelsey and Sable, and Belinda felt a sense of dread at having to mix with them. Much had changed over the years since Lostwell had been destroyed, but Belinda had missed it all. Karalyn's twins had been babies when Belinda had left Colsbury, and now they were eight years old. Of all the Holdfasts, Belinda wished to see only one – Corthie, and he was languishing in prison. It didn't seem right, but Kelsey had assured her that it had been Corthie's choice.

She opened the door, and peered out into the corridor. To her left sat Karalyn's rooms, while Kelsey and Van were living in the suite opposite Belinda's bedchamber. For once, there was no sign of Silva, and Belinda felt a twinge of relief mixed with guilt.

'Good morning, Ascendant,' said a cheerful voice.

Belinda turned, and saw Lucius Cardova approach, with Cael by his side. She didn't know the Banner soldier very well, but he had been part of the operation that had freed her from Implacatus; and she knew that he was in love with Karalyn.

'Cael and I have been out for a walk,' Cardova said, halting. 'The gardens are beautiful in autumn.'

'Did you see the graves?' said Belinda.

'Yes. You can't walk through the gardens without passing them.'

'That is why I haven't been there. Almost everyone buried in the gardens is dead because of me.'

Cardova smiled, though his eyes flickered with concern. 'That was a long time ago.'

'It feels like yesterday.'

'Can we get some breakfast?' said Cael.

Cardova nodded. 'Perhaps Belinda would like to join us?'

'She doesn't want to,' said the boy. 'She doesn't like Colsbury.'

'All the same,' said Cardova, 'it's our job to try to make Belinda feel welcome. It takes time to recover from what she's been through, Cael.' He smiled at Belinda. 'Just a coffee?'

Belinda suppressed her initial reaction, and nodded. They walked along the corridor, passing the rooms that held more Holdfasts, and entered the kitchen. Sable was there, along with a young woman called Lara, who had been introduced to Belinda as Sable's girlfriend.

'Good morning,' said Cardova. 'Is there any coffee?'

Sable looked up, a cigarette balanced in the fingers of her left hand. 'There might be enough for a couple of cups. There's plenty of food.'

'I'm not hungry,' said Belinda.

'I was thinking about Cael,' said Sable.

The boy sat down next to Sable, and she ruffled his hair, then pushed a bowl of bread towards him. Cardova went to the stove and lifted the coffee pot, as Lara eyed Belinda.

'Why are you looking at me like that?' Belinda said.

Lara shrugged. 'I'm still getting used to living alongside a bleeding Ascendant.'

'Belinda isn't like the other Ascendants,' said Sable.

'She doesn't want to be a god,' said Cael, between mouthfuls of bread.

'Is that right?' said Sable.

Belinda sat. 'It's none of your business.'

Lara snorted. 'How about a tiny bit of gratitude, eh? Sable nearly died saving your ass, Belinda. You seem like a god to me – all arrogant and cold. Is living with mortals beneath you?'

Sable frowned at the young woman. 'Leave her alone, Lara.'

'What? I thought you hated her?'

'I used to,' said Sable. 'A lot has changed since then.'

Cardova placed a mug of hot coffee in front of Belinda, then he sat and lit a cigarette.

Belinda coughed from the smoke, her eyes never leaving Sable. What had the woman meant by her words?

'Have you checked on Holder Fast's location this morning?' Cardova said. 'Is she any closer?'

Sable nodded. 'They're a few hours away. I offered to use the Quadrant to bring them here, but Daphne wants to enter Colsbury her way.'

'What's changed?' said Belinda.

Sable raised an eyebrow.

'You said that a lot has changed, and somehow that means you don't hate me any more. What has changed?'

Sable narrowed her eyes. 'Do you remember Old Alea?'

Belinda nodded. 'I remember a little.'

'Do you remember me, you and Corthie, fighting side by side to protect the Sextant from Edmond? That was the first and only time we have ever worked together. Then, later, I learned that you had sacrificed yourself to save Corthie and Aila. I can hardly hate you for that, can I?'

Belinda stared at her. 'Do you imagine that we are now friends?'

Sable laughed. 'No. But, I no longer loathe you. We have both made mistakes, and now we are both here; or should I say *back* here? We have things in common that I can't ignore, Belinda. We were both accused of treachery, and we were both sent away to Lostwell. Neither of us feels at home in Colsbury, and I can understand that. We are also the only two people here who have killed Ascendants.'

'Frostback and Kelsey have killed two Ascendants,' said Cardova.

'I meant, on our own,' said Sable; 'not with the aid of dragons or blocking powers. Belinda killed Arete, and I killed Kolai.'

Cardova smiled. 'You killed Kolai, Sable? This is the first time I have ever heard that story. No, wait – it's the hundredth time.'

'I'm the greatest mortal god-killer of all time,' said Sable. 'Can you blame me for mentioning it?'

'You're certainly not the most modest mortal of all time,' he said.

'Why would I be modest, Lucius? Anyway, I was saying that Belinda and I aren't as dissimilar as I had once believed.'

Belinda continued to stare at her. 'I don't like you.'

A shadow of disappointment passed over Sable's features, then her usual self-assurance re-asserted itself.

'We are not the same,' Belinda went on. 'You are cruel and dishonest; a liar and a cold-blooded murderer. You manipulated soldiers into slaughtering civilians in the markets of Plateau City. I haven't forgotten that, nor have I forgotten a multitude of other sadistic crimes you have committed.'

Sable said nothing, and took a draw of her cigarette.

'You cheeky bitch,' said Lara. 'Is that what we saved you for – so you could sit here and insult us?'

Belinda turned to the young woman. '*You* didn't help save me; and I was insulting Sable, not you. You are nothing to me, Lara.'

The young woman's eyes tightened. 'The Holdfasts should have left you on Implacatus.'

'It's too early for this shit,' said Sable.

Cael looked up. 'I'm telling mama that you said a bad word.'

Sable laughed. 'No one likes a snitch, Cael. People won't say things in front of you if they think you'll run off to tell your mother.'

Lara got to her feet. 'Come on, Sable. I ain't sitting here with Belinda; not after the way she spoke to us.'

Sable stood. She stubbed out her cigarette, and turned her eyes towards the Third Ascendant.

'I'm here if you want to talk.'

'Why would I want to talk to you?' said Belinda.

Sable shrugged, then she and Lara left the kitchen. Cardova sighed, then sipped from his mug of coffee.

'Do you hate me, too?' Belinda said to him.

'I don't know you enough to hate you,' he said. 'You're rude, cold and arrogant, but after everything you've been through, none of that surprises me. You don't trust anyone. Again, who could blame you for that? What you need to realise is that there are people here who care about you; people who are prepared to be patient. People like Karalyn; and Sable, too. Personally, I thought the plan to rescue you was insane, but Karalyn, Kelsey and Sable were determined to try. Three dragons also risked their lives in Cumulus – for you, Belinda.'

'Why did you help?' Belinda said. 'You admitted that you don't know me.'

'I didn't do it for you,' he said. 'I did it for Karalyn. Does that matter now? You're here, in one piece.'

'My mind is broken. My body may have healed, but my mind hasn't. I fear sleep, because I have the same nightmare, over and over; and I hate being awake, because all I think about is the nightmare.'

'The restrainer mask?' he said.

'I can still feel the nails in my eyes; I will always feel them.'

'Only fourteen days have passed since we brought you back from Cumulus,' Cardova said. 'It might take months before you start to feel normal again.'

'That's the problem. What is normal? I have never lived a normal life; not one that I can remember. I was the wise old Queen of Khatanax, but I have no memory of those days. After I was scoured, I spent less than three years on the Star Continent – with Karalyn, and then with Thorn; and then I was sent to Lostwell and the City of Pella. How would I know what normal felt like?'

Cardova met her glance. 'What do you want?'

'To die,' she said.

He shook his head. 'Please don't say that to Karalyn; it would break her heart.'

'The way she broke mine?'

'She loves you.'

Belinda nodded. 'And part of me still loves her, despite everything that passed between us. The only Holdfast who has never hurt me is Corthie. I miss him.'

'He'll be getting out of jail in just over a month. Karalyn or Sable can take you to Kellach Brigdomin to visit him.'

'I could use the Sextant to bring him here.'

Cardova smiled. 'Why haven't you?'

'Because I can't bring myself to look at the Sextant, let alone use it. Lostwell was my home, Lucius; my realm. Without it, I am nothing. Seeing the Sextant again would only remind me that my life has been a failure.'

She got to her feet, determined not to cry in front of the Banner soldier.

'Where are you going?' said Cael.

Belinda hurried from the kitchen without responding. To her relief, the corridor was empty, and she strode past the closed doors, then ran down the stairs of the Great Keep. She emerged into the open by the base of the keep, and filled her lungs with fresh air. On the other side of the large forecourt, dozens of workers were busy repairing and modifying the huge bulk of the Summer Palace, so that it would be ready for Thorn's return to Colsbury. Belinda couldn't bring herself to think about her old friend, nor about the fact that Empress Bridget was dead and gone. Thorn's ambitions had always annoyed Belinda, and yet it seemed as though half of the Empire was supporting her claim to be the new Holder of the World. It didn't make sense.

Belinda turned away from the palace, and walked towards the ruined quayside. She passed the scarred exterior of the tall Spire on her left, then noticed that the harbour was also swarming with workers. A new pier was being constructed, along with a wide boatshed, and Belinda changed her mind about visiting that location. She needed to be alone, not surrounded by workers. She turned right, and came to the gates by the western entrance of the castle gardens. Belinda paused, and glanced down at the spot where Lennox had died. Would Karalyn's husband still be alive if she hadn't opened the gates to Agatha? It occurred to her that she did share something with Sable – between them, they had destroyed Lennox.

She resumed walking, and passed through the gates. Despite what she had said to Cardova, the gardens would be peaceful, and she craved some quiet solitude. Many of the trees were starting to lose their leaves, and the grass was littered with them. She selected a path and walked deeper into the gardens, her sandals crunching on the gravel. She reached the central fountain, then began to veer away from the cemetery, the sight of it making her feel sick. She stopped. A lone figure was standing by a grave, a bunch of flowers clutched in her hands. Belinda watched as the figure crouched by the graveside. She laid the flowers down by the stone slab, and arranged them.

Belinda swallowed, then strode forwards.

The figure turned.

'Good morning, Karalyn,' said Belinda.

'Good morning, Belinda.'

'Why do you come here every day?' said the god.

Karalyn got to her feet. 'Why don't you?'

Belinda frowned. 'Because it would make me feel even worse than I already do. This is the first time I have been in the gardens since you rescued me.'

'I know. In answer to your question, I come here to talk to Lennox.'

'Do you believe he can hear you?'

Karalyn narrowed her eyes. 'No. He's gone, Belinda; I know that. All the same, I can't live here and not visit his grave. The time I spent with Lennox, both here and in Domm, was the happiest in my life.'

'What about Cardova?'

Karalyn turned back to stare at the grave.

'Are you in love with Lucius Cardova?' Belinda went on.

'Aye. I am. It makes me feel guilty, as if I am betraying Lennox. And then I think – what if I had died, and Lennox had lived? Would I want him to be alone? No. I would want him to find someone else; someone who made him happy.' A tear rolled down her cheek. 'The twins have no memory of their father, and they have no memories of me, not until I returned from Lostwell.'

'I'm glad you're not alone.'

'Are you?'

Belinda remained silent, unsure how to respond. Did Karalyn blame her for Lennox's death? Probably, though she had never said it.

'My mother will be arriving soon,' Karalyn said, 'along with Thorn.'

'I know.'

'My mother is unhappy that I left Colsbury to rescue you. She blames me for her nearly being executed.'

'Why are you telling me this?'

'To warn you. My mother might not be overjoyed to see you here, Belinda. She might lose her temper and say something stupid. Don't take it personally.'

'Will Thorn be happy to see me?'

'I have no idea. You used to be close, didn't you?'

'We were best friends for nine months, and then we weren't. I hated her by the time we got to Colsbury. She cared about nothing but attaining power.'

'And now she has it. As far as the Holdings and Sanang are concerned, Thorn is the new Empress.'

'Are you going to help her against Lord Bryce?'

Karalyn shrugged. 'I will if Colsbury is attacked, but I'm not going to go on the offensive. I've already missed too much time with my children. I intend to stay in Colsbury. Daimon won't be able to harm us if Kelsey and I are here.'

Karalyn lifted her head, as if she had heard something.

'Mother's wagon is crossing the bridge to the island,' she said. 'You should come with me, to greet them.'

'Why?'

'If there's going to be a scene, then I'd rather we got it over with as soon as possible.'

Karalyn began to stride away, then she halted and turned back to face Belinda. The god frowned, then walked after her. They went along another path, and took the tunnel that went under the Lesser Keep. They emerged into the castle forecourt, close to the front of the Summer Palace. Others were already waiting there, including the majority of the workers who had been busy repairing the palace. Belinda saw Sable and Lara among them. Kelsey and Van Logos were also there, chatting to Silva by the edge of the small crowd.

Karalyn walked to the front of the group, and Belinda remained by her side. Silva saw her, and rushed over.

'Where were you, your Majesty?' the demigod said.

'I went for a walk,' Belinda said.

'I was worried about you, my Queen,' said Silva.

Belinda turned away as a wagon rolled through the arched gatehouse. It was being pulled by four horses, and two young Sanang men were up on the driver's bench. They led the wagon over to the small crowd, and pulled on the reins. One of the men leapt down to the cobbles and walked to the rear of the wagon, while the other stepped up onto the driver's bench, and raised his arms.

'Bow your heads!' he cried. 'We have brought her Imperial Majesty Empress Thorn back to Colsbury. Bow your heads for the new Holder of the World!'

The workers obeyed the young Sanang man, and a few fell to their knees as Thorn and Daphne climbed down from the back of the wagon. Belinda kept her chin high, and watched them approach. Thorn was dressed in blue, and Belinda almost smiled at the sight.

'Thank you, Pechtang,' Thorn said to the man on the driver's bench. 'It is good to be home.' She scanned the crowd, then glanced over her shoulder. 'Olo'osso,' she said, 'I believe your daughter is here.'

An older man jumped down from the back of the wagon and charged into the crowd. He reached Lara, who grinned and laughed as he picked her up and whirled her around.

'My sweet little Alara!' he cried.

'Put me down, father,' she shrieked.

Daphne smiled, then her eyes roved over the crowd. She shared a long glance with Karalyn, then her gaze fell upon Belinda, and she frowned.

Belinda stepped forward. 'Don't blame Karalyn, Holder Fast,' she said.

'Who said anything about blaming anyone?' Daphne said. 'We survived the dungeons of the Great Fortress in Plateau City and, now that we have returned, we shall be too busy to apportion blame.'

Thorn glanced at Belinda. 'Hello, old friend.'

'Hello,' said Belinda.

Thorn walked forward a few paces, then stopped a couple of yards in front of the god.

'I am happy to see you safe,' Thorn said. 'Karalyn was determined to rescue you from the moment she learned you were still alive.'

Belinda nodded. 'You still like the colour blue, I see.'

Thorn smiled.

'Where's Keir?'

Thorn's smile evaporated. 'Has no one told you?'

'Sable told me that he had betrayed the Holdfasts and was working with Lord Bryce against you.'

'Then why did you ask?'

'She is doing it to be petty,' said Daphne. 'Ignore her, your Majesty. Come; we have much to do.'

Daphne led Thorn into the Great Keep, and the crowd dispersed.

Silva frowned. 'Holder Fast should not speak to you in such a tone, my Queen.'

'She has every right to,' said Belinda. 'I was being petty. Thorn always insisted that I would eventually realise that Keir was a better man than I thought he was; but I was right, and she was wrong.'

'She's the Empress now,' said Karalyn. 'And let's not forget that you fell for Naxor. You were both blinded by love for men who might not have deserved it.'

'You're right,' said Belinda. 'I loved Naxor, or I thought I did.' She looked around and saw Sable standing back from Olo'osso and Lara, who were laughing together. Belinda walked over to her. 'Sable,' she said.

Sable turned. 'Yes?'

'I'm sorry I blamed you for trying to seduce Naxor. I was wrong, and I know that now.'

Sable raised an eyebrow. 'To be honest, I wasn't aware that you blamed me for that.'

'Naxor tried to seduce you in Old Alea, but you rejected him.'

Sable laughed. 'That's right. I'd almost forgotten. What did you ever see in him?'

'I don't know. Will you take me to visit Corthie when he is released from prison?'

'Of course. I miss him, too.'

Belinda smiled. 'Thank you, Sable.'

Another older man approached. He passed Belinda and Sable, and embraced Van.

Van smiled. 'Father.'

'It's good to see you back, Caelius,' said Cardova, who was standing close by.

'You too, Lucius,' said Caelius. 'After fourteen days on a wagon with Olo'osso, I'm happy to see some Banner faces again.'

Olo'osso glanced over from where he was talking with Lara. 'The feeling's mutual, Banner rat.'

Cardova, Van and Caelius glowered at Lara's father.

'There are three Banner rats here now,' said Cardova. 'If you insult Caelius, you insult all of us.'

Olo'osso slapped his thigh and laughed, then Lara made an obscene gesture at the three Banner men.

'That's my girl,' said Olo'osso. His gaze fell upon Belinda. 'And who is this? Might it be the fabled Third Ascendant; the one Holder Fast complained so bitterly about all the way home?'

'I am the Third Ascendant,' said Belinda.

Olo'osso chuckled as he walked over to where Belinda stood.

'You don't look like one of the most powerful gods in all creation,' he said.

'Her Majesty could strike you down with a glance,' said Silva.

'No doubt,' Olo'osso said; 'but then again, so could Empress Thorn, or even Shella, for that matter. It thrills my heart to be in the presence of such deadly women. So, Miss Belinda, are you on our side, eh?'

'And which side is that?' said Belinda.

'The side of Empress Thorn,' he said. 'I notice you didn't bow your head towards her Imperial Majesty.'

'Queen Belinda bows to no mortal,' said Silva.

Olo'osso frowned at the demigod. 'Is this your personal sycophant, Miss Belinda? I always wanted one of those. Hey, Alara, perhaps you could walk by my side, announcing to all and sundry how wonderful I am.'

Lara snorted. 'Dream on, father.'

'I have yet to decide if I shall acknowledge the legitimacy of Thorn's claim to the throne,' said Belinda. 'When I do, it shall be to her that I will speak, not to you, Olo'osso.'

Olo'osso raised an eyebrow, then turned to Sable as if Belinda hadn't spoken.

'I hope you will forgive me, Sable,' he said, 'but I intend to steal my daughter away from you for a short while, so that I can catch up with her. I hope you have been treating her well.'

'Don't embarrass me, father,' Lara said, tugging at his arm.

Olo'osso performed a mock bow, then strode off with Lara. Sable chewed her lip for a moment, then exhaled.

'Mother will expect us all upstairs,' said Karalyn. 'She probably has a hundred plans cooking in the back of her mind.'

'Have you given them their powers back?' said Sable.

'Aye,' said Karalyn; 'the moment their wagon entered Colsbury. Daimon will be able to see them now, but he won't be able to touch them, not with me and Kelsey here.'

'I'm sorry I got you into trouble,' said Belinda.

Karalyn turned to her. 'Mother can be as angry as she likes, but I'll never regret saving you from Edmond.'

The rest of the group began to make their way into the Great Keep, but Belinda stayed where she was.

'You go,' she said to Karalyn. 'I don't belong in there.'

Karalyn nodded, then she followed the others, leaving only Silva and Belinda outside.

Belinda lowered her gaze. 'I don't belong anywhere.'

CHAPTER 2
THE FUNERAL PROCESSION

Plateau City, The Plateau – 17th Day, First Third Autumn 534

Keir watched as the wagon pulled into the forecourt of Colsbury Castle. Four horses were hitched to the front, and the two young Sanang men on the driver's bench brought them to a halt in front of a small crowd. One of the men walked to the rear of the wagon, and helped the passengers down onto the cobbles. Keir ignored everyone else for a moment as he watched Thorn step down from the wagon's rear. She was dressed in blue, and was as beautiful as the day he had first met her in Rainsby.

His wife... No. Not any more. The divorce that Keir had both longed for and feared had come to pass; it had been one of Empress Bridget's final commands. Eight years of marriage – brought to an end with a few words. Keir watched Thorn walk to the front of the crowd, his mother by her side, and he noticed Belinda standing next to Karalyn. It was true, he thought – Thorn had a god on her side. He remembered Karalyn saying that she had restored Belinda's full range of powers; if that was true, then Belinda was as strong as Agatha had been. Keir tried to take a closer look, but something was blocking him from entering the minds of anyone in the crowd. He could watch from a distance, but get no nearer. Kelsey. It had to be. He couldn't see her in the crowd, but that made sense, as she was invisible to his powers.

Keir felt a tightness in his chest as he observed Thorn and his mother enter the Great Keep of Colsbury. Almost his entire family seemed to be there, gathered in the same place, united against the new Emperor. They were traitors, he told himself, disgusting traitors; and yet he almost wished he was in Colsbury with them, so strong was the feeling of isolation that dwelt within his heart. He had chosen the Empress over his own family, and then the Empress had died, struck down by the poison brought by Kelsey and Lord Naxor from the City of Salve. His thoughts hardened. Salve had robbed the Empire of Bridget, and those responsible for the wicked conspiracy deserved to die for their crimes, even Kelsey. Yes, even his sister. The little girl who had slavishly followed him around the Hold Fast estate in his youth had gone forever, replaced by a young woman who was just as spiteful as Karalyn. For peace and justice to prevail, the entire nest of traitors had to be rooted out and destroyed.

That's right, Keir, said a voice in his head. *Rooted out and destroyed.*

Keir froze. He hated sensing Daimon within his mind, but was also fearful that the dream mage would perceive his discomfort. He tried to smother his revulsion at the intrusion into his thoughts.

Daimon laughed. *You have nothing to fear from me, Keir,* he said. *I know which side you're on.*

Keir composed himself. *Did you see Thorn and my mother arrive?*

Aye. I was watching, just like you. Our enemies are gathered in the one place. This is good. It means they are too scared of me to go on the attack.

Keir glanced down at the castle forecourt. The crowd had dispersed, leaving only Belinda and her faithful demigod Silva standing on the cobbles.

They have Belinda, he said.

I see her.

Can you read her thoughts?

No. Her mind has been moulded by Karalyn. She wiped the god's head; wiped it clean, then rebuilt it from nothing. Impressive work, but I've read the thoughts of her servant. Lady Silva has her doubts about Belinda. She doesn't want the Third Ascendant to assist Thorn; she thinks the gods should remain aloof from the petty struggles of mere mortals such as you and me, Keir. Silva shall be my instrument. Through her, I will ensure that Belinda does not interfere with our plans.

Keir smiled.

Do you understand, Keir? Daimon said. *There's nothing to worry about; I have it all in hand.*

Keir felt a surge of confidence flow over him. Daimon was right. There was nothing to worry about.

Daimon severed Keir's connection to Colsbury. Keir blinked, and glanced around the small office within the upper levels of the palace in Plateau City. He got to his feet and left the chamber. The palace was busy, but subdued. Soldiers and courtiers were milling around, but almost no one was speaking, and their faces reflected the deep sense of grief and shock at the death of their sovereign ruler. There was an undercurrent of anger, too; a deep feeling of rage that Bridget had been taken from them in her prime; and a longing for revenge.

Keir strode along the corridor, nodding to those who bowed their heads to him as he passed, and entered the grand audience chamber, where Bridget had held countless meetings with her subjects over the many years of her reign. The deceased Empress's children were all in the chamber, standing close to the empty throne, and Brogan glanced in Keir's direction.

Keir bowed as he approached.

'Your Majesty,' he said to Bryce, 'I have finished scouting Colsbury. Thorn has returned, along with my mother, and the others who escaped from the Great Fortress.'

Bryce nodded, his eyes dark and lined with grief. 'I know,' he said. 'Daimon has informed me of this.'

'We should kill them all,' said Bethal, her features almost covered by a black veil.

Berra let out a sob, and lifted her hands to her face.

'The time for tears is over, sister,' snapped Bethal. 'It is time for vengeance.'

'Let us get today over with first,' said Bryce. 'Once our mother has been interred in the ground, then we shall be free to think of the future.'

A tall Kellach soldier entered the chamber and bowed low.

'The funeral procession is ready to leave, your Majesty,' he said to Bryce.

'Thank you,' said the Emperor-elect. He glanced at his siblings. 'Follow me.'

Bryce led the way out of the audience chamber, his brother and sisters trailing after him. Keir joined them, walking to their rear, as more courtiers and soldiers followed Bryce down the stairs. Mage Tabor emerged from a room, and strode next to Keir, his eyes red and lowered; then Daimon also joined them, taking his place just behind the five children of Bridget. No one uttered a word as Bryce led them down into the fortress, and the only sounds were coming from the tears of several courtiers, and the tread of their feet on the stairs. They reached the ground floor of the Great Fortress, where a huge crowd was awaiting them. Soldiers in shining steel armour were flanking a long open-topped carriage, upon which sat a large coffin, fashioned from dark wood and edged in gold. Berra cried out at the sight and burst into tears, as Brogan supported her with an arm. Next to them, Bedig's face was a mask of fury, and his hands were shaking with rage.

The crowd parted for the royal party, their eyes on the five children of the dead Empress, the harsh silence punctuated only by sobs. Bryce walked to the front of the carriage, then his hand reached out to brush the flank of one of the six white horses that had been hitched to the reins. He nodded to an officer, who raised an arm, and the gates facing the Old Town were pushed open. A great roar of noise entered the fortress, from the thousands who had gathered on the streets to say farewell to their beloved Empress. The procession set off, the six white horses pulling the carriage through the gates and down onto the road outside. Every space on either side of the road was packed with people, and more were hanging out of the windows of the tenements. Flowers were thrown onto the cobbles, creating a carpet of blooms over which the horses walked, as they pulled the carriage along the street. Keir kept his head down as he strode through the gates, trying to lose himself in the crowd of courtiers and soldiers that was following the carriage. He was a member of the most hated and reviled family in Plateau City, and fear was bubbling in the pit of his stomach. Bryce had been careful to announce Keir's loyalty to the people of the city, but many of the citizens seemed almost deranged by grief, and he had no doubt that if any Holdfasts came into their grasp, they would be torn to pieces.

At the front of the procession, Bryce walked alone, his head bowed as he led the carriage through the streets of the Old Town. His four siblings were directly behind the carriage, and soldiers were flanking them, to protect them from the more enthusiastic sections of the populace. People were screaming and howling their lamentations in an outpouring of grief that Keir felt was bordering on mass hysteria, and soldiers were using their long shields to keep the people from swarming over the carriage bearing Bridget's coffin.

Bryce turned left at a large junction, the press of the crowds leaving only a narrow channel free for the horses and carriage as the noise rose and rose. Thousands of voices rang out, smothering the sound of the horseshoes clipping over the cobbles. To the right, on the roads leading to the harbour, hundreds of Rakanese citizens of the Empire had gathered, while Holdings and Kellach Brigdomin people were jostling to get a view of the coffin. Bryce passed through a gate in the Old Town walls, and the procession entered the old peasant district. The roads grew wider, but they were just as packed as before. The procession approached the edge of the Kellach Quarter, and the noise reached new heights. Thousands of Kellach civilians were kneeling by the side of the road, their grief and anger rippling through the air like a vast wounded beast. The route the procession would take had been published a few days before, and it seemed as though every Kellach Brigdomin citizen had left their homes in the Quarter to be present as the coffin passed. Keir glanced at the raw emotions on the faces of those lining the streets.

How could his mother believe for a second that she could prevail over people like that? The Kellach had idolised Bridget as one of their own, and it was clear from their reaction to Bryce that they were prepared to follow him anywhere, no matter the cost. Thorn was delusional if she thought she could compete with that. No, she wasn't delusional. The little witch knew exactly what she was doing. She would attempt to use cunning and sly tricks to gain the throne of the Empire, but she would never succeed.

The procession reached another large junction, and Bryce turned left again, heading for the gate in the Emergency Wall, the line that divided the Kellach Quarter from the city's New Town. Soldiers were massed by the arched gate, keeping the passage clear for Bryce. The carriage passed through the gate, and the volume of noise lowered a little as the procession entered the huge open-air market on the other side of the Emergency Wall. Thousands of Holdings citizens were lining the route, and packing out the marketplace, but many were standing in a respectful silence, their heads bowed, and the lamentations of the Kellach soon began to fade away. Bryce led them through the market, and then turned left again, passing the homes of the wealthy merchants. They reached the main road that led from the northern gates of the city, and turned left for a final time. The rich inhabitants of the aristocratic and diplomatic districts were on the streets, along with hundreds of students from the university. They were more subdued than the Kellach and the citizens of the Old Town, but their grief was just as tangible, and many were openly weeping as the carriage passed them. Keir saw a few mages who worked at the university – Ravi, Nadia and Dean. None of them were powerful warriors, and they looked a little uncomfortable as they stood side by side among their students. Ravi caught Keir's glance for a brief second, then the Rakanese clay mage looked away, his cheeks flushing.

Ahead of the procession, the Great Fortress loomed up, its dark exterior reflecting the sombre grief that hung over the city. It had been Bridget's capital for twenty-seven years, and now it belonged to Bryce. The Emperor-elect reached the bridge over the dry moat and carried on, leading the procession back into the shadows of the Great Fortress. In a choreographed move, the horses were halted, and six Kellach soldiers lifted the coffin from the back of the carriage, as the rest of the procession filled the ground floor of the fortress. The six soldiers waited for Bryce, then the Emperor-elect led them down a wide set of stairs into the basement of the fortress. The others queued up and filed after them, and Keir walked next to Tabor as they descended into the crypt. They passed the dungeons to their left, where Bridget had died, and carried on until they reached a large chamber, lit by oil lamps hung from the ceiling. The base of a massive, unfinished sarcophagus sat at the rear of the chamber, and the six soldiers carried the coffin on their broad shoulders over to it, as Bridget's children stood in a line.

Bryce nodded, and the soldiers lowered the coffin into the stone sarcophagus. The sound of weeping rose up from the watching crowd, filling the chamber as the six soldiers bowed towards the coffin, then took a pace backwards. Bryce reached forward with a hand, and touched the dark wood that encased his mother's body; then he turned to face the crowd.

'Citizens of the Empire,' he said, and the chamber hushed. 'For twenty-seven years,' Bryce went on, 'Empress Bridget ae Brenna ae Brig ruled this world. She brought peace and prosperity to every nation of the Empire, and fought off the attempts of Agatha and her band of archmages when they tried to usurp power. She loved this world, and she loved this city, and today we shall honour her memory. This day, we shall mourn, but we shall also be glad, as we remember what it was about my mother that made her so beloved by her people. She put their needs before her own; she defended them from all enemies, and cared for the weak and powerless, ensuring that no citizen ever starved or was left destitute. She also ruled with justice and mercy. I saw how she suffered, and my sisters and brother saw it, too; how she would feel the pain of even her lowliest subject. She strived day and night to make this world a better place, and the Empire that stands today is a testament to all she achieved.' He paused, his eyes flashing with anger. 'Now, we are faced with a new threat. Not a threat from another world, such as

Agatha represented, but a threat from within; a threat from those who once called themselves loyal. The government of the Holdings and the Matriarch of Sanang have rallied round a pretender to the throne...' He paused again, as a swell of anger rippled through the crowd filling the crypt. Bryce raised his hand for silence. 'Rest assured,' he went on, 'that we shall destroy this nest of vile traitors. I do not blame the people of the Holdings, nor do I hold the folk of Sanang responsible for the path their leaders have chosen. No. The fault lies with the former Herald of the Empire, and her duplicitous apprentice, Lady Thorn of Greyfalls Deepen.' The boos and jeers intensified. 'But that is for tomorrow,' Bryce went on, raising his voice to be heard over the tumult. 'Today, we mourn. Tomorrow, we fight. Are you with me?'

The crowd roared, the noise deafening Keir for a moment. The rage emanating from those present made him want to crawl into a corner and hide, and he could barely look at the faces of those around him. He felt a fist strike his shoulder.

'Here's one of them!' someone cried. 'A Holdfast is here!'

More people turned to stare at Keir, their eyes consumed with hatred and anger.

'Kill him!' a man shouted.

'No!' Bryce cried. He gestured to a squad of soldiers, who charged into the crowd. They shoved the mob back from Keir and surrounded him.

'Lord Keir is an ally and a friend,' said Bryce, as the crowd threatened to erupt. 'He is living proof of my mother's mercy. Lord Keir saved my mother's life from the blade of an assassin. Do not blame him for the crimes of Daphne Holdfast.' He beckoned with a hand, and the soldiers moved forwards, escorting Keir to where Bryce stood. The Emperor-elect reached out and shook Keir's hand, then he turned to address the crowd again.

'This Empire judges people on their actions,' he said, 'not on the crimes of their relations. Lord Keir is loyal to the Empire and, in time, he will become the new Holder Fast, once the traitors in his family have paid for their transgressions.'

The crowd settled a little, but many were still staring at Keir.

Brogan stepped forward. 'Citizens of the Empire; let us return to the palace, to honour my mother's memory. Do not sully this day with misplaced violence. As Empress Bridget forgave Lord Keir, so shall we. It is what her Majesty would have wanted. Lord Keir saved her life, and for that, we shall always be grateful.'

The soldiers began pushing the crowds from the chamber, and up the stairs. Keir turned to Bryce.

'Thank you, your Majesty.'

Bryce nodded. 'I meant every word I said, Keir. You are one of us now.'

A few hours later, Mage Tabor was showing Keir around his new apartment.

'There are stairs at the rear,' the mage said, pointing to a door leading from the spacious living area, 'that go to the roof garden.'

Keir smiled. 'I have my own personal access to the roof?'

'Yes,' said Tabor. 'The Emperor-elect wishes to favour you. He would also like you to refrain from smoking within the interior of the palace. Please use the roof for that.'

Keir nodded.

'And here is your bathroom,' Tabor said. 'You also have a study. It's a little on the small side, but you can use it as a place to work.'

'You'll be pleased about that,' Keir said. 'You'll have your office to yourself again.'

Tabor smiled. 'Indeed. And, finally, here is your bed chamber.'

Keir gazed through the open door. There were no windows in his new apartment, but it scarcely mattered, not if he could go up onto the roof whenever he pleased.

'Please pass on my thanks to his Majesty,' he said.

'You can tell the Emperor-elect yourself,' Tabor said. 'You are expected to be in his Majesty's presence an hour after dawn tomorrow morning, to begin work. The period of mourning ends at midnight tonight, and there is much to do.' The mage smiled. 'I also have a surprise for you. It wasn't my idea, I hasten to add, but the Emperor-elect hoped it would please you.'

'A surprise?' said Keir. 'What is it?'

'You'll see. Remain within your apartment for the rest of the evening. It's been fully stocked with wine; ring the bell if you require food.'

Tabor strode to the main entrance of the apartment, smiled, then left, closing the door behind him. Keir pulled off his outer coat, and laid it over the back of a chair, then he explored his new home. It was several times larger than the cramped rooms where he had been living up until that point, and made him feel less isolated. Bryce was trying to prove something to him – that he had been accepted by the children of Bridget as a friend. Well, maybe not as a friend, but as a loyal and useful servant. It occurred to Keir that the Emperor-elect was wise to keep him close. It showed the masses of civilians that Bryce was not spiteful, or blinded by his hatred for the Holdfasts. How could he be, if one of the Holdfasts was a member of his inner council?

There was a knock on the main door, and Keir strode over the polished floorboards to open it. A couple of servants were in the passageway outside, with Keir's belongings.

'My lord,' said one, bowing, 'may we bring your possessions into your apartment?'

Keir nodded, and moved to the side. The two servants picked up the luggage, and carried it into the living area.

'Put it down by the long couch,' said Keir. 'Tell me, did you go to the Holdfast townhouse in person to collect my things?'

'Yes, my lord,' said one, as he laid a trunk down by the couch. 'We visited the townhouse yesterday, to avoid the crowds from today's funeral procession.'

'Was anyone home?'

'Just a sole servant, my lord. We handed over the eviction papers to her, and told her she had until sunset to leave Plateau City. The keys are now in the possession of Lady Brogan.'

Keir smiled, wishing he could have seen Tabitha's face when the imperial staff had arrived at the front door of the townhouse.

The servants bowed and left the apartment, and there was another knock on the door almost immediately.

'What is it now?' said Keir, opening the door. His mouth opened. Standing outside, looking a little lost and bewildered, was Tilda Holdwain.

'Keir,' she said, her voice betraying her nerves.

'Tilda? What are you doing here?'

'Didn't you summon me?' she said. 'I was told to leave the Holdings Embassy an hour ago, and soldiers brought me here. They said I would be living here, with you.'

Keir stared at her. Was this Tabor's surprise?

'Please don't leave me standing out here in the corridor,' she said.

'Come in,' he said.

She walked into the apartment, and he closed the door.

'Where are your things?' he said. 'I mean, if you're supposed to be living here.'

'The soldiers are going round to my apartment,' she said. 'They told me to expect them later today, once the crowds have cleared a bit.' She glanced around, her eyes darting over the chamber. 'Did you ask for me, Keir? I wish you had let me know in advance. I was terrified when the soldiers marched into the embassy. They informed the ambassador that I no longer worked for him.'

Keir frowned. Were Bryce and the others playing games with him?

'I had no idea you were coming,' he said. 'Mage Tabor told me to wait here for a surprise, but I wasn't expecting this.'

'Oh.' Her face flushed, and she looked down. 'After you left Plateau City, I didn't hear from you in thirds, and I thought you'd forgotten all about me. And now... now, you're telling me that you don't want me here? Should I leave?'

'I had to go back to Colsbury for a while,' he said. 'The Empress was angry with me for killing Brannig, and it took a while to sort it all out.'

'Yes. I heard about that.'

'And then I had to deal with my wife. Or, should I say, my ex-wife. Thorn and I are divorced.'

She nodded, her eyes remaining downcast.

Keir started to grow angry. Why hadn't Tabor told him what to expect? Were they all laughing at him? Perhaps Daimon was watching at that moment, and relaying Keir's awkwardness and Tilda's embarrassment to an amused Bryce.

Don't be silly, he told himself. Everything was fine. There was nothing to worry about. It was all in hand. He should relax, and be glad that he had someone with which to share his new apartment. Tilda was pretty, very pretty, and he should try to make her feel at home.

He smiled. 'I'm glad you're here, Tilda. I missed you.'

She glanced up at him. 'Truly?'

'Yes.'

'I missed you, too,' she said.

'Come and have a look round,' he said. 'The bathroom alone is bigger than my last apartment; and wait until you see the back stairs. We have our own private access to the roof garden.'

He took her hand.

'Am I really living in the palace?' she said. 'It's like a dream. I can't wait to tell my family.'

They grinned at each other like excited children.

If you're listening, Daimon, Keir said to himself; *thank you.*

A voice drifted into his mind. *You're welcome.*

CHAPTER 3
CLACKENBAIRD FARM

Marchside, Kell – 20th Day, Second Third Autumn 534

Aila steered the cart into the village square, and brought the two ponies to a halt in front of the town hall. She pulled her coat round her, tucked her scarf in, and jumped to the ground. She glanced up at the sky as she lifted Killop down to the muddy track. Clouds were drifting by to the south, but there was no sign of rain. Yet. She reached into the back of the cart, and picked up Konna. The baby was wrapped up in a harness, and Aila slipped her arms through the loops, so that Konna was hanging against her chest.

'Don't wander off,' she said to Killop, who pretended he hadn't heard her.

Aila tied the reins to one of the wooden posts that ran by the front of the town hall, gripped Killop by the hand, and approached the building. She took her time with the stairs, as Killop was still learning how to master them, then they entered the hall.

A Kellach man glanced down at her from where he was standing by a side door. 'Yer a wee bit early, hen.'

Aila nodded. 'I was worried the cart might get stuck in the mud after last night's rain. Do you want us to wait?'

'Nah,' the man said. 'What's half an hour after ninety days, eh?' He pulled a set of keys from a deep pocket. 'Say, did ye hear about Empress Bridget?'

'Yeah.'

'What a shame, eh? A terrible business. Poisoned, apparently.'

Aila decided not to comment. The news of the Empress's death had taken a while to filter down to Kellach Brigdomin, and the specifics were vague; but Aila had her suspicions.

'That Bryce lad'll make a fine Emperor, but,' the man went on, as he unlocked the side door. 'You were travelling with two of his sisters back in spring, weren't ye?'

'That's right,' Aila said. 'Brogan and Bethal. We met Bryce in the *World's End*, up in the Domm Pass.'

The man raised an eyebrow. 'Did ye? What was he like?'

Aila shrugged. 'He seemed all right, I suppose. I only spoke to him for a few minutes.'

The man swung the door open, then he took a wall lamp, lit it, and they descended down a flight of stairs.

'Hey, Corthie,' the man cried, as they reached the bottom of the stairs.

He shone his lamp over the interior of the basement, and Aila saw Corthie's face at the barred slat in his cell door.

'Is it time?' Corthie said. 'Am I finally getting out of here?'

'Aye, son,' said the man. 'That's yer ninety days over. Yer wife and bairns are here to collect ye.'

He selected another key, slid it into the lock, then twisted it. The door opened, and Corthie stepped out. He smiled at Aila, then gathered her up in his arms.

Aila kissed him. 'Careful with Konna,' she said. 'Don't squish her.' She sniffed. 'Malik's ass; you stink.'

'Aye?' Corthie said, laughing. 'I'll have to put in a complaint about the bathing facilities in this dungeon.' He glanced at the man. 'Is that it? Am I free to go?'

The man nodded. 'Aye. The chief was wanting a wee word with ye, but. Do ye fancy waiting upstairs? She should be here in a minute.'

'No bother,' said Corthie. He stretched his arms, then leaned down and picked up Killop. He kissed the boy on the top of his head. 'Damn, it's good to hold my family again.'

The man with the lamp led them back to the ground floor of the town hall, and Aila took a seat, while Corthie began throwing Killop up into the air. She had taken the children to see their father nearly every day of his incarceration, but she had usually only seen his face through the barred slat, and she smiled at the sight of him, while Killop shrieked with laughter.

'What is that stench?' came a voice from the hall's entrance.

They turned, and saw Kallie walking towards them.

'That'll be me, Chief,' said Corthie.

Kallie smiled. 'I might have to give ye another twenty days for offending my nostrils. And what's going on? The noon bell hasnae rung yet.'

'Aila was early,' said the man with the lamp.

Kallie shook her head. 'What kind of jailor are ye? Corthie's not supposed to get out until noon. Yer a soft touch, and no mistake.'

The man grinned.

Kallie's eyes turned back to Corthie. 'Well, son; yer ninety days are done. I hope ye've learned yer lesson. No more beating up folk, right? That's you got a record now.'

'Aye, boss,' said Corthie. 'I'll be a good boy. Oh, and thanks for not adding any more days to my sentence on account of me escaping before.'

Kallie shrugged. 'That would have been unfair, under the, uh... circumstances. And thank you, Corthie, for coming back. Handing yerself in like that has fair raised the amount of respect for ye among the folk round here. Nobody thought ye'd ever come back; but ye did.'

'The rest of my family think I was mad for doing it,' he said, 'but I still want to live down here, and there was no alternative.'

'Are ye heading back up to Clackenbaird Farm?'

'Aye, for a long bath.'

'Praise Pyre for that.' Kallie smiled at the two children, then nodded at Aila. 'I hope it all works out for the four of ye. Come down here and see me if ye need anything, aye?'

'Thanks, Chief,' said Corthie.

He and Aila strode from the town hall, each carrying a child. Aila scanned the skies. A chill wind was blowing from the west, but there was still no sign of rain.

'Pyre's arse,' said Corthie, glancing at the bare branches of the trees in the village square; 'what happened to summer?'

'You spent it locked up, Corthie,' said Aila. 'It's a minor miracle that it isn't raining. The weather's been awful these past few days. Malik knows what winter will be like.'

'It's no worse than Freshmist.'

'Corthie, Kell is like Freshmist for nine months of the year. I'm already longing for spring, and it's still autumn.'

Aila loosened the cords round the wooden post, and they climbed up onto the cart. Aila took the reins, and they moved off. Konna was still strapped to her front, but the child was sleeping, and she didn't want to risk moving her. Corthie glanced at the village of Marchside, as if seeing it for the first time. A couple of men were crossing the road in front of them, and they waved up at the cart. Aila waved back.

'He's out, is he, hen?' one of them shouted.

'He certainly is,' Aila called back. 'I've just got to keep him out of trouble now.'

The man laughed. 'Good luck with that, hen.'

Corthie glanced at her as the cart rolled forward. 'Do you know them?'

'I know every damn person in this village, Corthie,' she said. 'I've been here for eighty days on my own. Some folk took pity on me, others gossiped; and some came up to the farm to help out. Not only are you famous, we're the richest people in Marchside, by a long way. The money your mother gave us before we left Colsbury might have seemed like a trivial sum to her, but it's worth a fortune down here. I've even been asked if I want to join the village council.'

'Aye? What did you say?'

'I told them that I couldn't consider it until you had been released. There's too much work to do on the farm, and I couldn't spare the time.' She eyed him. 'Listen; I have news from the outside world.'

He frowned. 'If it's about Bridget, then I heard. The jailor told me this morning.'

'Did he tell you how it happened?'

'He said she was poisoned.'

'Yes. That's not the whole story, though. The poison in question is rumoured to have come from another world, and was disguised as a healing substance. It healed the Empress, then it killed her.'

Corthie narrowed his eyes. 'Oh.'

'Exactly. Does that not sound like salve to you? If it was salve, then some kind of terrible mistake must have occurred. Perhaps the Empress took too much, too quickly. Regardless, the story I heard stated that the new Emperor is going to hunt down and punish those responsible.'

'Is Bryce the new Emperor? What about Thorn?'

'No one down here knows much about Thorn, or any of the other Holdfasts, for that matter. We're too cut off from the rest of the world. The Empress died a third and a half ago, and we're only just hearing about it now. As far as everyone in Marchside is concerned, Bryce is the new Emperor, his sister Brogan is the new Herald of the Empire, and Daimon is his chief mage.'

'Daimon? Pyre's knackers.'

'We should be safe down here,' Aila went on. 'As long as the iron, coal and whisky barrels keep flowing north, no one should interfere with Kellach Brigdomin. That's what you wanted, right? To get away from it all?'

Corthie remained silent for a moment, then he nodded. 'Aye.'

Aila guided the cart out of the village, and they took the road leading to the Brig Pass. They slowed in front of a group of workers who were toiling to pave the road, transforming it from a muddy, rutted track into something more solid and enduring. A few of the workers smiled and waved at them, as Aila steered the cart around the piles of sand and cut flag stones.

'Guess who's paying for the road improvements?' she whispered to Corthie, as they carried on.

'Us?'

'You got it. I was fed up with the cart getting stuck in the mud, so I loaned the village five thousand in gold to upgrade the road that runs by the farm. I say "loaned", but I doubt we'll ever see the money again. Still, it'll be worth it once it's finished.'

Corthie laughed. 'It sounds as though we're doing our bit to civilise Kell.'

Aila smiled, then glanced up at the sky. The grey clouds in the south had been joined by a darker front moving in from the west. Rain was coming, but Aila was confident they would be home by the time it started. The paved road ended, and the cart bumped down onto the muddy track. A few minutes later, Aila steered the ponies on to the side road that led to their land. They passed a hedgerow that marked the boundary, and began to climb a gentle slope.

'We still haven't given the farm a name,' she said.

'It already has a name,' said Corthie.

'Well, yeah; but I don't know if I like Clackenbaird.'

Corthie shrugged. 'I don't think we should go around renaming places. If that's what it's called, then that's what it's called.'

Killop pointed into an enclosed field on the right flank of the hillside. 'Sheeps.'

'That's right, wee man,' said Corthie. 'Big fluffy sheep. Em, Aila, when did we buy sheep?'

'About a third ago,' she said. 'We have cattle, too, and a few goats. We also planted turnips in the fields on the other side of the hill, and I've purchased enough barley seed to sow acres of the stuff come spring.'

Corthie raised an eyebrow at her. 'You're taking this farming stuff seriously, I see.'

'I've been keeping busy.'

'But you've had two children to look after.'

Aila nodded. 'I've brought in some tenants.'

'How many?'

'Five. We might need more after winter. We'll see.'

'And where are they living?'

'I've had two of the little cottages renovated; three live in one, and two are in the other. They're nice; you'll like them.'

They reached the crest of the hill, and Aila saw Corthie's eyes widen as he saw the refurbished farmhouse for the first time.

'Pyre's arse, Aila,' he cried. 'You did all this in eighty days? The house looks amazing; and, without the scaffolding, it's much bigger than I remember.'

'Are you pleased?'

'Pleased? I'm... speechless. It looks like a damn palace; big enough for twenty people.'

She laughed. 'Don't get carried away. I wanted it finished by the time you were released, and I work better under a little bit of pressure.' She pointed to a track that led off to the right. 'The tenants' cottages are down there. Close, but not too close.'

She steered the cart into the yard in front of the house, and pulled on the reins to bring the ponies to a halt. They climbed down to the flag stones, and Aila looped the reins round a horizontal post.

'We can deal with the cart later,' she said. 'I want you cleaned up before we do anything else. I began heating the water before I left to pick you up, so it should be hot enough for a bath.' She smiled. 'And before you ask, yes – we have an inside toilet.'

Aila put Konna down for a nap, then went back outside with Killop to stable the ponies while Corthie scrubbed himself clean of eighty days' worth of grime. The rain was starting by the time both ponies had been fed and watered, and she pulled the small cart into a shed to keep it dry, while Killop played in the yard. She picked him up as the rain grew heavier, and ran into the house. She checked on Konna, then went to their living room, where Corthie was standing in a clean pair of shorts, a towel in his hands.

'I've been thinking,' he said, as he dried his hair.

'Yeah?'

'About the outside world. There *is* something that I want to know about. When we left Colsbury, Sable and Kelsey were talking about going to Implacatus to rescue Belinda. I don't suppose you've heard anything?'

'No, sorry,' she said.

He nodded, then pulled a tunic over his head. Aila watched him for a moment, then set Killop down onto the thick rug.

Corthie glanced out of the window. 'The rain's stopped already.'

'It's going to be one of those days,' Aila said. 'Rain, sun, rain, sun, with a lot of wind thrown in.'

He laughed. 'You're becoming an expert on the weather. What is there to eat? I could...'

A loud knock came from their front door.

'Are we expecting anyone?' he said.

'No,' said Aila, as she began to walk to the door. 'I specifically asked the tenants to give us some time together before introducing themselves.'

She left the living room and strode down the hallway. If it was the farm's tenants, and they had brought alcohol, then she was going to get annoyed. The Kellach Brigdomin sense of hospitality seemed to revolve around drinking to excess, and Aila had wanted to shield Corthie from that, at least for a while. He hadn't touched a drop in eighty days, and part of her was a little surprised that he hadn't mentioned the fact.

She reached the door, and swung it open.

'Surprise!' cried Sable.

Aila blinked. Standing outside the front door were three women, including Sable Holdfast. Her eyes went to one.

'Belinda?'

'Hello, Aila,' said the god.

'And this is Lara,' Sable said, gesturing to the other woman. 'She's from Dragon Eyre. Is your criminal husband in?'

'You already know that Corthie is here,' said Belinda.

Sable nodded. 'Yes, that's true. I was just being polite.'

'Were you watching us?' said Aila.

Sable nodded again. 'I was. I promised Belinda that I would bring her here once Corthie had been released, and then I waited for the rain to stop. Can we come in before it starts again?'

Aila moved to the side, and the women filed in past her.

'Nice house,' said Lara, glancing around.

'Thanks,' said Aila. 'Daphne Holdfast's money paid for it to look this way. I thought, you know, if we were going to live in Kell, then I needed some level of comfort.'

She led them into the living room, and Corthie glanced over. His eyes locked with Belinda's, and the god rushed up to him and threw her arms round his wide frame. Corthie hugged her, and Belinda started to cry.

Lara frowned, then opened her mouth to speak.

'Let them get on with it,' said Sable. 'Belinda has been waiting a long time for this moment.'

Tears rolled down Corthie's face as he held the weeping Third Ascendant, and Aila felt a little jealous at the sight. She knew they saw each other as brother and sister, but the intensity of their emotions had caught her off guard.

'Would anyone like some tea?' she said.

'Yes, please,' said Sable. 'Plenty of sugar in mine.'

'We have honey.'

'That will do. Do you need a hand?'

Aila nodded, then Sable followed her into the kitchen. Aila filled the kettle with water and placed it on to the stove.

'So,' she said, 'you rescued her.'

'Yeah. We killed a few gods in the process,' Sable said, 'but Belinda's not coping well with it all. She spent a couple of years in a restrainer mask, at the mercy of Edmond, and it's taking time for her to recover.

That's why I brought her here so quickly; she's been counting the days until Corthie's release.'

Aila frowned. 'And you're helping her? You?'

'I've been making a special effort to get on with her.'

'Why?'

'She feels lost, just like I did. Some of the Holdfasts in Colsbury have been pretty cold towards her. Karalyn's gone the other way, and has been smothering her with maternal affection; while Silva's barely left her side.'

'Silva's back?'

'Yes. She's reverted to her old sycophantic ways in the presence of her beloved Queen, and it can get a little over-bearing at times.'

'How did you persuade Silva to remain in Colsbury while you brought Belinda here?'

'Easy,' said Sable. 'I didn't tell her we were coming. Listen; be prepared for Belinda to ask if she can stay here for a while.'

Aila nodded as she lined up five mugs on a tray. She filled the teapot with hot water, and set it down on the tray next to the mugs. She gathered the honey and a small jug of milk, then picked up the tray, and they walked back into the living room. Corthie and Belinda were sitting side by side on a long couch, while Lara was gazing out of the window at the view of the hills.

Corthie glanced up. 'Belinda's going to be staying for a few days,' he said. 'Is that alright?'

'Of course,' said Aila. 'You're all welcome to stay.'

'Thanks,' said Sable, 'but Lara and I need to get back to Colsbury. I'm due to transport Thorn and Daphne to Holdings City tomorrow. Thorn's making a speech to the Holdings parliament.'

'That's Sable's job now,' said Lara; 'taking folk round the world whenever they demand it. Even though Karalyn and Kelsey could do the same thing.'

'Karalyn and Kelsey have to remain in Colsbury to defend it from Daimon,' said Sable. 'And I wanted to come here.' She crouched down onto the rug, and ruffled Killop's hair. 'He's getting big, Aila.'

Belinda's gaze snapped over to the young boy. 'You have children?'

'Two,' said Aila. 'This is little Killop, and Konna is sleeping in her cot in the next room.'

Belinda frowned at the boy. 'I can sense self-healing powers.'

'That's right,' said Aila. 'Both of the children are demigods.'

'Holy crap,' said Lara. 'Demigods, eh? You raising a family of immortal Holdfasts?'

Aila nodded, unsure of what to say.

'How old are they?' said Belinda.

'Killop is two-and-a-half,' said Aila, 'and Konna was born in the Second Third of Summer, on the tenth of Koralis in the City calendar.'

Corthie smiled. 'And I hope we'll be trying for number three soon?'

Aila smiled back at him. 'I hope so, too.'

'This is dangerous,' said Belinda. 'This could alter the long-term balance of power on this world. You can't just introduce a new generation of gods on to the Star Continent.'

'Why not?' said Corthie.

'Think of the future,' the god said. 'Not in your lifetime, but in the centuries to come. When every mortal alive today is dead and gone, your children will still be here.'

'Not necessarily,' said Aila.

'What do you mean?' said Corthie.

Aila frowned. 'I don't like to talk about this, Corthie. I don't want to think about what happens after you...'

'After I die?'

'Exactly. I had planned to go back to the City, once you... were no longer here. But with Yendra's death, and Mona's, I'm not sure any more.'

'Your children will most likely be adults by the time Corthie dies,' said Belinda. 'You won't be able to tell them what to do. This is very irresponsible of you both. What if your children decide that they are entitled to rule the mortals of this world? After a few centuries, they might feel they deserve power. That's how it begins; that's how history repeats itself.'

Corthie and Aila glanced at each other.

'Do they have powers?' Belinda went on.

'They will,' said Aila. 'Karalyn saw it. They'll both have the full range of vision abilities, and fire, and a bit of dream as well.'

Belinda swallowed, and the room fell into an awkward silence, as the adults watched Killop playing on the rug.

'Let's change the subject,' said Sable. 'You mentioned the City, Aila. Salve City. If you want, I could take you, Corthie and the kids there for a holiday. Not right now, of course, but in a while, once Corthie's settled in. Belinda told me that she would quite like to see the City again.'

'I would,' said Belinda.

'I don't know,' said Aila. 'As much as I respect Queen Emily and King Daniel, I don't have many friends left alive in the City. And Amalia is there, and she hates me.'

Sable stirred honey into her tea. 'Amalia died in Implacatus,' she said. 'She was part of the operation to rescue Belinda, and was arrested, tortured and executed, because she wouldn't reveal the location of Salve City to the Ascendants.'

Aila put a hand to her mouth.

'She died a hero,' said Belinda. 'She gave her life to save me, and to protect the City.'

'Wow,' said Aila. 'That, I was not expecting.'

'There is someone in Salve City who you might like to see,' Sable said. 'In fact, you might be the only person pleased to see him.'

'Who?'

'Naxor.'

Aila smiled. 'Naxor's there? Oh. Perhaps I could be persuaded to visit, for a while.'

'You can count me out,' said Corthie. 'I have no interest in seeing that little weasel again.'

'Nor I,' said Belinda.

Sable laughed. 'See what I mean, Aila? Naxor spent some time locked up after Simon's regime fell, and then the King and Queen released him, so that he could sell salve to the Empire. I presume you know how that worked out?'

'So,' said Corthie, 'it was salve that killed the Empress?'

'Yes,' said Sable, 'and now Bryce is swearing revenge on Naxor for poisoning his mother. Kelsey was there when Bridget took her first dose of salve. Naxor gave her a sample vial, of the concentrated stuff, and Bridget glugged the entire thing down in a couple of days.'

'Then, it wasn't Naxor's fault?' said Aila.

'No. He's innocent, this time. Alright; here's what I propose. Lara and I will leave Belinda here, and then we'll return in a while, and take you all to the City.'

'I agree,' said Belinda.

'No, thanks,' said Corthie. 'I've just spent eighty days beneath the town hall. I need to stay in Clackenbaird and learn how to run the farm.'

'It would only be for a little while,' said Aila. 'I could do with a break.'

'I don't mind if you go,' he said. 'As long as it's not for too long. I could look after the children; I want to spend more time with them, especially Konna. I've barely seen her since she was born.'

'But I would need to take Konna with me; I'm still breast-feeding. I could leave Killop with you, and you two could have some father-son time.'

Corthie frowned, then nodded. 'Alright. Just for a few days, aye?'

Sable sipped her tea, then stood. 'Excellent. We have a plan. Lara, let's go.'

'Wait,' said Corthie. 'When will you be coming back?'

Sable shrugged. 'I don't have an exact date in mind. Maybe half a third from now? Oh, and your sisters send their greetings. Kelsey said she hopes you don't stink of pig shit.'

'There are no pigs in Kell,' said Corthie, laughing. 'It'll be sheep-shit.'

'I'll be sure to correct her,' said Sable.

'Any word from my mother?'

'Only that she would prefer you to be in Colsbury with the others. Bryce is gathering the imperial armies, and we think he might strike against the Holdfasts.'

'I'm not interested in getting involved in politics,' Corthie said.

'It's your family,' said Lara; 'not politics.'

'They're fighting over the crown, aren't they?' he said. 'I like Thorn, but I don't want to kill people just to further her ambitions. I want to live a quiet life, as a farmer. Why do you think I willingly went back to prison?'

'That's what I thought you'd say,' said Sable. 'Right; see you all later.'

The air shimmered, and Sable and Lara vanished.

'I didn't see Sable use a Quadrant,' said Aila.

'She keeps it in her pocket,' said Belinda, 'and uses her thumb to trigger it. She likes to show off, in other words.'

Aila nodded. 'You seem to be getting on very well with her. I thought you two loathed each other.'

'We used to. It's strange but, out of all of the Holdfasts, Sable's been among the nicest to me since I was rescued from Implacatus. I mean, Karalyn's been nice, of course; but Sable treats me as an adult, while Karalyn... well, she mothers me. And Silva behaves like my shadow, following me around wherever I go. Sable acts normally around me, and I like that. She's still an arrogant show off, though; that hasn't changed.' She turned to Corthie. 'I wish you would come to the City of Pella with us.'

'Maybe next year,' he said. 'But, we'll have plenty of time here to catch up.'

Belinda nodded, and Aila tried to imagine what the next few days would be like. She had been looking forward to getting Corthie on his own, and now she had the Third Ascendant staying in the farmhouse as a guest.

Belinda smiled. 'What shall we do first?'

CHAPTER 4
ONE STEP CLOSER

Colsbury Castle, Republic of the Holdings – 21st Day, Second Third Autumn 534

Thorn stared at her reflection in the dresser mirror. Her hair was sitting perfectly on her bare shoulders, and she had spent far too long applying her make-up. She wondered about the dress. Was it too revealing? Perhaps the members of the Holdings parliament would prefer a more conservative outfit, one that covered her shoulders and arms. She decided against changing. Sable had been waiting to take her and the others to Holdings City, and she was probably starting to grow impatient.

She took a breath as her chest tightened. Nerves were making her stomach ache, and she wanted to get her speech to the parliament over with as quickly as possible, so that she could concentrate on the coronation, and the formation of her first, legitimate, government. There would be no coronation without the support of the Holdings, however; and she knew it had to be done, and done well. News of the mass hysteria and waves of grief that had taken place at Bridget's funeral had reached Colsbury some time before. As far as Plateau City was concerned, Lord Bryce was now Emperor Bryce, and Thorn needed to act, before her campaign withered away.

She stood, then walked out of her bedchamber. Daphne was standing by a pile of luggage, her eyes on Sable, who was arguing with Lara about something. Pechtang and T'Lang were also present, and both were dressed in fine new uniforms, with gleaming steel breast-plates and polished leather boots. Agang Garo was the last member of their party, and he was wearing long black robes that made him look like a statesman.

'Sorry about the wait,' Thorn said.

'Never apologise, your Majesty,' said Daphne. 'We are at your service.'

Lara smothered a snigger.

Daphne turned to her. 'Perhaps you should remain here, Alara'osso, with your father.'

'I like visiting new places,' said Lara. 'And Sable told me that it'll be warm down on the plains of the Holdings; well, warmer than Kell was. It was freezing down there. Oh, and call me Lara. Only my father uses my full name. Are you angling to be my new stepmother?'

Pechtang laughed, then he fell silent at a glance from Daphne. 'Any relationship I might have with your father is none of your concern, Lara,' she said. 'You are an adult, just as we are.'

'Let's not bicker,' said Sable, getting to her feet.

Daphne and Lara shared a glare of mutual contempt, and Thorn almost felt sorry for Sable, who was trying to keep her girlfriend and her half-sister happy at the same time. The atmosphere between Lara and Daphne had been frosty from the very beginning, and time had not improved it.

'Are we all ready?' Sable said. 'I want to leave before Silva realises I'm here. She hasn't forgiven me for taking Belinda to Kell, and if she shouts at me again I might have to punch her.'

Daphne glanced at Thorn, who nodded. Sable reached into a pocket, and the air shimmered. The party arrived in the gardens of the residence of the First Holder, their luggage piled up on the dry lawn next to them. Thorn breathed in the air of the city. It was much warmer than Colsbury, and the sun was shining down from a perfectly blue sky, in a shade that matched her dress.

'Ah, this is better,' Lara grinned. 'This feels more like Dragon Eyre, except there ain't no damn sea. And, you know, no dragons flitting about in the sky.' She nudged Sable with an elbow. 'What are we going to do while Thorn makes her speech? Are there any decent taverns?'

'There are several,' said Sable. 'I'll need to be careful, though. My face is known to a few people in Holdings City, and I'd rather not bump into any of them.' She turned to Daphne. 'Shall we meet you back here at sunrise tomorrow?'

'Yes,' said Daphne. 'Thank you.'

Sable smiled, then she and Lara vanished.

Daphne sighed. 'I do wonder at times about my sister's choice of romantic partner. I know it's none of my business, but Sable could do so much better for herself.'

'I hope you don't say that in front of Olo'osso,' said Agang.

'Olo'osso is besotted with his daughters, and I suspect that Lara, being the youngest, is his firm favourite. So, no, Agang; I wouldn't dream of bringing it up with him.'

'It's weird,' said T'Lang. 'Your sister's seeing the daughter of the man you're seeing; whereas before, with Caelius, you were seeing the father of your daughter's man. It's hard to keep track.'

Daphne smiled.

'Have you chosen one of them?' said Pechtang. 'Has that old pirate won out over Caelius?'

'I like them both,' said Daphne. 'Do I have to choose?'

T'Lang elbowed his brother in the ribs. 'She wants them to fight over her again.'

'Give me a hand with the luggage, lads,' said Agang. 'Let's not leave her Majesty standing here.'

The three Sanang men lifted the cases, and they all walked along a garden path towards the residence. An old man was pruning some bushes, and he glanced up, then bowed his head towards Daphne.

'First Holder,' he said; 'it's good to have you back.'

Daphne gave him a nod, then they came to the side door of the mansion. Daphne felt for her keys, then pushed at the door, and it opened. They entered the cool hallways of the residence, and a courtier's eyes widened as he saw Daphne.

'Summon the servants and staff,' Daphne said. 'I wish them to greet their new Empress.'

***

'Here is my list,' said Thorn, leaning across from the couch to pass the slip of paper to Daphne.

Daphne took the piece of paper and studied it.

'Shella as my Chief of Staff, your Majesty?' said Daphne. 'Does the Herald of the Empire require a Chief of Staff?'

'I tend to think so,' said Thorn. 'I'll need you to organise our secret army, and that will presumably take you away from the Star Continent for some time. Shella can fill in for you in your absence.'

'If she's willing to take the role, your Majesty.'

'I need her. She organised the Migration, and built an entire city in Rahain for the refugees. She keeps her talents hidden, but she is exactly what I require. She can run the day to day affairs of the Empire while we attend to other matters.'

Daphne nodded. 'And Agang Garo for Imperial Chamberlain? Is that a Sanang position? What does a chamberlain do?'

'He shall run my household. Colsbury, in other words. I need someone from Sanang in a position of high authority, so I thought I would invent a new role for him. He can look after supplies, logistics, personnel; that sort of thing. It will relieve the pressure on you and Shella. Pechtang and T'Lang will be part of my Imperial Guard, but they're too young and inexperienced to be given more responsibility. Agang has plenty of experience. He was a king, and then he governed the Mya enclave for over a decade.' She smiled. 'And it helps that neither he nor Shella are Holdfasts.'

Daphne nodded. 'I see you have left the space next to Caelius's name blank, your Majesty.'

'Yes. I want him to work for me, but it will most likely be as part of the secret army. The same goes for Lucius Cardova and Van Logos. If our plan is successful, then someone with Banner experience will be needed. They can help explain the situation to the soldiers on Dragon Eyre.'

'Won't their contracts with Salve City be a problem, your Majesty?'

'Caelius's contract has expired,' said Thorn, 'so he's available. And I suspect that Lucius Cardova might be tempted to allow his to expire. He is clearly in love with Karalyn, and I think he could be persuaded to stay on the Star Continent permanently. Van, though, I believe will return to the City in time. He's only here to see Kelsey, and she wants to return to the City once the crisis is over.'

'Is there no role for Olo'osso, your Majesty?'

Thorn smiled. 'No. I don't wish to offend you, but Olo'osso is too unreliable. He openly boasts about being a thief and a criminal, and I've seen no sign of him attempting to mend his ways. If I put him into a position of power, he will abuse it.'

'He's going to be upset, your Majesty, especially if Caelius gets a role.'

'I'm not in the business of handing out favours, Daphne. I intend to rule in an open and transparent manner, just as you taught me.'

Thorn noticed a slight frown crease Daphne's lips.

'I also left Sable's name off the list,' Thorn went on; 'but I hope she will continue to support me. She will be needed to transport the Banner army from Dragon Eyre to this world, now that Karalyn has refused to do so. I think Sable's role would be best left informal. Off the books, as it were.'

'And Belinda, your Majesty?'

Thorn sighed. 'I have no idea what to do about Belinda. Silva has been trying her best to persuade her to withhold her support from our cause, but, even without that, I would doubt that Belinda would help me. The days of our friendship seem a long time ago. Back then, I had imagined her as my Herald, were I ever to attain power. Now, I will be happy if she doesn't get in my way. She could destroy us all if she wished it. Why did Karalyn have to return all of her powers?'

'I asked my daughter the same question, your Majesty. She did it on Lostwell, at a time when she thought she would never see Belinda again. It's our misfortune that the Third Ascendant has ended up back on our world. I admit it was a relief when Sable took her to Kellach Brigdomin; and, after that, Sable is going to take her to Salve City. With any luck, she might decide to stay there.'

Thorn lowered her eyes. 'I feel sorry for her.'

'She's one of the most powerful beings in history, your Majesty.'

'I know, but she has suffered so much. And she looks so sad. You must have seen the way she has been walking around Colsbury on her own. If only I knew what to say to her, to find the right words to express how much I wish we could be friends again; but every time I try to talk to her, I end up making it worse. She seems so lonely.'

'She is with Corthie now, your Majesty. My son will know how to cheer her up.'

There was a knock at the door of the office, and Agang entered.

He bowed before Thorn. 'Your Majesty, the carriage is ready to take us to the parliament building.'

Thorn got to her feet and smoothed down the front of her dress. Daphne, Agang, and the two young Sanang men joined her as she strode from the office, and they walked down the wide hallway towards the front of the residence. Courtiers and staff were lining the walls, and each bowed their head as Thorn passed. Pechtang and T'Lang moved into flanking positions next to her – with one at each shoulder, while Daphne and Agang remained a pace behind. A servant opened the front door, and Thorn emerged into the soft sunlight of autumn. A large carriage was parked a few yards from the front entrance, and a footman extended a hand to assist Thorn. She stepped up into the carriage, then Daphne and Agang followed her in, as the two young Sanang men took up their positions by the rear rails. The side door was closed, and the driver pulled on the reins. The carriage moved forwards, the four horses pulling it along the driveway leading to the busy streets of Holdings City.

'Today's parliamentary agenda is straightforward,' Daphne said. 'The members shall listen to the new Empress's speech, then they shall hold a debate, and then they shall vote.'

'What are the terms of the vote?' Agang said.

'It's simple,' said Daphne; 'do they acknowledge Thorn as the new Empress? Yes or no. In theory, the result should be a foregone conclusion; after all, they have already voted to confirm that they accepted the outcome of the conference that selected Thorn in the first place. The untimely passing of Empress Bridget has, however, made this new vote necessary.'

'Where will our majority come from?' said Agang. 'Is anyone likely to oppose our claim?'

'As you probably know,' Daphne said, 'the Holdings is not a full democracy, such as Rakana was in the past. Out of the hundred members of parliament, thirty are selected by the Holders, who come together every six years to choose from their own number. That is the means by which I have twice been selected to sit in parliament. Fifty members are directly elected by the people who live in Holdings City and the River Holdings – that is where I hold much of my support; among the poorer sections of society. The final twenty members are elected from the larger towns dotted over the Holdings – Royston, Blackwater and so on. The First Holder is then elected by a vote of the hundred members. For my first term, I garnered sixty-four votes, but that fell to fifty-three for my second term. For the vote today, we can expect the vast majority of the members from Holdings City and the River Holdings to support us, along with a few from the towns. As for the aristocratic Holders, some of them will vote against us simply because they oppose every policy I put forward. Holds Clement, Cane, Wain, Wick and Greening are firmly on our side, but many of the others loathe me and my government. Any result where we get more than sixty votes should be counted as a great success.'

Thorn glanced out of the window as the carriage rolled through the streets of the city. There was nothing on the exterior of the carriage to denote who was inside, and Thorn wondered what the people would think if they knew. Would they bow to her, ignore her, or call her a traitor and a pretender to the throne? She took a breath to calm her nerves, and wished Acorn was with her. Her sister had possessed the ability to keep Thorn's feet firmly on the ground, and had been fond of ascribing her every act to her long-term plan of becoming Empress. Thorn smiled at the memory. If only Acorn had known how close she was to her achieving her dream. One speech, one vote, and the coronation would be happening.

The First Holder's residence was located close to the parliament, and Thorn saw the building rise up in front of her. The carriage went through an open set of iron gates, and drew up by the side of the parliament building.

Agang peered up at the structure. 'Is this an old building? Has it always been the parliament?'

'Yes, and yes,' said Daphne. 'Back when the Holdings was a monarchy, it housed the Merchants' Guild; it was where they used to debate and decide trade policy. I had it requisitioned when I first assumed power. Constructing a new parliament would have been rather expensive, and so I evicted the merchants.' Daphne glanced at Thorn. 'You are being very quiet, your Majesty. Is everything all right?'

'It's just nerves,' Thorn said. 'I'm so close, and yet so much could still go wrong.'

Daphne smiled. 'You'll be fine. Trust yourself. Show them the same qualities that you have shown me, and everything will work out.'

The side door was opened by Pechtang. He held out a hand, and Thorn took it, then she stepped down from the carriage. A crowd of onlookers had gathered by the iron railings surrounding the parliament building, and many were staring at her. An older man approached, leading a group dressed in fine robes.

'Your Majesty,' said Daphne, 'this is Weir, the Deputy First Holder of the Republic, and an old and trusted friend. He has been running the country while I have been in Colsbury.'

Weir bowed low before Thorn. 'It is a great honour to meet you, Empress.'

'The honour is mine,' said Thorn. 'Daphne has often spoken about the great faith she places in your abilities. I understand that you have been nominated to replace her as First Holder?'

'That is correct, your Majesty,' he said.

'She is not a "majesty" yet,' said an older woman in the group that had accompanied Weir. She glanced at Daphne. 'So, you do remember where Holdings City is located? It's been so long since you have deigned to visit us that I had assumed you had forgotten.'

'This is Holder Terras, your Majesty,' Daphne said. 'The first king of the Holdings originated from Hold Terras, and that has led them to believe that they are more important than the rest of us.'

'Whereas everyone knows how modest the Holdfasts are about their dubious achievements,' the old woman said.

'My greetings, Holder Terras,' said Thorn. 'I shall not attempt to persuade you to vote for me this day, as I do not wish to insult your intelligence. If you haven't been persuaded of the truth and justice of my claim by now, then I would presume that you never shall.'

Holder Terras looked Thorn up and down. 'Well, she's presentable, at least. She'll make a fine figurehead for your rule of the Empire, Holder Fast.'

Thorn smiled. 'It is clear that you know very little of me, Holder Terras,' she said, 'if you believe that I would settle for being anyone's figurehead.'

Holder Terras snorted and walked away.

Daphne smiled. 'This way, your Majesty.'

Thorn and the others followed Daphne up the steps and into the interior of the building. A bell rang out through the hallways, and groups of people began filing through an open door.

'The bell is used to summon all members into parliament,' Daphne whispered. 'Pechtang and T'Lang shall have to remain outside the debating chamber, but you have been invited, your Majesty, and I am allowed to bring Agang Garo as my guest.'

Thorn gave a slight nod. She walked through the door, and entered a large hall. The seating looked antique, and was arranged in semi-circular rows, with a tall podium set upon a platform facing the rapidly-filling chairs. A low hubbub of noise greeted Thorn as she walked towards the podium. A clerk bowed to her, then he gestured for Holder Fast and Agang Garo to go to their seats. He then led Thorn up onto the platform, and the parliamentary secretary stepped up on to the podium and raised his hands for silence.

Thorn gazed out at the members of parliament as they began to quieten down. It was easy to see where the thirty aristocratic Holders were sitting. They were bunched together in a group by one side of the hall, their expensive robes and jewellery marking them out.

When the hall had descended into silence, the secretary lowered his hands.

'My greetings to all honourable members,' he said. 'We are gathered here today to consider a bill that has been presented to this parliament by Member Weir of the River Holdings, Deputy First Holder of the Republic. The bill asks this parliament to come to a decision concerning the validity of a claim to the succession to the imperial throne; a claim put forward by Member Weir, and seconded by Member Daphne Holdfast, First Holder of the Republic. The claim itself is held by one Lady Thorn of Greyfalls Deepen, who has come here today to address the honourable members. After she has spoken, there will be time set aside for a debate, and then there shall be a vote.'

The secretary stepped down from the podium, and gestured to Thorn. 'You may speak.'

Thorn ascended the podium. 'Honourable members,' she said, her voice clear and strong, 'let me begin by expressing my deep sorrow over the death of Empress Bridget. Her Imperial Majesty was the greatest leader this world has ever known, and I mourn her loss keenly. No one did more for the people of this world, and perhaps no one shall ever equal her accomplishments. As we all know, Empress Bridget prided herself on governing this world via the rule of law, and it is the rule of law that must now be followed in her absence. The law is clear on matters of the imperial succession – each new Emperor or Empress is selected by a conference of the world's high mages. Empress Bridget was selected in this manner, just as I have also been selected. It is deeply unfortunate that Lord Bryce has decided to dispute my legitimate rights to the throne. He seems to think that he deserves the crown, simply because his mother wore it. If he succeeds, then the imperial crown will forever become a possession of the Kellach Brigdomin, passed down through the random selection of children who happen to have been born in a palace. Was it for this that we fought the Creator? Is this why we toiled against the armies of Agatha – to gift the Empire to a single family in perpetuity? Fortunately for this world, Lord Bryce will not succeed. He is a usurper, and he will be held to account for his acts of treason. I will hold him to account. I shall reign as Empress, and then, when my time is over, my successor shall be selected according to the law.'

She gazed out over the crowd, and sent a gentle flow of her powers into the hall, soothing the minds of the members of parliament, and lifting their spirits.

'As proof of this,' she went on, 'I hereby renounce any desire or intention to have any children of my own, so that there can be no doubt that I shall not follow in Lord Bryce's footsteps. Such is my love for the Empire, that I can make such a pledge. Such is my love for the people of this world, that I will consider myself to be the mother of all; a mother who protects, nurtures, and cares for all of the inhabitants of this Empire. My claim is legal, but more importantly, it is just. Today, you have a chance to show the world that the Holdings shall defend the law; and to prove that this parliament shall not shirk from its duty. Thank you.'

Thorn stepped down from the podium, and strode from the platform.

'That was short and sweet,' said Agang, as they relaxed in a small ante-chamber close to the debating hall.

'No one likes a long speech, Agang,' said Thorn. 'The majority of the members will have already made up their minds long before I spoke to them.'

'I was expecting a few policy statements,' Agang went on; 'some substance that would tell them how you intend to rule. Tax, trade, our policies towards Rakana and Rahain; anything, really.'

'None of that matters. I was selected to be Empress; that is the only relevant point I wished to convey.'

'I once gave a speech in Broadwater that lasted five hours,' Agang said.

Thorn smiled. 'Then, no offence, but you won't be writing any speeches for me.'

The door opened and Daphne walked in. She closed the door behind her, and exhaled.

'We did it,' she said. 'We won the vote, by sixty-two to twenty-four, with fourteen abstentions.'

Thorn rose to her feet and embraced Daphne. A surge of relief struck her and she closed her eyes. One step closer.

'Well done, your Majesty,' said Agang, standing. 'This means we can press ahead with the coronation.'

Daphne smiled. 'The parliament also decided to send representatives to Colsbury to attend the ceremony.'

'Did you pick a date?' said Thorn.

'We did, your Majesty. The eleventh of the Last Third of Autumn. That will allow time for delegates from the Matriarch's court in Sanang to also attend. I shall send them a message tonight.' She glanced into Thorn's eyes. 'Why didn't you tell me that you have decided against ever having children?'

'Because I wasn't sure if I would go through with it,' Thorn said. 'It was only when I was standing by the podium that I realised I would need to make a personal sacrifice, for the sake of the Empire.'

'But what a sacrifice,' Daphne said. 'I hope you don't live to regret it, your Majesty.'

'Being Empress shall be enough for me,' Thorn said; 'more than enough.'

55

CHAPTER 5
EMPEROR BRYCE

Plateau City, The Plateau – 2nd Day, Last Third Autumn 534

Keir gazed down at the city from the low wall that enclosed the roof garden. A holiday had been declared to celebrate Bryce's coronation, and the streets were full of people, just as they had been on the day of Bridget's funeral. Forty-five days had passed since then, and the atmosphere in Plateau City had slowly altered, from uncontrolled grief, to relief that a civil war hadn't erupted with the Holdfasts, to a steady sense of continuity, edged with anger. The people seemed to think the Holdfasts should be punished, and were hoping that Emperor Bryce would be the man to do it, but, at the same time, very few were advocating all out war on the Holdings and Sanang.

Coronation day was providing another moment of pause among the citizens of Plateau City. Festive bunting had been draped across most of the main highways, and flags and banners were fluttering in the chill autumnal breeze. The crown had donated plenty of gold to ensure that street parties could take place in each of the city's Quarters and districts, and the celebrations were in full swing. Unlike the funeral, the vast majority of the citizenry would be unable to witness the actual crowning of Bryce, but the new Emperor was planning to tour each part of his city in the coming days, from the Rahain Quarter on the far banks of the river, to the aristocratic district in the New Town, and everywhere in between.

Tilda shivered by Keir's side, and his arm drew her closer to his body. She pushed him away.

'What's wrong?' he said.

Tilda said nothing, and Keir sighed. He had given up trying to predict her mood swings. On some days, she acted as if she was besotted with him, and on others, she was like a different person – cold, and resentful about having to live in the palace. She had been forbidden from leaving the Great Fortress by an express order of the new Emperor, and Keir knew she felt trapped. It was for her own safety, they had been told. Her father, Holder Wain, had voted in the Holdings parliament to confirm their view that Thorn was the legitimate sovereign of the Empire, and Tilda was being shielded from any over-zealous citizen of Plateau City who might want to take revenge upon her family.

'I can almost see my old apartment from here,' she said, her eyes scanning the area to the north-west of the Great Fortress.

'Do you wish you were back there?' he said.

She hesitated, as if fearful of giving an honest answer.

'You can tell me,' he said. 'There's no one else up here.'

She shook her head. 'He's always watching.'

'Who, Daimon?'

Her eyes tightened at the mention of the dream mage's name.

'He can't look everywhere at once,' said Keir. 'Recall what happened when the Holdings voted to support Thorn. The Emperor was furious with Daimon, because he had completely missed it. As a vision mage myself, I actually sympathised with Daimon – he can't be watching Colsbury, Plateau City, and Holdings City all at the same time. And he's supposed to be keeping an eye on the imperial garrisons, to ensure none of the Holdings soldiers desert. Whatever happens in the world, the Emperor expects Daimon to have witnessed it, and that's simply not possible. I doubt he has much time to spare watching us.'

'He still does it, though,' Tilda said. 'Sometimes, when we're alone at night, I'm certain that he's spying on us. Worse, sometimes, I don't even care. Something's happening to me. I feel happy and relaxed one minute, and then terrified the next.'

Keir nodded. He had a strong suspicion that he knew the cause of her worries – that Daimon was manipulating her thoughts and emotions, but he felt it would only make her more anxious if he revealed this to her. He also suspected that the same thing was happening to him; it was the only rational explanation for his own sudden changes of mood. He could switch from despondent to elated in the blink of an eye. He recognised the signs from his own youth, when Karalyn had routinely manipulated those around her, and it left him with a bitter taste.

'Are we guests,' Tilda said, 'or are we hostages?'

'Whatever occurs,' Keir said, 'you can rely on me. I won't let anything bad happen to you.'

She shook her head. 'You are as much of a prisoner here as I am, Keir. You just don't realise it yet.'

That was nonsense, he thought, though he kept his opinion to himself. He wasn't a hostage, or a prisoner, he was a vital part of Emperor Bryce's court. His vision abilities were far greater than Tabor's feeble skills, and he was second only to Daimon; while Tilda, for all her good looks, was powerless. That was why she had been given to Keir. There was nothing to worry about.

He gazed down into the streets of the city. He and Tilda were standing above the wall that divided the Old Town from the New. To their left, the narrow lanes of the Old Town were heaving with people. Every road seemed to have its own party, and the sound of the celebrating citizens was providing a constant background noise. On their right, the tall spires of the university gave way to the elegant streets of the aristocratic district. Among them lay the old Holdfast townhouse, now requisitioned by the crown. Keir wondered if Tabitha had managed to get out of the city without being harassed or lynched. She was a silly bitch, but she didn't deserve to die.

The noon bells began to ring, and a great cheer rose up from the city.

Keir nodded. 'That's it. Bryce is now officially the Emperor.'

Tilda scowled at him. 'Do you not wonder why we weren't invited to the coronation?'

'Only a small handful of people were invited,' he said. 'Just family, and a couple of others. They wanted a private ceremony. That's understandable, I guess.'

'Then why was Daimon invited?'

'He is the chief mage of the Empire.'

Tilda leaned in closer to him. 'If they're all busy, then...'

'Yes? Then what?'

'Then maybe we should try to run for it. We could slip away, and be out of the city in an hour.'

'Are you mad?' he said. 'Why would we want to do that?'

'I'm scared, Keir. I'm scared of Daimon. I hate the way he leers at me; and the way he speaks now, as if he were trying to pretend he is an aristocrat. The Emperor has changed, too; don't you see that? It must have been the death of his mother that made him change. He never smiles like he used to, and he seems consumed with anger all of the time. Even Lady Brogan's different. All she talks about is how much she wants to kill your mother and Lady Thorn.'

'My mother is a traitor, and Thorn is an evil witch. They deserve to die.'

Tilda stared at him. 'How can you say that about your own mother?'

'Because it's true. My mother was never loyal to Empress Bridget – I can see that now. For years, all she's been doing is defying the orders of the Empire, and grooming her nasty little protégé. They only care about power. Things might seem unsettled now, but once the Empire has been reunited, everything will be fine again.' He stretched his arms. 'Come on; we should go downstairs. Lady Brogan asked us to return to the palace a few minutes after the noon bell.'

Tilda looked reluctant to leave the roof garden, but she nodded, and they walked to the stair turret. Keir led the way back down to their apartment, and Tilda followed in silence. They were already dressed in their finest clothes, and passed through their rooms, Keir locking the front door behind him. Two Kellach soldiers were waiting outside in the corridor.

'We are here to escort you to the throne room, my lord,' said one, bowing his head.

'Thank you,' said Keir. 'Lead on.'

The soldiers about-turned and set off down the carpeted passageway. Keir glanced at Tilda as they walked, but she was keeping her head lowered. They descended a wide flight of stairs, and approached the large throne room. Its doors were lying open, and the soldiers led them inside. Bryce was sitting upon his mother's throne, a golden crown on his brow, while Daimon and Bryce's four siblings were gathered next to him. Keir and Tilda walked to the area in front of the throne, and both bowed. Keir noticed Daimon smirking at them, and then Tilda began to smile, as if all her cares had evaporated.

'Congratulations on your coronation, your Majesty,' Tilda said, beaming in joy.

Bryce nodded. 'Thank you, Miss Holdwain.'

'May your reign be long and successful, your Majesty,' said Keir, keeping his gaze down.

'I hope it will,' said Bryce.

The soldiers ushered Keir and Tilda to the side, and then Keir noticed that a queue had formed behind him. It seemed as though every courtier and soldier in the Great Fortress was lining up to congratulate their new sovereign. They approached the throne in small groups, each bowing low as they praised the Emperor, and the hall began to fill with people. Tabor was near the front of the queue, and he joined Keir and Tilda once he had said his piece.

Keir grew bored as the endless procession made its way past the Emperor. The flow of people seemed unceasing, and the long minutes dragged out. When the hall was full, soldiers opened a side door, and began to shepherd some of the people out again, but Keir, Tilda and Tabor were left where they were. Keir noticed other mages arrive. Dean was first. He bowed awkwardly in front of Bryce, and muttered a few words, then Ravi and Nadia walked forwards. Both looked nervous, and kept their gazes down; then all three mages were led over to where Keir was standing. A few minutes later, Sanders, the old Holdings vision mage, shuffled in front of the throne. She murmured something inaudible, and Bryce frowned.

Lady Brogan took a step forward. 'What did you say, Mage Sanders?'

Sanders glanced up. 'I wished for peace to return to the Empire, my lady.'

'You are here to congratulate your new sovereign,' Brogan said. 'I would like you to do so. Now.'

Sanders swallowed. 'I wish the best for the new Holder of the World.'

Brogan frowned.

'This woman believes that Lady Thorn is the rightful ruler of the Empire,' Daimon exclaimed, pointing at the old mage.

The hall hushed, and Sanders began to tremble.

'Is that true?' said Bryce.

'I... I believe in the law,' Sanders said.

'Address the Emperor correctly,' cried Brogan, 'or you shall be deemed as treacherous as Daphne Holdfast.'

Sanders bowed her head, and began to weep. 'I cannot call a man something he is not. That would be wrong.'

Brogan glanced at a squad of soldiers and snapped her fingers. 'Take her away. Chain her and lock her in the dungeons, until she learns some respect.'

'No!' cried Sanders. 'I am an old woman; the dungeons will be the death of me.'

'Don't forget to hood her,' Brogan went on. 'Her vision powers are feeble, but she may try to use them to escape.'

The soldiers approached Sanders. Two grabbed her arms, and the old woman began to struggle.

'Help me, someone!' she cried. 'You all know the truth – am I the only one here with the courage to say it? Bryce is not the Emperor; the throne does not belong to him. He...'

A Kellach soldier struck Sanders across the face with the back of his hand, and she went limp. The squad dragged her from the hall, as everyone stared, but no one spoke.

Brogan nodded to the queue, and it started moving again as if nothing had happened. To Keir's right, Ravi was trembling, but, on his left, Tilda was still smiling inanely. Keir kept his features impassive. Sanders was an idiot.

The queue went on and on, with even the lowliest servants of the Great Fortress afforded the honour of congratulating Bryce. After an hour or so, Tilda's smile began to fade, and she blinked as if awakening from an unpleasant dream. Keir willed her to keep quiet, but she wasn't as foolish as Sanders, and she behaved herself, despite the fear in her eyes.

Eventually, the queue petered out, and the hall began to empty again, but Keir and the other mages were told to remain where they were. The last of the servants left the hall, then Tilda was escorted away. She glanced at Keir as the soldiers led her back to their apartment, but he kept his eyes on the floor. The doors to the hall were closed, leaving only the royal family, the mages of Plateau City, and over a dozen heavily-armed soldiers present.

Daimon stepped forward. 'Mages, kneel before your supreme lord and master.'

The five mages strode forward. Keir ensured he was in the lead, while the others followed behind him. They lined up in front of the high throne, and then each of them fell to their knees, their heads bowed.

'You are all now in the service of the Empire,' Daimon said. 'His Majesty has asked me to probe deeply, to ensure that none of you secretly harbour the same seeds of disloyalty as Sanders displayed to us earlier.' He glanced along the line. 'Mage Tabor, you have no need to prove anything – your loyalty is already well known. Rise, and join us on the platform.'

Tabor gasped in relief, then got to his feet. Keir frowned as Tabor took his place next to Brogan and the other children.

'Mage Keir,' Daimon then said; 'despite the treachery of your insidious family, you are also trusted. You and Tabor shall now hold the titles of Court Mages, and you will both report directly to me. Join us.'

Keir grinned. He walked up onto the platform, where Brogan gave him a nod.

'And what have we left, eh?' said Daimon, his accent slipping a little. 'A feeble fire mage, who prefers reading obscure old books to venturing out of the university grounds; a sly wee clay mage, who considers certain members of the Holdfast family to be his friends; and a useless old stone mage, who once betrayed her own daughter to Sable Holdfast. What shall we do with you three?'

'If we are so useless,' said Nadia, 'then perhaps you should allow us to return to our jobs at the university.'

'Shut it, ya auld cow!' Daimon cried, his aristocratic accent abandoned. He paused, smiled, and took a breath. 'It was a rhetorical question. I have a real question for you – are you prepared to obey every command of our new Emperor?'

'We are at the service of the Empire,' said Nadia, keeping her head down.

The Emperor glanced at Dean. 'Fire mage,' said Bryce. 'Is it true that you were on the roof of the Great Fortress the night Emperor Guilliam was killed?

'Aye, your Majesty,' Dean said. 'And I was with Empress Bridget the following morning when she was crowned.'

'Then tell me – how did you end up hiding away in the university? The others on the roof that night all went on to lead lives of prosperity and fame, and yet you became a humble librarian? Why?'

'I had no desire to seek wealth or fame, your Majesty.'

'He's lying,' said Daimon. 'The truth is that Dean is too scared to leave his library and his books. Crowds frighten him, and he had to be compelled against his will to attend the palace this day. Worse, his powers are too weak to be of any use to us. Even if he had any courage, which he doesn't, he'd be no good against the Holdfasts.'

'Is he loyal?' said Brogan.

Daimon snorted. 'He's too afraid to be anything else. I could strengthen his mind if his powers were decent, and make him brave, but is there any point?'

Bryce nodded. 'You are dismissed from my presence, Dean. Go back to the university and continue with your work.'

Dean exhaled as he rose to his feet. 'Thank you, your Majesty,' he said, then he hurried from the throne room, a soldier opening the door for him.

'One down, two to go,' said Daimon. 'Stone mage – what do you have to offer your new Emperor?'

'My expertise lies in hydraulics, my lord,' Nadia said. 'I specialise in waterworks, sewage and heating systems. I studied in the finest institutes in Rahain before… before Agatha and the wars ruined my homeland. Now, I help maintain the underground pipes and cisterns of Plateau City, and teach advanced Rahain technology to the students of the university.'

'That actually seems quite useful,' said Brogan. 'Do you ever have occasion to use your powers in the course of your work?'

'Very rarely, my lady. It is true that I possess stone powers, but not to a great extent.'

Daimon peered into her eyes. 'She once stabbed Sable Holdfast in the back, killing her. Unfortunately, Thorn was on hand at the time to revive the Holdfast witch.'

'Is that so?' said Bryce. 'Mage Nadia, do you still desire to kill Sable Holdfast? Before you answer, know that Daimon will be able to perceive any lie that passes your lips.'

Nadia looked down. 'I do desire her death, your Majesty. Sable tricked me into betraying my own daughter, then she cut her down in cold blood in the university quad. Sable promised me that she would leave Nyane unharmed, but she broke her word, and I cannot bring myself to forgive her.' She glanced at Ravi, who was kneeling to her right. 'Sorry.'

'Why are you apologising to him?' said Brogan.

'Because I have lied to Ravi in the past, my lady. I told him that I had forgiven Sable Holdfast, and that it was all in the past, but my heart has never healed.' She began to sob, and put her hands to her face.

'We shall let her go,' said Bryce. 'Nadia's enemies are our enemies, and that is enough for me. She is too valuable in her present role to throw her life away against the Holdfasts. Nadia, return to the university.'

Nadia bowed her head, and fled from the chamber.

'That leaves you,' Daimon said to Ravi. 'I heard you offer your congratulations to our new sovereign, but I've seen the disloyalty that rots your soul. You wish you were far from here; you wish you were in Colsbury with the other traitors. Is that not right?'

'You're the one reading my thoughts,' said Ravi; 'you tell me.'

Daimon laughed. 'At least you have a backbone, clay mage. Alright, I'll tell you what I can see. You love Sable Holdfast. You love Kelsey Holdfast, too, but not in the way that you lust after Sable. That witch pulled your mind in a hundred different directions, until you were completely besotted with her. You know this is true, and yet you can't help yourself.'

'I remember Ravi from the siege of Colsbury,' said Brogan. 'He and Nadia created some kind of protective substance, and they coated the outer walls of the castle with it, so that Agatha's fire and stone powers couldn't work.'

'That's right, sister,' said Bryce. 'I recall it, too. Ravi is more powerful than Dean and Nadia combined, but his heart lies with our enemies. Perhaps we should execute him, to ensure that he doesn't try to defect to the Holdfasts.'

'There is an alternative, your Majesty,' said Daimon. 'Ravi has a very rare and peculiar ability – he can turn coal into diamonds.'

Ravi groaned.

'Any conflict with the Holdfasts will be expensive, your Majesty,'

Daimon went on. 'Perhaps it would be wise to imprison Mage Ravi, and put him to work. I could help persuade him to work hard, and he might prove to be a profitable source of income.'

'I agree,' said Brogan. 'Ravi is physically weak, and he has no powers that would enable him to escape from the chains and shackles of the dungeons. If he produces diamonds for our cause, then we should let him live.'

'Oh, come on,' said Ravi, his eyes wide. 'You don't need to shackle me. I spent a year in a Rahain dungeon making diamonds for Agatha, and then Sable forced me to do the same thing for her. What if I promise to be a good boy? If you send me back to the university, then I swear I'll start making diamonds for you. I could do about five decent-sized gems every third or so; and I won't try to leave the university grounds. Please don't chain me up again.'

Daimon squinted into Ravi's face. 'He's telling the truth. However, I would advise against letting him leave the palace, your Majesty. His thoughts are fickle – he could easily change his mind.'

'I have the solution,' said Bryce. 'We shall find Ravi a small room within the palace, and shackle his ankles together, to make it impossible for him to run away. Brogan, assign two soldiers to guard him at all times. If he proves himself to be useful and dependable then we might, in time, consider removing the shackles.'

Brogan nodded. 'Would Keir's old rooms be suitable, your Majesty? They remain unoccupied.'

'Yes, sister. Please see to it. This meeting of the mages is over. Tabor, instruct the merchants' guild that I am ready to receive them. Keir, you are dismissed. Return to your quarters.'

Keir and Tabor bowed low before the Emperor, as Brogan gestured for two soldiers to accompany her and Ravi. The Rakanese mage looked close to tears as he was led away, then Keir and Tabor left the hall by a different door.

Tabor glanced at Keir. 'We are very fortunate, the two of us,' he said. 'The Emperor trusts us.'

Keir nodded. 'Is there any work for me today?'

Tabor shrugged. 'Lord Daimon didn't give us anything to do, so, no. Remember, we work for him now. I imagine things will get busier for us once things have settled into a new routine. See you later.'

Tabor strode away, and Keir turned for the stairs. He ascended one flight, and walked to his apartment. The front door was unlocked, so he assumed that Tilda was inside. He entered his rooms, and glanced around.

'Tilda?'

Nothing. He looked into each room, but saw no sign of the young Holdings woman. He lit a few lamps and quickly changed out of his fine robes, hung them up in a wardrobe, and pulled on more comfortable clothes. He grabbed his cigarettes and headed for the rear stairs. The sun was low in the western sky when he emerged from the gloom of the stair turret. Keir breathed in the evening air, and strolled among the trees, flower beds and bushes of the beautiful roof garden. He went to the bench where Tilda often sat, but there was no sign of her.

Where was she?'

He turned, and his mouth fell open in fright. Tilda had climbed up onto the wall that ringed the garden, and was looking down at the hundred-foot drop to the streets below. Her bare feet were balanced on the lip of the wall, as if the slightest gust of wind would send her over the edge. Keir looked at her face, and saw nothing but despair.

'Tilda!' he cried.

She turned her head, and gave him a look of desperate sorrow.

'I'm sorry, Keir,' she said, then she stepped off the wall.

Keir launched himself towards her, and managed to grab hold of her right arm as she fell. He slammed against the wall, his fingers gripping her arm as she dangled over the edge. He braced his feet, and pulled her back up, then used both hands to haul her over the wall and into the garden. She struggled in his grasp, weeping uncontrollably.

'It's alright,' he said, his arms enveloping her. 'You're safe now.'

'Let me go,' she cried. 'Don't you understand – I want to die.'

'No,' he said; 'don't say that, Tilda.'

'I'm trapped here, forever,' she sobbed. 'I know what's happening to me, Keir – I felt it in the throne room. I was sad and angry, and then Daimon looked into my eyes, and it was as if someone had lit a lamp in my mind, and I felt happy, so happy. He did it to me, didn't he? He can make me feel whatever he wants me to feel.'

Keir didn't respond.

Tilda glared at him. 'You knew, didn't you? You knew what he was doing to me, and yet you said nothing. You're just as bad as the others. Am I your slave?'

Keir pushed his way into her mind. *Sleep.*

Tilda's eyes closed and she slumped in his tight embrace. Keir released her, and sat on the grass, his head in his hands. Perhaps he should have let her jump, he thought, then he chastised himself. She was his responsibility. He was supposed to be taking care of her, not allowing her to leap from the roof of the Great Fortress. He picked her up in his arms, and carried her down into their rooms. He laid her on their bed, and left the apartment. He knew where to go, and conducted his business quickly, even though he knew Tilda would remain asleep for a while. When he got back to their quarters, he locked the door, and went into the bedroom.

Awaken.

Tilda's eyes opened, and she rubbed her head. 'What happened?'

'Here,' he said, passing her something.

'What is it?' she said.

'Dullweed.'

She frowned at him.

'Trust me,' he said, raising a lit match to the end of the weedstick. 'It will help.'

CHAPTER 6
QUEEN OF NOWHERE

Marchside, Kell – 5th Day, Last Third Autumn 534

Corthie held the gate open as the rain pelted down from the grey skies. Belinda urged the ponies forward, and the cart rolled through the gate and onto the rough, muddy track. Corthie closed the gate, and jumped back up onto the cart.

'This damn weather,' he laughed.

Belinda smiled. 'I don't mind it. I love it down here.'

Corthie rolled his eyes and laughed even louder. His clothes, face and hair were drenched with the persistent rain, and his boots were coated in a thick layer of brown mud.

'Shall we check on the sheep?' said Belinda.

'Not in this rain,' Corthie said. 'Let's head home, and dry off for a bit before we venture outside again.'

Belinda nodded, then she guided the cart up the gentle slope that led to the farmhouse. It had been a good day – hard-working and busy, and Belinda had appreciated the way that physical labour had drowned out the anxieties in her mind. She wondered if that explained why Corthie had chosen that life; she knew that he also suffered from the ghosts of his past. Maybe hard work was his way of blocking it from his thoughts.

The wind howled across the flank of the hill, sending the cold, driving rain into their faces. Every sensible inhabitant of Marchside was probably keeping indoors, she thought, but neither she nor Corthie were particularly sensible. Expert killers, yes; but not very sensible ones. She smiled as she glanced at him. She felt safe next to Corthie, not because she was afraid that anyone would physically hurt her; there was no one on the Star Continent able to do that; but more because he accepted her for who she was, and she felt that she never had to explain herself to him. He understood her, and yet he loved her all the same.

She steered the ponies into the courtyard in front of the farmhouse. A curtain flickered.

'Aila will be thinking we're crazy,' Corthie said.

'Maybe we are,' Belinda said.

'Aye. Maybe.'

Corthie jumped down from the cart before Belinda had brought it to a halt, and he started untying the two ponies from their harnesses. He gripped the reins, and led them towards the dry confines of their stable, while Belinda dealt with the cart. She powered her battle-vision, and pushed it into a shed, then closed the door once it was inside. She and Corthie ran for the front door of the farmhouse, and Corthie pushed the door open.

Aila was standing in the wide hallway waiting for them, with Konna in her arms. 'Shoes and coats off before you go any further,' she said, as Corthie and Belinda entered. 'I'm not having you drag mud all over the house.'

'Aye, boss,' said Corthie, leaning down to unlace his heavy boots.

Aila threw a dry towel to each of them, and shook her head.

'We fixed the fence,' Belinda said, as she rubbed her hair with a towel. 'No more cattle should be able to escape.'

'At least you achieved something,' said Aila. 'It's horrible out there today.'

Belinda pulled off her boots, and set them down next to Corthie's by the front door.

'I've put the kettle on for you,' Aila said.

Corthie kissed her. 'Thanks. Tea, Belinda?'

She smiled. 'Yes, please.'

They hung their sodden coats up by the main door and walked down the hallway and into the kitchen.

'I'll make the tea,' said Corthie, striding to the long stove in his bare feet.

Aila and Belinda sat down by the sturdy dining table, and Aila cradled Konna in her arms. The sight made Belinda broody for a brief moment, and she thought about the many children she had given birth to, and then forgotten about. Silva was the closest thing she had to a child, and she acted like an old woman. She even looked older, as if to show everyone that she wasn't a salve-addled demigod.

'How old do I look?' she asked Aila.

Aila narrowed her eyes a little. 'Um, let me see. Twenty-five? Early to mid-twenties, I'd guess. I wish I looked a little bit older. I can't tell you how much I regret sniffing that salve in Ooste. It'll take a century for me to look as old as you; maybe longer.'

Belinda nodded. 'I think I am jealous of you, Aila.'

'Why?'

'The children. Staying here with you and your family has been wonderful, but perhaps it's made me want to have children of my own. I mean, more children. Silva told me that I've had many children over the millennia, and I even saw some of their tombs in Dun Khatar. I can't remember any of it, of course.'

Aila smiled. 'Do you have any particular father in mind?'

'Corthie is a good father,' said Belinda.

'He is,' said Aila, 'but he also happens to be my husband.'

'I know that. Do you think I could find someone like Corthie? Someone dependable and loyal; someone I could trust. Someone who wouldn't try to seduce Sable at the first opportunity.'

Corthie laughed. 'We could start looking around Kell for you.'

'I think I would prefer an immortal,' Belinda went on, 'but not one who has already lived for countless ages. A young immortal.'

Corthie poured hot water into the teapot. 'You could wait until wee Killop's old enough.'

Aila glared at him.

'It was a joke!' he said.

'Not a very good joke,' said Aila.

Belinda smiled, though she hadn't quite understood the exchange. Was there something funny about Corthie's suggestion?

'We should have asked Sable to bring down more tea,' Corthie said. 'I doubt we have enough to get us through winter.'

'If you're short of tea,' said Belinda, 'then I could drink whisky.'

'We haven't got any,' said Aila. 'You can buy some down in the village.'

Belinda nodded, then she turned to Corthie. 'Why haven't you drunk any alcohol since I arrived? You used to drink all the time. I've been meaning to ask for a few days, but I got the feeling that it might be an awkward subject.'

'Well,' said Corthie, as he brought the teapot and mugs over to the broad table, 'I was in jail for eighty days, and couldn't have any in there. You arrived the day I got released, and I thought, if I've been without it for so long, then I might as well continue. This winter will be the big test; all those dark nights, and weather too terrible to work in. We'll see how it goes.'

'You've done very well,' said Aila. 'I'm proud of you.'

Corthie frowned. 'Don't say that. If you say that, then what are we going to say to each other if I start drinking again? The chances are that I'll slip up now and again.'

'Sorry for bringing it up,' said Belinda.

'You are the queen of the awkward conversation, Belinda,' said Aila.

'Still? I thought I was getting better.'

'You are,' said Aila. 'A while ago, you wouldn't have realised that we'd been having an awkward conversation.'

Belinda laughed. 'I'm going to say something else that might make you feel awkward. Aila, Corthie, I love you both very much. This has been the happiest I've been in... I don't know how long. All the pain I feel, and all of the horrible memories of being stuck in that mask; they don't seem so bad here. When Karalyn and the others rescued me from Implacatus and took me to Colsbury, I wanted to die. I don't want to die any more. You have shown me that I can be happy again; that it's possible. Thank you.'

Corthie and Aila sat in silence for a moment, and Belinda wondered if she had offended them.

Aila sniffed. 'That's the most beautiful thing anyone's ever said to me.'

'You wanted to die?' said Corthie, his voice strained.

Belinda nodded. 'The pain was too much. Not the physical pain; my body was healed. The pain in my mind. It's still there, but I think I might be able to live with it.'

Corthie puffed out his cheeks.

'Am I interrupting?' came a voice from behind them.

They turned, and saw Sable leaning against the kitchen doorframe.

'You are,' said Belinda, standing, 'but it's all right. It's good to see you, Sable.'

Sable raised an eyebrow as Belinda hugged her.

'We were getting our feelings out in the open,' said Aila.

'Then I'm glad I wasn't here for that,' Sable said. 'Is that fresh tea? How about you pour me a mug, nephew, while Aila and Belinda pack their things? I assume you're ready to go?'

'Go?' said Aila. 'Now?'

'Well, not right now,' said Sable, sitting at the table, 'but in the next few hours. I did say that I would be back in around half a third; and guess what – that's today. Had you forgotten?'

'Shit,' muttered Corthie. 'You mean I'm going to lose my wife and my best friend at the same time?'

'That's a little melodramatic, nephew,' said Sable. 'I'm not taking them away forever. It's just for a few days, and you are still more than welcome to come with us.'

Corthie chewed his lip. 'Maybe another time. I need to work on the farm.'

'Is that the real reason?' said Belinda.

'Partly,' he said. 'Another part of me worries about visiting the place where I killed so many greenhides. I need to divorce myself from violence, and the City reminds me of blood and death. I'm not ready to face it. Not yet.'

Sable shook her head. 'Well, it's up to you. There go my dreams of embarking upon some mad rampage with Corthie Holdfast. I guess that makes me the greatest mortal warrior of all time.'

'You're welcome to the title,' Corthie said. 'It's been nothing but a burden round my neck.'

'The people of the City of Pella would disagree,' said Belinda. 'You are a hero to them.'

'I wasn't there for Simon,' he said. 'Kelsey's their hero now.'

'Do you mind if I go?' said Aila.

'No,' he said. 'You should go; get a break from Clackenbaird – you deserve it. I'll look after Killop, and you can take Konna.'

Aila stood, and handed the baby to Belinda. 'I'll pack.'

Belinda gazed down into Konna's sleeping face. 'She's beautiful. Dangerous, but beautiful.'

Sable grimaced. 'What have I come back to? Corthie's sworn off violence, and Belinda's swooning over a baby? I think I need a drink.'

'There's no alcohol in the house,' said Belinda. 'Corthie's given up.'

'That's it,' Sable cried. 'The world has gone mad.'

Belinda gave Corthie a last hug, then stepped back so that he could embrace Aila. The demigod had Konna strapped to her chest, while Killop was looking up at his parents.

Aila kissed her husband, then leaned over and kissed Killop on the head.

'Have a good time,' Corthie said, 'and take care. Don't let Sable lead you all astray.'

'See you in a few days,' said Aila.

Sable reached into a pocket, and the air shimmered. The three women and the baby appeared in the large forecourt outside the Great Keep of Colsbury, surrounded by hundreds of armoured Sanang soldiers.

'Holy crap!' Sable yelled. 'These guys weren't here when I left.'

There was a loud commotion as several soldiers jumped in shock at their sudden appearance, and Konna started to cry. Belinda powered her battle-vision and shielded Aila, her eyes narrowing at the ranks of muscular soldiers.

Sable raised her empty hands. 'We're friends of Empress Thorn. We didn't mean to startle you.'

A young man shoved his way through the crowd towards them.

'These women are on our side,' he yelled.

'Thanks, Pechtang,' said Sable. 'What are all these guys doing here?'

'They've just arrived, Sable,' Pechtang said. 'The Matriarch sent them to reinforce Colsbury. Their officers are speaking to Daphne and the Empress just now. T'Lang and I are organising where they're all going to be living.' He cleared a path through the lines of soldiers. 'There are eight hundred – a full regiment; and they brought their own weapons and equipment. They marched all the way from Broadwater.'

'Didn't Daimon see them?' said Belinda.

Pechtang shrugged. 'If he did, then he didn't do anything to stop them.' He halted when they reached the entrance to the keep. 'I'd better return to work. Good to see you back, Belinda.'

Belinda frowned as the man ran off.

'Of all the times to Quadrant to the courtyard,' muttered Sable, as they entered the keep. 'I usually arrive in the Sextant chamber, but I knew that Belinda doesn't like that room, so I thought I'd be clever. Eight hundred Sanang? That will stiffen the defences.'

'Those soldiers were massive,' said Aila. 'And their arms were huge. They're from Sanang?'

'Yeah,' said Sable. 'Is that the first time you've seen Sanang men?'

'I've met Agang Garo,' Aila said.

'He's old,' said Sable. 'Sanang women, like Thorn, look pretty similar to Holdings women, except for their skin colour; but Sanang men are almost like a different species.'

'The Sanang are a different species,' said Belinda. 'The only fully-human species on this world are the Holdings people.'

They carried Konna and their luggage up the stairs to the inhabited levels of the keep.

'I'd better take you to see Silva,' Sable said to Belinda. 'She's not been happy that I left her here while you were in Kell.'

They heard sounds coming from the dining room, and Sable opened the door. The tall shutters were wide open, and autumnal sunlight was filling the chamber. Down one side of the long dining table sat Karalyn, the twins, Cardova and Caelius, while Kelsey, Van, Olo'osso, Lara and Silva were on the other side. At the far end of the table, four places had been set, but their seats were empty.

'This looks cosy,' said Sable.

Silva leapt to her feet and ran towards Belinda. 'My Queen!'

Belinda felt embarrassment wash over her as Silva fell to her knees and started to weep.

Kelsey sighed. 'The effect you have on Silva never fails to amaze me, Belinda. One minute, she's acting like a mature adult, then she turns into this as soon as she sees you.'

'Hello, Aila, Belinda,' said Karalyn. 'How's Corthie?'

'He's fine, thanks,' said Aila.

'He's sober and working hard,' said Belinda, lowering her heavy bag to the ground. 'Should we go to the City of Pella now?'

'In a few moments,' said Sable. 'Where are Daphne and the others?'

'They're speaking to the commanders of the Sanang regiment that arrived,' said Karalyn.

'Aye,' said Kelsey. 'Shella and Agang work for Thorn now; or Agang works for Thorn, and Shella works for mother. It's complicated.'

Sable nodded. 'What's the story about the regiment?'

'There's not much to tell,' said Kelsey. 'They arrived an hour ago. The Matriarch sent them, and now she's demanding to know where the huge army is; the one that mother promised her would be here by now.'

Sable nodded. 'I guess this means we'll be going to Dragon Eyre soon.'

Karalyn frowned. 'You know I don't agree with this plan.'

'We'll be doing Dragon Eyre a favour by evacuating thousands of Banner soldiers,' said Sable. 'For Dragon Eyre to be at peace, it's essential that we remove them from the Home Islands.'

'I don't mind that,' said Karalyn; 'it's the bringing them here that I don't like. If we were going to send them to Implacatus, then I would help, but does the Star Continent need a hundred thousand Banner soldiers to suddenly appear?'

'Your mother seems to think so.'

'But what do you think, Sable?' said Karalyn.

'If we can afford to feed them and arm them, then I think it's a good idea. How else are we supposed to resist Bryce's imperial army?'

Karalyn groaned. 'There are what – two hundred thousand soldiers in the imperial army, aye? Where are they all? There's no field army of any size. The vast majority of them are garrisoning scores of fortresses and border posts – the Great Tunnel leading to Rahain, the Frontier Wall between the Plateau and Rakana. Rainsby, Westport, and so on and on. Two hundred thousand is a big number, but there's no way that Bryce will ever be able to gather them all together into a coherent force. The only possible reason that he would even attempt such a drastic course of action is if we transport a huge number of Banner soldiers here. If we do this, then he'll be forced to respond. We'll be escalating an already tense situation.'

'I don't agree,' said Sable. 'Bryce might not be able to rustle together the entire two hundred thousand he has under arms, but he could manage a force of sixty or seventy thousand, and that would be more than enough to overwhelm Colsbury, and blockade Sanang and the Holdings into submission.'

The three Banner men glanced at each other.

'I agree with Sable,' said Caelius.

'You would,' scoffed Olo'osso. 'You'd like a few thousand more Banner rabble to arrive here, wouldn't you, little soldier-boy?'

'Listen to the mortals squabble as they discuss slaughtering each other, my Queen,' said Silva. 'You should have no part in this sordid quarrel, your Majesty.'

'Belinda hasn't even said anything, Silva,' Sable snapped.

The demigod glowered at her.

'Can we leave now?' said Belinda.

Sable sighed. 'Fine. Lara, are you ready?'

The young woman shrugged. 'Where is it we're going this time?'

'Salve City.'

Lara stood. 'Are we going to be staying for a while?'

'We could stay for a few nights, I suppose.'

'You'll be back for the coronation, aye?' said Kelsey.

'When is that?' said Sable.

'On the eleventh. Six days from now.'

'Yeah. We'll definitely be back for that.'

Lara nodded, and strode out of the room.

'One other thing before you go,' said Cardova. He reached into a pocket and withdrew an envelope. He stared at it for a moment, then took a breath, stood and handed it to Sable.

'What is it?' said Sable.

'It's my resignation letter,' Cardova said. 'I am resigning my commission from the Banner of the Lostwell Exiles. I will need the permission of the King and Queen of the City in order to leave, but I'm hoping that it will be a formality. Could you please give it to them when you get to Tara? Tell them it has been an honour to serve, but I want to make a new start here.'

Sable smiled at Karalyn. 'You got your man, niece.'

Karalyn nodded, then glanced at Cardova. 'I only hope he doesn't grow to resent me for it. Being a soldier is all he's ever known.'

Cardova took her hand. 'I have a funny feeling that the new Empress might be requiring my services before too long.'

Sable tucked the envelope into her tunic, then she glanced at Van and Caelius. 'What about you two?'

'My contract with the City was always temporary,' said Caelius. 'It expired a while ago.'

'I have another month of leave before I'm due to go back,' said Van. 'You can assure their Majesties that I fully intend to return to the City and resume my duties on the correct date.'

Lara strode back into the dining room, a packed bag over her shoulder. 'I'm ready.'

Sable withdrew the Quadrant from her pocket.

'Take care, my sweet girl,' said Olo'osso.

Lara smiled. 'And behave yourself, father.'

'Say hello to everyone for me,' said Kelsey.

Belinda watched as Sable's fingers brushed the surface of the copper-coloured device. The air crackled, and then Belinda, Aila, Konna, Sable, Silva and Lara found themselves standing at the top end of Princeps Row in Tara. The red sky overhead was clear, and the air was crisp and cold. Belinda smiled, and took a deep breath. Then she turned, and noticed that Maeladh Palace was a blackened ruin. She stared at the vast expanse of charred debris and collapsed walls, then Aila did the same.

'Cuidrach Palace is in a similar state,' said Silva.

'Really?' said Aila. 'My old home looks like that?'

'Every palace in Auldan was destroyed in the fight with Simon,' Silva went on. 'Medio fared a little better – the palaces there are still standing.'

'Were you here for the whole thing?' said Belinda.

'Yes, my beloved Queen. I was on this world from the moment you transported the survivors of Lostwell here, until shortly after Simon's death. It was a time of tears.'

Aila sighed. 'Malik's ass. Where do we go now?'

'The King and Queen are living in one of the big mansions on this street,' said Sable. 'That's where we'll go first, to let them know that we've arrived, and to hand over Lucius's letter.'

'Do they have any idea that we are coming?' said Belinda.

Sable shook her head. 'I haven't been here since before we rescued you. Kelsey was back for a while, to collect Van and more of her things. She might have mentioned that you were back.'

They started walking down the wide road, and Belinda glanced around. She didn't know Tara very well, having spent most of her time in Ooste, Icehaven and Pella while in the City. They passed a good view of Warm Bay, and Lara pointed down at the small number of ships.

'There's a harbour down there,' she said. 'Can we visit it later?'

Sable nodded. 'We could take a boat over the Straits to Jezra, or sail to Port Sanders.'

'I might sail to Port Sanders,' said Aila. 'Naxor will be there, I imagine.'

Silva shuddered at the mention of the demigod's name. 'I will most certainly not be accompanying you on that particular voyage,' she said. 'Not unless I was going there to kill that little traitor.'

Aila raised an eyebrow at Silva, but said nothing. Sable led them to a huge mansion on their left, and they walked up a long driveway, shielded from the road by trees and thick shrubs. Banner soldiers were on duty outside the mansion, but they recognised Sable from her previous visits, and allowed them through.

Aila shook her head. 'Typical. I lived here for nearly eight hundred years, and it's Sable they know.'

'I get around,' said Sable. 'I'm famous on four different worlds. No, I'm infamous. Yes, I prefer infamous.'

Belinda smiled at Sable's display of arrogance. In the old days, it would have made her angry, but she had come to realise that Sable was more complicated than she had previously imagined. More importantly, Sable had been one of the few Holdfasts to offer her unconditional friendship. If her old foe could put their torrid past to one side, then Belinda felt that she should also try.

More Banner soldiers were standing by the side entrance to the mansion, and they nodded at Sable.

'Good afternoon, Miss Holdfast,' one said. 'Bringing guests this time?'

'This is Lady Silva,' said Sable, 'Lady Aila, Lady Belinda and Captain Lara.'

The soldiers' eyes widened at the roll call of names.

'Don't rush inside to tell the King and Queen,' Sable went on. 'I want to surprise them.'

One of the soldiers laughed. 'I'll listen out for the screams.'

The soldiers moved to the side and opened the door for them.

'Thank you,' said Belinda.

'Our pleasure, my lady.'

The party walked into the mansion, and Sable led them down a long hallway to their left. She knocked on a door, and waited for a response.

'Enter,' came a voice.

Sable pushed open the door, and they strode into a large audience room. It didn't look much like a palace, Belinda thought. There were no thrones, and very few courtiers were on hand. It reminded her of Bridget's first palace in Plateau City, which had also been based within a mansion. Sitting at the end of a table were King Daniel and Queen Emily, who were staring at the new arrivals with wide eyes.

Emily got to her feet. 'My friends,' she said, her voice breaking.

'Welcome back to the City,' said Daniel, a huge smile on his face.

Belinda bowed her head. 'Your Majesties. How are you?'

'Much better for having seen you all,' Emily said, dabbing her eyes with a handkerchief. She walked round from the rear of the table, and embraced Belinda, Aila and Silva in turn. 'It's so good to see you.' She glanced at Lara and smiled. 'And who is this?'

'This is Captain Lara of Dragon Eyre, your Majesty,' said Sable.

'Ah,' said Emily. 'Kelsey mentioned you, Captain Lara. She also told us that Belinda had been rescued from Implacatus, and I admit that I have been nurturing a hope that you would visit us. Are you staying long?'

'I'm not sure,' said Belinda. 'A few days, at the very least.'

'Some of us intend to return for Thorn's coronation as Empress of the Star Continent,' said Sable, 'which is in six days' time.'

'We shall throw a banquet in your honour this evening,' said Daniel.

Emily turned to Aila, and gazed down at the baby slung to her chest. 'May I?'

Aila lifted Konna out of the harness, and passed her to the Queen. Emily cradled the child in her arms.

'This must be your second, yes?'

'Yes,' said Aila. 'She's called Konna. I left Killop Junior in Kell with Corthie.'

'It is a pity that Corthie isn't also here,' said Daniel. 'I understand that he was in prison?'

'He's out now,' said Aila. 'He wanted to come to the City, but he's worried that it might push him back into his old life of violence. He's trying hard to live a peaceful life.'

'He will come when he is ready,' said Belinda.

Emily smiled as she rocked the baby in her arms. 'And I thought today was going to be another day. But no, we have Belinda, who saved the City by sealing the breach in the walls; Silva, who was a rock of strength during Simon's reign; and Aila, who ended the rule of Marcus. Three heroes of the City. You might have to excuse me, so I can hide somewhere and cry in secret for a while.'

'I do have some business to discuss,' said Sable. 'Banner-related business. I have a letter from Lucius Cardova.'

Emily nodded. 'I think I can guess the contents. And the dragons? Will Frostback and Halfclaw ever return?'

Sable frowned. 'I've barely seen them recently. They've been exploring the mountains to the north of Colsbury, looking for some-where to raise the baby dragons they're hoping to have. I don't think they will be returning to the City any time soon.'

Emily sighed. 'I suppose it was always too much to expect that they would settle here forever. Still, I shall miss them. I miss them already.'

'We still have Dawnflame,' said Daniel. 'She and Lady Jade seem happy to live in the Eastern Mountains. There are four young dragons there also – Firestone, and Darksky's three infants; as well as Burntskull and Bittersea, who live a little to the south of Lady Jade's location. This world will have dragons for a long time to come.'

'I know that, darling,' said Emily, 'but Frostback and Halfclaw seemed like *our* dragons, although I know that wasn't really true.'

'Things change,' said Belinda. 'People move on, and I suppose dragons do, too.'

'Indeed,' said Emily. She looked into Belinda's eyes. 'What you did during the last moments of Lostwell's existence affected us profoundly. Forty thousand exiles arrived here, along with the Banner forces who have served us so well. In the darkest days of Simon's reign, it was those exiles who sustained us. I cannot ever thank you enough, Belinda. I know you paid dearly for what you did. If there is anything I can do to make your life more comfortable, then all you have to do is ask.'

Belinda lowered her gaze. 'I spent two and a half years as Edmond's prisoner. I… have nightmares, I…'

Emily passed the baby back into Aila's arms, then she took Belinda's hand.

'You sacrificed yourself for the people you love,' Emily said. 'You are a true queen.'

'I am not a queen,' Belinda said. 'My realm was obliterated.'

Emily smiled. 'You shall always be a queen in my eyes. Always.'

CHAPTER 7
BETTER THAN GOAT-HERDING

Port Sanders, Medio, The City – 29th Marcalis 3423

Aila sipped the rich wine from her glass, and savoured the view from the balcony of Tonetti Palace. The harbour of Port Sanders lay spread out before her, and the Warm Sea was shimmering into the distance. The air was cold but the sky was clear, and radiant in shades of peach and red. Next to her, Konna was wrapped up warm in her cot, sleeping in the afternoon light.

'It wasn't my fault,' said Naxor. 'I warned Bridget about taking too much salve. I expressly told the Empress to take only one tiny sip each day, not to gulp down the lot as if it were whisky. Did she listen? No, she did not. Regardless, it is safe to say that I am no longer welcome in Plateau City, not while Bryce is claiming to be Emperor.'

'You could always come to Kell to visit us,' Aila said.

'Kell? Is that where you and Corthie are living? You have a farm, I believe? Kelsey was quite scathing about it.'

'It's a farm, yeah. I was running it for a few months, while Corthie was serving his sentence for assault.'

'Know much about farming, do you, cousin?'

'No, but I've hired several people who do.'

'Ah, the smart approach. I do hope you haven't been getting your hands filthy. You are a demigod, after all.'

'I've been too busy getting the farmhouse looking nice,' she said. 'Daphne Holdfast paid for it all. Her wealth is beyond anything I could have imagined.'

'Really?' said Naxor, his eyes twinkling.

'Yes, really. And you can wipe that look off your face. You're cunning, but you're no match for Holder Fast, cousin.'

'That sounds like a challenge.' Naxor shook his head. 'You know, Aila, you have changed over the last few years. It doesn't seem too long ago that you were skulking about in the shadows of the City, assassinating gang leaders and plotting against Duke Marcus. And now you live in domestic bliss, with young children and a husband. What would Stormfire think if she could see you now?'

'Things were different back then,' Aila said. 'Having immortal children has changed everything. In the City, all of the gods were related to each other, and any child I had would have been mortal. You must have heard me talk about this a thousand times, about how I would never have children that would grow old and die before my eyes. When Karalyn told me that Killop was going to be a demigod, my entire attitude changed in an instant. Now, Corthie and I can have lots of children, and they will live on as we do. Let me enjoy the next half century, cousin; I want to savour every moment of it.'

'Very well,' he said. 'You should know that I shall be on hand to help guide your children into immortal adulthood.'

Aila nodded, and put her glass down. 'Alright. It's time for a difficult conversation.'

'Oh? And I was enjoying our pleasant afternoon. It is truly lovely to be in your company again, Aila; I appear to be rather short of friends at present.'

'And why is that? This is what I wanted to talk about. I understand why Belinda doesn't like you – you were mean to her, and don't try to deny it. The same goes for Silva. What Belinda thinks, Silva thinks. Except, Silva also dislikes you for another reason. Everyone's been far too polite to tell me why, but I know it must have something to do with Simon.'

Naxor groaned.

'Well?' said Aila. 'What happened?'

'I betrayed King Daniel and Queen Emily,' he said. 'I sided with Simon, and helped him take over the City.'

Aila gasped. 'You did what? And... you're just openly admitting it to me?'

'I have to. Karalyn's delightful children did something to my head, making it exceedingly painful if I try to lie. I could have obfuscated, I suppose, but the truth would come out eventually.'

Aila sighed. 'Why would you side with a tyrant?'

'It was complicated, cousin. I started by siding with Queen Amalia, our late grandmother. I wanted a return to the old days, when our family was in charge. But, as soon as we had launched our ill-fated coup, we had dragons, Banner soldiers and Kelsey Holdfast swarming all over us. We had to flee to another world and, in the process, we inadvertently freed the Tenth Ascendant from his four-millennia-long exile. After that, we had little choice. We either assisted him, or we died. I chose to live.' He smiled. 'But look at me now – free again. My reputation will take a few centuries to recover, but my present plight is infinitely better than many of the alternatives.'

'Lucius Cardova told me about the deaths in our family. I think he might have also mentioned that you had helped Simon, but my mind was spinning by that point. Did every demigod who resisted Simon die?'

'Most of them. Jade didn't, clearly. Lydia was a reluctant supporter of Simon, but she was a supporter nonetheless, while poor Doria had little choice in the matter. Simon abused her horribly.'

'And you did nothing to help her?'

'I was trying to persuade Simon to stick to his original promise. He insisted that he would only be in the City for a very short time, and I was eager to see him move on. In hindsight, I should have done more; I can see that now. Fortunately, Doria appears to have forgiven me. Don't forget that, when Simon was going to execute Emily, Daniel, Kelsey, and everyone else, I was chained up next to them. Simon turned on me before the end. He knew I hated him. The problem was, by then, everyone else hated me, too.'

Aila shook her head.

'Do you also hate me now, cousin?' he said.

'Of course not. You and I… Let's just say that I can be quite tolerant of your flaws, Naxor; just as you have been tolerant of mine.'

Naxor smiled again. 'That pleases me greatly.'

'It would be different, Naxor,' she said, 'if you'd had a hand in Yendra's death. I doubt I could have ever forgiven you if that were the case.'

'Fortunately, that was nothing to do with me. Prince Montieth did that all on his own. He killed Amber, too. Did you know that?'

'It doesn't surprise me. I'm glad he's dead.'

'We have Jade to thank for that.'

'Do you ever see her?'

Naxor snorted, and nearly spilled his wine. 'Are you crazy? Jade would kill me if she knew I was sitting here. She believes me to be safely locked up beneath the ruins of Maeladh Palace. Luckily, she never visits the City, or I would have to go into hiding.'

Aila considered asking Naxor for more information about why Jade loathed him enough to want to kill him, but decided against it. Knowing that he would be compelled to tell the truth held some attractions, but she wasn't sure she wanted to discover every sordid detail of what he had done during Simon's reign. Konna began to squirm in the cot, and Aila tucked in the blanket where it had come loose.

She glanced at Naxor, who was gazing out to sea. Was she wrong to continue to be his friend? Naxor had done many despicable things throughout his long life, but he had always been there for Aila when she had needed him. Well, not always. She decided she didn't care. She liked him, and that was that. If, despite all the odds, Belinda and Sable could become friends, then why couldn't she remain Naxor's friend?

'Do you know about Daphne Holdfast's plan to transport thousands of Banner soldiers from Dragon Eyre to the Star Continent?'

He eyed her. 'No. Nor does it particularly interest me, cousin.'

'No? Feeding and housing that amount of soldiers is going to cost the Holdfasts an exorbitant sum. Many of them will be sick, injured, or simply worn out.'

Naxor raised an eyebrow. 'What are you suggesting? I assume you are suggesting something?'

'The deal with Plateau City has fallen through, right?' she said. 'Yet the City still needs the supplies and resources that Bridget agreed to send. We're in winter now, and things are only going to get worse. I've been a little shocked at how shoddy and rundown Port Sanders is looking, and I dread to think what living conditions are like in the Circuit. And Auldan looks like a warzone. Might not a clever negotiator be able to work something out?'

Naxor narrowed his eyes, then smiled. 'You mean sell salve to Daphne Holdfast? She needs it for her poor Banner soldiers, and we need the supplies that she can provide. Aila, my cousin, perhaps I have underestimated you all these years.'

'You would need to persuade the King and Queen, of course.'

'That would have been difficult only a few short months ago,' Naxor said. 'They were adamant that they would only deal with the legitimate government of the Star Continent. But, with the Empress's demise, and the onset of winter here, there might be an opening. Desperation can result in all kinds of compromises that might have previously been deemed undesirable.'

Aila smiled. 'Such as releasing you from prison early?'

Naxor laughed. 'Indeed. When the Empress breathed her last, I wondered if soldiers would come calling at the gates of Tonetti Palace to haul me back to my little cell. I was wrong to worry. The King and Queen have stuck to their word. Perhaps, cousin, when you return to Colsbury, you could quietly mention to Daphne that I am willing to divert the trade in salve to the Holdfasts? If she were then to ask Daniel and Emily directly, then it would save me the effort of trying to persuade our beloved monarchs. It would sound a lot better coming from Holder Fast.'

'I was thinking along those lines,' she said. She smiled. 'I must say, plotting and planning with you makes a nice change from trying to coax a herd of goats into a field in the pelting rain. Don't get me wrong, I miss Corthie and Killop, but, by Malik's ass, I don't miss the damn weather.'

There was a noise from the glass doors behind them, and Lydia and Doria walked out on to the balcony.

Lydia took a seat, her right hand clutching a golden goblet filed with white wine. 'What a fine evening. What were you two discussing?'

'The weather,' said Aila.

Lydia smiled. 'A likely story. I hope you haven't been encouraging my brother's more nefarious tendencies, Aila. I am being held partly responsible by the crown for his good behaviour.'

'I would never dream of such a thing, cousin,' said Aila.

Lydia narrowed her eyes, but said nothing.

'Have you missed the City?' said Doria, as she stood by the balcony railings.

'Yes,' Aila said, 'but it's not the same, is it? There has been so much loss, and so much suffering. I'm relieved I wasn't here for Simon, but at the same time, I wish I had been able to help.'

'And how would you have helped, dearest cousin?' said Lydia. 'I assume you would have sided with the rebels, as is your wont. Simon would have disposed of you in seconds. Or, if you were less fortunate, he would have thrown you into his harem.'

Doria glanced away, her eyes dark.

'My apologies, sister,' said Lydia, her stern features softening slightly.

'Do you want to talk about it, cousin?' said Aila.

Doria kept her eyes on the horizon. 'No. I never want to talk about it. Ever.'

The balcony fell into silence, and Aila noticed that Naxor was avoiding Doria's glance.

Lydia cleared her throat. 'Sable and the others are on their way to Port Sanders. That's why we came out here – to let you know. They are currently on a boat sailing from Tara. Apparently, the mortal girl among them wanted to travel by sea.'

'Is it time for you to go home?' said Doria.

Aila sighed. 'I think so.'

'I wish you could stay a bit longer,' Doria said. 'With so few of our family left in the City, I've enjoyed you being here.'

'I couldn't agree more,' said Naxor. 'Perhaps, if Sable is willing, then you might be able to stay for a few more days, cousin? Are you planning on attending the coronation of the new Empress?'

'I wasn't intending to,' said Aila. 'I try to stay aloof from the politics of the Star Continent.'

'But, my dear cousin, if Sable whisks you off today, then you shall be expected to attend.' He smiled. 'Perhaps it would be wise if you remained here for a little longer; to avoid giving the impression that you wish to entangle yourself in the politics that you are trying so hard to avoid.'

Aila laughed, then tried to think it through. Naxor had a point. It would seem rude, at the very least, if she returned to Colsbury, then refused to attend the coronation. Things were probably going to be too busy for anyone to divert time to take her back to Kell; and she was most certainly tempted by the offer to stay in Port Sanders for a few more days.

'Let me think about it,' she said.

Naxor grinned and clapped his hands together. 'The old Naxor charm still works, I see.'

Aila shook her head at him and got to her feet. She lifted Konna from the cot, and cradled her close to her chest.

'I need to feed Konna now,' she said. 'And then, when Sable and the others get here, I'll let you know what I've decided.'

Aila opened her eyes. She was lying on her bed in the guest room in Tonetti Palace, while Konna lay sleeping in her arms. Aila sat up, careful not to awaken the baby, and rubbed her face. She hadn't meant to fall asleep, but it had been so nice to lie down with Konna that she must have drifted off. She glanced at the window. The shutters were half-open, but it was night outside, and the skies were swirls of purples and deep reds. She wondered if she would have enjoyed her stay in the City so much if it had been Freshmist or Sweetmist. She wasn't dreading her return to Kell, but she wasn't looking forward to three months of harsh winter. Would it hurt if she spent a couple more nights in the City? She had cared for two young children on her own for eighty days; Corthie would manage fine with only one for just a short while longer.

She heard voices coming from the hallway outside, and she recognised Belinda's tones. Aila got out of bed, closed the shutters, and lit a lamp to make it look as though she hadn't been napping, and then someone knocked on her door.

'Come in,' she said.

Belinda opened the door and walked into the room.

'Konna's sleeping,' Aila said, 'so please be quiet.'

Belinda glanced at the bed, and nodded. Aila picked up the baby and carried her to the cot that lay by the window. She placed her down, then backed away, creeping over the floorboards. She ushered Belinda out of the room, and eased the door shut.

'Are you ready to leave?' said Belinda. 'I would rather not be in Tonetti Palace for any longer than necessary. The sight of Naxor makes me want to hurt him.'

'He has that effect on many people.'

'Have you packed?'

'Not yet. Where are Sable and the others?'

'They're out on the balcony. Well, not Naxor. He fled as soon as we arrived.'

'Let's join them for a moment,' Aila said. 'I'll be able to hear Konna from the balcony if she wakes up – it's directly above our room.'

They began walking along the marble-lined corridor.

'Have you enjoyed being back in the City?' Aila said.

'Not as much as I enjoyed living with you, Corthie and the children in Kell,' said Belinda; 'but it's been pleasant enough to take my mind off Implacatus. I went on a tour of the ruins of Cuidrach Palace, and saw the designs for its reconstruction. Then we went on a boat trip to Jezra for the day, and I spoke to several of the Lostwell Exiles that I transferred to this world with the Sextant. I liked that. I also went to Ooste, but the ruins of the Royal Palace are closed off because they're unsafe, so I couldn't go inside.'

'You've done a lot in a few days,' Aila said. 'I've mostly been sitting on the palace balcony drinking wine and watching the sun go up and down.'

'You deserved the rest.'

'I'm not going to argue with that.'

They ascended a flight of stairs and emerged out onto the wide balcony. Doria and Lydia were there, along with Sable, Silva and Lara.

Sable glanced up at Aila. 'There you are. The sight of so many women sent Naxor running away in sheer terror,' she said. 'Are you ready to go back to Colsbury?'

Aila pursed her lips. 'Um, what would you think if I stayed here for a few more days? I have no particular desire to attend Thorn's coronation. Do you think you might be able to collect me once that's all over and done with?'

Lara rolled her eyes. 'Sable ain't a bleeding ferry service, Aila.'

'I know that,' said Aila. 'I would be very grateful.'

Sable shrugged. 'It's no problem, Aila. I don't know how Corthie will react, though.'

'Well, we didn't give him an exact date, did we? And, how long is a "few days"? That could be interpreted in a number of ways. Three days? Seven? It's a bit vague, you know.'

'It's your marriage,' said Sable. 'I'll try to come back here the day after the coronation, but I can't guarantee it. It might be a day or so after that.'

Aila sat. 'Thanks.' She glanced at Lara, who was frowning. 'Did you enjoy all of the boat trips you went on?'

Lara shrugged. 'Yeah. Most of the ships were standard masted galleys; nothing I ain't seen before. And they were in a terrible state of disrepair. It was a marvel that the ship we were on today didn't bleeding well sink into the Warm Sea. Still, crappy boats are better than no boats, which is the situation in Colsbury.'

'The City needs wood, and many other supplies,' said Aila. 'There are lots of shortages.'

'No kidding,' said Lara. 'And worse, there ain't no bleeding coffee. What kind of world has no coffee? And no cigarettes. And the food is shit. I ain't eating no damn seaweed, nor no sea worms. Colsbury might not have any boats, but at least the food's edible.'

'Sable,' said Aila; 'could I have a quiet word before you leave?'

'Best make it now,' said Sable, 'as I plan on leaving in a few minutes.'

The two women rose to their feet and stepped back into the interior of the palace.

'What is it?' said Sable.

'You're going to be involved in the plan to transport all those Banner soldiers from Dragon Eyre to Colsbury, aren't you?'

'Yes. Karalyn has refused to help, so it'll be me that does it.'

'I was thinking. All of those soldiers – some of them will be in poor condition. Injuries, malnutrition, illness, and so on?'

Sable nodded. 'That seems likely.'

'Well, the City still needs resources. Wood, especially, as Lara pointed out. The King and Queen had negotiated a deal with Empress Bridget, but clearly that has fallen through. I have spoken to my cousin...'

'Which one? Naxor?'

'Yes. He is willing to assist in arranging a new deal, exclusively with the Holdfasts. Salve for supplies. Daphne could use salve to bring her new army up to full health in a very short time.'

'Salve's reputation in the Star Continent has taken quite a blow with the Empress's death, Aila. I'm not sure Daphne will want it now.'

'But you've taken it before, haven't you? You know that it's basically safe, as long as it's not abused.'

Sable exhaled. 'I've taken it once. Funnily enough, it was Naxor who gave it to me, in Old Alea, after I'd been tortured by Maisk.'

'And it worked for you? No side effects?'

'None. It healed me fine. It didn't grow back my missing finger, though.'

'You didn't take enough, which was probably a good thing.'

'I could bring it up with Daphne, I suppose.'

'You could also ask Van, Lucius and Caelius about it. Being Banner, they know a lot about the effects of salve on mortals. If they think it's a good idea, then they could help persuade Daphne.'

Sable narrowed her eyes a fraction. 'Why is this important to you?'

'You must have seen the state of the City, Sable. It's a wreck. I know that you didn't see it before the recent troubles, but it was beautiful, believe me. And worse, people are going hungry, because the fishing fleet was destroyed, and there are no resources to rebuild or repair the ships. Everything's falling apart, and it hurts me to see the City like this. Lara was right about the ships, and the food, but it wasn't always like that. If I could help with this, then I will be able to return to the Star Continent knowing that the future of the City is secure.'

'Are you going to speak to Daniel and Emily about this?'

Aila lowered her glance. 'No. It would be better if Daphne approached them directly. If Naxor or I suggest it, then they might oppose the idea in principle. After all, look what happened the last time Naxor led the negotiations. Bridget ended up dead.'

'Was this Naxor's idea?'

'No, it was mine. Do you disapprove?'

'I happen to think your plan has some merits. It would certainly bring the Banner forces into a state of readiness far quicker than any other method. We would need a fairly large quantity of salve in a relatively short time. Could the City manage that?'

'Yes. I think so. There are refining facilities at the mine in the Eastern Mountains, and Jade will know everything there is to know about the process. How much would a hundred thousand Banner soldiers require?'

'No idea, but the Banner lads in Colsbury will probably know. Alright; I'll try to sell the plan to Daphne, and see what she says. Perhaps, by the time I come back here to get you, something will have been worked out.'

Aila smiled. 'Thanks, Sable. You would be doing the City a massive favour.'

'It's not a favour, Aila; it's business. Come on. Let's go back out on to the balcony before the others wonder what we're up to.'

They strode back out into the evening air, and Aila poured herself a glass of wine. Lara eyed her with suspicion for a moment, then turned to Sable.

'Are we going now?'

'I thought you liked it here?' said Sable.

'I do, but I don't like hanging around waiting to travel. Also, I've run out of cigarettes, and I'm gasping for a smoke.'

Lara, Silva and Belinda stood.

'Take care, Aila,' said the Third Ascendant. 'I'm sure I'll see you again soon.'

Aila and Belinda embraced, then Sable removed the Quadrant from a pocket. She winked at Aila, then the four women vanished.

Naxor emerged from the shadows. 'Have they gone?'

'Yes, brother,' said Lydia; 'the scary women have gone.'

'Thank Amalia's sweet breath for that,' he said, striding out on to the balcony.

'Is that an appropriate thing to say?' said Doria. 'Amalia's dead.'

Naxor shrugged as he took a seat. 'If Aila can call upon Malik's divine ass, then I don't see any problem with invoking Amalia. It's what our grandmother would have wanted.'

'Does anyone miss her?' said Aila.

'I imagine that Kagan and poor little Maxwell might,' said Lydia.

'No one else?'

'I would seriously doubt it, cousin,' Lydia said. 'The former God-

Queen was not the most popular person in the City, despite everything she did to help end Simon's reign. The mortals of the Circuit celebrated when they heard the news of her demise.'

'That makes me a little sad,' said Aila. 'She and Malik founded the City, after all, and she did more than anyone else to destroy the greenhides.'

'I thought you hated her, cousin,' said Doria. 'I certainly hated her.'

'I did hate her,' said Aila, 'but she died a noble death. She refused to reveal the location of this world to the Ascendants, and they killed her for it. Those of us left in this family should try to remember that.'

Doria snorted, and looked away.

Lydia reached over a low table to pour more wine, and Naxor gave Aila a pointed look while his sisters weren't watching. He mouthed the word 'salve'. Aila nodded, and he smiled.

'This is the life,' he said, stretching out his legs. 'You know – I have a feeling that things will shortly improve for our beloved City.'

CHAPTER 8
BORN FOR IT

Colsbury Castle, Republic of the Holdings – 11th Day, Last Third Autumn 534

Shella lifted the crown from the soft, velvet cushion.

'Kneel,' she said to Thorn.

Thorn glanced at the crown as she got down onto both knees in front of the packed hall. It was a modest band of white gold, with a large sapphire mounted upon the front. Thorn had designed it many years before, while dreaming about becoming Empress of the world, and now the dream was coming true. She held her breath.

Shella held the crown out, inches above Thorn's brow.

'Thorn of Greyfalls Deepen,' she said, 'the lawful and chosen successor to the imperial throne, fairly chosen by a free vote of the world's high mages, with this crown, you are, and shall be, the Holder of the World, from this day until death takes you.'

Shella lowered the crown, and set it upon Thorn's head.

'Arise, Empress Thorn, sovereign and true ruler of the Star Continent, Holder of the World.'

Shella got down to her knees, and every person in the large hall did the same. Thorn rose to her feet, her silver-threaded dark blue dress rustling as she moved. She smiled.

'Hail the Empress!' cried Daphne.

'Hail!' echoed the crowd. 'Hail!'

Thorn kept her back straight and her head held high, as the cries of the people, her people, resounded through the circular hall of the Summer Palace. Behind her, the huge, curved windows were letting in the soft autumnal light, illuminating the old wooden throne that sat upon a dais. The throne had once belonged to the monarchs of the Holdings, and its charred sides betrayed signs of the damage inflicted at the time of Agatha's assault on Colsbury. Thorn stepped up onto the dais and sat on the throne. The crowd cheered again, and Thorn suppressed an urge to grin.

She had done it.

The mocking words of her sisters and mother reverberated through her mind as she watched the crowd kneeling before her. For years, her family had made fun of her ambitions, and how she wished that they could have been there to see that they had been wrong. They had all been wrong – Acorn, Clove, Keir, Bridget, Belinda. Thorn caught a glimpse of the Third Ascendant among the people packing the hall. Belinda was kneeling like the others, though her expression was unreadable.

Daphne approached the throne, and knelt before it.

'I pledge my loyalty and service to you,' she said, 'the one true Empress.'

'Stand, Herald of the Empire,' said Thorn. 'Take your place at my right-hand side.'

A queue formed as Daphne did as she had been ordered. The others in the crowd began to swear their fealty to Thorn, as, one by one, each approached the throne. Thorn smiled at them all. The Holdfasts were near the front of the queue, followed by representatives of the Holdings Republic, and delegates sent by the Matriarch of Sanang. The words each said had been coined by Thorn herself. Daphne had wanted a longer statement of loyalty, but Thorn had opted for simple brevity; as simple as the crown upon her brow. Karalyn's turn came, and she repeated the vow without emotion, then Kelsey knelt next, and smiled up at Thorn as she said the words, an irreverent gleam in her eyes. Agang was close to tears as he recited his pledge, while Sable looked uncomfortable, as though she was well aware of all the wrong she had done to Thorn's family. Their individual reactions counted for little, Thorn knew. The effect was the same.

The delegates from Sanang had brought gifts, and they laid them before the throne, piling up gold and gems mined from her forest homeland that sparkled in the morning sunshine. Thorn had organised every last detail of the coronation, but the weather had been beyond her control. She had worried that it would rain; the fact that it hadn't was merely an added bonus. She revelled in the sunlit spectacle she had created, and smiled at everyone who knelt before her. Once the main crowd of attendees had sworn allegiance, Belinda stepped forward. Silva was nowhere to be seen. Thorn had been informed that the demigod had refused to enter the Summer Palace, but her non-attendance was an irrelevance. Silva was from another world, and Thorn knew that she was loyal to Belinda alone.

The Third Ascendant walked up to the throne, and Daphne's eyes narrowed slightly.

Like the weather, Belinda was also unpredictable.

'You are a Queen,' said Thorn, 'and Queens do not bow to other Queens. Your friendship is all I long for, Belinda, not your fealty.'

The hall stilled as everyone watched.

Belinda glanced down, then tilted her head. 'You are the Empress of this world,' she said. 'I acknowledge this openly and freely before you. You followed the law, and Bryce did not. I recognise your authority over the people and nations of this world, your Majesty.'

Thorn smiled, though she noticed no sign of the friendship she desired.

'Thank you, Queen Belinda,' she said. 'Your words have touched my heart. Please remain here for my first council; I crave your advice on certain affairs of state.'

Thorn nodded towards Daphne, and the Herald of the Empire took a step forward.

'Refreshments are available in the lower hall,' Daphne said. 'All guests are invited to make their way to the stairs. For her Imperial Majesty's first council session, the members of the Empress's court will remain here.'

Sanang soldiers in blue-enamelled steel breastplates opened the doors of the hall, and the delegates and guests began to file out. Courtiers entered as the guests departed, and set up tables and chairs, laying them out in two semi-circles in front of the wooden throne. Thorn watched as the people she had selected to be in her court took their seats. In the row of chairs closest to her, Daphne, Shella and Agang took the central seats, flanked by Karalyn, Kelsey and Sable, while the others made their way to the rear. Belinda hesitated for a moment, then sat next to Lucius Cardova and Caelius Logos in the second row.

When they were all seated, Thorn smiled.

'Thank you, friends,' she said. 'I shall not keep you long. I do not intend to bask in the glow of joy I feel at today's events, as each of us here knows that, two hundred miles to the south of Colsbury, an illegitimate regime has decided to rebel against the lawful rule that has been bestowed upon me. The Empire is ruptured, with Sanang and the Holdings upon one side, and the Plateau and Kellach Brigdomin upon the other. Rather than celebrate, we must act. I have orders for each person seated here before me. Daphne Holdfast, as Herald of the Empire, I am entrusting you with the task of bringing the Banner army currently languishing on Dragon Eyre to this world. To assist you in this endeavour, I am appointing the following people to serve under your command – Sable Holdfast, Caelius Logos, and Lucius Cardova. Together, you will travel to Dragon Eyre at the earliest opportunity, and return with as many soldiers as are willing to commit themselves to a new contract. Shellakanawara shall take over the duties of Herald in Daphne's absence, while, as Chamberlain of the Empire, Agang Garo shall run the affairs of Colsbury. While Bryce's usurping court consists of untried children, I shall instead rely on the deep experience and knowledge of those who have proved themselves many times over. I have also taken Sable's advice to heart. Kelsey Holdfast shall return to the City of Pella and the Bulwark, and there, she shall negotiate with the rulers of that world, and return with enough salve to ensure that our Banner army is fit and ready to defend our rule. Karalyn Holdfast shall remain here, to protect Colsbury from Daimon.'

Thorn paused for a moment, her eyes watching the expressions on the faces of those gathered before her.

'It is likely,' she went on, 'that Bryce will attempt to sever communications between Sanang and the Holdings. Until the arrival of the Banner forces, there is little to be done about this state of affairs. The soldiers under Bryce's control may also place Sanang and the Holdings under blockade, and Colsbury itself may come under direct assault. Indeed, our position may worsen before it gets better. We must be resolute. We must hold firm during the tests that will come our way. Above all, we must remember that the ordinary soldiers serving under Bryce's command are not our real enemies. They have been manipulated into fighting for a cause that is wrong, and, one day, we shall need to forgive, and come together again as one Empire. We must do nothing to alienate those with whom we must reconcile. Anyone who surrenders to us shall be forgiven, and only those responsible for the crime of usurpation shall be held to account. That number is small. Bryce, Brogan, Keir Holdfast, and Mages Tabor and Daimon I now declare to be wanted for treason against the Empire. These criminals have brought this world to the edge of conflict, but even so, if they repent, then they too shall be forgiven. I shall not start my reign with vengeance upon my lips. Compassion and hope are more powerful than revenge and bitterness. We shall defend Colsbury, but we shall not reduce Plateau City to ruins. I shall not deploy Kelsey and her dragons against the capital of this Empire, nor do I yearn for the obliteration of Bryce's armies. Our rule shall be tempered with mercy and love, but do not mistake this for weakness. I shall not give an inch, nor shall I compromise with the usurpers – they must repent, or they will die. I will do whatever it takes to reunite this Empire and, though it pains me, the path I have chosen will lead to blood, fire and death. In such a situation, it is the love we each feel for this world that shall see us through. Remember that, in the dark times to come. I shall remain faithful to our cause, no matter what occurs – you can depend upon me. I am the mother of this world, and I shall be unflinching as I face the future.'

Thorn paused again, to allow her words to settle among those present.

'I shall brook no disloyalty,' she went on, 'but here, within this council, I wish to encourage dissent and debate. I have chosen you all for a reason, and will not tolerate any sycophantic behaviour. Within this council, you are free to speak your minds. Disagree with me, point out where you think I am mistaken, and, together, we shall steer the Empire back on to its true course.' She smiled. 'Thank you.'

Daphne got to her feet, and bowed her head towards Thorn. 'Her imperial Majesty has spoken. As Herald, I shall chair the meetings of the imperial council. Raise your hand if you wish to speak.'

Kelsey's hand shot into the air.

Daphne frowned a little. 'Yes, my daughter?'

'I thought I was meant to stay here,' Kelsey said. 'Am I not supposed to be shielding Colsbury from Daimon?'

Daphne glanced at Thorn, who nodded.

'It is a risk,' Thorn said, 'but you know the rulers of the City of Salve, Kelsey. I ask that you be back as soon as possible. One or two days should suffice for the task I have set you. Karalyn shall defend Colsbury in your absence.'

Kelsey chuckled. 'You asked Karalyn to go first, didn't you, your Majesty? I assume that she refused?'

'Karalyn Holdfast has made it clear that she wishes to take no part in the operation to transfer the Banner army from Dragon Eyre to the Empire,' Thorn said. She turned her gaze to Daphne's eldest child. 'Due to all that Karalyn has previously done for this world, I am prepared to respect her wishes on this, as she has pledged to defend Colsbury to the best of her ability. The dragons shall also remain in the vicinity of Colsbury, on hand to repel any invasion force that attempts to breach our defences. Frostback and Halfclaw have agreed to this, and I am in their debt. Colsbury will be safe while you attend to the salve, Kelsey.'

'Fair enough, your Majesty,' Kelsey said.

Belinda raised her arm.

'Speak,' said Daphne.

'The new Empress announced that she had roles for each of us,' the Third Ascendant said, 'but I did not hear my name mentioned.'

'As I previously stated,' Thorn said, 'you are a Queen. I shall not be giving orders to a fellow sovereign. However, I very much hope that you will willingly assist our cause, Belinda. With you on our side, the future of the Empire seems more secure. Will you assist me, old friend?'

Belinda frowned. 'I don't know how. I have thought through your claim to the throne, and I agree that you are the lawful Empress of this world; but I am not of this world. Silva thinks I should have nothing to do with you, but I am conflicted. Would you be content if I observed at first, until I am clearer in my own mind about what action to take?'

'I am satisfied with that,' said Thorn. 'I would now like to discuss money. The cost of supplying and housing the Banner army will be high, and we are also prepared to pay a vast sum in the form of raw materials to the City of Pella in return for salve. Necessarily, these expenditures shall place a strain upon the imperial treasury. I would like to publicly thank the Holdfasts for placing their great wealth at my disposal. The loan shall be repaid in full once the Empire has been reunited. I am an adopted Holdfast, but the finances of the Empire shall be kept separate from the finances of my family. As Chief of Staff to the Herald of the Empire, Shella will have responsibility for the financial health of my rule. Everything in this regard shall be transparent and lawful, and be published openly. Imperial taxation from the Holdings and from Sanang shall now come to Shella, and she shall have the authority to disburse such funds as required.'

Thorn glanced at Daphne, who nodded.

'This first session of the council is at an end,' Daphne said. 'The Empress shall retire to her personal quarters, and then come downstairs to greet the delegates and representatives from the Holdings and Sanang. Dismissed.'

The members of the council rose to their feet, bowed, then began filing out of the grand chamber. Thorn waited until only Daphne, Shella and Agang were left, then she stepped down from the wooden throne.

'That went very well, your Majesty,' said Agang, bowing.

'Today has been a good start,' said Thorn, 'but we have much to do.'

'Belinda worries me, your Majesty,' said Daphne. 'Was it wise not to have insisted that she pledge allegiance?'

Thorn smiled. 'And what would I have done had she refused? Belinda is not someone who can be easily compelled. If I tried to force the issue, then she might decide to heed the words of Lady Silva, and oppose our rule.'

'Silva's been spreading all kinds of nonsense,' Shella said. 'I heard her telling Belinda that you were the true usurper, your Majesty; and that Bryce is the lawful Emperor.'

'Should she be arrested for sedition, your Majesty?' said Agang.

'Absolutely not,' said Thorn. 'Lady Silva is to be treated as a foreign dignitary, with diplomatic immunity. Besides, she has become so hysterical in her denunciations of me that I actually feel as though she has become an asset to my rule. We shall let her say what she pleases, and do nothing but smile and remain dignified. With any luck, Belinda will see through her schemes. I shall go upstairs now, and change into something a little less cumbersome. Give me ten minutes, and then please ask Sable to join me.'

Her three closest advisors bowed, then Thorn strode from the hall, her long dress trailing on the ground behind her. She ascended her private stairs to the upper level of the Summer Palace, where her quarters were located, and asked her courtiers to leave her in peace. She had a staff of a dozen men and women to attend to her needs, but she needed to be alone for a while, so that she could try to grasp the events that had taken place without interference. She walked into her massive bed chamber. The shutters were all open, and she had several excellent views to choose from. There would be time for that later, she thought. She undid the clasps on her dress and stepped out of it, then she opened the door to her large closet. Along one wall were dozens of dresses, all in differing shades of blue, and she selected one. She pulled it on and gazed at her reflection in the tall mirror.

For years, she had fantasised about becoming Empress, ever since she had first been in the presence of Bridget in Plateau City. That image had been emblazoned into her mind; the moment she had realised what she wanted from life. She wished her mother had survived to see her achieve her dreams. Bracken, too. Bracken would have loved to have become one of her favoured courtiers, and her death at the hands of Sable still hurt. Thorn had loathed Sable Holdfast for a long time, but the ruthless witch had knelt before her and sworn allegiance. If Thorn had meant what she had said about compassion and forgiveness, then she would need to apply that to Sable, no matter how much it pained her.

Thorn walked into her main living room as the door was knocked.

'Enter,' said Thorn.

One of her young courtiers opened the door.

'Your Majesty,' she said, 'Sable Holdfast is here to see you.'

'Let her in,' said Thorn, 'then ensure that no one disturbs us.'

The young woman bowed her head, then Sable strode into the living chamber, her eyes wary. Thorn gestured to a chair, as the door was closed behind her.

'Take a seat, Sable.'

Sable chose the chair closest to the door, and Thorn sat across from her.

'Do you know why you are here?' Thorn said.

'Do you want me to read it out of your mind, your Majesty?'

Thorn smiled. 'You mean you haven't done so already?'

'No. Not on your coronation day. That seems a little rude.'

'Ruder than destroying my family?'

Sable said nothing.

'I apologise,' said Thorn. 'That was uncalled for.'

'Was it?' said Sable. 'I sense you have been wanting to say that, or something similar, for a long time, your Majesty.'

'You have already apologised for killing Bracken,' Thorn went on; 'in Plateau City, moments after Karalyn brought you from Dragon Eyre. It surprised me greatly. Did you mean the words you said to me that day?'

'I did. Killing Bracken was a stupid mistake, born out of anger and frustration. It wasn't the worst thing I've done in my life, but I regret it all the same. I also regret taking your mother to Rahain. I could say that I was only obeying the orders of Lord Ghorley, but that might sound a little hollow. Is that why you summoned me?'

'No. After you return from Dragon Eyre with Daphne, and once you have transported all willing Banner soldiers to this world, I want you to kill Daimon.'

Sable narrowed her eyes. 'I see.'

'Do you?'

'Yes. Daimon is the biggest threat to your rule, and the biggest threat to the Holdfasts. Unchecked, there is little he couldn't do to ruin everything for us. Eliminate Daimon, and Bryce's regime will collapse.'

Thorn smiled. 'I am glad we see eye to eye on this, Sable.'

'Presumably, you wish me to keep this order a secret, your Majesty?'

'Does that concern you?'

'No. Why wait, though? Wouldn't it be better to make the attempt now, before the Banner forces are brought here?'

'I don't think so. Bryce's actions will be unpredictable if we strike now, and I shall need soldiers to reassert order in the Plateau. We shall do this my way – methodically. Banner first, assassinations later. I have one other favour to ask.'

'Yes?'

'Do you think you might be able to persuade Belinda to accompany you on the operation to Dragon Eyre?'

Sable frowned. 'Do you want rid of her?'

'No. Certainly not. I want her to feel as though she has a role to play, if she wants such a role. She would be an observer. I sense a most unlikely friendship is developing between Belinda and yourself, and I would like her to spend more time with you. When she first arrived in Colsbury, she looked as sad and forlorn as anyone I have ever seen. Then you took her to Kell and to the City of Salve, and her spirits have markedly improved. Whatever you are doing, I would like you to keep doing it.'

Sable nodded. 'I had already thought about inviting her along. I had imagined that you might object, your Majesty; Daphne will object.'

'Leave Daphne to me. It is vital that Belinda does not turn against us. If she remains neutral, then that would be a favourable outcome. However, if she could be brought to the conclusion that assisting our reign is the right thing to do, then Belinda's power could easily tip the scales.'

'I can't manipulate Belinda, if that's what you're getting at, your Majesty. Nor would I wish to do so.'

'I didn't mean that. If you are her friend, then be her friend; that is all I am asking. Now, walk with me. I wish to join the celebrations in the lower hall, and I want you by my side.'

'Do you still hate me, your Majesty?'

'I am unclear as to my feelings regarding you,' Thorn said, getting to her feet. 'I confess that I will always struggle to forgive you for what you made Lennox do to my hospital in Rainsby, and for the abduction of my mother and the death of Bracken. However, I believe that your attempts to redeem yourself are genuine. Please do not make me out to be a fool for the trust I am now placing in you.'

Sable stood, saying nothing, and the two of them walked to the door. A courtier opened it for them, and they began to descend to the lower floors of the Summer Palace. Sanang soldiers were guarding the main stairwells, and were posted by the doors of the great lower hall, where hundreds had gathered. Food and drink had been laid out on long tables, and the delegates from Sanang and the Holdings were mingling with the villagers from Colsbury, and the workforce that Daphne had brought in to carry out the repairs to the buildings on the isle. Daphne had been waiting by the stairs for Thorn to arrive, and she stepped forward as soon as she saw the Empress.

'Welcome the Holder of the World!' Daphne cried, her voice cutting through the hubbub.

Thorn smiled as the crowd turned to gaze at her.

'Please,' Thorn said, 'carry on enjoying yourselves. I shall make my way to you.'

Despite her words, several groups began to approach her. A dozen Sanang men and women fell to their knees on the floor in front of her, and prostrated themselves.

'A Sanang Empress of the world,' one gasped, as tears ran down his cheeks. 'Your people love you, your Majesty.'

'As I love them,' said Thorn.

A group of Holdings dignitaries were getting closer from the other side, each seemingly eager to pay their respects to their new sovereign. One of them, a middle-aged man, bowed his head before Thorn, then his hand moved, and a knife flashed out. Sable caught the man's arm, then she gripped his wrist and twisted. The man fell to one knee, crying out in pain. The knife clattered to the marble floor tiles, and the hall hushed into silence.

Soldiers bounded forwards.

'Nobody panic,' said Thorn. 'A mere knife cannot harm me. Release him, Sable.'

Sable let go of the man's arm, and he slumped to the floor, clutching his wrist. Thorn raised a hand to halt the gathering soldiers.

'Wait,' she said. She glanced down. 'What is your name?'

'I know who he is, your Majesty,' said Daphne.

'Let him speak,' said Thorn. 'I wish to know why a Holdings member of parliament would like to see me dead.'

The man glanced up, his eyes wet with tears. 'I had no choice, your Majesty. They have my daughter.'

'Who has your daughter?'

'Lord Bryce, your Majesty,' the man said. 'Poor little Tilda is trapped in the Great Fortress, and Daimon told me that he would make her suffer if I didn't kill you. I'm sorry.'

'You must be Holder Wain,' said Thorn. She glanced up. 'Did everyone hear that? So low has Bryce fallen, that he has resorted to threats against a young Holdings woman. Tilda Holdwain is a prisoner of the false Emperor, and his pet Daimon has tried to use her plight to blackmail her father.' Her eyes glinted with defiance. 'That is what we are fighting against. Our enemies will use every horrible little trick against us, but they shall not prevail. Stand, Holder Wain; you are free to go.'

The crowd around them stared as Sable helped Holder Wain to his feet.

'I might have broken his wrist,' said Sable.

Thorn extended her hand and touched Holder Wain. He shuddered, then gasped in relief.

'You... healed me, your Majesty,' he said. 'I came here to kill you, and you healed me.'

'I will heal the entire world if that is what it takes,' said Thorn. 'Furthermore, I shall use the resources at my disposal to monitor the situation of your daughter, and to rescue her, if possible. You have my word.'

Holder Wain burst into tears, then he bowed his head before the Empress.

Sable smiled, and leaned in close.

'You're not bad at this Empress stuff,' she whispered in Thorn's ear.

Thorn kept her expression serene. 'I know.'

CHAPTER 9
NOTHING TO WORRY ABOUT

P lateau City, The Plateau – 12th Day, Last Third Autumn 534
'That fucking Sanang bitch!' Bryce screamed.

Keir kept his glance down, and the others in the audience chamber said nothing.

Bryce hurled his full glass at the wall, where it shattered, showering red wine and fragments of glass over the soldiers positioned close by.

The Emperor pointed at Daimon. 'You told me that the coronation wouldn't go ahead. You told me that Silva would persuade Belinda to rebel against Thorn. You told me that Holder Wain would kill that Sanang cow. You told me everything would be fine, if only I left you to deal with things.'

'Your Majesty,' said Daimon, 'the Holdfasts remain powerless. What does an empty coronation mean? Nothing.'

'Powerless, you say?' cried Bryce. 'Then tell me, why haven't you brought Colsbury to its knees?'

'The presence of Kelsey and Karalyn Holdfast are frustrating my powers, your Majesty,' said the dream mage. 'I have been unable to act freely.'

'Your pathetic failure has only made things worse,' Bryce went on, his eyes wild with fury. 'Thorn has a crown on her head, and thousands of foreign soldiers will soon be pouring into the Star Continent. When that happens, our advantage will evaporate into thin air. We must act now, before the Banner bastards get here. Brogan, when will the imperial army be ready to march?'

Bryce's twin sister raised her head. 'Your Majesty, we are still in the process of detaching the regiments from their garrisons. Orders have been sent out across the Empire, recalling individual units to Plateau City; but we cannot leave our borders undefended. Rakana and Rahain remain dangerously hostile, and trouble could erupt if we stripped every garrison.'

'Stop prevaricating, sister,' said Bryce. 'Give me numbers and dates.'

'Very well, your Majesty,' Brogan said. 'We should have a force of around seventy thousand ready in about a third from now. Many units are embarking upon ships to cross the Inner Sea as we speak. At present, however, we have approximately ten thousand soldiers to spare within Plateau City.' She lowered her gaze. 'We have also been experiencing some problems, your Majesty.'

'What problems?'

'There have been disciplinary concerns among the Holdings soldiers within the ranks of the imperial army, your Majesty,' Brogan said. 'A large minority are conflicted. Their morale is low and, in some cases, mutinous. Just yesterday, several Holdings officers were arrested in the cavalry headquarters, after they were found to be conspiring to desert the imperial capital.'

Bryce's face twisted with anger. 'Those treacherous bastards.'

'Indeed, your Majesty. It seems that they were planning to lead a large number of disaffected Holdings soldiers north, to join the rebels in Colsbury. Luckily for us, they were betrayed by a few Kellach Brigdomin officers within their regiment before they could proceed with their plan. The Kellach have remained steadfastly loyal.'

Bryce sighed, and put his head in his hands. 'Why would the Holdings soldiers betray us like that? Don't they realise that Thorn is nothing but a pretender to the throne?' He glanced up. 'Keir, any insights?'

Keir cleared his throat. 'The soldiers from the Holdings will have heard about the decree issued by their government, your Majesty. The Holdings parliament voted to ratify Thorn's accession and, for many folk from that nation, that will be tantamount to an invitation to desert the imperial army. They have no love for Thorn, but some will have been falsely persuaded that your accession was illegal.'

Bryce turned back to his sister. 'What proportion of the seventy thousand soldiers are from the Holdings?'

'About six out of every ten soldiers in the imperial army hale from the Holdings, your Majesty,' Brogan said.

'Can't we replace them all with Kellach soldiers?'

'The Kellach Brigdomin already volunteer for imperial service at a far higher rate than any other people, your Majesty. There simply aren't enough of them to replace those from the Holdings. The Sanang, Rakanese and Rahain elements within the army are also in short supply. We might be able to introduce conscription to Amatskouri, but the Rakanese make better sailors than soldiers, and there could be trouble if we force them into the army. I fear Amatskouri might refuse to cooperate if we pressed too hard.'

'We should make an example of the arrested Holdings officers, your Majesty,' said Daimon. 'If we show the world that we shall not tolerate disloyalty, then the ordinary Holdings foot-soldiers will fall into line.'

The Emperor nodded. 'Where are the condemned officers?'

'They are being held in the dungeons below us, your Majesty,' said Brogan. 'I would counsel caution, however. Many of the officers are popular with the rank and file. It would be better for us if we attempt to win them over, rather than have them executed.'

Bryce stared at his sister. 'I do not compromise with traitors. Have them brought up here. We shall take a recess for an hour, and then I shall deal with them in person.'

The Emperor got down from his throne and strode away, Daimon hurrying after him.

Keir puffed out his cheeks, glad that none of the Emperor's anger had been directed towards him. He watched as Brogan headed towards the stairs, then he walked to the apartment he shared with Tilda. The air was thick with dullweed smoke when he entered his room, and he coughed. Despite the ban on smoking within the palace, no one had brought up Tilda's new habit with him. He was sure that they all knew, but they appeared content to ignore it. He walked through to the bed chamber, and saw Tilda lying stretched out on top of the covers. He removed a half-smoked weedstick from her fingers, set it down in an ashtray, then he sat on the bed. Tilda was sleeping, her thin features relaxed. A plate of uneaten food lay on the bedside table. It had been a while since he had seen her eat a proper meal, especially one that she hadn't promptly thrown up. The dullweed had destroyed her appetite, but it had made her more compliant, and she hadn't tried to hurl herself from the palace roof again.

He nudged her, but got no response. The dullweed had also killed her desire for him physically, and the few times that they had slept together had been awkward and uncomfortable, as if she were doing it only to please him, and to ensure that he kept her supply of dullweed flowing. Sooner or later, he would have to cut off her supply, but he had been finding excuses to put it off. It was the only thing that seemed to make her happy, and he dreaded having to live with her if she started suffering from withdrawal symptoms.

He nudged her again, and she groaned and rolled on to her front, her eyes remaining closed. Keir sighed. If Daimon had brought him Tilda for company, then he could have chosen someone better. Keir got to his feet and strode from his quarters. He still had nearly an hour before he was due back in the audience chamber. He decided to visit the captured clay mage, so that he could gloat. He had vague memories of Ravi from both Rainsby and Colsbury, but had never liked him. He approached the hallway where Ravi's small room was located. Two soldiers were outside the door, and they glanced at Keir.

'I want to see the prisoner,' he said.

'Right you are, Lord Keir,' said one of the soldiers. He took a key from a belt pouch, and unlocked the door. 'Knock when you wish to leave, sir.'

Keir pushed the door open and entered what had once been his old quarters. He glanced around at the mess. Unwashed clothes and empty plates were littering the floor, and a rank odour was pervading the air.

'What do you want?' snapped a voice from behind him.

Keir turned, and saw Ravi sitting at a small table, his right fist clenched.

'What a disgusting pig you are,' said Keir. 'Imagine living in this mess.'

'Piss off, Keir.'

Keir's temper bubbled up. 'How dare you speak to me in that manner?'

'Oh yeah? And what are you going to do about it, eh? You're as bad as that maniac Daimon. I don't know what Thorn ever saw in you.'

'I could have you chained up and sent to the dungeons.'

Ravi laughed. 'No, you couldn't. You know why? I've been working my ass off in here. In the last ten days, I have produced three large gems for Emperor Bryce. All top quality, all expensive. He was very grateful, and told the soldiers to remove the shackles from my ankles. Right now, I'm worth more to him than you are, you useless twat.'

The Rakanese mage opened his clenched fist, revealing an off-colour gemstone the size and shape of a smooth pebble.

'Here's number four,' Ravi said. 'Am I going to have to tell the Emperor that you've been hindering my work?'

'I'm not hindering your work.'

'Yes, you are. Your presence is making me feel sick. I dislike the stench of traitors.'

Keir tipped a chair over, spilling its contents of dirty socks on to the floor, then sat down.

'I am not a traitor,' he said.

'Do you really believe that?' said Ravi, closing his fingers round the gemstone. 'Has Daimon been inside your head and messed with your thoughts?'

'Of course he hasn't.'

'Oh yeah? And how would you know? Sable did the same thing to me, and I didn't know she was doing it. Maybe you'd be in Colsbury with your family if you hadn't met Daimon.' He crinkled his nose. 'Actually, I have felt Daimon in my head, so I don't think he's as good at mind-manipulation as Sable is. She used to be quite subtle with my feelings, whereas Daimon's about as subtle as a brick in the face.'

Keir thought about Tilda for a moment, and knew that Ravi's hunch had some truth to it.

'But then again,' Ravi went on, 'there might have been times when Daimon was in my head, and I didn't feel a thing.' He shrugged. 'Who knows? So, what do you want?'

'Thorn was crowned yesterday.'

'So? Do you think I'm remotely interested? Missing her, are you?'

'No. I hate her. She's nothing but a conniving little witch.'

'You must have loved her at some point.'

'That's none of your business.'

Ravi snorted. 'You're the one who brought it up. Wait; I get it – you're bored and needed someone relatively sane to talk to? Is that it? Your girlfriend's too far gone on dullweed to get any sense out of her, and the rest of this imperial court is a damn madhouse. You know, I've met Brogan a few times. She came to visit the university, and I remember her quite well. She was a lovely girl. Polite, sensible, funny. Look at her now, Keir. She's as crazy as her brother. Why?'

Keir frowned. 'How do you know about Tilda?'

'The entire palace knows. I overheard the guards gossiping. I can sympathise. I had a girlfriend who became a dullweed addict. She was force-fed it by Agatha and her merry band of archmages in order to keep her sedated. I don't know which was worse: seeing her in a state of oblivion; or seeing her struggle with the after-effects once she had come off it.' He sighed. 'Poor Kerri. I wonder what happened to her.'

Keir said nothing.

'So,' Ravi went on, his voice lowering, 'is Daimon keeping her on dullweed, eh? Is that why you're here? Are they forcing you to work for them, by keeping Tilda under their control? You don't need to say anything. I know that bastard can read our minds whenever he feels like it. If that's the case, then maybe I've made a mistake about you, Keir. Agatha kept Kerri on dullweed so that I would have to make gems for them. It didn't occur to me until now that Daimon might be pulling the same trick on you.'

Keir lowered his gaze. Part of him wished that what Ravi was saying was true.

'She tried to kill herself,' he whispered. 'She tried to throw herself off the roof of the Great Fortress.'

'Oh shit, mate,' said Ravi. 'That's terrible. Poor girl. How long has she been on dullweed?'

'Ten days.'

'Then there's hope. Ten days isn't too bad; she'll barely be addicted at all. Kerri was on the stuff for over a year. Ten days is nothing. Try slipping some dreamweed into her stash, and weaning her off it. She might feel like shit for a couple of days, but she'll recover. Wait; is Daimon controlling what she smokes?'

Keir had no idea how to respond. The truth was out of the question. If Ravi knew that he had been the one to supply dullweed to Tilda, then he could guess the Rakanese mage's likely response. Why did he care what a stupid clay mage thought? Yet, he did. It was because Ravi had made the mistaken assumption that Keir was a better man than he really was, and the thought depressed him.

Ravi nodded. 'This little chat has been quite enlightening, but I'd better get back to work, eh? This diamond isn't going to squeeze itself.'

Keir got to his feet without a word, then walked to the door and knocked. A key sounded in the lock, and a soldier opened the door. Keir stepped outside, and the door was re-locked behind him. He considered going back to check on Tilda, but guilt was squirming its way through him, and he thought better of it.

He walked back into the large audience chamber, and found Brogan there, along with a group of seven Holdings army officers in chains, while armed Kellach Brigdomin soldiers stood guard by the doors.

'You're a little early, Keir,' said Brogan.

'I was at a loose end.'

Brogan smirked, then shook her head at him. Keir frowned, wondering if she was mocking him about Tilda. If Ravi knew, then Brogan would definitely know. He glanced at the group of prisoners. They had each been beaten, and their faces were bruised and swollen. Two of the seven were women; not that it made any difference, Keir thought. Traitors were traitors.

'Should I interrogate them?' Keir said.

'Leave them for Daimon,' Brogan said.

'Shame on you, Keir Holdfast,' said one of the prisoners.

'Shut up,' whispered one of the other arrested officers. 'Are you trying to get us killed?'

'We are officers of the Imperial Cavalry,' said the first prisoner. 'They shall not execute us.'

'Are you an idiot?' said the other. 'Are you forgetting who is advising the Emperor? Daimon would enjoy killing us.'

'You are deserters,' said Keir; 'and you will pay the price.'

An older prisoner shook his head. 'We are Imperial Cavalry, son. That means we work for the Empire, and Thorn is the new Empress. We weren't deserting; we were seeking the rightful sovereign of this world. As should you, before Daimon swallows you whole.'

Keir opened his mouth to issue an angry retort.

'Don't waste your breath on this trash,' said Bryce as he entered the hall.

The Emperor strode towards the throne, as Daimon walked by his side, then Bryce stopped in the centre of the chamber and turned to face the prisoners.

'Who are they, sister? What are their ranks?'

'We arrested three lieutenants, your Majesty,' said Brogan, 'two captains, and two majors.'

Bryce stared at the captives. 'I should kill you myself,' he said. 'You swore an oath to me, and you have each broken your word.'

Keir noticed that Bryce had a war axe strapped to his belt, and the Emperor's fingers hovered over the handle.

The seven prisoners eyed each other in alarm.

'Well?' Bryce cried. 'Nothing to say?'

'With all due respect,' said one of the older officers, 'we swore an oath to the Holder of the World; and you, sir, are not the Holder of the World.'

Rage flashed over Bryce's features. He pulled the axe from his belt and lunged forwards, raising his arm. The axe swung down and struck the officer who had spoken, the blade driving deep into his chest. The other prisoners cried out, but their chains were preventing them from being able to run away. Bryce ripped the axe from the officer's chest, and the body slumped to the floor, blood spilling out over the marble tiles. The officer mouthed something, but no sound came from his lips. Bryce raised his arm again, and brought the axe down, splitting the officer's skull open.

'That is how we deal with traitors,' Bryce said, his eyes lit with a savage excitement.

Brogan took a step back, her face lit with horror, then Daimon glanced at her. The princess's expression changed in an instant, and she laughed at the cowering prisoners.

'Kill them all, brother,' she said.

'No; please!' cried one of the lieutenants, her eyes pleading with the Emperor.

Bryce rushed into the group of prisoners. He grabbed the woman by the hair, and forced her to her knees, then ran the blade of the axe across her neck, ripping out her throat. Blood sprayed over the Emperor's arms and clothes as the young lieutenant collapsed to the floor.

'Aye!' crowed Daimon. 'That's it! Wade in the blood of your enemies, your Majesty. These traitors deserve to die. They are in love with the false Empress; they worship her. Make them pay for their crimes.'

A frenzy seemed to overtake the Emperor, and he tore through the chained prisoners, hacking and lunging with the axe, and carving them up as if they were carcasses in a butcher's shop. The officers screamed, but the chains were holding them in place, and they succumbed to the wild axe blows one by one. Keir remained frozen to the floor as he watched the slaughter. They were condemned prisoners, he told himself, destined for execution. Did it matter how they died? He began to feel sick. The sight of the blood and dismembered body parts on the marble floor were stamping themselves into his mind. Was this how the ruler of the world was supposed to behave? He pulled his glance away, and saw Brogan staring at the carnage her brother was causing. Her eyes were lit with a sadistic pleasure that seemed a million miles away from Brogan's true personality.

The last prisoner fell to the floor, his neck almost severed, but Bryce did not stop. He went from body to body, hacking the corpses into pieces, as the sweat rolled down his flushed face, his clothes soaked in blood. The Kellach soldiers standing by the doors glanced at each other, but none spoke. Bryce panted as he crouched over the bodies like a vulture, his eyes wide and lost.

A door opened, and the Emperor's three younger siblings entered the audience chamber. Bethal and Bedig were chatting as they walked in, but both fell silent as they caught the scene laid out in front of them. Berra lifted her hands to her face, and made a strange sound – half-choking, half-sobbing.

'Brother,' said Bedig.

Bryce turned his head, and saw them. His eyes changed, as if awakening from a bad dream, and he stared down at the carnage by his feet; then vomited onto the floor. He fell to his knees amid the blood and gore, and dropped the axe.

'Our work isn't finished,' said Daimon. 'The people must know what happens to traitors. Order the soldiers to collect the remains, and have them dumped in the middle of the Old Town, so that the citizens can see how the treacherous die.'

Bryce turned towards the dream mage, and for a moment Keir thought the Emperor was about to refuse, then he swallowed.

'Do as Daimon commands,' he told the soldiers by the door. 'Clean this mess up, and take it to the Old Town. Make a sign, telling the people that these officers betrayed me, and so I killed them. It shall serve as a warning.'

One of the soldiers gestured to a colleague, and the two of them left the hall.

'You beast,' said Berra.

'Silence, sister,' said Brogan.

'And you,' Berra shouted at Brogan; 'did you just stand here and watch while Bryce butchered these prisoners? How could you?'

Daimon raised a finger at the young princess, and Berra's outraged expression transformed into a thin smile, and her features calmed.

Bedig and Bethal noticed the sudden change, and both cowered back a step, their glances lowered.

More soldiers entered the chamber. One was carrying a large bed sheet, and he laid it onto the floor by the dead officers. Bryce straightened his back and stepped away from the carnage, then he watched as the soldiers piled up the body parts on to the sheet.

Keir started to edge towards the doors. No one was paying him the slightest attention, and he felt a driving urge to escape the nightmare that had taken place in the audience chamber.

'And where do you think you're going, Keir?' said Daimon.

Keir halted. 'I felt I wasn't required, Chief Mage.'

'Oh, you are needed,' said Daimon. 'Stay where you are.'

Keir's limbs refused to respond, and he was forced to stand still. Ravi had been right, he thought. Daimon's powers were blunt and crude, with no trace of subtlety.

The soldiers finished placing the body parts onto the sheet. Two of them raised the corners of the sheet and tied them in the middle, then four soldiers lifted the bundle, their hands red from the blood seeping through the thin fabric.

A sergeant exhaled, then lifted his head. 'The Old Town, your Majesty?'

'Yes,' said Bryce. 'In the central square, close to the harbour. And don't forget the sign. The people must know why these officers died.'

'Aye, your Majesty,' said the sergeant.

He nodded to the others, and the soldiers carried the bundle out of the audience chamber, leaving pools of blood smeared over the marble floor. Bryce picked up the axe and stared at it for a moment. The blade was notched from striking the chains that had held the captives, and it was streaked in gore. The Emperor placed the weapon back on to his belt, then turned, and strode towards the low platform at the rear of the hall. He climbed the steps and sat in his throne, the blood dripping from his clothes.

'What has this achieved, brother?' said Bethal, her voice quavering as she kept her eyes low.

'It sends a message, sister,' said Bryce; 'to anyone thinking of deserting the army. It shows the people that I shall not tolerate disloyalty.'

'Shouldn't they have been hanged?' Bedig said. 'Did you have to kill them yourself?'

'It was to me that they each swore an oath,' Bryce said. 'It is fitting that I should be the one to make them pay for breaking their word. Do you disagree, brother?'

Bedig shook his head. 'No! You're the Emperor.'

Bryce smiled. 'Yes. I am.'

Daimon walked up onto the platform and took his place by the Emperor's side.

'There was one other item of business, your Majesty,' he said.

'That's right,' said Bryce. He glanced up, and his gaze fell upon Keir. 'Step forward, my Holdfast.'

Keir felt his limbs become free again, and he walked up to the platform and bowed his head before the throne.

'I have a task for you,' said Bryce.

'Yes, your Majesty?'

'I want you to take the ten thousand soldiers that are currently stationed within Plateau City, and march them north.'

'North, your Majesty?'

'That's what I said. You shall strike at Colsbury before the Banner forces have a chance to arrive, and end this rebellion. Do you understand?'

'I think so, your Majesty.'

'You have strong powers,' Bryce went on; 'powers that you haven't used in some time. However, I recall your boasting from past days – about how you destroyed the armies of Rahain when they assaulted Rainsby. You are the only warrior mage at my disposal, and therefore you shall have the honour of wiping out the Holdfasts who linger in Colsbury. Kill them all, and reduce the island to smoking ruins. Then, bring the head of the pretender to me. I want to mount Thorn's skull on the battlements of the Great Fortress.'

'But... your Majesty, Karalyn and Kelsey will be in Colsbury; and Sable, too. I...'

'Are you scared?' said Daimon.

'I'm being realistic, Chief Mage,' said Keir.

'You have the ability to use your fire powers at a distance,' said Daimon. 'You'll be beyond the blocking range of your sisters. And I will be watching, and helping.'

'See?' said Bryce. 'Your fears are unjustified, Keir. You want revenge against your family, don't you? Revenge against Karalyn, for what she did to you as a child; revenge against Kelsey, for abandoning you; revenge against Sable, for all the crimes she has committed – and revenge against your mother, for choosing Thorn over you. Take your revenge, Keir, and you shall be elevated to Holder Fast, your place in my court secure forever. Brogan, how soon will the ten thousand be able to depart Plateau City?'

'The regiments are equipped and poised to leave, your Majesty,' Brogan said. 'They could depart in the morning.'

Keir's spirits sagged, then Daimon gazed into his eyes, and a sudden burst of confidence flooded him.

'I will do as you command, your Majesty,' he said, his chin high. 'I will destroy the enemies of the Empire, and I shall bring you Thorn's head.'

'Then go,' said Bryce. 'Prepare yourself for the journey, and kiss Tilda goodbye, for you shall be leaving her here, where she shall be safe.'

Keir bowed. 'At once, your Majesty.'

He strode from the hall, but already the sense of confidence was dissipating, and he was nearly in tears by the time he reached his apartment. He unlocked the door, and his senses were assailed by the acrid scent of dullweed smoke. Tilda was sitting in an armchair, her finger clutching a weedstick, as her eyes stared out blankly.

Keir rushed over to her, and crouched next to the armchair.

'Tilda,' he said. 'I have to go away for a while.'

Her expression changed to one of anxiety. 'Go?' she said, her voice slow and slurred. 'Where?'

'To Colsbury,' he said. 'The Emperor wants me to lead the assault.'

'But,' she said, 'who will give me dullweed if you're not here?'

A tear rolled down Keir's cheek.

Tilda grew agitated. 'Who will give me dullweed, Keir? You can't leave me here without any.'

'Is that all you care about?'

'No... No.' She tried to smile, and reached out for him. 'Don't go, Keir. I love you.'

He went into her mind, but all he could see was her desire for more dullweed, and her fear that her supply was about to be cut off.

'I'll make sure you have enough before I go,' he said.

'Do you promise?'

'Yes. I promise. There's nothing to worry about, Tilda. Everything's going to be fine.'

CHAPTER 10
TOO GOOD TO BE TRUE

Colsbury Castle, Republic of the Holdings – 14th Day, Last Third Autumn 534

Belinda packed fresh clothes into her small bag, aware that Silva was watching her from the corner of the room.

'You don't have to come with us,' Belinda said. 'You can stay here if you'd prefer.'

'I shall not leave your side, my beloved Queen,' Silva said, 'and I am not opposed in principle to you travelling to Dragon Eyre.'

'No? I thought you didn't want me to help Thorn.'

'I don't want you to help Thorn, your Majesty,' Silva said. 'She is a criminal and a usurper. If anything, you should be fighting her. Strike her down, and this world shall be at peace.'

Belinda shook her head. 'You shouldn't say such things. You are fortunate that the new Empress tolerates your dissent. Another ruler might well have had you arrested and executed for treason.'

'It cannot be treason to support the rightful sovereign of this world, your Majesty.'

'I'm used to you telling me to stay out of the affairs of mortals, Silva,' Belinda said, as she tied the cords on the bag. 'Since when did you care who rules this world? It sounds as though you *do* want me to get involved, but on the side of Bryce. Why?'

'He is the legitimate Emperor, my Queen.'

'I disagree. I greatly admired and respected Bridget, but there is no doubt that she broke the law when she appointed her son as her successor without going through the proper procedures first. You might not like the Holdfasts, but the conference they held was lawful, and their decision final. But, that didn't answer my question. Why do you care?'

Silva narrowed her eyes, as if she hadn't understood what Belinda had meant. The Third Ascendant sighed, and slung the bag over her shoulder.

'Are you coming?'

'Yes, your Majesty,' said Silva, bowing. 'Perhaps, once we are on Dragon Eyre, you will forget any foolish notions about assisting the Sanang usurper.'

'Are you calling me foolish, Silva?'

The demigod's cheeks flushed. 'No, my beloved Queen. I misspoke. I am sorry.'

Belinda strode from the bed chamber, growing more exasperated with Silva with every moment that passed. The demigod followed her out into the hallway, and they walked to Daphne's office. Belinda knocked on the door then pushed it open.

Daphne glanced up from her desk. Lucius Cardova and Caelius Logos were sitting opposite her, while Olo'osso was standing red-faced next to them.

'Good morning, Belinda,' said Daphne. 'Give me a moment, if you please. Olo'osso was just leaving.'

'This is unjust!' Olo'osso cried, a finger in the air. 'I am a native of Dragon Eyre. If anyone should be accompanying you, it should be me, not this Banner filth.'

Daphne frowned. 'That kind of attitude is counter-productive, my friend. How are we to recruit Banner soldiers to our cause if you insist upon calling them "filth"?'

'But I know the islands of my home world better than anyone alive!' Olo'osso roared. 'These Banner… scoundrels shall betray you at the first opportunity. You need someone there who will watch your back.'

'I will have Sable for that,' said Daphne.

'And me,' said Belinda. 'I won't stand by if anyone attempts to betray us.'

Daphne smiled. 'Thank you, Belinda. You see, Olo'osso? There is nothing to fear. We shall be back within a third, with thousands of fresh soldiers to defend Colsbury.'

'And what should I do while you are away?'

'You are not a prisoner here,' said Daphne. 'If you wish, you can oversee the repairs to the island's harbour. It would be nice to have it up and running before we return.'

Olo'osso glared at her, then stormed from the room, brushing past Silva on the way out.

'I thought he'd never leave,' muttered Caelius.

Cardova chuckled. 'To be honest, I wouldn't mind swapping places with him. Dragon Eyre is at the top of my list of places I would rather avoid, and that's after going to Cumulus.'

Daphne turned her eyes to the two Banner soldiers. 'You swore an oath to Empress Thorn, did you not, Captain Cardova?'

'I certainly did, ma'am; and I wasn't suggesting for a moment that I intend to shirk my duty.'

'I'm glad to hear it,' said Daphne.

Sable and Lara entered the room. Sable glanced at Belinda, and gave her a slight nod.

'What's up with father?' said Lara. 'I saw him in the hallway, but he just cursed under his breath and walked away.'

'I was explaining to him why he couldn't come along with us today,' said Daphne. 'He took the news badly.'

'I ain't surprised. Why isn't he coming? He knows Dragon Eyre better than a couple of Banner guys.'

'He doesn't know the Home Islands,' said Caelius; 'and that is where we will find the vast majority of Banner soldiers.'

'He raided Gyle once,' said Lara.

'Whereas Captain Cardova and I have been posted to Gyle several times, along with Ectus and Na Sun Ka. If we were going to Olkis, then your father's presence would be essential, but Sable informed us that the last Banner garrisons have long since been evacuated from that island.'

'That's true,' said Sable. 'I watched them leave. Nine out of ten Banner soldiers will be on the Home Islands, and the rest will probably be up in Alef, guarding what remains of the oil fields. However, we'll be going to Ulna first, to let Blackrose know we're back.'

'I would like to see Blackrose again,' said Belinda. 'I didn't get a chance to speak to her when we returned from Implacatus.'

'Perhaps we should remain in Ulna, your Majesty,' said Silva. 'You could reacquaint yourself with your old friends, and forget about this insane idea to bring foreign soldiers to this world. The vile Sanang usurper does not deserve your assistance.'

'Be quiet, Silva,' said Sable. 'You're like one of those annoying little flying insects, always droning and whining in your ear.'

'I have a suspicion that her attitude might change once we have left Colsbury,' said Daphne.

'What do you mean?' said Belinda.

'Isn't it obvious? I thought it was obvious. To my mind, there is one strong possibility that could explain Silva's sudden and incessant support for Bryce. Daimon. The young dream mage has probably been in her mind, trying to drive a wedge between Belinda and the rest of us.'

'What nonsense!' cried Silva.

'It seems reasonable to me,' said Sable. 'However, I'm not optimistic that anything will improve in Dragon Eyre. Daimon might have driven his powers deep into her mind.'

'We shall see,' said Daphne. 'Are we all packed and ready to go?'

'Yes,' said Sable, patting the pocket where she kept her Quadrant.

Daphne got to her feet. 'I have briefed the Empress in full, and I have spoken to Kelsey and Karalyn regarding their duties while we are in Dragon Eyre. Kelsey will remain here for another day or two after we're gone, in case Daimon tries anything; then she and Van shall travel to the City in order to obtain the salve we require.'

Sable withdrew the Quadrant from her pocket. The two Banner soldiers glanced at each other, then rose to their feet.

'Dragon Eyre, again,' muttered Cardova.

'Chin up, lad,' said Caelius. 'We have a job to do.'

Sable's fingers brushed against the Quadrant. The air crackled, and the travellers found themselves standing outside the enormous reception chamber within the bridge palace in Udall. Belinda glanced around, remembering the last time she had been there. She had been weak, dizzy, and barely conscious, she recalled; her mind flayed by the spikes in the crown.

'Leave the talking to me,' said Sable, as she strode into the vast chamber.

The others followed her inside, and Belinda saw several huge dragons in the centre of the hall, their scales illuminated by shafts of light coming through the large apertures in the ceiling.

'Greetings,' Sable called out.

The dragons turned to observe the small party.

'To what do we owe this pleasure?' said Blackrose, her red eyes flaring in the shadows. 'I recognise some, but not all of you.'

'This is my sister – Daphne Holdfast,' said Sable.

'Ah, the matriarch of the fabled and infamous Holdfast tribe?' said Blackrose. She lowered her head to sniff Daphne. 'I was almost expecting someone ten-foot tall with horns and a tail.'

'It is a great honour to finally meet you, Queen Blackrose,' said Daphne, tilting her head a fraction. 'May your enemies be torn limb from limb.'

'Oh, I like you, Daphne Holdfast, Sable-sister, and Corthie-mother. May your enemies wither into dust as you dance upon their graves.'

Daphne smiled. 'I have a feeling that we might share the same enemies, renowned Queen of Ulna. The gods of Implacatus have been a plague upon my world, as they have been on this world.'

'Your sister has proved to be more than a match for them, Holder

Fast,' said Blackrose. 'Not only did she rid Dragon Eyre of its foul and loathsome gods, but she also destroyed many upon Implacatus itself, not so long ago.'

'She does the family proud, your Majesty,' said Daphne.

'I am glad to see you reconciled,' said Blackrose. 'I understand that this was not always the case.'

'That is true,' said Daphne. 'Sable and I were enemies for a long time.'

'Let's skirt over that part,' said Sable.

'Very well,' said Blackrose. 'Are you here to see Maddie, or perhaps Austin and Ashfall? They are not in the palace at present, although I could send Ahi'edo down to the harbour to fetch them.'

'We are here to talk over a plan we have in mind,' said Sable. 'With the power of the Sextant, I have the ability to remove thousands of Banner soldiers from this world. Would that be something that would satisfy you?'

'Indeed it would, Holdfast witch. My companions and subjects are still astounded by what you achieved with regards to Wyst. At a stroke, you removed the greatest threat to my realm that still existed, and now you intend to do the same with the detested remnants of the Banner armies? My heart would sing for joy were this to happen.'

'We probably won't be able to extract every single Banner soldier,' Sable said, 'but we should be able to gather up the vast majority. We shall start with Ectus, and then move to Gyle and Na Sun Ka.'

'Be careful, witch,' said the black dragon. 'Na Sun Ka has seen heavy fighting in recent days. Unk Tannic units have been in conflict with rogue detachments of Banner forces for control of the island; while those who were once slaves now rule Gyle. In turn, they have enslaved large numbers of settlers and former Banner soldiers. Only Ectus remains under the control of those elements who came from Implacatus, and the situation there is reported to be chaotic.' Her eyes narrowed as she gazed at Sable. 'The consequences of your bloody work upon this world shall be felt for a very long time, my dear witch.'

Sable nodded.

'May I stay here for the night?' said Belinda.

'You are all welcome to stay for the night,' said Blackrose. 'In fact, I insist upon it. Lara can visit her sisters in the harbour, and I know that Maddie, Millen and Austin will wish to spend some time with you, Sable-witch. And I would like to talk with you, Belinda-god, and you, matriarch of the Holdfasts. Let us feast. There is wine and food in abundance, and the sun is shining over my beautiful island realm.'

'I would be delighted to accept your kind offer, your Majesty,' said Daphne.

'It is decided,' said Blackrose. 'Stay, and you can leave for Ectus in the morning. I wish to hear all the news from your world.'

Belinda sat on the edge of the harbour and watched as the sun cleared the horizon. The night had been warm, and the sky was transforming from pinks into a perfect shade of blue. The town of Udall was pretty in parts, while other sections had been destroyed in the recent wars and troubles; but it was vibrant with life, and Belinda could understand why Sable liked it so much. There were dragons everywhere – in the skies, perched upon the roofs of the town, and coming in and out of the palace that spanned the wide, brown river. Belinda had spent the evening with Blackrose and Daphne. She had sat quietly for most of the time, as Holder Fast and the dragon discussed politics and the states of their respective worlds in an atmosphere of mutual, though competitive, respect.

Belinda felt the warm sunshine touch her skin, and she savoured it, content to do nothing but sit. She wondered where Silva was. The demigod had been offended when Belinda had brought up the possibility that her opinions on Thorn had been formed by Daimon, and had stormed off halfway during the evening. Silva had been crying as she had left, but Belinda didn't know if they had been tears of sorrow or of anger. Blackrose and Daphne had then roundly mocked the demigod, and Belinda felt a little guilty for having said nothing in Silva's defence.

She needed to do better. Despite her irritation with the demigod, Silva was the only member of her family that Belinda knew. She had also been unfailingly loyal to her for centuries.

A shadow crossed her path, and she glanced up to see two men approach.

'Good morning, Belinda,' said Cardova.

'Good morning, Captain.'

'Call me Lucius,' he said. 'Enjoying the view?'

'Yes. Why did no one tell me how beautiful Dragon Eyre was?'

'Caelius and I are Banner,' he said. 'We tend to think of Dragon Eyre differently. But, you have a point. It is very beautiful.'

'The last time I saw Ulna,' Caelius said, 'it was infested with greenhides, and there was no one living here.' He shook his head. 'The damn gods and their greenhides. It's Gyle that I'm dreading the most. That's where the Unk Tannic murdered my wife. My pain blinds me to this world's beauty.'

Belinda wanted to ask more, but it felt like prying into someone's grief, so she remained silent.

'We saw you from the deck of the *Flight of Fancy*,' Cardova said. 'Daphne and Sable are there, and they're saying that it is time to go.'

'The *Flight of Fancy*? Is that one of the ships in the harbour?'

'Yes. It belongs to the Five Sisters – a pirate clan. Lara is one of them, which probably explains why she and I don't see eye to eye. The pirates of Dragon Eyre have had a troubled relationship with the Banner over the years.'

'That's putting it mildly,' said Caelius.

Cardova smiled. 'I was trying to be diplomatic.'

'Is Silva there?'

'Yes,' said Cardova. 'Did you fight? She seemed a little upset.'

'I suggested to her that Daimon might be responsible for her opposition to Thorn. She didn't take it well.'

Belinda got to her feet, and walked with the two soldiers along the busy quayside. Fishing boats were crowded by the wooden piers, and gulls were squawking and calling out to each other as they circled the masts. Four large ships were lined up by the widest pier, and they were all flying the same flag.

'That's the fleet of the Five Sisters,' said Cardova. 'A brigantine, two frigates, and an old merchant vessel.'

'The brigantine is a real beauty,' said Caelius.

Cardova nodded. 'It's Lara's pride and joy.'

Belinda gazed at the ships as they walked, and she wondered if she had crossed the oceans of Lostwell while she had been Queen. As they approached the first ship, a figure began running down the gangway. It was Silva. The demigod hurried over to where Belinda was.

'My Queen,' she said. 'I am so sorry. I shouldn't have walked away from you last night.'

'No,' said Belinda, coming to a halt. 'It is I who need to apologise.'

'For what, your Majesty? You were right. I have been thinking about it all night, and I realise that what you said must be the truth. Daimon has poisoned my mind. I should have realised sooner. He made me think that Bryce's claim was right, and that Thorn's was wrong, when, in truth, I care nothing for the petty squabbles of mortals. Can you forgive me?'

'Of course, but it will not affect my own opinions. I am involved in the affairs of the Star Continent, whether you agree or not.'

Silva bowed her head. 'Yes, your Majesty. Does this mean that you intend to support Thorn?'

'I haven't decided yet. But, I will not oppose her.'

They walked up the gangway and on to the deck of the ship. Several sailors stared at Belinda, and she wondered if word had spread that the Third Ascendant was in town. Cardova led them to the rear of the ship, and they climbed up some steps onto a higher deck, where the ship's wheel was located. Belinda saw Daphne there, along with Maddie, Sable and Lara, and a few others she didn't recognise.

'Good morning, Belinda,' said Daphne.

'I have decided not to oppose Thorn, Holder Fast. I thought I should tell you.'

Daphne gave her a look that Belinda found wearily familiar, and the Third Ascendant wondered what had been so stupid about what she had said.

'I wish you wouldn't look at me as though I were a fool,' Belinda said.

'I don't think you're a fool,' said Daphne. 'You just say things at the oddest times. I was expecting a simple "Good morning", or something similar, not news of that magnitude. I assure you, I am very glad that you will not oppose Thorn. She is the rightful Empress.'

'I agree. And, good morning.'

Sable stepped forward. 'Lara and I have agreed that she will stay here in Udall while we travel back and forward across Dragon Eyre. Her ship is almost ready to sail again after its repairs and, naturally, she wants to be the first to captain it. We'll use Udall as our main base, and visit other locations from here.'

'That seems sensible,' said Daphne. 'Are we going to Ectus first?'

'Yes.' Sable turned to Caelius and Cardova. 'I assume you have both been to Ectus before?'

'More than once,' said Caelius.

'It's changed,' said Sable. 'I changed it. I unleashed waves of greenhides, bombs and dragons over the island, killing thousands. Maybe tens of thousands. It was where Badblood was slain, and I held a passionate hatred for the place for a long time. Be prepared.'

Cardova nodded. 'Where shall we arrive?'

'Along the northern coast,' said Sable, 'in the western suburbs of Sabat City. Watch out for any stray greenhides that might have survived. Belinda, if you see any approach, I would be most obliged if you could deal with them.'

'You mean kill them?' said Belinda.

'Yes. Kill them. Stand close together, everyone. When we arrive, I will remain quiet and in the shadows. It is highly unlikely that any Banner soldiers will recognise me, but I'm not taking any chances.'

Daphne, Belinda, Silva, and the two Banner soldiers gathered round Sable, and those who were carrying weapons placed their hands on to their hilts. Sable reached into a pocket, winked at Lara, then the air shimmered.

The small group found themselves standing in the midst of desolate ruins. Blackened walls lay everywhere, along with tons of refuse and debris. Holes pitted the surface of the road, and an awful odour was emanating from somewhere close by.

Cardova gasped, his eyes wide as he stared at the devastated landscape.

'I think I know where we are,' said Caelius. He pointed at the burnt-out façade of a building. 'Wasn't that the *Colonial Arms*? I used to drink there.'

A few faces peered out of the ruins at them, and Daphne stepped forward from the group.

'Men and women of the Banners, hear me,' she cried. 'The gods of Implacatus have abandoned you. They are not coming back to Dragon Eyre. We are here to offer you a new deal, and a new contract. We have a Quadrant, and are from another world, but we have heard of your suffering, and wish to save you from despair.'

Belinda glanced around as Daphne spoke. She could see the many pairs of eyes that were watching them, but no one left the shadows of the ruins. Daphne gestured to Cardova, and the tall soldier raised his hands.

'I am Captain Lucius Cardova, formerly of the Banner of the Black Crown. I have served on Dragon Eyre, and Lostwell, and several other worlds. This woman speaks the truth. We guarantee a new contract to any of you who wish to get off this damn world. You will be housed, equipped, trained and fed according to Banner principles – this I swear.' He nodded to Caelius.

'I am Sergeant Caelius Logos, formerly of the Banner of the Golden Fist. I too have served on Dragon Eyre, more times than I care to recall. This offer is fair and just. We shall be on Dragon Eyre for many days to come, travelling round the Home Islands, and recruiting all Banner personnel who want a new life. Or rather, a return to your old lives. Lives of security and discipline; of order and duty. All petty crimes that may have been committed after the gods fled this world will be overlooked. The world where we live is in need of good soldiers. Spread the word.'

'Thank you,' said Daphne. She reached into her shoulder bag, and removed a pile of leaflets that had been printed in Colsbury. 'For more information,' she said, 'take one of these. It will tell you the locations and the dates where we shall be recruiting. If there are any officers listening, then be assured that you will retain your rank in the new Banner that we are founding.'

A solitary figure emerged from the ruins of a housing block. He was thin, and his face was unshaven and haggard-looking. He glanced over his shoulder for a moment, then strode forwards.

'I am, or was, Lieutenant Anius of the Banner of the Winged Serpent,' he said. 'Forgive me for being sceptical, but this sounds like an Olkian trick. Are you trying to lure us out of hiding?'

'Greetings, Lieutenant Anius,' said Daphne. She thrust a leaflet into the man's hands. 'This is not a trick. I need an army. The Empress of my world is under threat from a rebel usurper, and I hear that the Banners have the best soldiers in the known worlds. Is that so?'

The lieutenant gave her a wry smile, then he glanced down at the words printed onto the small leaflet.

'Have a think about it,' said Cardova. 'There's no need to make a decision now. Talk to your old colleagues, and those who served under your command.'

'Show me your tattoos,' the lieutenant said.

Cardova and Caelius each pulled up the sleeve on their left arm, and showed the lieutenant the tattoos of their respective Banners.

The lieutenant nodded. 'This seems too good to be true. In fact, it seems too good to possibly believe. Are you seriously suggesting that you will remove the Banner forces from Dragon Eyre with a single Quadrant?'

'No,' said Daphne. 'We intend to do it with a Sextant.'

The lieutenant laughed. 'Now I know you're bullshitting me.'

'You must have heard the rumours about there being a Sextant on Lostwell,' said Cardova. 'Well, those rumours were true. I have seen the Sextant with my own eyes, Lieutenant.'

'Lostwell was obliterated.'

'I know. I was there,' Cardova said; 'but three thousand Banner soldiers survived the destruction, along with forty thousand civilians, thanks to the Sextant. Come to the meeting at sunset tonight; the details are on the leaflet.'

The lieutenant chewed his lip. 'Say it is true; say that you're being honest – do you plan on transporting every able-bodied Banner soldier to another world? What about the sick and injured? What about the service personnel? The cooks, tailors, shoe-makers, armourers? We have been through too much to leave anyone behind.'

'We will take any who are willing,' said Daphne. 'The new Banner will need service staff just as much as your old Banners did. As for the sick and wounded, we are organising a large shipment of salve to heal those who require it.'

'Do you have any salve with you?' said the lieutenant. 'There are a lot of sick folk in the ruins behind me. If you could heal them, then we might start to believe you.'

'The shipment has yet to arrive,' said Daphne.

'I can do it,' said Belinda.

The lieutenant frowned at her. 'Who are you?'

'I am the Third Ascendant,' said Belinda. 'Bring out your sick and wounded.'

The lieutenant sighed. 'I knew it. You're all full of shit. The Third Ascendant was taken to Implacatus years ago.'

Belinda raised a hand, and she sent her powers into the soldier. 'I can sense you are carrying a hip injury,' she said. 'You have been hiding it well, but it has been causing you considerable pain, and has been preventing you from sleeping. There. It is healed.'

The lieutenant gasped, and nearly fell over as he stumbled backwards. A hand went to his right hip, and his eyes widened.

'What happened?' cried a voice from the ruins. 'Did they hurt you, Anius?'

'No!' he cried. 'They damn well healed me. This woman healed me. Quick – bring out everyone who is injured.'

Soldiers in tattered uniforms began carrying out men and women on stretchers, while others supported the walking wounded, and the area around the small group filled with people.

'Who are they?' said someone.

'Never mind that for now,' said the lieutenant. He glanced at Belinda. 'Please, whoever you are; heal these people. So many of us are suffering here. Please.'

'I wasn't lying about my identity,' said Belinda; 'but, whether you believe me or not, I will do this.'

She raised her hands, and sent a massive burst of healing powers throughout the vicinity, healing every wound and injury in an instant. Cries rose up from the crowd, along with tears of relief and shock, and the crowd pressed closer.

'Thank you,' said a weeping woman. 'My pain has gone. Who are you?'

'I have already told Lieutenant Anius my name, but he didn't believe me.'

'She wasn't lying,' said Cardova. 'This is Queen Belinda of Lostwell, the Third Ascendant. Join us, and you shall have an Ascendant on the same side as you.'

Several soldiers fell to their knees, their heads lowered, while others looked sceptical. Daphne began handing out leaflets, and they spread among the growing crowd.

'Are you forming a new Banner?' said someone.

'We are,' said Daphne. 'The Banner of the Sapphire Throne.'

CHAPTER 11
AN OUTSTAYED WELCOME

Port Sanders, Medio, The City – 5th Monan 3423

Aila rocked the agitated baby in her arms as she paced up and down the balcony of Tonetti Palace. Her eyes scanned the harbour, as if a boat containing Sable Holdfast was about to dock at any moment, though she knew it was irrational. Sable was far more likely to appear in a shimmer of air than on a ship. Where was she? Aila had been in the City for eleven days, demonstrably longer than the 'few' she had promised Corthie. Thorn's coronation would have taken place five days before, so why hadn't Sable turned up to collect her?

'Don't worry, cousin,' said Naxor.

'That's easy for you to say,' Aila said. 'Corthie will be wondering where I am. I hate being reliant upon someone else's Quadrant.'

Naxor took a seat and sipped from his glass of wine. 'You could always steal Emily's Quadrant. She still has the device that belonged to the God-Queen, if I'm not mistaken. Steal it, and I could take you to Corthie in a heartbeat.'

'Really? Steal a Quadrant? Is that your advice? What if something's happened? Maybe Daimon has slaughtered the Holdfasts, and Colsbury is in ruins. What if I'm stuck here forever?'

'Don't be so melodramatic, cousin. There are far worse places to be.'

'My son and husband are in Kell, or had you forgotten? Malik's ass, I miss them. I even miss the farm. I left Corthie a list of what needed to be done, but it didn't extend beyond four or five days, which is how long I thought I was going to be here. This is your fault. I shouldn't have listened to you. I should have returned with Sable when she was last here.'

'I always was a useful scapegoat for other people's problems,' said Naxor. 'I merely suggested that you avoid the coronation. The decision was yours, cousin. Besides, I have enjoyed your company, and shall miss you when you leave.'

'If I leave.'

'If you continue to complain in this fashion, then I might be tempted to steal Emily's Quadrant myself, just to send you on your way.'

Aila eyed him. 'Would you hand it back afterwards?'

Naxor smiled. 'Sometimes, cousin, I doubt that you know me at all.'

'Where would you go? You couldn't take me back to Kell. You don't know how to get to Dragon Eyre or the Star Continent.'

'Don't I?'

'But, how could you know?'

'I have my ways. Now, if I could get my hands on the Sextant, then I would be free to visit countless other worlds. Some of them are bound to be utterly devoid of gods. Think, I could be the only immortal there with powers. I could live like an emperor, instead of living off the hospitality of my sisters.'

'Is that your new ambition? Have you given up trying to control the salve trade?'

'No. I am still optimistic that I shall be required to sell salve to the Holdfasts. It has only been a few days, Aila. Really, you are acting like a mortal. What are a few days to those such as us? Your son would still be alive in Kell, even if you were stranded here for a century.'

She narrowed her eyes at him.

The air shimmered above the palace, and a figure fell through the air towards them. Aila screamed, and shielded Konna in her arms as the figure crashed into the balcony table, sending glasses and plates flying.

Naxor laughed. 'Oh my. Kelsey?'

The figure groaned from the floor of the balcony, as Aila stared down at the young Holdfast woman.

Naxor leaned over. 'Are you quite all right?'

'Bloody Quadrants,' Kelsey muttered. 'I must have got the height wrong.' She sat up, and rammed the Quadrant into a shoulder bag. 'Still, as Sable says, better too high than too low. At least I got the distance right. Thank Pyre the maps in Tara are accurate.' She got to her feet, and wiped some pottery fragments from her long dress. 'Sorry about the mess.'

Naxor righted a chair. 'I'll have the servants clean it up. Take a seat.'

'What are you doing here, Kelsey?' said Aila. 'Did Sable send you to take me home?'

'Sort of,' said Kelsey, sitting. 'Van and I have been in Tara, speaking to Emily and Daniel about getting salve for mother's army. It turns out that they were quite open to negotiating. The tons of timber and iron that we brought with us might have smoothed the way.' She rifled through her shoulder bag, and took out a wrapped package. 'Here's some coffee for you.'

'Thank you,' said Naxor. 'Tell me more about this deal. Am I required?'

'Aye,' said Kelsey. 'Emily and Daniel want you to supervise the trans-action. Mother wants five tons of refined salve as soon as possible, in exchange for everything that was on Emily's original list – the one we gave to Bridget before she keeled over. My next task is to speak to Jade.' She glanced at Aila. 'After that, I can take you back to Corthie and wee Killop.'

Naxor frowned. 'Five tons? That's rather a lot.'

'You're going to the Eastern Mountains?' said Aila.

'Obviously,' said Kelsey. 'Are you both coming? Jade and I... well, we've had our differences. We parted on good terms, but I'd rather have you two with me when I speak to her.'

'I think I shall decline,' said Naxor. 'I am happy to take the refined salve to your world, and I will handle all of the details regarding the trade, but I shall not be visiting my charming, homicidal, cousin Jade. Aila can go. I'll even volunteer to hold the baby while you are gone.'

Aila snorted, then walked to the balcony doors. 'Doria!' she cried. 'Could you come out here?'

'Am I not trusted to babysit?' said Naxor.

'Do I have to answer that?' said Aila.

Doria emerged from the shadows of the palace. Her eyes flitted over the broken glasses and plates, then settled on the young Holdfast woman.

'Hi, Doria,' said Kelsey.

'Good day, Miss Holdfast,' the demigod said. 'You called for me, Aila?'

'Kelsey is going to take Konna and me home, but she has to visit Jade first. Could you look after Konna for a while? We shouldn't be too long.'

Doria frowned. 'How I wish I was more useful to everyone than merely being thought of as a minder of children.'

'I know how you feel,' said Kelsey.

'But, of course I shall do it,' Doria went on. 'Has she been fed? Does she need a nap?'

'She's a little unsettled at the moment,' said Aila, passing the baby to her cousin, 'but that might be because I've been pacing up and down the balcony impatiently. She's probably picked up my own anxiety.'

Doria cradled the baby, who immediately calmed, her eyes closing. Doria smiled.

'Thanks,' Aila said.

'This next part might be tricky,' said Kelsey. 'I've never used the Quadrant to get to the Eastern Mountains before, and there are no maps of the area. I'm told it's about two hundred miles from here, but we might have to walk for a while, if we don't end up appearing in the middle of a mountain.' She glanced at Naxor. 'Unless…'

'Unless I show you how to get there?' said Naxor. 'My dear Holdfast, I am always glad to be of service. Hold out the Quadrant.'

Kelsey grinned, then rummaged in her bag. She withdrew the copper-coloured device, and displayed the surface to the demigod. Naxor leaned over, and extended a finger.

'The salve mine is not exactly due east from here,' he said. 'You have to adjust a little towards sunward, and the distance is two hundred and seventeen miles. The mine is located in a narrow valley, but it is wide enough for your purposes. Glide your finger to this point, and you will appear close to the little stream that flows down from the waterfall.'

'Cheers, Naxor,' said Kelsey.

'Might I offer a little advice? Five tons of refined salve represents at least ten tons of the raw material. Jade might not have the facilities to process such a large amount in the timescale that Daphne Holdfast requires. If that turns out to be the case, then I would suggest transporting much of it here, to Port Sanders, where I can operate a parallel refining operation. The alcohol needed would also be far easier to source here. I could set up the basic equipment in the palace basement, with Lydia's permission, of course.'

'Why are you being so helpful?' said Kelsey.

'Because I'm bored, Miss Holdfast; and I wish to see more of the Star Continent. Excepting Plateau City, naturally. I have no desire to run into Bryce or Daimon.'

'Fair enough. I have one more question, and remember not to attempt to lie.'

Naxor frowned.

'Have you seen my notebook, Naxor?' Kelsey said. 'The one where I'd written down the instructions on how to get to the different worlds. Did you take it?'

'Lost it, have you?'

'Answer the question, Naxor.'

'Yes,' said Aila; 'though I think I already know what he's going to say.'

'I haven't got it,' Naxor said.

'That's not what I asked,' said Kelsey.

'I did happen to see it, and I memorised its contents. But, I didn't take it. I saw it in the Banner headquarters in Tara. You really should be more careful, Kelsey.'

'You sneaky little rat,' Kelsey said.

Naxor shrugged. 'What was I supposed to do upon discovering it? Close my eyes?'

Kelsey shook her head. 'But, if you haven't got it, then where is it? You said you didn't take it. Did you do something else to it?'

Naxor squirmed uncomfortably. 'I hope your memory is good.'

'Why?'

'Because I destroyed it. That notebook was far too dangerous to leave lying around. I felt it was my duty.'

Kelsey groaned. 'Well, I suppose that's better than letting it fall into the wrong hands. Thanks for being honest.'

'I had no choice, my dear Holdfast. You know, at some point the twins' powers will cease to work within my mind. I can already feel them starting to fade. I'm quite looking forward to the day they disappear completely.'

'I bet you are,' said Kelsey. She stood. 'Come on, Aila. Let's visit Jade.'

Aila nodded, and Kelsey swiped her fingers over the Quadrant. The air shimmered, and they appeared in the sky above the narrow valley in the Eastern Mountains. Kelsey cursed loudly as they fell, then they splashed into the cold waters of a deep pool. Aila's head went under the surface, then she kicked out with her legs, and bobbed back up again.

'That bastard!' Kelsey yelled.

'I thought he couldn't lie,' said Aila.

'Technically, he didn't,' Kelsey spluttered. 'He said "close to the stream", and I guess we are.'

Aila swam to the side of the pool, and hauled herself out on to the soft grass. She had heard of the little valley that Blackrose had discovered, but had never been there before. A waterfall was tumbling down a cliffside, where a series of caves lay, and the bare branches of a few trees were swaying in the chill breeze. Kelsey pulled herself out of the water, and the two women sat shivering on the bank, their clothes and hair soaked through.

'Jade,' called a deep voice; 'we have visitors. It appears that one of them is the rude Holdfast girl you dislike.'

Aila and Kelsey turned, and saw a massive red dragon sitting behind them.

'Where in Pyre's name did you come from?' yelled Kelsey.

'I happened to be flying when you crashed into our little pool, insect,' said the dragon. 'It was most amusing.' She turned to regard Aila. 'Have you brought a gift for my son Firestone to devour, Holdfast insect?'

'This is Aila,' said Kelsey, 'and no, Dawnflame, you aren't allowed to eat her.'

The figure of a woman appeared by the entrance to a cave.

'Cousin Jade?' said Aila.

The demigod walked down the slope from the cave, her eyes narrow, and a frown upon her lips.

'What do you want, Aila? I thought I had seen the last of you. I haven't missed you at all. Has your mortal boyfriend died already?' She raised an eyebrow. 'You're wet.'

'We are,' said Aila. 'We fell into the pool.'

'That wasn't very clever,' said Jade. She glared at Kelsey. 'I presume you are here for salve? I can't imagine that you have travelled to our valley for a pleasant chat.'

Kelsey stood. 'Do you have any spare clothes we can change into? I don't know about Aila, but I'm freezing.'

'Of course I have spare clothes. Do you think this is the only dress I own? But you can't have any. They're mine.'

'I could dry you with some flames, insect,' said the dragon.

'Perhaps we could build a fire,' said Aila, pulling herself to her feet. 'We could sit close to it and warm ourselves while we talk.'

'Talk about what?' said Jade. 'That time you abandoned me in Port

Sanders? Or about the time you ran off with your mortal boyfriend, and left the City undefended against Simon?'

'What difference would Aila have made to Simon's rule?' said Kelsey. 'You're talking out of your arse again, Jade.'

Jade smiled. 'You're right, for once. Aila's feeble powers would have been useless against Simon. He would have crushed her with a glance.'

Aila sighed. 'I've been hearing all these stories about how you saved the City, Jade. I guess I had been hoping the experience might have changed you, but you're just as petty-minded as you've always been.'

'How dare you? I have changed. In the old days, I wouldn't have been standing here talking to you. I would have asked Dawnflame to incinerate you both.'

'And I would have happily obliged,' said the dragon.

'You have my permission to build a fire,' said Jade. 'See? I can be nice. Did you bring me a present?'

Kelsey reached into her shoulder bag and took out a small parcel, wrapped in wet paper.

'Here,' she said. 'It's a bit soggy.'

Jade held the package between her thumb and forefinger, as if it contained something nasty.

'What is it?' she said.

'Chocolate,' said Kelsey.

'And what do I do with it?'

'You eat it, Jade.'

'If it's poisonous, it won't work on me.'

'Why would I bring poison?' said Kelsey, waving her arms around in exasperation.

'I shall investigate it in the privacy of my cave,' said Jade. 'Build your fire.'

She turned and strode away, and Kelsey puffed out her cheeks.

'Do you see what I've had to put up with?' the Holdfast woman cried. 'Thank Pyre she lives in the damn mountains.'

Half an hour later, Aila was warming herself by a small fire, while Kelsey poked it with a stick. The red dragon had remained in the valley to keep an eye on them, and had laughed at their several failed attempts to get the fire going. Aila had removed her shoes, and was drying them by the flames, and steam was rising from her clothes.

'You're sitting too close to the fire,' said Kelsey. 'You're going to burn yourself.'

Aila raised an eyebrow. 'Have you forgotten that I'm a demigod? A fire this size cannot harm me.'

'Dragon fire would do the trick,' said Dawnflame. 'I incapacitated Simon long enough for Van to steal his Quadrant.'

'You would have been very useful in our raid on Implacatus,' said Kelsey.

'You raided Implacatus, insect? You are braver than I thought. Did you slay any gods?'

'Frostback did. Her big sister helped – Ashfall.'

'I remember Ashfall from Lostwell. She was a fine-looking young dragon. She broke her father's heart by going off with Blackrose.' The red dragon moved her head closer. 'So, Frostback and Ashfall were fighting gods on Implacatus?'

'Aye, and Deepblue, too.'

The dragon roared out in laughter, and the ground shook beneath Aila.

'That little runt was on Implacatus?' Dawnflame bellowed.

Kelsey and Aila glanced at each other, as they waited for the laughter to stop. Jade strode out from the caves, and walked down to the side of the fire.

'Do you have any more chocolate, Kelsey?'

'Not on me,' Kelsey said. 'Did you like it?'

Jade sat and crossed her legs. 'Yes. How can I get more?'

'I'll bring you a crate of the stuff if you help us.'

'A crate? How big?'

'Huge,' said Kelsey.

'What do you need?'

'Five tons of refined salve, as soon as possible.'

'Five tons?' cried Jade. 'Is this a joke?'

'No,' said Kelsey. 'King Daniel and Queen Emily have negotiated a deal with my home world. My mother will send iron, and timber, and whatnot, and the City will supply five tons of refined salve in return.'

Jade pulled a face. 'That's ridiculous. Do you know how many tons of raw material I shall have to excavate to make five tons of refined salve?'

'Em, ten tons?' said Kelsey.

Jade looked annoyed. 'Yes. Ten tons. Well done. This is going to ruin my nails. Is that why Aila is here? Is she going to help me dig it all out?'

'Dawnflame can use her claws,' said Kelsey. 'I'm taking Aila home after this.'

'We do have a large amount of raw salve that has already been excavated,' said the red dragon.

'Aye? How much?'

'About four tons, I think,' said Dawnflame.

'We could take that with us now,' said Kelsey.

'And who would refine it?' said Jade. 'Amalia is the only person in the City with the requisite skills. Is she prepared to refine salve for you?'

Aila glanced at her cousin. 'Amalia is dead.'

'No,' said Jade. 'Someone would have told me.'

'We're telling you now,' said Kelsey. 'It happened when we were on Implacatus. Amalia came with us, but the gods killed her.'

'She died a hero,' said Aila. 'After everything she did in her long life, our grandmother died rather than reveal the location of this world to the Ascendants.'

'The God-Queen...' Jade mumbled. 'Our family is in ruins. The God-King, the God-Queen, and every one of the God-Children; gone. Who's left but a handful of demigods? I miss Yendra the most.'

'I miss her, too,' said Aila.

'Then why did you run off to another world?'

'You know why – for Corthie.'

'Has the mortal made you happy?'

'Yes. We have two children; both demigods.'

Jade stared at her. 'Your mortal can sire demigods? I now understand why you chose him.'

Aila decided not to argue with her cousin. Jade *had* changed. She was as blunt as ever, but she seemed more reflective, more thoughtful, than she had been in the past.

'You didn't answer my earlier question,' Jade said. 'Who is going to refine the raw salve if you take it away from here?'

'Don't worry about that,' said Kelsey.

'Don't worry about it? What are you keeping from me, Kelsey? Who else knows how to refine salve? I can think of only one person, but that's impossible. Naxor is in prison.' She stared at Kelsey. 'He is in prison, isn't he? He'd better be.'

Kelsey hesitated. 'Um...'

Jade's eyes narrowed. 'Why aren't you giving me a straight answer?'

'Shit,' Kelsey muttered. 'I guess you'll find out sooner or later. The King and Queen decided to release Naxor, so that he could...'

'What?' Jade cried. 'They released that nasty weasel?'

'Eh, aye, Jade. Naxor's been quite useful. He...'

'Useful? Kelsey, he tortured me! He tied me to a wooden frame, right here in this little valley. Me, Flavus, and Rosie Jackdaw. If Dawnflame hadn't turned up, he was going to murder us all, slowly. Where is he? I'm going to kill him. Dawnflame, get ready to fly to the City. We're going to hunt that bastard down.'

'You can't,' said Aila.

Jade stood. 'Don't tell me what I can't do, cousin. Let me guess – he's staying in Port Sanders with his gullible sisters, isn't he? I think Tonetti Palace will be burning tonight.'

'I can't let you do this,' Aila said, getting to her feet.

'If Simon couldn't stop me, what chance do you think you'll have, Aila?'

'But Lydia and Doria are in Tonetti,' said Aila, 'along with dozens of mortal guards and staff. Are you going to kill them, too?'

'If they're stupid enough to shelter Naxor, then they deserve to burn. Dawnflame, where's your harness?'

'In the second cave to the right, demigod,' said the red dragon.

'My baby daughter is in Tonetti Palace,' Aila cried.

Jade shrugged and strode away towards the caves, and the dragon cackled with laughter.

'There is nothing I enjoy more than burning the palaces of the gods,' Dawnflame said. 'Tonetti shall be my first in Medio.'

'Did Naxor really torture Jade and Maddie's sister?' said Aila.

'I don't know the exact details,' said Kelsey.

'He was on the verge of torturing them when I intervened,' said the dragon.

'Then he might have been bluffing,' said Aila.

'Stop making excuses for that worthless insect,' said the dragon. 'Naxor sold himself to Simon, and was a most willing accomplice in the Ascendant's sadistic schemes.'

'We should warn him,' Aila said.

'You will not,' said the dragon.

'Stay close to me,' Kelsey whispered. She reached into her bag and the air shimmered. The dragon cried out in anger as Kelsey and Aila appeared by the entrance to the caves, fifty yards from the fire. Kelsey ran into the opening, and Aila chased after her. They came to a large cavern full of crates of raw salve, and Kelsey reached into her bag again.

'This is going to make a mess of the balcony,' she said, then she swiped her fingers over the Quadrant.

The air shimmered again, and they appeared a foot above the balcony in Port Sanders, with crates falling around them. Two split open as they slammed into the floor of the balcony, and raw salve leaked out. Aila slipped as she landed, and fell into the pile of crates. She wriggled free before any loose salve could touch her exposed skin, and backed away into the building, her eyes wide.

'What was that noise?' came Naxor's voice. He rushed to the balcony doors, and stared at the crates of raw salve. 'Oh my.'

'Jade knows you're here,' said Aila.

'You told her?' Naxor cried. 'Why would you do such a thing? You know how much she hates me.'

'And why does she hate you so much?' said Aila. 'So much that right now she's getting ready to fly on Dawnflame to come here to kill you. Is it true? Did you torture her, and Rosie Jackdaw?'

'I was trying to get information out of them,' he said. 'I made a lot of threats, but I didn't actually do anything. Remember, I cannot lie. You have to believe me.'

'But you were going to hurt them, weren't you? I mean, if the dragon hadn't stopped you?'

Naxor's face fell. 'I… well… yes.'

'Oh, Naxor,' she said.

'Quit chatting and help me move these crates,' Kelsey cried from the balcony.

'I have a better idea,' said Naxor. 'If Jade is coming here on Dawnflame, then the only way to ensure the safety of my sisters is if I leave the City, immediately. Kelsey, take us to Colsbury. And the salve, too, of course. I don't need to be here to refine it.'

Kelsey frowned, then nodded.

'Wait,' Aila cried. 'I need to get Konna.'

She ran into the palace as flecks of raw salve flew off her clothes, and raced towards Doria's quarters. She reached the door and burst through. Doria was singing to the baby, who was settled on the demigod's lap.

'Jade and Dawnflame are coming!' Aila yelled. 'They found out that Naxor's here. Kelsey and I are taking him to the Star Continent, and I need Konna.'

'Jade and Dawnflame?' said Doria, her face paling.

'You should evacuate the palace,' Aila said. 'Get everyone out, in case Jade doesn't believe that Naxor has really gone.'

Konna started to cry, the shouts having awoken her. Doria stood, and passed the child to Aila.

'What have you done, cousin?' Doria said. 'Jade may have saved the City, but she is a ruthless killer. She and her dragon burned the palaces of Auldan in their war against Simon. Why did you tell her that Naxor was here?'

Aila thought about blaming Kelsey, but did it matter where the fault lay?

'Sorry,' she muttered.

'Well, you had better go, I suppose,' said Doria. 'I need to warn Lydia, and begin the evacuation.'

Aila held Konna close to her chest, as guilt rolled through her.

'Go!' said Doria.

Aila nodded, then she turned and ran.

The air crackled, and three figures appeared in a courtyard, surrounded by the crates of salve. Overhead, the sky was threatening rain, and black clouds loomed to the west.

'This doesn't appear to be Colsbury,' said Naxor.

'Well spotted,' said Kelsey. 'It's Kell. We'd better get these crates under cover before the rain starts. Is there a shed or a barn we could use, Aila?'

Aila pointed at a large outbuilding. 'Put it in there. I'll find Corthie.'

She strode towards the farmhouse, feeling alarmed about what had happened in the City, but relieved to be home. She walked through the front door, and found Corthie in the kitchen. Killop was sitting next to him eating from a bowl with his hands.

'He's supposed to use a spoon,' Aila said.

Corthie turned, and smiled. He jumped off his chair and hugged her, then took Konna into his hands. Aila walked over to Killop, and kissed him.

'Mummy's home, my little boy,' she said.

'There's my beautiful girl,' Corthie said, holding Konna up in front of him. 'My two beautiful girls.'

Aila glanced around the kitchen. 'The house seems to be still standing.'

Corthie raised an eyebrow. 'Eleven days, eh? Is that what you meant by "a few"?'

'Can you come outside? I need your help with something. It'll require strength, so you should leave Konna here.'

Corthie placed Konna into the cot that stood by the window, and then Aila led him outside.

'Pyre's arse,' Corthie said, as he surveyed the dozens of crates. 'Is that salve?'

'It certainly is, brother,' said a voice.

'Kelsey?' he said.

'Aye, and I'm not alone. I brought along a good friend of yours. Someone you've really missed.'

'Aye? Who?'

Naxor emerged from the outbuilding, salve particles covering the front of his tunic.

He smiled at Corthie, and waved his hand at him. 'Hello, there.'

Corthie groaned.

CHAPTER 12
DERELICTION OF DUTY

C olsbury Castle, Republic of the Holdings – 27th Day, Last Third Autumn 534

Thorn gazed out at the view, a long set of pale blue robes protecting her from the chill wind. Winter was fast approaching, and the top of the Summer Palace was a cold place to be. The peaks of the nearby mountains were already flecked with snow, and more would soon be arriving.

'There's good news and bad,' said Kelsey, who was standing next to Agang on the long, circular balcony that ringed the uppermost floor of the palace.

'I'd like to hear the good news first,' Thorn said.

'Alright. Jade didn't burn down Tonetti Palace. Just as Dawnflame was about to unleash an inferno, Lydia and Doria managed to persuade Jade that Naxor had gone.'

Thorn stifled a shrug. What did she care if a palace on another world had avoided destruction?

'And the bad?' she said.

'Jade is so furious with the King and Queen of the City that she's refusing to cooperate. She said that she won't excavate any more salve; not for us, not for anyone.'

'Could someone else be sent to the mine to replace her?'

Kelsey frowned. 'I don't think you quite understand the situation. The salve mine is two hundred and seventeen miles from the City, and there are millions of greenhides in between. The only ways to get to the mine are by Quadrant, or by dragon; and with Frostback and Halfclaw now living here, and Dawnflame siding with Jade, no one else can get there.'

'I see. How much salve did you manage to retrieve from the mine when you and Aila fled?'

'About four tons. We lost a little bit in Port Sanders, and then some got all wet and muddy in Kell before we could move it into a big barn. That's where Naxor has set up his refining equipment. He ordered a huge amount of Severton gin, and he estimates that he'll have about two tons of the refined stuff ready within ten days or so.'

'We asked for five tons.'

'Aye. I know. Still, two's better than nothing.'

'Cut the amount of raw materials being sent to the City. Two out of five is forty per cent; therefore, we shall give forty per cent of what was agreed. Agang, see to it.'

The old Sanang man bowed. 'I shall, your Majesty.'

'Is that fair?' said Kelsey. 'It's not Emily's fault that Jade is unhinged.'

'Despite outward appearances, Kelsey,' Thorn said, 'the Holdfasts' funds are not unlimited. Forty per cent still represents a massive amount of timber, iron, copper, luxury goods, and everything else that is on the list. I would like you to return to the City for a brief visit. The King and Queen can prioritise their needs. That's fair.'

'If I take a huge crate of chocolate to Jade,' Kelsey said, 'then I might be able to win her over.'

Thorn turned to Kelsey. 'Really? Her wrath would be assuaged by chocolate?'

'Probably not, but it's worth a try.'

'Chocolate?'

'You're from Sanang, where chocolate is so plentiful that kids eat it for breakfast. Alright, I'm exaggerating, but you have to realise the impact these so-called luxury goods have on other worlds.'

'Fine. You have my permission to try. Don't be gone for too long. I need you here in case Daimon tries to interfere.'

'You'll have Karalyn. She can watch out while I'm gone.'

'And have you seen Karalyn recently? She stays in her rooms with the twins, and has no interest in anything else. You have done far more for me than your sister has, Kelsey. It hasn't gone unnoticed or unappreciated.'

'Thanks, I guess.'

'Tell me; when you are in the City, do you address the King and Queen in the same manner that you address me?'

'You mean, do I call them "your Majesty"?' She smirked. 'Not often, your Majesty.'

Thorn smiled. 'I am glad to know that I am not the only sovereign from whom you withhold respect.'

'Oh, come on, Thorn. I do respect you. I wouldn't be working for you if I didn't. I've known you for ages, ever since Rainsby; but it was the four years when you looked after the twins that really won me over. How you managed to do that while retaining your sanity is beyond me. I'll never forget your face when Karalyn returned from Lostwell. Most people would have been relieved, but you looked heartbroken.'

'I was heartbroken. By that point, I sincerely believed that Karalyn would never return, and I had started to think that the twins would be mine forever. Cael and Kyra caused me so much pain, but I loved them dearly. I always will.'

'You were a good mother to them.'

'Thank you, Kelsey. That means a lot.'

'And now you're the damn Empress.'

'I am.'

'How does it feel? Bridget never wanted to be Empress; that was obvious. But you – you've always wanted it. I knew that from the first time we met. So, how does it feel?'

'It feels wonderful. Despite Daimon, despite Bryce; it feels right, and natural. I know that I have to prove myself, but I am determined to be a fair, compassionate and generous ruler; the mother of the world.'

Kelsey shook her head. 'I don't know how you can say that with a straight face.'

'Because I truly believe it, Kelsey. I love this world and its people, and I will defend even the lowliest subject, as a mother defends her children. I don't mind if you laugh at me. People have laughed at me for years. My sisters, especially. The ridicule of others means nothing to me. I know who I am.'

They fell into silence, and gazed out at the view from the high balcony. The waters of the lake were rippling in the breeze, and the little village on the shore was basking in the soft sunshine.

'I have a report on the recent influx of deserters from the imperial army, your Majesty,' said Agang.

Thorn nodded. 'What are the latest numbers?'

'In Colsbury itself, your Majesty,' Agang said, 'over three hundred men and women have arrived, and handed themselves in. They claim that the false Emperor is gathering an army, and that they were members of garrisons being sent to Plateau City when they deserted. The news from the Holdings frontier is a little older, your Majesty, but the indications are that at least a thousand soldiers have crossed over from the Plateau in the last third.'

'Are the soldiers all from the Holdings?'

'Almost all, your Majesty. A small number of Rakanese and Sanang volunteers have also surrendered to our forces. Only the Kellach Brigdomin seem unaffected. Some of the deserters have reported tensions within individual imperial regiments, with those from the Holdings pitted against those from Kellach Brigdomin. They also said that many more from the Holdings are dissatisfied with the false Emperor, and would desert if they had the opportunity.'

'That sounds like good news,' said Kelsey.

'It's not,' said Thorn. 'The Empire is splitting along racial lines, and that holds trouble for the future. For unity to prevail, indeed, for the Empire itself to exist, the differing nations of this world have to work together; and the partnership between the Holdings and Kellach Brigdomin has been the foundation upon which this Empire has flourished. If those two nations learn to hate and mistrust each other, there may be lasting damage. We need to find a way to appeal to the Kellach Brigdomin. Their love for Bridget has clouded their position, and has devolved into a misplaced sense of loyalty towards Bryce. Perhaps if we had a warrior like Corthie with us; someone the Kellach could identify with, then many might not view us so unfavourably.'

'He's not interested in getting involved,' said Kelsey.

'Doesn't he care about the future of this world?'

'He doesn't want to slaughter soldiers from the imperial army. He's worried that if he fights, he won't be able to stop. He said that if gods or greenhides ever attack this world, then he will help, but that's the only thing that will get him to take up arms again.'

Thorn said nothing for a moment. There was no point in blaming Kelsey for her brother's intransigence. She had toyed with the idea of sending Corthie a direct order, summoning him into the service of his rightful sovereign; but she had feared the consequences of his likely refusal. Like Belinda, Corthie needed to be coaxed into supporting her, not given strict orders that she would be unable to enforce.

'We have been integrating all deserters into the units defending Colsbury, your Majesty,' Agang said.

'Good,' said Thorn. 'However, I think we need to stop calling them deserters. Deserters are cowards, and it takes courage to leave Bryce's army to join our forces. The soldiers under my command represent the true imperial army, and those who cross over are returning home, as it were. We must welcome them, and show them that we trust them. It is possible that some may well be spies working for Bryce, but as Daimon can watch us whenever he pleases, I am not overly concerned about that.'

Kelsey pointed towards the mountains to the north. 'Frostback and Halfclaw are approaching.'

Thorn turned, and saw the two specks in the sky. She smiled. She might not have Corthie Holdfast on her side, but she had two fine young dragons. They, too, were difficult to command, but they had given every sign that they were prepared to support her cause, and defend Colsbury if necessary. The sun was catching on the silver wings of Frostback, and the dragon glistened in the air as she swooped down. Her blue and green mate followed her, and they descended over the island. Many of the Sanang soldiers on guard along the walls and towers of Colsbury stopped what they were doing to gaze up at the sight. It was always impressive to see the dragons, and Thorn liked the way everyone was growing to love them.

Frostback circled the Great Keep, then she saw Thorn, Kelsey and Agang up on the high balcony of the Summer Palace. She and Halfclaw banked, and grew closer.

'Greetings, my rider,' said Frostback, 'and greetings to you, Empress Thorn. Just as you have moved into this palace, Halfclaw and I have found our new home, and we have come to tell you about it.'

'After scouting the mountains for many days,' said Halfclaw, 'my beloved and I discovered a large network of wide and airy caves, some twenty miles to the north-west of Colsbury. It is there that we shall raise our young.'

'Have you finally decided to have children?' said Kelsey.

'Indeed, we have, my rider.' Frostback turned her head towards Thorn. 'Might we request some assistance?'

'What kind of assistance?' said the Empress.

'Human workers,' said Halfclaw. 'The caves are fine, but some tunnels and openings require widening, while others would be better sealed off and closed. In the world of the City, the rulers sent workers, who greatly improved the living conditions in the mountain refuge where Deathfang had chosen to dwell. Would you extend to us the same courtesy, Empress?'

'You shall have everything you need,' said Thorn. 'Is there a road or path that leads to your new home? We could send wagons with workers and equipment.'

'The way is hard for mere humans to travel,' said Halfclaw, 'but we can pick up and carry any such wagons that you supply. The workers can live with us, under our protection, while they perform their tasks; and then we shall bring them all back.'

'Agang shall see to it,' said Thorn. 'Give him a list of whatever you need, and he shall make the preparations.'

'I can help with that,' said Kelsey. 'I have a lot of experience of this sort of thing. They'll need pick-axes, shovels, timber, saws; all kinds of things. I can make a list.'

'Thank you, Empress, and thank you, my rider,' said Frostback. 'We shall also need a way to communicate. If Colsbury were to fall under threat, then Halfclaw and I will rush to your assistance, but we shall require a means to be alerted to your plight.'

'Would you be able to see a plume of coloured smoke from your new home?' said Agang.

'Quite possibly,' said Halfclaw, 'though we would not always be looking in the right direction.'

'We could ask Karalyn,' said Kelsey. 'She could send you a message.'

'We shall speak to her,' said Thorn. 'Return tomorrow at dawn, dragons, and we shall have the workers and wagons ready to leave. With winter approaching, it would better to have the work carried out as soon as possible.'

'You have our gratitude, Empress,' said Frostback. 'Kelsey, do you wish to travel with us, to see our new home?'

'Aye; that sounds great,' said Kelsey.

Frostback lowered herself in the air, then moved alongside the balcony. Agang helped Kelsey climb up onto the railing, then the Holdfast woman stepped on to Frostback's shoulders, and strapped herself into the harness.

'I shall bring my rider back at dawn when we return, Empress. I know that you require her presence here, to block the powers of Daimon. However, once the threat from Bryce and his dream mage has passed, then I shall expect my rider to dwell with me. I miss her company.'

'I understand,' said Thorn.

The two dragons beat their wings and ascended into the sky. They circled over the island twice, then raced off to the north-west. After a moment, Thorn felt her soulwitch powers return.

'Was it wise to let Kelsey leave, your Majesty?' said Agang.

'We cannot keep her locked up in Colsbury,' said Thorn, 'and we are relying upon her dragons to defend this island if we are attacked.'

'She left without leaving me a list, your Majesty.'

'I'm sure we can imagine what they shall require. Two wagons of equipment and a dozen workers should suffice. Please see to it personally, and then ask Karalyn to come to the palace.'

Agang bowed. 'Yes, your Majesty.

Thorn turned back to the view as her chamberlain left the balcony. The circular walkway jutted out from the top floor of the palace, leaving only a needle-like spire to rise into the sky behind her. She glanced down. The Summer Palace was piled up in tiers like a Holdings wedding cake. Each tier contained more than one floor, and they grew progressively narrower as they climbed. Workers were still repairing parts of the exterior, re-pointing stone blocks and painting over the war damage, but the interior was almost finished. Almost a hundred people had moved in, from the servants and staff who ran the building, to the clerks in their new offices, and the soldiers who were there to guard Thorn. Pechtang and T'Lang had each been given a fine apartment, and Agang had a whole level of the palace to himself, just beneath the Empress' two-storey quarters. It was luxurious, but Thorn believed an Empress should live in a proper palace, and not a fortress. On the other side of the large forecourt, Daphne had reserved the Great Keep for her offices as Herald of the Empire, and it too had dozens of staff now living there, including some experienced officials who had been lured away from the government of the Holdings. It was a fine place from which to run the Empire, though Thorn knew that she would be expected to live in Plateau City once Bryce had been defeated.

Forty minutes had elapsed before Karalyn was shown into the Empress's quarters. She had brought the twins with her, and they both ran up to Thorn, who crouched down and embraced them in turn.

Karalyn frowned. 'You asked for me?'

Thorn stood. 'Yes. Thank you for coming. Did you walk here?'

'No. There are far too many stairs between my rooms in the Great Keep and your rooms in the palace.'

'Are you well?'

'Aye.'

'Good. I was wanting to ask you something. The dragons were here earlier, discussing their new home in the mountains. It's about twenty miles away. In the event of an emergency, I would need you to summon them here as quickly as possible. Would you be willing to do that?'

'Of course.'

'Kelsey can give you the exact location tomorrow.'

'Was that everything?'

A slight frown creased Thorn's lips. 'Not quite. I am sensing some hostility from you, Karalyn.'

'I'm not hostile; I'm busy. I was in the middle of giving the twins a reading lesson.'

Thorn nodded. 'In the conference of the high mages where I was selected, you voted for me, did you not?'

'Aye. I did.'

'Why? You have displayed no enthusiasm for my rule, you neglect to address me by my correct title, and, frankly, you treat me with an attitude that borders upon disdain. Have I done something to offend you?'

Karalyn shrugged. 'You talk a lot about love and compassion, but your first act has been to assemble a massive army that will cause bloodshed and destruction across the Plateau; and it annoys me that you have embroiled Lucius into your plans. I also know that you have commanded Sable to assassinate Daimon. I voted for you because Bridget shouldn't have appointed her son as heir. On a personal level, I like you. I'll never forget what you did for the twins while I was in Lost-well. Does that mean I think you'll be a decent Empress? I don't know yet, but the initial signs have not been good.'

'I make no apologies for wishing to defend my rule. Bryce has two hundred thousand soldiers in uniform under his authority. And yes, I am aware that he will not be able to gather that entire number into one giant army, but without troops of our own, he would walk all over us. He could use his forces to separate Colsbury from the Holdings and Sanang, and place a blockade on to both of those nations. He could cut off our supply routes and starve us into submission. Without an army, my reign would be over by the end of winter.'

'And what about assassinating Daimon? He's just a boy, a misguided boy.'

'Firstly, you should not be eavesdropping on my private conversations. Secondly, and forgive me for saying this, but you are being hopelessly naïve if you believe that Daimon is merely a misguided child. He murdered elected councillors in Kellach Brigdomin, then he saw to it that your own mother was arrested in Rakana. Furthermore, he was clearly behind Brannig's attempt at killing Bridget; and these are just the things we know about. I also believe he was responsible for persuading Bridget to have me and your mother executed. His heart is rotten.'

'You don't have any proof about Brannig.'

'No? You read Brannig's mind, didn't you – and yet you saw no signs that he harboured a desire to kill the Empress. Keir also reported that the man's eyes were glazed over when he was carrying out the attempt. You would have to be wilfully blind to imagine that Daimon was not responsible.'

A flicker of anger passed over Karalyn's features.

'Am I being unfair?' said Thorn.

'Aye, you are. Your problem is that you've already made your mind up about Daimon. You need him to be evil. The same goes for Bryce. I know Bryce. He's a good man. If it's compassion you're after, then Bryce exemplifies it. It was his compassion that saw Daimon pardoned by Bridget in the first place. You talk about it, while Bryce actually lives it.'

Thorn sighed. 'Perhaps you have not been keeping abreast of events, Karalyn. Were you aware that Bryce personally hacked seven Holdings officers to death with a war-axe? The officers had been arrested for trying to encourage soldiers to leave the imperial army, and join us. Now, one might imagine that such officers would be court-martialled, and yes, perhaps even executed. However, that is not what occurred. Bryce slew them all in the audience chamber of the Great Fortress, and then the body parts were taken to the main square in the city's Old Town, and left there for the public to see. That is how we know what took place. Bryce had a sign written, explaining what he had done. Does that sound compassionate, Karalyn?'

The tall Holdfast woman stared at the Empress.

'I also know Bryce,' Thorn went on; 'or rather, I thought I knew him. This savage act does not seem like something Bryce would have done. I required several witnesses who saw the gruesome display, and who read the sign in question with their own eyes before I could bring myself to believe it. Tell me, Karalyn; why would kind and compassionate Bryce do such a thing? And not only do it, but revel in it to such a degree that he wished the entire city to know what he had done?'

'I will look into this myself,' Karalyn said, her eyes tight.

'Please do.'

The two women glared at each other, then Thorn noticed that the twins were peering up at them both with anxious expressions on their faces. Thorn forced herself to smile.

'Why are you arguing?' said Cael.

'Sometimes adults disagree about things, Cael,' said Thorn. 'Your mama and I are still friends.'

'Can I live here in the palace with you?' said Kyra.

'It is very important that you do as your mama asks, children,' said Thorn.

'I'm in your head,' said Kyra, 'and I know that you're angry with mama.'

'Come out of Thorn's mind, now,' said Karalyn. 'I've told you about this before, Kyra. It's rude to go into someone's head without asking.'

'I'll try not to be angry, Kyra,' said Thorn.

There was a sharp knock upon the entrance to Thorn's quarters, and Agang opened the door, looking flustered.

'Apologies for the interruption, your Majesty,' he said, as he hurried towards the Empress.

'Is something wrong?' said Thorn.

'I have just been speaking to a batch of deserters that arrived in Colsbury today, your Majesty,' he said. 'They claim to have fled from a force led by your former husband.'

Thorn blinked. 'Keir is leading an armed force?'

'Yes, your Majesty; and he is bringing it to Colsbury. The soldier said that he has ten thousand under his command, and they are approaching Colsbury by the southern road. They told me that the army will be here in the next day or so, and that Keir intends to destroy us.'

'That seems unlikely,' said Thorn. 'Karalyn has been using her powers to monitor the roads leading to Colsbury. She would have seen them if they were that close.'

Karalyn bit her lip. 'Uh, I might not have checked the roads for a few days.'

Thorn suppressed a cry of anger, conscious that the twins were gazing up at her.

'I was busy,' Karalyn went on, 'and forgot.'

'You forgot?' cried Agang. 'Monitoring the approaches to Colsbury was your responsibility, Karalyn!'

'Don't raise your voice,' said Thorn. 'Remember who is present.'

'I... yes, of course, your Majesty. Apologies. Karalyn, I would be most obliged if you could confirm the reports from the deserters.'

Karalyn swallowed, then nodded, and her eyes glazed over.

'Is Uncle Keir coming?' said Cael.

'That is what your mama is going to find out,' said Thorn. 'Would you like a drink? Agang, pour the twins some apple juice, if you would.'

'Of course, your Majesty.'

Agang led the twins over to a cabinet by the entrance, while Thorn kept her gaze upon Karalyn. The dream mage coughed after a few moments, and her eyes cleared.

She glanced at Thorn. 'It's true. My brother is leading ten thousand imperial soldiers north towards Colsbury. I would guess that they will be here tomorrow. They have catapults and trebuchets, and I could sense Daimon watching them. Should I summon the dragons?'

'The dragons will be here at dawn, and they will be bringing Kelsey back with them. That will suffice.'

'I, uh... sorry.'

'The important thing is that we were alerted before the army arrived before the walls of Colsbury.'

'I should have been watching.'

'Yes. However, there is no point in lamenting about that now. What's done is done. I imagine that you would be unwilling to kill your own brother?'

'Is that what you want me to do?'

'No. I would never ask you to do something that would clearly disturb your conscience. All the same, there is a reasonable chance that Keir shall not survive the coming days. I will strike him down myself if I have to. But, I am no Bryce. We shall wait to see what Keir does, before we act. Killing him would be a last resort.'

'My brother's powers are extensive,' said Karalyn. 'He can manipulate fire from a distance of several miles. Kelsey will be too far away to block him.'

'I am perfectly aware of Keir's powers. I saw them in action many times in the war against Agatha. So, the storm witch wishes to challenge the soulwitch? So be it. We shall muster our troops and defend our walls.'

'Maybe I should go to Dragon Eyre?' Karalyn said. 'I could recall Sable and Belinda; and my mother. We might need them.'

'No. I do not wish the recruitment of the Banner force to be interrupted. We have you and Kelsey, and me, if it comes to it. We also have Shella, and two dragons. Could you please do me a small favour, and fetch Shella from the Great Keep? I wish to discuss the defences with her.'

Karalyn called for her children, and they joined her. She directed a guilty-looking glance at Thorn, then she and the twins vanished.

Agang shook his head. 'I don't know how you managed to keep your temper, your Majesty.'

'It is wise not to get too angry in front of Cael and Kyra,' she said.

'Karalyn was completely negligent, your Majesty. What use is a dream mage, if she cannot be trusted to do her duty?'

Thorn smiled. 'I would imagine that Bridget often asked herself the same question.'

CHAPTER 13
BROKEN BY THE SHORE

Colsbury Castle, Republic of the Holdings – Winter's Day 534

Keir strode into the command tent.

'Good morning, my lord,' said an aide. 'Coffee?'

Keir nodded, then he joined his senior officers, who were standing round a table. They bowed their heads at his approach, and he glanced down at the map.

'Any changes overnight?' he said.

'Nothing of any substance, my lord,' said a tall Kellach major. 'A few supply wagons were intercepted on the road leading from the Holdings, though far fewer than on the previous evening. They must be getting the message that Colsbury has been blockaded, and that we are allowing nothing through.'

'There was also the usual number of Holdings deserters, my lord,' said another Kellach officer. 'A further seven troopers absconded in the night. They evaded the pickets in the hills to the east, and slipped through under cover of darkness. Another four were arrested trying to flee. That brings the total in custody to seventy-three.'

'What about Colsbury itself?' Keir said. 'Any movement reported?'

'None, my lord,' said the major. 'Our scouts are in the abandoned village on the opposite shore from the isle. The gates of Colsbury are closed, and no one has attempted to cross the bridge in either direction.'

'There are over a thousand people besieged in there,' Keir said. 'Their supply situation must be precarious by now.'

'In truth, my lord,' said the major, 'our own supply situation is more fragile than that of those besieged inside Colsbury. The captured wagons have helped, but if we intend to starve Colsbury into submission, we shall need to double what we are currently receiving from Plateau City. Ten thousand soldiers require several dozen wagons' worth of food every day, my lord.'

'I am aware of that.'

An awkward silence fell over the officers.

'If I may, my lord,' said a colonel. 'I was under the impression that the Emperor expects us to assault Colsbury, not place it under a long siege. Our soldiers are not equipped to sit here all winter, as only a brief campaign was planned. Have our orders changed, my lord?'

'If a long siege is our intention, my lord,' said the major, 'then we should consider sending at least half of our force back to Plateau City. We shall also need to requisition winter clothing, fuel for campfires, and specialist teams to construct vessels to patrol the lake. At present, there is nothing to stop those inside Colsbury from sending out their own boats to gather supplies from the opposite shore.'

'The two dragons would burn any vessel we launched on to the lake,' said Keir.

'Then we should order up ballistae from Plateau City to deal with them, my lord. Our trebuchets and catapults are sitting uselessly in camp. If we were to move them closer...'

'Then the dragons would destroy them,' snapped Keir.

'Perhaps, my lord,' said another major, 'if you were to disclose to us your plan for taking Colsbury, then we might be better able to offer more constructive advice.'

Keir hesitated. He knew that his force was ill-equipped to carry out a siege, but any frontal assault on Colsbury would lead to carnage. With two dragons, Thorn and Shella guarding the bridge to the mainland, any soldiers attempting to cross would be cut down in seconds. He had placed his command post two miles to the south of the isle, alongside the road leading to the Plateau, and kept his soldiers back from the area directly opposite Colsbury, shielding them from the power of the island's defenders. He remembered being on the isle when Agatha had placed it under siege. Her army had only penetrated the defences when Belinda had opened the gates to them.

'I have no further orders at present,' Keir said. 'Maintain our current positions.'

The officers bowed their heads. 'Yes, my lord.'

Keir strode out of the command tent and filled his lungs with the cold mountain air. All around him, rows of tents were spread across the hillside, and soldiers were gathered by their entrances, eating breakfast, and getting ready for another day of inactivity. For three days, Keir's army had done nothing but block the roads leading to Colsbury. They had been getting through their supplies at an alarming rate, devouring their way through tons of bread, meat and ale each day, without making any progress towards their objective. Keir climbed the incline, and strode to the edge of a ridge that rose above the lines of tents. At the top of the ridge, he glanced down at the road. It snaked its way along the banks of the lake before reaching the evacuated village. In the distance, Keir could make out the island of Colsbury. The top of the Summer Palace was rising clear of the cliffs flanking the southern side of the isle. Was that where his former wife was now living, he wondered. Keir sat down on the edge of the ridge, and let his powers slip free of his body. He sped them towards Colsbury. Sanang soldiers were guarding the curtain wall that encircled the island, but Keir could sense nothing in the interior, as if his powers were being deflected. It was Kelsey. His little sister was on the island, and her mere presence was preventing him from spying on Thorn and the others. He was able to see some things outwith Kelsey's range, but the area around the Summer Palace and the twin keeps was shielded.

Why are you still here, Keir? said a voice in his head. *You cannot win.*

Keir frowned. *Piss off, Karalyn.*

No. I don't think so, brother. Why are you disobeying the commands of the false Emperor? Bryce told you to attack, and yet you have done nothing. Are you thinking about changing your allegiance? It's not too late, Keir. As of this moment, you have done nothing irredeemable.

If you have come into my mind to offer your surrender, then I shall listen. Otherwise, I have nothing to say to you, sister.

Surrender? Are you deluded? Bryce wishes to execute every Holdfast within the walls of Colsbury. My children are here, Keir. Do you imagine I would ever surrender them to Bryce? I could wipe your mind from here, brother. It is only because you have refrained from assaulting Colsbury that I have not done so. Kelsey hopes that you will come to your senses, but I have my doubts. Know this, brother – if you put my children in danger, I will destroy you. I have done nothing in this petty conflict so far, but I will not tolerate any threat to Cael or Kyra. Do you understand?

Keir said nothing. His sister's presence lingered in his mind, then it vanished. It had been predictable that Karalyn would threaten to wipe his mind. She knew it was his weak spot; she knew it terrified him more than anything else. He stared at the distant sight of Colsbury as help-lessness swamped him. If he attacked, he and his army would be oblit-erated; but if he marched back to Plateau City, then Bryce and Daimon would probably have him killed. The image of Bryce hacking through the seven Holdings officers was still strong in his mind. The same thing would likely happen to him if he returned to the imperial capital in fail-ure. They would probably kill Tilda, too. He thought about slipping away. He could run, or he could walk over the bridge to the isle and beg his ex-wife for mercy. Either way, Tilda would die.

Is your loyalty wavering, Keir?

Keir stifled a groan. Daimon.

I have been watching you closely, Daimon went on. I wanted to see how you would react to your sister's presence in your mind. Did she threaten you, Keir? Or, did she make you any promises? Were you tempted by her words? You can hide nothing from me, Keir. I can see into your soul.

The only way to defeat them is through a long siege, Chief Mage, Keir said.

Not so. You have powers, Keir. Use them. If you do nothing, then the fresh army from Dragon Eyre shall be arriving soon, and they will destroy the forces under your command. The Emperor grows impatient, disturbed by your lack of progress, and your wavering will. You shall strike today, Keir; you have no choice. Hear my words, Keir. You have no choice.

The voice disappeared from Keir's mind, but he knew that Daimon was still watching him.

He had to attack. He had no choice.

He got to his feet, then turned and gazed down at the rows of tents on the far side of the ridge. The soldiers were useless. Keir would have to do it alone. If he struck quickly, then Karalyn might be dead before she could summon her powers to destroy him. He glanced up at the clouds, then raised his right hand. Daimon's powers hadn't given him any confidence, but there was nothing else he could do. Compelled or not, he would attack.

Keir sent his vision powers high into the sky. It had been a long time since he had attempted to combine his vision skills with his mastery over fire. He felt his way through the clouds, then gazed down at Colsbury. He wouldn't need to see what was happening within the palace or Great Keep; he just needed to make sure his aim was true. He sensed the darkest clouds, and focussed his powers, feeling the energy swirl around him. He grunted, as sweat rolled down his forehead, then the clouds crackled and rumbled as his power grew. He built up the tension within the clouds, and unleashed it upon Colsbury.

A huge streak of lightning ripped through the air. Keir aimed it at the isle, and it struck the smaller of the two keeps in a flash of light and smoke. Keir cursed. He had been hoping to hit the Great Keep, where Karalyn lived. Flames were leaping up from the Lesser Keep, and Keir encouraged them to spread, knowing that he had mere moments in which to act. He returned to the clouds, as two black specks streaked through the sky towards him.

Keir smiled. He might have missed the Great Keep, but he wasn't going to miss two dragons. He stoked the energy held within the clouds again, and jagged, twin forks of lightning exploded from the sky. One struck the blue and green dragon, and its right wing burst into flames. The other lashed out like a whip, and hit the silver dragon in a crescendo of light and noise. The dragons screamed. The silver one plunged down, and crashed onto the island of Colsbury, disappearing beyond the high curtain walls; while the blue and green dragon slammed into the shallow waters by the side of the lake. Smoke rose in twisted plumes from the surface of the water, and the ripples sent waves against the shoreline.

Keir dropped his powers and sprinted down the ridge, mingling with the soldiers gathered there. All of them were staring up at the sky, their eyes wide. Keir grabbed a helmet from a pile, put it on, and kept his head down. If Karalyn was hunting for him, she would need to look through the entire army to find him; as long as he didn't use any more of his powers, he might be safe. He noticed a captain among the others.

'Send a company down to the shore,' Keir shouted. 'If the blue dragon lives, it shall be our hostage.'

'Aye, sir,' said the captain.

Keir watched as the officer summoned a detachment, then he joined them, staying near the rear as the captain led them over the ridge. Flames and thick dark smoke were still rising from the island of Colsbury. With any luck, the occupants of the isle would be gripped with panic and despair, stunned by the loss of their two dragons. Keir smiled. At last, he had some good news to report to Plateau City. Not even Daimon would be able to fault him. In a matter of moments, he had removed the most potent part of the island's defences. Without dragons, the siege could be tightened, and the artillery could begin pounding the Summer Palace into rubble.

The detachment reached the road at the bottom of the slope, and the soldiers ran towards Colsbury. The blue and green dragon had crashed several hundred yards to the south of the isle, and a soldier pointed at the lake.

'Something's moving!' he cried.

They ran on, and Keir saw a scaled forelimb rise above the surface of the lake, then a blood-streaked head emerged from the water.

'The beast is trying to drag itself out,' cried another soldier.

'Quickly!' shouted the officer. 'Don't let it escape.'

The soldiers increased their speed. The lead unit reached the shore where the dragon was struggling to pull itself free of the water, and aimed their crossbows at its head. More soldiers arrived, and they formed up into three thick lines, each levelling their bows at the enormous beast.

'Move and you die, lizard!' shouted the captain, his sword drawn.

The dragon collapsed, its head and forelimbs lying on the shore, while the rest of its bulk remained submerged. It was still alive, its chest rising and falling, but its scales were scorched and bloody, and its eyes were barely open.

The captain noticed Keir among his men, and his eyes widened.

'My lord,' he said, 'should you be exposing yourself to such risks? This dragon might be dangerous, sir.'

'It was I who brought the beast down,' Keir said.

'What shall we do with it, my lord?' said the captain. 'We have no chains or nets. If we intend to keep it as a hostage, then we shall need to bring ropes, and have the gaien drag it from the lake.'

Keir glanced up at the curtain walls of Colsbury. He couldn't see the Lesser Keep from his position, as the Summer Palace was blocking it, but smoke was still rising in thick plumes. He wondered if Thorn was watching.

'I have decided against keeping the beast as a hostage,' Keir said. 'It would eat too many supplies, and would serve better as an example to our enemies. Kill it. Remove its head, and then we shall use a catapult to launch it into the castle.'

The captain saluted. 'As you wish, my lord.' He gestured to two soldiers. 'Run back to camp, and fetch the largest saw you can find.'

The two soldiers saluted and sprinted back down the road.

'The rest of you,' said the officer, 'keep your weapons trained on the beast. Do not hesitate to loose if it moves. Aim for its eyes.'

Keir paced up and down the shore, his gaze flicking between Colsbury and the wounded dragon. He wondered if the other one was dead.

He hoped that was the case. If it still lived, then there was a chance that Thorn might be able to heal it, and the value of Keir's achievement would be lowered by half. It was unlikely that Karalyn would allow him to use his powers again. Once the green and blue dragon had been dealt with, Keir would order half of his force back to Plateau City, and settle down for a long siege. At least he had tried. If he had managed to strike the Great Keep, and killed his elder sister, then the rebellion would be over in all but name. He cursed his luck.

Why have you stopped, Keir? said Daimon's voice in his mind. *Why do you hide among your soldiers? Strike! Rain lightning down upon Colsbury, and raze it to the ground.*

My sister will destroy me if I try again.

She will not be able to harm you with me inside your head. I shall remain here, to guard you from her powers. Be brave. Be ruthless. Do not let it be said that you were too weak to destroy the rebels. People will think that you are still loyal to your family, Keir. Prove to them all that you are not weak. Kill them.

Keir hesitated, then he felt a burst of confidence fill his body. He laughed, and strode away from the dragon and the soldiers, until he was standing alone on the shoreline. Why had he been scared? He turned to face the dark clouds, and raised his arms again. Twenty yards away, the air shimmered, and Karalyn appeared, flanked by Thorn and Pechtang.

Thorn lifted a hand, and the soldiers guarding the green and blue dragon cried out in agony. Their skin fell in shreds from their faces, then they collapsed to the ground, their blood pooling over the rocky shore. Karalyn glanced at Keir, and he felt Daimon's powers surge within him, blocking his sister's attempts to invade his mind. Thorn turned from her bloody handiwork, and nodded to Pechtang.

'Do not kill him,' Thorn said. 'Leave him bloody and broken by the shore of the lake.'

Pechtang smiled, then raced forwards. Keir's confidence evaporated. He tried to use his powers on the Sanang warrior running towards him, but Karalyn was blocking him, just as Daimon had blocked her. Pechtang reached Keir and his clenched fists lashed out. Keir took a blow to the face, and another in his stomach, then Pechtang ripped Keir's helmet off and used it to club him. Keir doubled over, his hands raised to protect his head, but the Sanang warrior was fast and strong. Keir felt a boot batter into the side of his head, and he fell to the ground. He sensed Karalyn and Thorn watching in silence as Pechtang issued a savage beating. The Sanang man laughed as he stamped down onto Keir's face, breaking his nose and teeth, then Keir felt his fingers snap as Pechtang brought his boot down again. Pain such as he had never experienced tore through Keir, as Pechtang battered him.

Help me, Daimon.

I can do nothing, Keir. Karalyn is preventing me from using my powers, just as I am preventing her from using hers. There is nothing I can do against fists and boots. If you hadn't hesitated before, you would have been victorious. You have brought this upon yourself, Keir.

Pechtang's boot slammed down onto Keir's left forearm, and the bones snapped.

'Enough,' said Thorn.

'Yes, ma'am,' gasped Pechtang, his efforts leaving him out of breath. 'Are you sure you don't want me to kill him?'

'I'm sure,' said Thorn. 'I want his army to see him like this.'

Keir sensed Karalyn looking down at him.

'What did I tell you, brother? I warned you, and yet you still attacked. If Cael or Kyra had been harmed, you would be dead right now.'

'If your army remains here, storm witch,' said Thorn, 'we shall kill them all. Order the withdrawal, and we will allow you to retreat in peace. You have until sunset.'

The air shimmered again, and his sister, former wife, and Pechtang vanished, along with the green and blue dragon. Keir lay still for a moment, every inch of his body screaming in pain, then he closed his eyes, and oblivion took him.

As soon as Keir regained consciousness, he wished he hadn't. Agony was rippling through him, and his head was in torment, his nose and mouth the epicentre of a fierce and all-consuming pain.

'Try not to move, sir,' said a voice.

Keir opened his left eye. His right was swollen shut, and his vision was blurry. He was inside a tent, surrounded by officers and medical orderlies.

'Is it sunset?' Keir whispered, his voice slurred and hoarse, while the pain in his jaw almost made him pass out.

'Not yet, sir,' said an officer. 'You were only unconscious for a couple of hours.'

'Give him this,' said another voice.

Keir felt a cigarette being placed against his lips. On instinct, he inhaled, then he realised that it wasn't a cigarette. The dullweed's effects were quick in coming, and he felt the levels of pain recede. His thoughts became foggy, but he didn't care. All that mattered was that the pain was less than before. He took another draw, and lay back on the camp bed.

'What shall we do?' said an officer, his voice drifting into Keir's consciousness.

'We shall carry out Lord Keir's last orders, Colonel,' said another voice. 'He commanded us to maintain our current positions, and that is what we must do. I have already sent a scout to rush back to Plateau City with all haste, bearing the news of today's events.'

'It will take twenty days to run there and back, sir,' said a further voice.

Keir wondered what they were talking about. He could hear the words being spoken, but their meaning confused him.

'It's more than likely that Mage Daimon, or perhaps Mage Tabor, has been watching us,' said the first officer. 'As the next in command of this expeditionary force, it is my duty to await fresh orders from Plateau City. Until we receive word, we shall stay here, and continue to blockade the roads to Colsbury.'

'Sunset,' Keir slurred.

'Sir?' said a voice.

'He's rambling,' said another. 'The dullweed will prevent him from making any sense. Lord Keir is fortunate to be alive.'

'Sunset,' Keir went on. 'We leave at sunset.'

'What's he saying?' came another voice. 'Was that an order?'

'Pay no attention, Lieutenant,' said an older voice.

'Listen to me,' croaked Keir. 'We must leave at sunset, or my sister will kill us all.'

The tent fell into silence.

A head loomed into view, and Keir saw a man looking into his eyes.

'Can you tell us what happened on the beach, my lord?'

'Karalyn… she rescued the dragon, and told me… she told me to withdraw the army. If we don't, she will destroy us all, just as she destroyed the Rahain who fought for Agatha. Order the withdrawal. Now.'

Keir panted from the effort of speaking, as the officers glanced at each other.

'The chain of command is clear,' said a voice. 'We are obliged to follow Lord Keir's orders.'

'But he could be out of his mind on dullweed, sir.'

'He seemed lucid enough to me,' said another voice.

'I agree,' said the first voice. 'Return to your units, and order the immediate evacuation of the area around Colsbury. We shall dismantle the camp and return south. The decision is Lord Keir's. Dismissed.'

Keir heard the sound of a dozen officers leaving the tent. Orderlies approached the camp bed, and the weedstick was placed against Keir's lips again.

'I don't need any more,' he gasped.

'You will, sir,' said a voice. 'We're going to attempt to set your broken limbs, and clean up your wounds. We shall work as quickly as possible, but it won't be pleasant.'

The weedstick was thrust against Keir's lips again, and he inhaled. Two men took hold of his left arm. One nodded to the other, and they pulled the shattered bones into alignment. Keir's screams tore through the tent, and he blacked out.

When Keir next awoke, the sky was dark. He was moving, and every judder from the wagon was sending spears of pain through his bandaged body. His right eye remained swollen shut, but he could see the columns of marching soldiers filling the road behind him. The lake was nowhere to be seen, and trees lined the way on both sides.

Keir wept in silence, wishing that Thorn and Karalyn had simply killed him. His face was a raw, bloody pulp. With half of his teeth gone, and his nose smashed in, he would never be handsome again. Those vile witches had ruined him. What would Tilda think? Would she cower from him in horror? Wherever he went, people would stare at him. Mothers would shield the eyes of their children from the sight of him, and it was all his sister's fault. If he survived the wrath of the Emperor, he would dedicate the rest of his life to ensuring Thorn and Karalyn suffered the same as they had done to him. He vowed it to himself. Thorn valued her beauty, and he would take it from her, leaving her as ugly on the outside as she was on the inside.

'More dullweed, sir?' said a voice from beside him on the wagon.

Keir nodded. He felt a weedstick brush against his lips and he inhaled. His pain retreated, his memories feeling as though they had been nothing but a bad dream.

CHAPTER 14
THE TEMPLES OF SUN TA

S un Ta, Na Sun Ka, Western Rim – 21st Essinch 5255

Belinda and Sable walked through the enormous plaza, stepping over the bodies of the fallen. Above them, the sun was shining in the midst of a blue sky, but the huge dragon temples of Sun Ta were casting long shadows that spilled across the worn, blood-spattered paving slabs. Groups of exhausted Banner soldiers were standing together, drinking from water skins and smoking cigarettes. A few of their colleagues were among the fallen, but the majority of the dead were men in black-robes. Belinda glanced at the corpses. Most were without any visible injury, their hearts halted by her death powers.

Many soldiers stopped talking as Belinda passed them, and some bowed their heads towards the Third Ascendant. She wondered if they had heard the rumours about her identity, or perhaps they had witnessed what she had done to raise the siege of the temple. How many had she killed – two thousand? More? Regardless, her act had freed the hundreds of Banner soldiers who had been trapped within the walls of the vast temple – soldiers who had been starving to death; soldiers who were now staring at her in awe.

'Did I do the right thing?' she said.

Sable glanced at her as they walked. 'Yes. They were Unk Tannic.'

'Does that mean they deserved to die?'

'Don't feel sorry for them, Belinda. The Unk Tannic are fanatics. They used to blow up taverns.'

Belinda frowned as they approached the great gates of the temple. They had been opened, and Banner soldiers who had already been recruited by Daphne in Ectus were distributing food and water to those who had been besieged. Lucius Cardova was overseeing the wagons, and was speaking to a group of emaciated officers. Belinda couldn't hear what he was saying, but his role was to explain the details of the new contract on offer to any Banner soldier who wished to take it.

'Didn't you blow up taverns, Sable?' Belinda said, as they entered the thick shadows created by the tall flank of the temple.

Sable nodded. 'Yes. Taverns, supply depots, barracks – anything I could reach. I killed more Banner soldiers in a few months than the Unk Tannic managed in years. That was then, and this is now. Either way, I'm still helping Dragon Eyre.'

The two women entered the gates of the temple, and a rancid odour reached Belinda's nostrils. Sick and wounded Banner soldiers were lying by the walls of the entrance tunnel, groaning for salve and water. Belinda raised her hand, sending a burst of healing powers into the soldiers. It wouldn't cure their hunger or thirst, but she could see the looks of relief develop across their faces as their pain was lifted.

'What would they do,' said Belinda, 'if they knew who you were?'

Sable shrugged. 'They would probably try to kill me.'

'They all know that their new contract is being arranged by the Holdfasts,' Belinda said; 'and Lucius Cardova seems to think that the Banners are too professional to hold grudges.'

'I know what he thinks. All the same, I'm keeping the Quadrant close to my fingers. We can reveal who I am when we're safely back in the Star Continent. There's no point in upsetting them; I killed a lot of their friends.'

They reached the heart of the temple – a vast indoor space, its high ceiling held up by a forest of slim pillars. Old frescos covered the walls, but the paint had faded in places, while much was lost in the impenetrable shadows that shrouded the interior. Hundreds of Banner soldiers were present, along with dozens of support staff and civilians, including several small children. Daphne's recruits were moving through the crowd, spreading the news of their rescue.

'This reminds me of the cathedral in Holdings City,' said Sable. 'Dark and gloomy. It's gone now, reduced to ruins by the Creator, but I remember going there as a girl.'

'Is that where you worshipped Nathaniel?'

'Yes. It sounds stupid now, but my faith was the most important thing in my life when I was young.'

'It doesn't sound stupid. It was rational for the Holdings to believe in the Creator. You weren't to know the truth.'

'You won't remember this, but we were allies for a while,' Sable said; 'before Karalyn wiped your mind. We both worked for Agatha. I did it because I believed in the Creator, while you were doing it to get revenge on those who had killed him.'

'Did we ever meet?'

'No. I was aware of you; I knew that you had gone to Plateau City, but I was on an operation in Silverstream while you were trying to overthrow the Empress. I thought you were a young mage at that point. I had no idea that you should have been in charge of the entire invasion. Why was Agatha the leader?'

'Silva told me that I had abdicated all authority to her,' Belinda said. 'I was overcome with grief and anger over Nathaniel's death. I wanted revenge, just as you said. I wanted to kill everyone connected to Nathaniel's death.'

'That sounds familiar. I wanted to kill everyone after Badblood was slain. In my case, there was no Karalyn around to stop me.'

Belinda gazed at her right hand. 'And now I have killed again.'

'A cheer for the Third Ascendant!' cried a voice.

Belinda glanced up, and saw dozens of faces staring at her. A roar of noise sounded as the soldiers and civilians packed inside the temple cheered. Belinda tried to smile at them, but her heart was conflicted. She had fought Banner soldiers on Lostwell, and Sable had been slaughtering the same regiments that were now cheering wildly. She tried to think of the reasons why she had cut down the hordes of black-robed Unk Tannic who had been camped outside the walls of the temple. Were they worse than the Banner soldiers? More evil? She didn't know. A few soldiers got down onto their knees in front of her, their heads bowed, and Belinda's cheeks flushed.

Sable nudged her, and she glanced up to see Daphne and Silva approach.

'Good job, Belinda,' said Daphne, her right hand resting upon the hilt of her sword. 'Your little demonstration was witnessed by hundreds of Banner soldiers watching from the other temples. This will be a good day for recruitment.'

Belinda nodded. She noticed that, while Daphne had a grim smile on her lips, Silva was frowning and looking away, her eyes filled with disapproval.

'Shall we go back to Ectus?' said Sable.

'Not yet,' said Daphne. 'I want to speak to the senior officers based here in Sun Ta. I was holding a meeting in the Temple of Haurn while you and Belinda were clearing up the siege. The major-general of the Banner of the Silver Wing was there. He was undecided about our offer, but I suspect that he might have changed his mind after watching Belinda in action. Once we've spoken again, I would like you to return to Colsbury, Sable. It's time to start bringing soldiers to the Star Continent.'

'Good,' said Silva. 'I will be glad to get off this world. It is filled with nothing but pain and misery.'

Daphne gave a gentle shrug. 'Really? I quite like it here. Summon Captain Cardova and Sergeant Logos. They shall accompany us to the Temple of Haurn.'

The others followed Daphne as she led the way back out of the temple structure. They collected the two Banner soldiers by the gates, leaving some of their recruits to continue handing out food and water to the rescued soldiers; then they crossed the plaza.

'Which temple belongs to Haurn?' said Belinda.

Daphne pointed at a towering structure of grey marble and granite. Each of the twelve temples was different in appearance, but all seemed ancient; far older than the buildings of the town that lay at their feet. On the far side of the plaza, a large crowd of Dragon Eyre natives had gathered, their eyes on the Banner soldiers. Daphne had spread the word that all foreign soldiers would soon be leaving, and Belinda wondered if they had come to see if the rumours were true. A squad of new recruits moved into position around Daphne and the others as they crossed the vast open space.

'The natives hate us,' said Belinda, her eyes still on the crowds by the side of the plaza.

'They do,' said Daphne; 'but soon they will be singing our praises. Not only will we be removing the Banner soldiers from their midst, but we have also dealt a savage blow to the Unk Tannic.' She glanced at her half-sister. 'This was your ambition, was it not, Sable? To destroy the Unk Tannic?'

Sable nodded.

'I thought you would be happier.'

'I was thinking about Lara,' said Sable. 'The destruction of the Unk Tannic doesn't seem all that important to me any more.'

'It should,' said Cardova. 'If we're pulling the Banners out of Dragon Eyre, then the last thing we want to do is leave this world at the mercy of those black-robed fanatics.'

Caelius nodded. 'Well said, Captain. It's just a pity that we aren't staying long enough to wipe out every last one of them. There will be a few still hiding out among the volcanoes to the west of here, ready to crawl out of their holes as soon as we've gone.'

'We can't do everything,' said Daphne. 'Gyle remains a considerable challenge, for instance. The natives there have enslaved at least sixty thousand Banner soldiers, but we can't simply slaughter the natives the way we killed the Unk Tannic. Sable, I shall need you to transport all of the enslaved soldiers directly to the Star Continent. Can the Sextant do that?'

'Yes,' said Sable.

'Good. We will have to explain what has happened to them once they have arrived on our world. We can always send back any who refuse to sign the new contract.'

They reached the massive Temple of Haurn, and passed the guarded entrance gates. The interior of the temple was lit by a series of deep shafts that cut through the structure, and groups of soldiers were staring at Daphne and Belinda as they passed. A lieutenant greeted them, and led them to a large side chamber, where a dozen high-ranking Banner officers were assembled.

Daphne strode into the middle of the chamber, flanked by Sable and Belinda.

'I trust you have had sufficient time to think over our offer?' Daphne said. 'You all saw the power of the Third Ascendant. In a matter of minutes, she destroyed the Unk Tannic forces that have been camped in front of the temples for months.' She glanced at the seated group of officers. 'As of this moment, you are free to choose your own destiny again. You can remain here, on Na Sun Ka, and try to live side by side with those you occupied and oppressed for decades. Or, you can forge a new beginning, in a new Banner, with a new contract. The choice is yours.'

An older man with grey hair got to his feet.

'I have been selected to represent the views and interests of the other officers, ma'am,' he said; 'and we have a few questions.'

'Carry on, Major-General,' said Daphne.

'Firstly, how many have already signed up for this new Banner?'

'We have fifty thousand ready and waiting upon Ectus,' Daphne said, 'not including a further ten thousand support staff. More there are flocking to the new Banner every day. We have also visited Alef, and recruited another fourteen thousand soldiers from that archipelago. I understand that approximately twenty-five thousand Banner personnel are currently on Na Sun Ka. Your cooperation would be instrumental in securing their agreement.'

'What about those on Gyle, ma'am?'

'We have plans for them,' said Daphne. 'We cannot directly intervene on Gyle – to do so would lead to carnage among the natives of that island. We shall use the Sextant to transport every enslaved Banner soldier to our world. There, we shall explain to them what has occurred, and offer them the same contract.'

The officers glanced at each other.

'Your words comfort me, ma'am,' said the major-general. 'However, could you clarify one thing for us? We have heard that the Holdfasts are behind this new Banner. Is that true?'

'Yes,' said Daphne. 'I am Holder Fast, the senior member of the Holdfast family. I am working on behalf of Empress Thorn, who rules my home world. The contract would be with her Majesty, not with the Holdfasts, but I am her Herald.'

'One of your family killed countless thousands of our soldiers, ma'am,' the officer said. 'It might be hard for the lower ranks to accept that we will now be working for the family that slaughtered so many of us.'

'I was led to believe that the Banners are professional mercenaries,' Daphne said; 'the best in existence. Times change. Allegiances alter. None of you are being compelled in any way to join the new Banner; it must be a choice freely made. You are perfectly able to remain here if you so desire.'

'We are minded to accept your terms, ma'am, but we have one condition.'

'Name it.'

'We refuse to serve directly under Sable Holdfast's command, ma'am. We think the witch is based upon Ulna at the moment, working alongside Queen Blackrose. If you swear that she will not lead us into battle, then we are prepared to recommend to our forces that they accept your offer.'

'I can agree to that condition,' said Daphne. 'Summon all willing volunteers to the temple district of Sun Ta, and we shall transport them all to our world in a few days. A tented city is currently being constructed within the Holdings, and there shall be food, equipment and salve available to all who join the Banner of the Sapphire Throne. You have my word.'

The major-general strode forward, and extended his hand. Daphne took it, and smiled.

'We accept the terms of your offer,' said the officer; 'and shall abide by our new contract.'

'Thank you, Major-General,' said Daphne. She glanced at Sable. 'If you would be so kind as to begin the process of transporting the first batches to the Star Continent, sister, I would be much obliged. Leave Captain Cardova and Sergeant Logos with me.'

Sable nodded, then placed her hand into a pocket. The air shimmered, and Belinda, Sable and Silva appeared by the base of the bridge palace in Ulna.

'This isn't the Star Continent,' said Silva.

'Well done,' said Sable. 'Your powers of observation are to be commended.'

Silva frowned. 'There's no need for sarcasm.'

'The way I'm feeling, you're lucky you only got sarcasm, demigod,' Sable said. 'Come on; we need to find Lara, and then we can leave.'

'Are you angry?' said Belinda, as they began to walk towards the harbour.

Sable glanced at her. 'Did you hear the way I was discussed back there? If those officers had known my name, do you think they would have agreed to help us? And Daphne removed me from command of the new Banner without a word of consultation. Not that I wanted to command them, but still. I thought I was past being treated like a pariah by the other Holdfasts.'

'You reap what you sow, witch,' said Silva.

Sable fell into silence, and Belinda turned to look at the boats sheltering within the breakwaters of the large harbour. Alongside the multitude of small fishing vessels, the four ships of the Five Sisters were easy to see, their tall masts rising over the stone quay. Gulls were circling overhead, following a group of fishing boats as they sailed into the harbour, their cries echoing across the shore. They passed Captain Tilly's ship, then climbed the gangway leading to the deck of the *Giddy Gull*. The smell of fresh wood and bitumen hung heavy in the air, and sailors were busy preparing the vessel for a voyage. Sable led the way to the quarter deck, and they walked up the steps. A couple of carpenters were touching up the paintwork on the new cabin that sat at the rear of the ship, and a small group was standing by the wheel.

Sable swallowed, then approached Lara.

'We're back,' she said. 'Are you ready to return to the Star Continent, Lara?'

The captain of the *Giddy Gull* raised a hand for silence in Sable's direction, then she continued speaking to the small group surrounding her.

'Fifty miles should do us,' Lara was saying; 'then we'll bring the *Gull* back into port. We'll hug the coast as far as Gliden, and see how the ship holds up. I want the bosun and his team on standby throughout; they'll report to you, Master.'

A man Belinda recognised as Maddie's romantic partner saluted. 'Aye, ma'am.'

Lara turned to Sable. 'You were saying?'

Sable frowned. 'I'm going back to Colsbury. Daphne's staying on a little longer, but my part in recruiting the new Banner is over, and I need to start transporting the soldiers off this world.'

Lara nodded. 'I see. And then?'

'Then, I intend to help defeat Bryce and Daimon, just as I promised.'

'And what about the promises you made to me, Sable? Don't they count?'

'They count,' said Sable. 'I just need to do this first.'

Lara's eyes flashed with rage. 'When will it bleeding well end, Sable? There will always be one more thing that you need to do. I'm sick of it. You promised me that you would settle down, here in Dragon Eyre, with me, as soon as you had forced the gods to withdraw. That was bleeding months ago. You care more about impressing your sister than you do about me.'

'That's not true, Lara. I love you.'

'Yeah? You don't seem to bleeding show it. You've dragged me about from world to world, while you carry out your little errands for the Holdfasts. I ain't your puppy, Sable. I have a life here – a life of my own.'

'What are you saying?'

'I want you to keep your damn promises; that's what I'm saying, Sable. Stay here. Forget this bullshit about who should be Emperor or Empress on your home world. Who cares? Let them fight it out among themselves; it ain't none of my damn business, and it ain't yours neither. We were happy, weren't we, before you got involved with your bleeding sister?'

Sable lowered her gaze. 'I can't stay. I have a job to do.'

'Yeah? Well, so do I. The *Gull's* ready for sea trials, and I should be here to make sure Tilly doesn't mess it up. The *Gull's* my responsibility, and yet you expect me to drop everything, again, to follow you around. Well, I ain't doing it no more. Got it?'

'You're being unreasonable, Lara,' said Belinda.

'Shut yer face, god,' spat Lara. 'Keep your nose out of my damn business. I ain't afraid of you.'

'Are you saying that it's over?' said Sable.

Lara exhaled, and shook her head. 'No. I'm saying that if you want this to work, then you need to at least try. I came with you last time, didn't I? Why's it always me who has to compromise?' She sighed. 'You're not ready, Sable. You might think you are, but you ain't. You think you have to prove something to your family, and nothing I say will change that. Come back when you're ready. Until then, piss off and leave me alone.'

Belinda realised that every person on the quarter deck was staring at Sable and Lara in a deathly silence, and even the sailors up on the rigging were peering down at them, listening to every word.

The air crackled, and Belinda, Sable and Silva appeared in the Sextant chamber in Colsbury.

Belinda glanced at the large device, then turned away from it.

She looked at Sable. 'Shouldn't you have said goodbye?'

'I said everything I needed to say,' Sable muttered, as she walked towards the Sextant.

'Shouldn't we tell Thorn or Karalyn that we're back?' said Belinda.

'You can do it,' Sable said. 'I need to work on the calculations.'

'Lara was acting irrationally,' Belinda said.

'Was she? She was right – I did promise her that I would settle down. I've ruined everything, yet again; and for what? So that Daphne Holdfast would accept me.'

Belinda said nothing, then she glanced at Silva, and they strode from the chamber, leaving Sable alone with the Sextant.

'Poor Sable,' Belinda said, as they walked along the hallway.

Silva snorted. 'Pay no attention to the follies of the mortals, my Queen. You owe them nothing. Lara was correct in one respect – this fight is none of our business.'

'What would you have me do, Silva?'

'Is that a serious question, your Majesty? Are you seeking my advice?'

'I am.'

Silva frowned. 'In truth, your Majesty, I do not know what to advise. Lostwell has gone forever, and Implacatus is too dangerous. That leaves this world, Dragon Eyre and the world of the Salve City. If you wished to rule any of these worlds, then they are yours for the taking. The Holdfasts should be your servants, not your masters.'

Belinda smiled. 'They are not my masters.'

'They are mortals, my Queen. They are but dust in the wind.'

They reached the door to the main living room, and Belinda pushed it open. Inside, Karalyn was sitting with Shella, while the twins were at the table, writing out words in their lesson books.

'We have returned from Dragon Eyre,' Belinda said.

Karalyn glanced up, and rose to her feet. 'Is mother with you?'

'No. Daphne is still in Na Sun Ka, negotiating with the Banner officers. Sable is in the Sextant chamber, ready to begin transporting soldiers to this world.'

Karalyn and Shella glanced at each other.

'Is something wrong?' said Belinda.

'We were attacked by Bryce's imperial forces two days ago,' said

Shella. 'Keir was leading them. He used his lightning powers and killed over a hundred people who were living in the Lesser Keep, including a dozen children.'

'He also wounded the dragons,' Karalyn said, 'but Thorn healed them both.'

'And Kelsey? Was she on Frostback?'

'No,' said Shella. 'She stayed in the Summer Palace during the attack, to protect the Empress from Daimon. If she had been flying that day, she would be dead.'

Belinda felt her anger flare. 'Where is Keir now? Is his force still outside Colsbury?'

'No,' said Shella. 'They've gone. They pulled out at sunset, the day before yesterday, after... well, after one of Thorn's Sanang lads kicked the shit out of Keir.'

Belinda frowned. 'You let him live?'

'Aye,' said Karalyn. 'He's still my brother, despite everything. Thorn would have killed him without a moment's hesitation, but I managed to hold her back. We left him bleeding and broken on the shores of the lake.'

'You should have killed him. He tried to kill you.'

Karalyn nodded. 'I couldn't do it. What would I have told mother?'

'What's wrong with the truth?' said Belinda.

Karalyn shrugged.

'You should report to the Empress,' said Shella. 'Her Majesty will want to know all the news from Dragon Eyre.'

'Is she in the Summer Palace?' said Belinda.

'Yes, along with Agang and her staff. Karalyn can take you there; save you walking up and down a dozen staircases.'

'I will check on Sable first,' said Belinda. 'Is the tented city in Colsbrookdale ready to receive its first batch of soldiers?'

'It's been ready for days,' said Shella, 'but Sable will need the precise location.' The old Rakanese mage got to her feet. 'I'll come with you.'

'I'll tell the Empress that you're back,' said Karalyn. 'I have no desire to watch thousands of Implacatus soldiers arrive on this world.'

Belinda eyed her oldest friend. 'What if Keir had hurt your children?'

'Then he would already be dead,' she said.

Belinda nodded, then she left the living room. Silva and Shella followed her out, and they retraced their steps to the Sextant chamber.

'How was Dragon Eyre?' Shella said, as they walked.

'Hot and sunny,' said Belinda, 'and full of death and misery. I should warn you that Sable is a little upset. Lara refused to return with us.'

'Boo hoo. I have more things to worry about than Sable's love life.'

Belinda glared at her. 'Have you no room in your heart for a little compassion?'

Shella laughed. 'I never thought I'd be lectured on compassion by you, Belinda. I thought you were too ruthless for such petty emotions.'

'You don't know me, Shella. Don't pretend that you do.'

Shella rolled her eyes.

Belinda opened the door to the Sextant chamber. Sable was standing next to it, a palm placed upon its glass surface.

'Shella knows how to find Colsbrookdale,' Belinda said, 'where the tented city is located.'

'I've already found it,' Sable said. 'It wasn't hard to notice. There aren't many valleys in the Barrier Mountains with adequate space and water supplies to accommodate tens of thousands of soldiers.'

'There is enough food there to feed eighty thousand people for a third,' said Shella; 'and more has been ordered. I've also gathered three thousand local Holdings militia to welcome the new arrivals, and a rudimentary headquarters is being constructed for the senior officers. How many will be coming in the first batch?'

'About sixty thousand,' said Sable. 'We're going to clear out Ectus first. I've identified the population to transfer. Then, once they've had a chance to settle in, I'll start bringing the rest.'

Belinda approached the device. She had been avoiding the Sextant since her rescue from Cumulus, the memories of the last moments of Lostwell too painful for her to face. Sable glanced at her.

'Do you want to use it?' she said to Belinda.

'No.'

'I've been wanting to ask you,' Sable went on, 'how it was that you knew how to operate it. You shifted thousands of people to Salve City. How did you manage that if you have no memories of ever using it before?'

'I don't know,' Belinda said. 'I told it what I wanted, and it did as I asked. I don't know how.'

'I can answer that,' said Silva. 'The Sextant was built for the Ascendants, and it knows each one of them. It would have recognised your touch, my Queen. It is the same principle that allows the Ascendants to control the greenhides.'

Sable nodded. 'Place your hands onto the device, and you can watch me work.'

Silva and Shella did so, while Belinda hesitated. She swallowed, then put her palm on to the smooth surface.

What is your desire, most glorious Third Ascendant?

'The voice,' Belinda whispered. 'That's what I heard in Lostwell.'

Sable smiled.

'How can you control it?' Belinda asked.

'I can also control greenhides,' Sable said. 'So, if it's the same principle that governs both, then there's your answer. All right; here goes.'

Belinda's vision clouded over, then she saw the island of Ectus loom in front of them. The battered shoreline stretched out for miles in either direction, pockmarked with craters and littered with ruined buildings. Belinda felt Sable's commands reach the Sextant, and the power held within the device thrummed under her fingers. Her vision swept over Sabat City, until they reached a large barracks, which was filled with Banner soldiers and support staff.

'This is one of the assembly points,' Sable said. 'There are a dozen others on Ectus, but I can link to them all at once. Sextant, can you see the tented city at Colsbrookdale in the Barrier Mountains?'

Yes, Sable.

'How many people on Ectus have been marked for transfer?'

Sixty-one thousand, two hundred and ninety-three.

'Transfer them all to Colsbrookdale.'

Belinda watched as the sky burned and crackled over Ectus, then every man and women in the barracks below them disappeared. Belinda laughed, then she gazed around Sabat City. The streets were empty, the harbour front deserted.

It is done, said the Sextant.

'Is that it?' said Shella.

Sable lifted her hand from the device. 'Let's find out.'

She reached into her pocket, then the air shimmered, and they appeared on a hillside overlooking a wide, flat valley, surrounded by mountains. A river was running through the middle of the plain, and hundreds of canvas tents were lined up in rows upon either bank, along with wagons loaded with supplies. Amid it all stood thousands of Banner soldiers, who were gazing around in bewilderment and excitement. Some stared, some laughed, while others fell to their knees and wept. Squads of Holdings militia began approaching on wagons, throwing out parcels of food and clothing to the starving soldiers.

Shella grinned. 'Nice job, Sable. Now, find me a few of their commanding officers; our work here is just beginning.'

CHAPTER 15
THE PRICE OF SALVE

Marchside, Kell – 3rd Day, First Third Winter 534

Aila tried to ignore the sounds assaulting her ears. Outside, hailstones were battering off the windows and roof of the farmhouse, creating a constant background cacophony of drumming; while Konna was crying her lungs out, her tiny face red and wet with tears.

'Hush,' whispered Aila, as she changed the baby's nappy. She hurled the soiled garments into a laundry bucket, and plucked fresh clothes from a pile by the table. Aila picked Konna up as soon as the new nappy and clothes were on her, and rocked the child in her arms.

'Hush, little demigod,' Aila said, but it made no difference to the volume of noise being emitted from the baby's lips.

She heard a low laugh from the doorway, and saw Naxor standing there, his coat soaked, and his boots trailing mud over the floor.

'What have I told you about your damn boots, cousin?' Aila cried. 'Look at the mess you've made of my floor.'

'Put the baby down and have a glass of wine,' Naxor said, as he removed his coat and slung it over a chair. He sat and lit a cigarette.

Aila glared at him. 'You aren't supposed to smoke in here. You have the shed for that.'

'I can't smoke in the shed, my dear Aila. There are far too many combustible materials stored in there; and I'm certainly not smoking outside in this weather.'

'If Corthie notices it, then I'm not going to stick up for you again. You know he hates the smell of smoke.'

Naxor smiled. 'I had gathered that. Where is the large oaf?'

'Don't call him that,' Aila said, as she paced up and down the dining room with Konna in her arms.

'My, you are testy today,' said Naxor. 'It's the hailstorm, isn't it? You were always morose in Freshmist.'

'Take your boots off before I punch you in the face.'

Naxor raised his hands. 'I'm doing it. Look; see?' He leaned over and unlaced his boots, then slipped his feet out from them. 'Oh, I've finished, by the way. It's done.'

'You've finished?'

'Indeed. Just under two tons of refined salve is now neatly stacked up within the shed. Enough to kill several thousand Empresses.'

'That's not funny.'

'That's a matter of opinion. Be a dear and pour me a glass of wine. You might be denying yourself life's little pleasures, but I don't intend to suffer.'

'Do it yourself. I have a crying baby in my arms.'

'Yes. I had noticed that. What a frightful noise your progeny is making.'

Aila narrowed her eyes at him, and he shrugged and got to his feet. He walked round Aila, and pulled a bottle from a rack.

'We appear to be running low on wine,' he said. 'Could you see to that? Neither whisky nor ale agrees with my constitution, and I refuse to drink cider. Oh, for some Taran brandy.'

Aila said nothing as Naxor opened the bottle and poured himself a generous measure.

'Whatever shall I do now?' he said, as he returned to the table and sat. 'Without salve to refine, I will be at a loose end.'

'You could help Corthie on the farm.'

Naxor laughed so hard he nearly fell off the chair.

'No, but seriously,' he said, as he wiped his eyes. 'There must be something for me to do. I have talents, and they are being underused.'

Aila sighed in relief as Konna began to settle in her arms. She slowed her rocking motion, hoping that the child would drift off to sleep. Killop was taking a nap in the next room, and it was a miracle that his sister's cries hadn't awoken him. She silently urged Konna to fall asleep, so that she could have a few minutes of peace to herself.

Naxor opened his mouth to say something, and Aila shot him a look. She rocked Konna for a while longer, then she placed the child down into her cot, pulled a blanket over her, and crept back a few paces.

'Don't say a word,' she whispered. 'Come on; we can talk in the kitchen.'

They edged out of the dining room, and entered the large kitchen. Aila fell into a chair, and exhaled, her nerves jangling.

Naxor smirked. 'Are you savouring every moment of your new domestic life, my dear cousin?'

'Shut up.'

'I would tell you that I understand, but I would be lying,' Naxor went on. 'I never involved myself in the lives of any of the mortal children I fathered in the City. I viewed it as a complete waste of my time.'

'I know. I can remember.'

'It's different for you,' he said. 'With your children being immortal, I can see why you would want to take personal charge of their upbringing. Still, you should hire a wet nurse and a few servants for the more unpleasant tasks. Have a little self-respect, Aila; demigods should not be changing nappies.'

Naxor drained his glass of wine, refilled it, then sat, a smug expression on his face.

A loud crash came from the dining room, followed moments later by the sound of Konna crying. Aila jumped to her feet, then blinked as she saw Kelsey walk into the kitchen, a Quadrant clutched in her hand.

'Oops,' said the young Holdfast woman. 'I might have knocked over a few plates in there. Oh, and the baby's woken up.'

Aila resisted the urge to scream and hurried through to the dining room. Four or five large dishes were lying broken on the floor, next to an upturned chair. Aila ignored the mess and picked Konna out of the cot. She began rocking her again, then carried her to the kitchen, where Naxor was pouring wine for Kelsey.

'Are you here for the salve?' said Aila.

'Aye,' said Kelsey.

'Did you bring wine?' said Naxor. 'What about coffee and tobacco? We're living like Reaper peasants down here in the wilderness.'

'I only brought myself,' Kelsey said, 'but I can pick up some things for you. Where's Corthie?'

'Out with the sheep,' said Aila, as Konna began to settle again.

Kelsey frowned and peered through a window at the hailstorm. 'Is he mad? What a stupid question. He bought a farm. Of course he's mad. When's he getting back?'

'It might be another few hours,' said Aila. 'The sheep have been escaping through holes in the fence, and he's trying to repair them all before nightfall.'

'Pyre's knackers; what a life. I wanted to tell him about Keir. First things first, though – Sable started transporting Banner soldiers to Colsbury yesterday. Sixty thousand so far, with more to come. Basically, that means we need the salve as soon as possible.'

Naxor gave a mock bow. 'Then you will be delighted to learn that I have completed refining the stocks that you and Aila took from the Eastern Mountains. There were no small vials, but we bought a supply of ale bottles from Severton, and the shed is filled with crates of the stuff, all ready to go.'

Kelsey nodded. 'Two tons?'

'A little less than that. We had some wastage in Port Sanders, if you recall.'

'I'll take it all back to Colsbury, and then I'll deliver the resources on Emily's list to the City. You should know that Thorn has cut the amount I'm permitted to take back. She said that, as only forty per cent of the salve has been delivered, the City is only due forty per cent of the promised resources. You can say what you like about Thorn, but she knows how to count.'

'But forty percent isn't enough,' said Aila. 'The City needs everything that was on the list.'

'I know that, and you know that,' said Kelsey, 'but Thorn isn't budging. Listen; you could do me a huge favour, Aila. If you were to come with me to meet Emily and Daniel, then you could help explain the situation to them. We need to persuade Jade to restart mining operations in the mountains; otherwise the City will never get all that it needs.'

Aila frowned as she rocked her daughter. 'What makes you think that Jade will listen to me?'

'You're her cousin. Besides, I'll need to make several journeys back and forward to transport the forty per cent, and you can speak to them while I'm doing that. Naxor can stay here and look after the kids until Corthie gets back; we won't be too long.'

'What?' said Naxor. 'Excuse me, Miss Holdfast, but I am not a common childminder.'

'Shut up, Naxor,' said Kelsey. 'You're the reason Jade's refusing to mine any more salve. Watching the kids for a couple of hours is the least you could do.'

'And who do you think refined all that salve?' he said. 'I have been toiling away for days to get it ready for you.'

'I don't give a shit. When my brother gets back, tell him where we've gone. We should be back some time tonight.'

'I haven't decided if I should go yet,' said Aila.

'Don't you want a break from the kids for a few hours?' said Kelsey. 'You look worn out, Aila.'

Aila frowned. 'Thanks.'

'Don't mention it.'

Aila pondered her choices. She would gladly escape from Konna's crying for a while, but she doubted that Naxor would be diligent with his duties.

'If I write you a list, cousin,' she said, 'then will you do everything on it? And, before you answer, what if I bring you back some Taran brandy from the City? You can have it, if everything on the list has been done to my satisfaction by the time I get back. I'll also get you some cigarettes. Deal?'

Naxor groaned. 'This is not a deal; it's extortion.'

'Take it or leave it, cousin.'

'Fine,' he said. 'Write your damned list. That brandy had better be top quality. Now, Kelsey, was there a message for your over-tall brother? Something about Keir?'

'It'll wait,' said Kelsey.

'Give me a minute to put Konna down and I'll write the list,' said Aila. She smiled. 'No. Perhaps it's time for Naxor to start practising.'

She walked over to where her cousin was sitting and handed him the sleeping baby.

Naxor pulled a face. 'I think I would rather be repairing the holes in the sheep fence.'

Twenty minutes later, Aila and Kelsey appeared a few inches above the grassy banks of a stream. They dropped to the ground, while around them, the crates of refined salve did the same, the glass bottles clinking as they settled onto the grass. A squad of Holdings militia was standing close by, while Shella glanced up at them from where she was sitting on a boulder.

'That was longer than five minutes,' the Rakanese mage said.

Kelsey shrugged. 'These things always take longer than expected. The important thing is that the salve is ready.'

'Where are we?' said Aila, glancing at the high slopes and peaks surrounding them.

'Colsbrookdale, in the Barrier Mountains,' said Kelsey; 'about six miles north of Colsbury.' She pointed at a low hillock. 'The Banner soldiers are on the other side of that. Do you want to see what sixty thousand soldiers look like?'

Kelsey led Aila to the slope as Shella ordered the Holdings militia to load the crates of salve onto the backs of two wagons.

'We thought it would cause less excitement if we delivered the salve out of sight of the Banners,' Kelsey said, as she and Aila climbed the side of the hillock. 'Many are injured and ill, after months of hardship on Dragon Eyre.'

They reached the top of the hillside, and Aila gasped at the sight. Below them stretched a valley, but the ground was barely visible under the hundreds of tents that had been erected. Everywhere she looked, she could see soldiers. Some were sitting by their tents, or lying on stretchers by the river, while others had been organised into groups, and were working. Access roads were being constructed, along with a line of two-storey wooden buildings; while queues had formed by several enormous equipment stores. New uniforms, armour, weapons and kit were being handed out by Holdings militia.

'Behold,' said Kelsey, a grin on her face; 'the Banner of the Sapphire Throne.'

'I thought they only arrived yesterday,' said Aila.

'They did,' said Kelsey. 'Thousands of the numpties insisted on starting work immediately. This lot are from the first island that mother and the others went to on Dragon Eyre; they've been preparing to come here for days. We're expecting another fourteen thousand tomorrow, who are also in good shape; but then we're going to get sixty-odd thousand from a place called Gyle. Sable says that they will need more help, as they were enslaved by the victorious natives. And then, finally, we'll get the last batch of another twenty-five thousand from the island where mother is currently located.'

Aila did a quick calculation. 'That's almost a hundred and sixty thousand soldiers.'

'Aye. They're not all combat soldiers, but. Around seventy thousand will be formed into the main fighting force. The others will be reserve and support staff. Thorn wants twenty thousand sent to guard the southern approaches to Colsbury within a few days. Daimon will probably have seen the arrival of this batch, and after Keir's failure, he and Bryce might decide on an all-out attack.'

Aila glanced at her. 'What did Keir do?'

Kelsey's features darkened. 'He tried to destroy us. He marched ten thousand soldiers up from Plateau City; but he kept them a few miles away from the island, and tried to take Colsbury on his own. He used his powers to hit the island with lightning, but missed the Great Keep, and hit the smaller one instead, killing dozens. He also nearly killed Frostback and Halfclaw. It was horrible. I was watching from a balcony of the Summer Palace. The dragons were swooping down, and he blasted them with lightning, and knocked them out of the sky. Thorn exhausted herself healing them both, and Halfclaw's still too weak to fly.' She spat on the ground. 'I knew Keir was with Bryce, but I never thought for a minute that he would actually try to kill us. I could have been on Frostback's shoulders, and if he'd hit the Great Keep, then he might have killed Karalyn and her children. Didn't he care? I'm so angry with him that I can hardly put it into words. Part of me wishes that Karalyn had killed him, instead of just letting the Sanang beat him up.'

'They beat him up?'

'Aye. Pechtang kicked the crap out of him. Should we tell Corthie?'

'I'm not in the habit of keeping secrets from my husband.'

'Then be prepared for an explosion. If Corthie discovers that Keir almost killed us, he might decide to come looking for his brother.'

Aila sighed. 'Life in Kell seems so peaceful and secure, suddenly. Even with the terrible weather. I'll try to pick the right moment to tell him.'

'You should know that Thorn is hoping that Corthie will change his mind and decide to join the fight.'

'I never doubted that for a moment,' said Aila. 'Who wouldn't want the greatest mortal warrior in existence on their side?'

'Are you going to try to persuade him not to fight?'

'No. It's his decision. I worry, though. If he ever gets involved in another war, I might lose him forever. He keeps saying that he has a savage beast inside him. I deny it to his face, but I know that he's right. If he kills again, there might be no stopping him.'

Kelsey nodded. 'I saw what he did in the Falls of Iron, and I agree with you. Let's keep him out of this, if we can.' She took the Quadrant out of her shoulder bag. 'We need to travel to the depot where the resources for the City have been collected. Are you ready?'

'Yes.'

Kelsey brushed her fingers over the surface of the device. The air shimmered, and they found themselves in a forest clearing. Teams of workers were hauling beams of timber from the edge of the woods, while sacks of iron ore sat next to stacks of crates. Aila gazed up at the mounds of timber that had already been arranged into neat piles.

'I'm not sure how much I can transport each time,' said Kelsey, 'so I'll just take you first, along with the crates of luxury goods; then I'll come back and start shifting the rest.'

They walked towards the enormous heap of supplies, passing rows of iron ploughs and farming equipment, and came to a pile of crates that had been separated from the rest.

'This is the coffee, sugar and suchlike,' said Kelsey. 'We'll take this to Princeps Row, and arrange where to dump the rest.'

The Holdings woman activated the Quadrant again, and they appeared under the red skies of Tara. Aila took a long breath of the cold winter air and smiled. Regardless of her new life in Kell, the City felt like her true home. One day, she knew, it might be her home again.

Kelsey attracted the attention of a few Banner soldiers patrolling Princeps Row, and a squad was organised to help move the crates to the Aurelian mansion. Aila left Kelsey to oversee the soldiers, and walked down the wide tree-lined street. The guards on duty at the makeshift palace recognised her, and allowed her to enter the mansion, where a courtier escorted her to the audience chamber. Inside, the King and Queen were sitting at their high table, surrounded by Taran and Gloamer merchants.

'Your Majesties,' said the courtier, bowing; 'may I present Lady Aila of Pella and Kell?'

Emily and Daniel glanced up from the table, and the chatter of the merchants died away.

'Greetings, Lady Aila,' said King Daniel, without a smile.

'You carry on with the meeting, darling,' said Emily, 'while I speak to our visitor.'

Daniel nodded, and Emily got to her feet. She walked towards Aila, and guided her into a much smaller room, where the wide windows showed a view of the ruins of Maeladh Palace, silhouetted by the deep red sky.

'Drink?' said Emily, as she closed the door behind him.

'I was hoping for a bottle of Taran brandy, your Majesty,' said Aila, 'to take back for Naxor.'

Emily frowned at the mention of the demigod's name, but opened a cupboard and handed a bottle to Aila.

'And how is Lord Naxor?' Emily said.

'Fine,' Aila said. 'He's bored and making a nuisance of himself, but no change there. Sorry about the way I departed the last time I was here. We had to flee from Port Sanders in a hurry.'

'Yes,' said Emily. 'I am aware of the circumstances. Kelsey has been back to the City more than once since Jade attempted to burn Tonetti Palace to the ground. It was Kelsey who informed us that the new Empress had decided to cut the amount of resources that were being sent here.'

'Kelsey's bringing the forty per cent over today,' Aila said.

'Needless to say, I am displeased about how this has turned out. Forty per cent is a lot of resources, but we had budgeted for the entire list. Releasing Naxor, I now realise, was a mistake. I should have foreseen Jade's response.'

'Is she refusing to cooperate?'

'She is. And, to be honest, I can hardly blame her. Naxor tortured her in the Eastern Mountains. He also tortured Rosie Jackdaw, and Lieutenant Flavus, a scout in the Banner. I was a fool to have ignored this.'

'He didn't actually torture them,' said Aila. 'He threatened to, but he didn't.'

'Only because Dawnflame intervened. Please don't defend him, Aila.' Emily walked to the windows and gazed out at the view. 'Now, somehow, I have to persuade Jade to restart the mining operation in the mountains; otherwise we shall never get our hands on the remaining sixty per cent that was promised to us. Do you have any suggestions as to how I should proceed?'

Aila glanced away. 'What does Jade want?'

'Naxor's head on a stick.'

'I... uh, can't provide that, your Majesty. Naxor refined the salve we took from the Eastern Mountains. Empress Thorn deems him useful.'

'Come now, Aila; there is no mystery to the art of refining salve. We could issue the Empress some written instructions; she doesn't require Lord Naxor for this purpose.'

'But, he's my cousin. I know he's made mistakes...'

'Mistakes, Aila? He betrayed us all. He sold himself to Simon.'

'So did Lydia.'

'Yes, but her cooperation was clearly under great duress. She did the bare minimum to keep her life. Naxor, on the other hand, went out of his way to support Simon, becoming his lackey, and his spy. He conspired to bring down the mortal monarchy, even before Simon made his appearance. Did you know that he poisoned the water supply of Pella? He put death-salve into the cisterns, and killed hundreds.'

'Death-salve, your Majesty?'

'One of Prince Montieth's nasty little inventions,' said Emily. 'For that alone, I should have hanged Naxor.'

Aila rubbed her face. 'Perhaps I should go to the Eastern Mountains, so that I can apologise to Jade in person?'

'There is no need to go to the mountains for that,' said Emily. 'Jade is here, in Tara. Shall I summon her? Wait here.'

Aila groaned as Emily went to the door and opened it. The Queen spoke to a courtier, then re-closed the door.

'I might need that drink now,' said Aila.

Emily gave a half-smile, and gestured towards a cupboard. 'Help yourself.'

Aila extracted another bottle of Taran brandy and filled a glass. She wondered where Kelsey was, in case Jade tried to kill her.

'Is Dawnflame also in Tara?' she said.

'No,' said Emily. 'The dragon went back to the mountains, frustrated that she had been forbidden from razing Tonetti to the ground. She is due back in a few days, to collect her rider.'

'Jade is her rider?'

'So it seems. They developed a strong bond during the struggle against Simon. Were it not for that, there would have been no controlling Dawnflame. She only backed away because Jade ordered her not to attack. It was a perilous moment, to put it mildly.'

The door opened again, and Jade strode into the room, her dark green gown flowing to the floor. Her eyes went over the Queen, then she saw Aila, and her expression hardened.

'What do you want, cousin?' Jade said, her voice cold.

'I... uh, I'm sorry, Jade; about, you know, the whole Naxor thing.'

'Why are you sorry?' said Jade. 'Did you release him from prison?'

'No, but... I protected him from you and Dawnflame in Port Sanders. Look, I had no idea about what he did to you and Rosie in the mountains, or about the death-salve in Pella. I'm here to ask if you would please start extracting salve out of the mine again.'

Jade snorted. 'And why should I do that? This City – the City that I saved from Simon – holds me in such little respect that they freed a monster like Naxor; and then they neglected to tell me about it.'

'I have already made a formal apology regarding this,' said Emily.

'Just words,' said Jade. 'I want more than words. What can you offer me that is worth more than words?'

'I cannot have Naxor arrested, Jade,' said Emily. 'He lies beyond my jurisdiction.'

Jade shook her head as if bemused, then stared at Aila. 'Are you hiding him on Corthie's world, cousin?'

'He has been staying with me, yes,' said Aila. 'He told me he was very sorry for what he did to you, Rosie, and that Banner scout.'

'And you believed him?' said Jade, laughing. 'Are you utterly stupid, cousin? Naxor only cares about one thing – himself. He will betray you if he senses an opportunity to enrich himself; just as he betrayed us. Bring me his corpse, and I shall restart the salve mine.'

'Ask me for anything else, Jade,' said Aila. 'I know you hate Naxor; and he deserves your hatred, but...'

Jade's eyes narrowed. 'But what?'

'But I still love him. He's my cousin, our cousin.'

'So? Montieth was my father, and yet I slew him for his crimes.'

'I can exile him forever, Jade,' said Emily. 'I can forbid him from ever returning to this world, on pain of immediate arrest and execution. He has no Quadrant, and hence he is trapped upon the world of the Star Continent.'

'Trapped? He's probably living in luxury, while laughing at me.' A tear ran down Jade's cheek. 'It's not fair. Why does he always get away with his crimes? I hate him so much it hurts me. I will kill him one day; I swear it.'

'I will ask the Empress of the Star Continent to arrest him,' said Aila. 'If she knew what he had done, then she would do it. She can keep him locked up.'

Jade fell into silence, her gaze lowered.

'What do you think?' said Emily.

'This is my suggestion,' said Jade. 'If I deliver the rest of the salve that the Star Continent needs, then my price is simple – Naxor is placed into my hands. He will be brought, hooded and chained, to my home in the Eastern Mountains. If you promise this, then I will restart the mine.'

Aila grimaced. 'But...'

'That's my offer!' Jade cried. 'Decide what you love the most, Aila – this City, or our twisted cousin. I think I'm being generous.'

Aila glanced at Emily, who said nothing.

'Well?' said Jade. 'Answer me, Aila.'

'Fine,' said Aila, exhaling. 'I promise.'

Jade smiled. 'Thank you, cousin. For a moment, I thought you were going to refuse. Once you have brought me Naxor, then, who knows, you and I might even become friends.' She turned to the Queen. 'I will start extracting raw salve from the mine as soon as Dawnflame takes me home. There. Are you satisfied?'

'Thank you, Jade,' said Emily. 'I am more than satisfied.'

'As you should be.'

Aila and Emily watched as Jade strode from the room, then the Queen poured herself a brandy.

'That was quite a promise,' Emily said. 'I hope you intend to keep it, Lady Aila.'

It was midnight by the time Kelsey returned Aila to the farmhouse in Kell. The hailstorm had lessened, but the rain was lashing down from the dark skies. Kelsey vanished, leaving Aila to run across the courtyard and into the shelter of the house. She closed the heavy front door and pulled off her boots by the entrance, then she crept into the kitchen, where a lamp was lit. Corthie and Naxor were sitting in silence by the table, and both looked relieved to see her.

Corthie got to his feet and embraced Aila. 'Good to see you back. How was it?'

'Fine,' said Aila. 'We delivered a mountain of supplies to the City, and took Naxor's refined salve to the new Banner army. How are the children?'

'Sleeping,' said Corthie. 'I came home to find Naxor trying to put them to bed. It was hilarious and disturbing at the same time. Tea?'

'Yes, please.'

Corthie went to the stove, while Aila sat and unloaded the cigarettes and the bottle of brandy on to the table.

Naxor's eyes lit up.

Aila glanced at her cousin. 'I spoke to Jade while I was there.'

'Yes?' said Naxor. 'And how did that go? Is she still thirsting for my blood?'

'I persuaded her to restart the mine,' Aila said, 'but it came at a price.'

Naxor laughed. 'I'm sure it did. Pray tell; what was the price?'

Aila tried to smile. 'You.'

CHAPTER 16
IMPERIOUS

Colsbury Castle, Republic of the Holdings – 6th Day, First Third Winter 534

Thorn smiled. 'You have done very well once again, Kelsey, and you have my thanks.'

'Maybe you should thank me when the rest of the salve gets here,' Kelsey said, her arms leaning on the balcony railings.

'Your news has given me confidence that it shall arrive,' Thorn said. 'When it does, deliver it to Lord Naxor in Kell, and then bring the refined product here. The two tons the demigod has already produced have done wonders for the health of the Banner soldiers. However, those who have been enslaved on Gyle are due to arrive in Colsbrook-dale soon, and we shall need more. Please ensure Lord Naxor works as quickly as possible.'

Kelsey frowned. 'I'll see what I can do. I took him a load of food, cigarettes and other stuff yesterday; but we'll have to think about Aila's promise. We're supposed to hand Naxor over to Jade once the rest of the salve has been delivered.'

Thorn said nothing for a long moment, her eyes on the Sanang soldiers drilling in the castle forecourt below the Summer Palace.

'I made no promise,' she said.

'Aye, but Aila did.'

'Lady Aila did so without my permission. She was not authorised to promise anything to Lady Jade. What I promised was the remaining sixty per cent of the list, and I intend to keep my word. Lord Naxor was not on the list, as far as I recall.'

'You're putting me into an impossible position, your Majesty,' Kelsey said. 'What am I supposed to tell Emily and Daniel if they ask? Let's not forget that Naxor probably deserves to hang for what he did to the City.'

'Lord Naxor has broken no laws of the Empire, as far as I am aware,' Thorn said, 'and we have no treaty governing the extradition of suspects to the world of the Salve City.'

Agang cleared his throat. 'If I may, your Majesty? It might be imprudent to ignore the demands of Salve City's rulers. We may have more need of salve in the future. From all that Kelsey has told me, Lord Naxor's crimes are serious and manifold. Would we risk the supply of salve, not to mention the goodwill of our allies, by preventing him from facing justice?'

'I shall consider your words, Chamberlain,' Thorn said. 'Right now, the fate of Lord Naxor is the least of my concerns.'

Kelsey glanced towards a window in the Great Fortress. 'There's Sable's signal lamp,' she said. 'She's ready to bring mother back.'

Thorn nodded, then she, Kelsey and Agang turned. The air crackled, and Daphne appeared on the balcony of the palace next to them, along with Lucius Cardova and Caelius Logos.

'Welcome home,' said Thorn.

Daphne bowed her head. 'Your Majesty; it is good to be home.'

'Sable told me everything you have achieved upon Dragon Eyre,' Thorn went on, 'and I have seen the first arrivals with my own eyes. Such a feat was barely imaginable only a short time ago. When we prevail against the usurper, the Empire will be in your debt, my Herald.'

Daphne smiled. 'How is everything in the tented city, your Majesty?'

'Everything is proceeding well,' Thorn said. 'Shella has taken charge of the supplies and logistics, and Kelsey has delivered the first large batch of salve. I am now appointing you, my Herald, as overall commander of the Banner of the Sapphire Throne. Take what staff you need, and organise the Banner as you see fit.'

'Thank you, your Majesty.'

'I admit to being a little disappointed that Sable will not be able to take up a formal role within the Banner.'

'It was the sole condition of the officers based in Na Sun Ka, your Majesty. They wouldn't have agreed to join if there was a chance that Sable would be appointed to lead them.'

'You acted correctly, my Herald. I shall find another role for Sable; one that suits her many talents. I was also thinking that Lady Belinda should become involved in the Banner, and I would be pleased if you would find space for her within your staff.'

Daphne frowned for a moment, then bowed. 'Of course, your Majesty.'

'One more thing,' said Thorn. 'While you were gone, my Herald, Olo'osso decided to take advantage of your absence to abscond from Colsbury.'

Cardova and Caelius glanced at each other.

'Do you know where he has gone, your Majesty?' said Daphne.

'He left no message or note,' said Thorn. 'Perhaps he felt aggrieved that Caelius had been included on your expedition to Dragon Eyre, while he had been left behind. Regardless, for what it is worth, I believe you are better off without him.'

Daphne kept her gaze directed downwards. 'Perhaps, your Majesty.'

Thorn smiled. 'I shall let you rest and refresh yourself, my Herald. Let us reconvene in an hour's time, and we shall go over the disposition and organisation of our formidable new army. Captain Cardova and Sergeant Logos, my thanks to you also. I understand that your contributions were essential to the success of this operation. If every Banner soldier retrieved from Dragon Eyre is as professional and efficient as you two have proved to be, then no one will stand in our way.'

The two men bowed, then they and Daphne strode from the balcony. Thorn turned back to the view, and heard Kelsey start to laugh quietly.

'What is so amusing, Kelsey?' Thorn said.

'When my mother and Sable left for Dragon Eyre,' Kelsey said, 'it was like you were still her protégé, and it was mother who was really in charge. Not any more. You actually spoke like an Empress.'

'That's because I am, actually, the Empress.'

'And why am I still here? You used to keep mother by your side day and night, but now you always want to have me with you.'

'Do you mind?'

'Uh, no.'

'Good. Don't get me wrong, Kelsey – I will always love and respect your mother. After all, legally speaking, she is now my mother, too. However, I have recently found your advice and talents more suited to my way of working. You get things done, Kelsey, and you are not afraid to speak your mind.'

'You could be describing mother with the same words.'

'I know, but Daphne will always put the family first, above all else. Whereas you, Kelsey, are more... unbiased, let's say. Clear-headed. I will occasionally have to make decisions that may adversely affect the Holdfasts, and I trust you to retain a larger perspective.' She smiled. 'Of course, this goes no further. This little conversation will remain between me, you and Lord Agang.'

'Alright,' said Kelsey. 'If you want me as an advisor, then tell me – what have you got planned for Sable?'

'You mean to test me already? Very well. I intend to unleash Sable upon Daimon. I have already given her orders to eliminate the rogue dream mage, as soon as she has completed the transfer of the Banner army from Dragon Eyre to here. She has my permission to wipe out Bryce, Brogan and the others if she needs to, but her primary target is Daimon.'

Kelsey pursed her lips. 'Oh. Right.'

'Do you disapprove?'

'I don't know.'

'Do you think me ruthless?'

'It's not that I'm worried about. When Sable and I went to Plateau

City after Bridget's death, Daimon almost managed to force Sable to hand over her Quadrant. She's not immune to his powers. Hang on; I have an idea. Naxor used a set of eye-guards to stop Daimon from reading his mind when we were negotiating with Bridget over the salve trade. If he still has them, then I could see that they find their way into Sable's hands.'

Thorn laughed. 'My dear Kelsey, do you see how useful to me you have become? You know, one day, if you wish it, you could be my Herald.'

Kelsey glanced away. 'Thanks. There's Van, though. He's back in the City, and I miss him. His contract with the King and Queen is not something he would ever break without permission, and there's no way Daniel and Emily will ever let him go. I enjoy helping you; I admit it, but what about the future? I don't want to have to choose between you and Van.'

'You would pick Van, as you should. Perhaps I could strike a deal with King Daniel and Queen Emily. They give me Van, and I'll give them Naxor.'

'Are you serious?'

'Yes.'

'You know, I always thought that my home was in the City, but I've realised that the main reason I didn't want to come back here was that I refused to live in my family's shadow. For years, they ignored everything I said. To them, I was just stupid, annoying, little Kelsey. But you and Sable, and Corthie, too, if I'm honest, don't treat me like that. You actually seem to value what I have to say. It means a lot to me.' She puffed out her cheeks. 'Anyway, I'd better go. Frostback is coming to take me to their mountain cavern so I can check on Halfclaw. Perhaps he will be able to fly today.'

'Take some of the salve from Shella's stocks if it will help,' said Thorn.

Kelsey smiled. 'Thanks.'

Thorn watched as Kelsey left the balcony, then she turned to Agang. 'Your thoughts?'

'On what, your Majesty?'

'On Kelsey.'

'She's always been a very bright young woman, your Majesty; but I don't know her all that well.'

'I know her well enough,' said Thorn. 'No matter what it takes, I want her by my side.'

'Might I remind you that she voted for Bryce, your Majesty?'

Thorn smiled. 'So did I.'

Thorn and Agang walked into the large meeting chamber, and over forty senior Banner officers got to their feet and bowed. Thorn gave a serene smile and strode to her throne. She sat, and the officers retook their seats. Agang positioned himself by Thorn's right, and then Daphne approached, and bowed her head.

'Your Majesty,' Daphne said, 'I have assembled every officer of the rank of captain and above from the soldiers who have already arrived on the Star Continent. More are due to follow from the islands of Gyle and Na Sun Ka in the coming days, but I felt it prudent to invite those from Ectus and Alef to this discussion.'

'Thank you, Commander,' said Thorn; 'and my thanks to all those in attendance. As the holder of the Banner's contract, I am aware of my obligations towards each of you; and I hereby swear to abide by the terms of the contract negotiated by Commander Daphne Holdfast. As you may be aware, the Empire is under threat. A usurper by the name of Bryce, the son of the previous Empress, has illegally declared himself to be the sole sovereign of this world. Unfortunately, Bryce has the bulk of the imperial forces under his command, which made the formation of a new, loyal army of critical importance. Thank you for answering our call for help.'

An older man among the group of officers stood.

'Speak,' said Daphne.

The man bowed his head towards Thorn. 'I would like to offer you our thanks also, your Majesty. Were it not for your offer, we would still be languishing on Dragon Eyre. Too many of our soldiers met their deaths upon that accursed world, and I speak for every officer here when I say that your generosity has touched our hearts. We too swear that we shall abide by the contract we have mutually agreed.'

He gestured to a couple of captains, who stood and unfurled a large cloth banner. It had been dyed pale blue, and had a throne embroidered in the centre, woven from silver and sapphire thread.

'This was made on Ectus, your Majesty,' said the older man; 'in your honour. It shall be carried into every campaign we wage on your behalf.'

Thorn smiled. 'Thank you. It is beautiful, and I will treasure it always. Commander, if you would, please outline the command structure you propose for this fine army.'

'Yes, your Majesty,' said Daphne, as the older man sat. 'There are five major-generals present here today. That rank denotes the highest position any officer can attain within a Banner of Implacatus. Each Banner would be commanded by a single major-general, answerable only to the holders of the Banner's contract. For example, Van Logos is the major-general of the Banner of the Lostwell Exiles.'

'I was of the impression that a major-general ranked lower than a major or a general, Commander.'

'That is the case in the imperial armed forces, your Majesty, but the Banners of Implacatus have their own traditions. The equivalent of a Banner major-general would equate to that of a general in the imperial army. As the Banner of the Sapphire Throne is far larger than any individual Banner on Implacatus, I propose that we divide it into sixteen new divisions, each of ten thousand personnel. Once divided, I then propose that we place or promote a major-general to command each division. Numbers one to seven shall comprise the combat forces, and numbers eight to sixteen shall serve as the reserves and the support divisions. Separate to that shall be the Command Staff, under my authority, who will be responsible for coordinating the entire army.'

'Very good, Commander,' Thorn said. 'As for dispositions, I require at least two divisions to be transferred south of Colsbury, to construct defences that will prevent any attack from the usurper's forces. This must be carried out as soon as practicable. Once the other five combat divisions are ready, I want them to reinforce this defensive position, and then we shall wait for Bryce to strike.'

Daphne frowned, and Thorn could tell that her Herald wished to object, or to make a comment.

'That will be all for now,' Thorn said. 'You have your orders.'

'Might I speak with you alone, your Majesty?' said Daphne.

Thorn nodded, then she rose from the throne. As soon as she was on her feet, every officer present also stood, their heads bowed. She strode past them, and left the chamber by her private stairs, as Daphne and Agang followed her. She emerged out on to the middle balcony, which encircled the palace halfway up its height, and turned.

'Your Majesty,' said Daphne, 'may I offer some advice?'

'Of course, my Herald.'

'It concerns the disposition of the Banner forces. As far as I can see, the gravest threat to the Empire is that Bryce will sever the connection between Sanang and the Holdings. Do you have information that points to him deciding to strike Colsbury in force?'

'No. I have nothing specific,' said Thorn; 'but that is what I think he will do. Are you aware of your son's failed attack?'

Daphne's eyes narrowed. 'What, your Majesty? My son? You mean Keir?'

'I assumed that someone would have informed you. Agang, please provide the details to my Herald.'

'Yes, your Majesty,' said Agang. 'Just before the end of Autumn, Keir brought ten thousand imperial soldiers here from Plateau City. Then, on Winter's Day, he decided to attack Colsbury in person, with storms and lightning. The two dragons and the Lesser Keep were hit, but her Majesty and Karalyn put a stop to his attack, and it failed. That night, Keir withdrew his forces south.'

Daphne said nothing, her eyes wide.

'The dragons survived,' Agang went on, 'thanks to her Majesty's healing powers, but many civilians died in the flames that swept through the Lesser Keep.'

'I was tempted to kill him,' said Thorn, 'but Karalyn calmed my ire, and we let him leave with his life. He is very fortunate indeed.'

'Keir…' said Daphne, her voice low. 'No. How could he do such a thing? Was he being controlled by Daimon?'

'I personally doubt it, but possibly,' said Thorn. 'That was another reason we allowed him to live. You should know, however, that he endured a severe beating at the hands of one of my Imperial Guardsmen. Keir murdered dozens of civilians, including many children, and an example had to be made. Do you need a moment, Herald?'

Daphne swallowed. 'He killed children, your Majesty?'

'He did. He would have also killed Kelsey, had she been riding on Frostback's shoulders at the time of the attack. Fortunately, she was standing right here in this very spot, next to me.'

'Did he mean to strike the dragons?'

'Most certainly. Bryce seems to have placed a lot of trust in my former husband. He wouldn't have given him ten thousand soldiers if that were not the case. Daimon may have influenced his emotions, but there is no doubt that Keir is now our enemy. It grieves me to have to say this to his mother, but if he attacks us again, I shall not hesitate to end his life.'

Daphne began to sob. 'This is my fault. I should have forced him to return with us to Colsbury, instead of leaving him with Daimon and Bryce.'

'This is not your fault,' said Thorn. 'I was married to Keir for many years, and yet I never foresaw that he would act so callously. Do not blame yourself.'

Daphne wiped her eyes.

'It is my belief,' Thorn went on, 'that Keir was sent to attack us before we could summon the Banner from Dragon Eyre. Hence, it is now my conviction that they will strike with all forces at their disposal before the Banner can be organised. Do you see my logic?'

'Yes, your Majesty.'

'Thank you for not questioning my orders in front of the officers. You can understand why I did not wish to have this conversation with so many others listening.'

Daphne walked to the balcony railings and leaned against them, her head lowering.

'This news is hard to take, your Majesty,' she said. 'To think that one of my children would send lightning onto Colsbury. He could have killed Cael and Kyra. You mentioned that Karalyn helped you?'

'She did. She blocked Daimon's powers, and allowed me to get close to Keir.'

Daphne sighed. 'At least one of my children acted responsibly.'

'Do not forget Kelsey, my Herald. Your younger daughter has proved to be of great assistance. In fact, I have come to rely upon her.'

'Kelsey?' said Daphne, a look of annoyed disbelief on her face. 'You're relying upon Kelsey, your Majesty?'

'Yes. I am considering elevating her to a position of authority within my court. Imperial Legate has a nice ring to it. That way, she could act with my authority while conducting my affairs on her travels.'

Daphne stared at Thorn. 'And… you trust Kelsey to do this?'

'She is wise beyond her years, and has a sharp mind. Yes, I trust her to do this.'

For a moment Thorn thought Daphne was going to laugh, and she was pleased when she didn't. Instead, the Herald of the Empire nodded, her features an expressionless mask.

'You are the Empress, your Majesty.'

The air shimmered next to them and Sable appeared.

Daphne glared at her half-sister. 'You should ask permission before you Quadrant next to the Empress like that.'

'This is the middle balcony, my Herald, not my private quarters,' said Thorn. 'I have already granted Sable permission to visit me here whenever she needs to talk.'

Sable raised an eyebrow, her gaze going from Thorn to Daphne.

Daphne's eyes looked pained. 'Sorry, Sable. I have just been informed about Keir, and I didn't mean to snap at you.'

'And I thought I was the only one in a terrible mood,' said Sable. She glanced at Thorn. 'Your Majesty, I have word from Dragon Eyre.'

'Problems?' said Thorn.

'No. I was using the Sextant to inform Blackrose of our progress, and one of her court has a request. Ashfall wishes to travel here to see her sister. She has also heard about Keir's attack, and wants to make sure that Frostback has recovered. If we play this well, we might soon have three dragons to defend Colsbury.'

Thorn nodded. 'Is Ashfall a fighter?'

'Yes, your Majesty,' said Sable. 'A damn good one, too. She looks a little like Frostback, but is larger and stronger. Even better, she will be bringing along a good friend of mine – a demigod with flow and healing powers by the name of Austin.'

'And Queen Blackrose is willing to allow them to leave her realm?'

'Yes, now that the threat from the dragons of Wyst has passed. Ulna is at peace, and I suspect that Ashfall may be feeling a little restless. Should I use the Sextant to bring them here?'

'Please do. Thank you, Sable.'

'No problem, your Majesty.' Sable glanced at Daphne. 'After I do this, you and I should lay low for the evening and get drunk; if, you know, the Empress says it's all right.'

Thorn smiled. 'You should most certainly do that. You both deserve a rest. I couldn't ask for better friends.'

Daphne nodded. 'I will join you, Sable, but don't expect cheerful company.'

'I could say the same to you, sister,' said Sable. 'We can be miserable together.'

Sable vanished then, a moment later, she shone a lamp from the window of the Great Keep where the Sextant chamber was located. The air crackled overhead with energy, and then a huge grey dragon appeared in the vast forecourt between the Great Keep and the Summer Palace. Agang gasped as the dragon lifted its head to peer around. The Sanang soldiers in the forecourt backed away in terror, then Sable appeared on the ground next to them, and Thorn saw her speak to the soldiers, and then to the dragon. A man clambered down from the dragon's back, and he and Sable embraced on the flagstones of the yard, as Thorn, Agang and Daphne watched from the balcony. Sable pointed at them, and the dragon raised its head all the way up to the middle balcony. She gazed at each of the humans in turn, then stopped at Thorn.

'You must be the Empress of this world,' said the dragon. 'I am Ashfall of Lostwell and Ulna, sister of Frostback, and daughter of Deathfang the destroyer of the Sixth Ascendant.'

'Welcome to Colsbury, Ashfall of Lostwell and Ulna,' said Thorn. 'My home is your home, and I bid you avail yourself of all that you require while you are here.'

'Thank you, Empress; you are as gracious as Sable informed me you would be. I believe that you saved my sister's life some days ago?'

'I have healing powers,' said Thorn, 'and I did what I could.'

'Again, I thank you, Empress.'

'If you wish to visit your sister, then Sable can show you where she and Halfclaw are dwelling. Kelsey is also with them, as Halfclaw remains too weak to fly.'

Ashfall turned her gaze to Daphne. 'I believe it was your son who almost slew my sister.'

'It was,' said Daphne.

'Sable has asked me not to hold you to account for this, and for her sake I will do as she desires. However, I warn you that if I encounter this Keir Holdfast, I will rip his head from his shoulders.'

'I understand,' said Daphne, holding the dragon's gaze.

'Good day to you all,' said Ashfall, then she extended her great wings and soared off into the cloudy sky.

Daphne lowered her eyes as soon as the dragon sped off towards the mountains. Thorn gazed at her Herald, feeling nothing but sympathy for the obvious pain she was in; and she was glad she had taken Karalyn's advice not to have Keir killed. Sable appeared on the balcony a moment later, then she and Daphne vanished, leaving Thorn and Agang alone.

The Empress turned to her Chamberlain. 'Shall we inspect the troops?'

Two hours later, Thorn and Agang were standing next to Shella on a raised veranda jutting out from the side of one of the newly-constructed wooden buildings in Colsbrookdale. Two dozen Sanang warriors were flanking them, while before them lay the tented city. The fourteen thousand new arrivals from Alef were located far to their left, while the first fully-equipped Banner division was marching south along the road. As each company passed the veranda, the soldiers' heads turned, and they saluted the Empress.

'What a sight,' said Agang. 'All that shining armour and new weapons; it's a marvel.'

'It's bloody expensive, that's what it is,' said Shella. 'Do you realise we've spent more than the entire annual imperial budget in little over a third? Every munitions factory in the Holdings is working flat out, along with every canvas-weaver, every blacksmith, every seamstress, every farmer, every...'

Agang laughed. 'Alright, Shella; I get the message.'

'It's almost criminal,' said Thorn. 'All that money could have been spent on making the lives of the ordinary citizens of the Empire better; instead, it's being wasted on a futile conflict.'

Shella shrugged. 'It's not the Empire's money you've been spending, Thorn – it's the Holdfast family's personal fortune.' She laughed. 'Just wait until I get my hands on the imperial treasury.'

A Banner officer approached the veranda, and was escorted into the Empress's presence by two Sanang warriors.

'Your Majesty,' he bowed.

'Good afternoon, Major-General,' said Thorn. 'Might I say how impressive your division is looking?'

'Thank you, your Majesty,' the officer said. 'And might I say what an honour it is to be appointed commander of the First Division of the Banner of the Sapphire Throne?'

Thorn smiled.

'When will your division reach its destination, Major-General?' said Agang.

'We should be in position by sunset tomorrow, my lord,' said the officer. 'Once there, we shall dig in as ordered, and begin the construction of the defences to shield the southern approaches to Colsbury. The Second Division should reach us by noon the following day.'

'That is good news, Major-General,' said Thorn. 'Please carry on.'

The officer bowed, then left the veranda to rejoin his soldiers as they continued to march past. Thorn gazed out over the vast numbers of Banner soldiers flooding the valley. It seemed almost impossible to believe that, only a few thirds before, she had been on her way to Plateau City to beg work from Bridget, and now she was Empress, in command of a vast army. The power made her almost tremble with nerves, and her hands gripped the veranda railings until her knuckles turned white. She had finally got everything that she had desired, everything that she had longed for. It felt good. No, it felt better than good; it felt... liberating.

'Here comes trouble,' muttered Shella under her breath.

Thorn turned, and saw Karalyn step up onto the veranda, her twins trailing along behind her.

'Hello, Karalyn,' Thorn said. 'I thought you wished to avoid gazing upon our new army?'

'I do,' Karalyn said, 'but after what happened last time, I thought I'd bring you the news myself.'

'Yes?' said Thorn. 'What news?'

'I was doing my daily vision scan of the northern Plateau, your Majesty,' she said. 'Bryce has left the Imperial Capital.'

'And where is he going?' said Agang.

'He's heading north,' said Karalyn, 'and he's not alone. He has Daimon with him, along with close to a hundred thousand imperial soldiers. They've taken the road that leads to Colsbury. I estimate that they will reach the Barrier Mountains in seven or eight days.'

Thorn smiled. 'Thank you, Karalyn.'

'Why are you smiling?' Karalyn said. 'Do you know what this means?'

'Yes,' said Thorn. 'It means that the Banner have arrived just in time, and that the battle for the Star Continent will take place where I hoped it would, twenty miles south of Colsbury – which happens to be precisely where I have ordered my forces to construct a defensive line. Bryce has made a mistake. For the sake of this world, let us all hope it will be his last.'

CHAPTER 17
ADDLED

N orthern Plateau – 6th Day, First Third Winter 534

Keir felt every bump in the road. The wheels of the wagon would dip and judder, and the vibrations sent pain shooting down his limbs and across his broken jaw. His clothes were drenched in sweat despite the chill in the winter air, but he didn't know if he had a fever, or if his body was yearning for more dullweed. The medical orderlies had been attempting to wean him off the narcotic, but they hadn't completely ceased his supply, and his existence seemed to revolve around the daily dose he received each dawn. For six long and painful days he had been carried on the wagon, while his expeditionary force trudged south along the road leading to Plateau City. By the time they stopped every evening to camp, the dullweed had worn off, and Keir was left to face another sleepless night of agony. At times, as he had lain in the darkness, he had thought he was going mad, the pain playing tricks on his mind. He had imagined that Thorn and Karalyn had been standing by the wagon, laughing at him and mocking his disfigured face. He had cursed them aloud, his cries littered with threats and promises of revenge.

He would kill them both – he knew that as a certainty. His former wife he would strangle with his own hands, and watch as he squeezed the life out of her; while he would slowly drive a knife through his sister's heart. They would plead for mercy, but he would give them nothing but a painful death. The rest of his treacherous family could be left to Daimon, but Thorn and Karalyn would be his.

'Not long to go now, sir,' said an orderly. 'We will be back in Plateau City in a few days.'

Keir turned his head. The swelling that had closed his right eye had lessened a little, and he stared at the orderly. The man was checking the dressings covering Keir's wounds, while taking care not to cause his patient any more pain.

'Dullweed,' Keir gasped.

'Sorry, sir,' said the orderly, 'but you've had your dose for today. You'll get some more tomorrow morning, after breakfast.'

'I... I'll...'

'Yes, sir?'

'I'll fucking kill you,' Keir croaked. 'I need dullweed.'

The orderly ignored his words, as he had ignored every crude threat that had come from Keir's mouth during the torturous journey from Colsbury. A Kellach sergeant walking close to the wagon caught the orderly's attention.

'See that?' he said, pointing ahead. 'Dust, in the distance. Horses.'

The orderly glanced up and peered down the road. 'Is that a messenger, do you think, Sergeant?'

'It's a lot of dust for a messenger,' the sergeant said. 'Nah. Something big's on the move.'

The wagon went over another bump, and pain shot through Keir's face and broken arm. He cried out, unable to hide his agony.

'Damn this road,' said the orderly, shaking his head.

'I don't understand why they haven't sent a flying carriage for his lordship,' said the sergeant. 'I thought Mage Daimon could see everything? They must know how badly he was injured.'

'Maybe those horses are coming for him,' said the orderly.

'Nah. Did you not hear what I said? That dust cloud is coming from an entire regiment of cavalry, if I had to guess. It's a hundred yards wide, at least. And look – the front columns of our lads have stopped.'

The orderly raised a hand to shield his eyes from the sun. 'Where?'

'Up ahead.'

'Your eyesight's better than mine, mate.'

'Just wait a moment. We'll be coming to halt soon, I'd expect.'

As the sergeant had predicted, the marching column began to slow, and within a few minutes, the wagon had stopped on the road, as soldiers stood around on either side.

'My patient could be doing without this delay,' said the orderly. He lit a cigarette, took a single draw, then held it to Keir's lips. Keir inhaled, hoping in vain that it would be dullweed. Disappointed, Keir glanced down the road. His entire force seemed to have halted. Supply wagons carrying the disassembled catapults and ballistae were dotted among the stationary infantry. He saw the cloud of dust that the sergeant had noticed, and reckoned he could hear the pounding of hooves on the road ahead. A pair of horses came into view, trotting alongside the columns of soldiers. Each horse had a Holdings cavalry officer on its back, their steel breastplates glistening in the weak winter sunshine. They were calling out orders or instructions to the soldiers as they passed, and the halted infantry began to groan and complain loudly.

'Pyre's arsehole,' muttered the sergeant.

'What are they saying?' said the orderly. 'Can you hear them?'

'Aye. They're ordering us to turn around. The bastards are wanting us to march north again.'

'Back to Colsbury?'

'That's what the pricks are saying.'

The pair of horsemen came closer.

'About turn!' one of them was shouting. 'About turn. You're going the wrong way.'

The other officer was pointing to the north, back down the road Keir's force had been marching along for six days.

'North!' he cried. 'We're going north!'

The orderly got to his feet on the back of Keir's wagon.

'Hey! Sir!' he shouted, his arms raised. 'Lord Holdfast is here.'

The two horsemen saw him, then slowed to a halt by the wagon. One of them looked down, then grimaced as he saw Keir's injuries.

'What's happening, sir?' said the sergeant.

'Your force has run into the lead units of the imperial army, Sergeant,' said one of the horsemen. 'We've been ordered to turn you around – you're blocking the damn road.'

The other horseman dismounted, removed his helmet, and looped his mount's reins round the side of the wagon. He climbed up on to the back, and knelt by Keir.

'Can you hear me, Lord Holdfast?'

'Yes,' Keir groaned. 'I need dullweed.'

The cavalry officer nodded, then glanced at his colleague. 'Continue up the road, Lieutenant, and pass on the word to the rest of Lord Holdfast's force. We need to get them moving north soon, before the entire road is clogged up.'

The other horseman saluted, spurred his mount, and rode on.

The officer turned back to Keir. 'List his injuries for me, orderly.'

'Yes, sir,' said the medic. 'Lord Holdfast has fractures in his left arm, right leg, ribs, jaw, and in the fingers of his right hand. His nose is broken, and he has lost seven teeth, with severe bruising to the face and upper torso. We have been administering daily doses of dullweed for the pain, but we've cut the amount to prevent him from becoming dependant upon it.'

The officer nodded.

'Should we turn the wagon round, Captain?' said the sergeant from the roadside.

'My patient is in no state to travel back to Colsbury, sir,' said the orderly.

'The Emperor wants to speak to Lord Holdfast,' the officer said, 'but in the circumstances, it would be too disruptive to try to get this wagon to his Majesty.' He glanced at the sergeant. 'Have your squad move the wagon off the road, and remain by it until his Majesty has reached this position.'

'Is the Emperor leading the army in person, Captain?' said the sergeant.

'Yes. His Majesty is still a few miles away, so guard Lord Holdfast until he gets here. I'm going to continue up the road. Do you know where the senior officers can be found?'

'Aye, sir. They're about half a mile behind us, to the north.'

The officer climbed down from the wagon, fitted his helmet over his head, and pulled himself up onto his mount.

'I want this wagon off the road in the next five minutes, Sergeant. Understood?'

The Kellach soldier nodded. 'Aye, sir.' He waited until the cavalry officer had disappeared along the road, then he turned to his squad. 'You heard the captain, lads. Let's get this wagon shifted.'

Keir braced himself as the soldiers gripped the sides of the wagon. One of them led the oxen down into the ditch that ran by the side of the road, and the others pushed and shoved the wagon after them. The soldiers in the main body of Keir's force were already starting to march back to the north, amid a low chorus of complaints and grumbling. Keir's wagon was pushed up the side of the ditch, and the soldiers brought it to a halt by the edge of a wheat field, its soil trampled by their boots and the wide wheels of the wagon.

'Here will do, lads,' said the sergeant. 'Settle down for a long wait, and then, who knows – you might get to meet the Emperor.'

The soldiers in the squad relaxed. Some sat by the side of the wagon and lit cigarettes, while others chatted in low voices by the oxen. The orderly sighed, and leaned back against the wagon railings. Keir watched as his army of ten thousand marched past, returning north in the direction of Colsbury. Directly behind them were thousands of cavalry troopers, each mounted, who took over an hour to pass the wagon. A supply train followed them, composed of dozens of covered carts and wagons; and then unit after unit of marching infantry. Keir gazed at them all as if in a dream, the pain never leaving him, as the sun slowly lowered towards the western horizon.

'Pyre's cock,' muttered the sergeant, as yet another full regiment of imperial soldiers began to pass their position. 'It looks like the Emperor is bringing the entire army. There isn't enough space round Colsbury to fit this lot. Where's he going to stick them all?'

'I'm not sure I care, Sergeant,' said the orderly.

'The rebels have only got a handful of Sanang guarding that damn island,' the sergeant went on.

'I heard a rumour that the rebels have got themselves a new army,' the orderly said. 'Did you not hear about it?'

'Oh, I heard about it, alright. It's a load of bollocks. Where could they get an army from? They might have rustled up a few Holdings deserters and a company or two of half-trained militia; but that doesn't make an army.'

'Maybe the Matriarch of Sanang has been building an army in secret.'

The sergeant shrugged. 'Aye. Maybe.'

'Banner...' Keir gasped. 'They're Banner.'

'What was that, sir?' said the orderly.

'The rebels have a Banner army.'

'A Banner army?' said the sergeant. 'What's a Banner army, sir?'

'Mercenaries,' said Keir, his jaw hurting whenever he spoke. 'From another world.'

The sergeant frowned at the orderly. 'Are you sure he hasn't had more dullweed?'

'You saw the dragons?' said Keir.

'Eh, aye,' said the sergeant. 'We saw them, sir.'

'The Banner is from the same world as the dragons.'

The sergeant moved in closer. 'Are you saying that the rebels have moved an army over from the home of the dragons, sir?'

Keir nodded, then he noticed that the other members of the squad had quietened, and were paying attention.

'Thousands of Banner soldiers are coming,' Keir said. 'Our job was to take Colsbury before they arrived.'

'And, have they arrived, sir?' said the sergeant.

'I don't know.'

'You have vision powers, sir; that's what I heard. Could you take a look for us?'

'Leave my patient alone,' said the orderly. 'He needs to rest.'

'But, mate, if he's right, then there might be thousands of these Banner bastards waiting for us. Don't you think we should know something like that?'

'A minute ago you were saying the rumour was bollocks.'

'Aye, but if anyone knows the truth, it'll be Lord Holdfast.'

'I will look,' said Keir, 'if you give me some dullweed.'

'Sorry, sir,' said the orderly, 'but I am under strict instructions from my commanding officer.'

'I'm your fucking commanding officer,' Keir spat.

The sergeant nodded. 'He has a point, mate. He's a damn lord. Are you not supposed to obey his orders?'

'Not in medical matters,' said the orderly.

'Go on,' said the sergeant. 'Break the rules; just this once. None of the lads here will breathe a word of it. Let the lord have his dullweed, and then we can all find out what in Pyre's name is going on. Aren't you curious?'

The orderly sighed. 'Fine.'

'Thank you,' said Keir. 'I will vision now. Have the dullweed ready.'

Keir focussed, and allowed his powers to leave his body. His sense of pain diminished as he left his injuries behind, but he was weak, and would need to work quickly. He raced his vision to the north, passing the thousands of soldiers on the road, then increased his speed, until the ground beneath was a blur. He reached Colsbury, and slowed. He gazed around, and saw the Sanang warriors up on the battlements of the gatehouse. Others were drilling in the main courtyard, and he realised that Kelsey must be absent from the isle, as he felt nothing blocking his powers. He glanced at the village on the mainland, but it seemed normal. There was certainly no Banner army hiding there. He was about to give up, when he noticed movement along the road that ran by the side of the lake. He shifted his vision to take a better look. Soldiers. Soldiers were marching south towards the village, their new armour and weapons gleaming in the fading light. Keir raced over them, and followed the road to the north. The lake came to an end, and he crossed a high ridge, then looked down into the wide valley that lay beyond. He gasped. The entire valley was carpeted in row upon row of tents, and thousands of soldiers were crowding the banks of the river. To the left, a line of wooden buildings had been erected, and a large banner was flying from the tallest roof. It was pale blue, with a silver and sapphire throne in its centre.

Exhausted, Keir pulled his vision back, and coughed, the motion sending bolts of agony through his broken jaw.

'Try to relax, sir,' said the orderly. He reached out, his fingers clutching a lit weedstick.

The sergeant placed a hand on the orderly's arm. 'Wait a moment. Sir? Did you see anything?'

Keir nodded. 'The Banner have arrived.'

Keir lay cocooned in dullweed's sickly embrace, his mind blank and his injuries numbed. A small part of his consciousness was aware that the sun had set, and that the squad guarding him had lit a small fire by the side of the road, as the endless columns of the imperial army began to halt for the night. The sergeant and his squad had bickered continually about the meaning of Keir's message, but the dullweed had made it impossible for him to speak, and he had stared vacantly at their further questions. The sounds and smells of the night camp filtered through to his senses as if he were wreathed in fog, and he almost wept when he felt the pain start to return.

'Dullweed,' he gasped.

The sergeant nudged the orderly, who was leaning back against the wagon railings with his eyes closed.

'Mate,' said the sergeant; 'wake up. His lordship's coming out of his weed daze.'

The orderly's eyes opened, and he rubbed his face. 'What?'

'Lord Holdfast's waking up,' said the sergeant.

'What did he say?'

'Take a guess, mate.'

A few of the squad crowded round the wagon.

'How many soldiers did he see?' said one.

'Were there more dragons?' said another.

'Quiet, lads,' said the sergeant.

'What's going on here?' came an authoritative voice from the road.

The squad turned, then each stood to attention.

'Good evening, sir,' said the sergeant, saluting. 'We were assigned to guard Lord Holdfast, sir.'

An army officer approached and peered into the back of the wagon.

'Get a stretcher,' he said. 'We're taking Lord Holdfast to the Emperor's tent.'

'Be gentle, lads,' said the orderly, as two soldiers lifted a stretcher from behind the driver's bench.

The stretcher was placed next to Keir, then four soldiers lifted him, while another slid the stretcher under his body. Keir groaned in pain.

'Easy now,' said the sergeant. 'Lift him off the wagon.'

A soldier went to each end of the stretcher, then they raised it, and stepped down slowly to the ground.

The army officer nodded. 'Follow me.'

The orderly trailed along next to Keir as the two soldiers carried him back on to the road. They followed the officer for a few hundred yards, weaving their way through the thick columns of resting infantry, until an enormous tent loomed ahead. It was ringed by a line of Kellach marines, who made way for the officer and the stretcher-bearers. Keir was carried into the lamplit interior, where more officers peered down at him, many grimacing at the sight of his face.

'Over here,' said the officer, pointing at a table.

The soldiers laid Keir's stretcher down, then saluted and left the tent.

'You too, orderly,' said the officer. 'Wait outside.'

'Yes, sir,' said the medic. He glanced at Keir for a last time, then strode away.

A group of officers gathered round the stretcher.

'Who did this to him?' said one.

'A witness reports it was one of the false Empress's Sanang body-guards, sir,' said another. 'He stamped on his face, and broke an arm and a leg.'

'I have the full list of injuries here,' said another, holding up a slip of paper. 'A cavalry officer compiled it earlier.'

He handed the list to a major, and several officers leaned in to read.

'Make way for the Emperor of the world!' a voice cried, and the officers jumped to attention and backed away from the table.

Keir strained his neck to look, and saw Bryce approaching from a closed-off section of the tent, Daimon by his side. The Emperor reached the table, and gazed down.

'Clear the area,' said Daimon. 'Everybody out.'

The officers scattered in seconds, leaving Keir alone with Bryce and Daimon.

'What a mess,' Bryce muttered. 'You saw it happen, didn't you, Daimon?'

'Aye, your Majesty,' Daimon said. 'I was watching through Keir's eyes at the time, protecting his mind from his sister.'

'It's a pity you couldn't protect his body. Look at his face. Half of the soldiers in the damn army have seen him. We should have placed a hood over his head.'

'The Banner... your Majesty,' said Keir; 'the Banner...'

'We know about their arrival, Keir,' said Bryce. 'Daimon has been keeping me updated with every movement the rebels have made. Why do you think the entire imperial army is on the move? If you had done what I asked of you, I would be sitting in Plateau City right now. But, you failed. You didn't even kill the dragons, and now a third has arrived, this very day. I should have you executed for incompetence.'

'He may still be useful, your Majesty,' said Daimon.

'For what?' said Bryce. 'To frighten children?'

'I have stoked his desire for vengeance, your Majesty,' Daimon said. 'He longs for the blood of those who did this to him. If we were to set him loose upon his family, he would do everything in his power to kill them.'

'But his leg is clearly broken,' said Bryce. 'He won't be walking for quite some time.'

Daimon glanced at Bryce, and their eyes met. They were silent for a short moment, and Keir guessed that Daimon was using his powers to communicate something secret to the Emperor.

'Is that wise?' Bryce said to the dream mage. 'I was hoping to keep this to ourselves for now.'

'I can wipe Keir's memory afterwards, your Majesty.'

'And then what?'

'Then, your Majesty, we use Keir to help us crush the false Empress and her foreign mercenaries. Despite his previous failure, his powers are still formidable. Let's give him another chance.'

Bryce remained silent for a few moments. Keir lay still on the stretcher, trying to fathom what the Emperor and his Chief Mage had been talking about, but the pain was a constant distraction.

'Alright,' said Bryce. 'Bring her in.'

Daimon bowed, then left the main area of the tent, slipping into the enclosed section.

'Have you brought Tilda, your Majesty?' Keir gasped.

'Of course not,' said Bryce. 'Why would I do that? Your dullweed-addled girlfriend is safely locked up in your apartment in the Great Fortress.' He shook his head. 'You seem a little dullweed-addled your-self, Keir. At least you now share an interest with Tilda. We shall return to the city once we have destroyed your former wife and her army of paid foreigners. Daimon was right; you could be useful in the coming battle. You can deal with any aerial threat.' He paused. 'I should save my breath. You won't remember this conversation when Daimon wipes your memories.'

The canvas moved, and Daimon emerged from the enclosed part of the tent. He was leading an old woman by a chain attached to a collar round her neck.

'This way,' Daimon said.

Keir squinted at the old woman. Her wrists were shackled and she was dressed in a tattered old robe. She had a dejected air about her, and Keir guessed that she had been chained up for a long time.

'What's happening?' said Keir.

'You'll see,' said Daimon. He turned to face the old woman. 'I'm leading you to a wounded man. I'm going to place your hand on his brow, and you will heal him.'

The old woman didn't respond.

'I don't think she understands the Holdings language,' said Bryce. 'Try Rahain.'

'I don't know Rahain, your Majesty,' said Daimon.

Bryce sighed. 'Then I'll do it.' He glanced at the old woman, and repeated the instructions that Daimon had said, but in Rahain.

The old woman nodded.

'She's not Rahain,' said Keir. 'She's Sanang. What's going on?'

'Hush,' said Daimon. 'You are correct – this woman is not from Rahain, though she was imprisoned there for many years. Her captors forced her to serve them, but she has strength; enough strength to escape and make her way to the Great Tunnel, where she was picked up by an imperial patrol. Can you imagine the torments she has been through? And yet, she had the will to struggle across the Grey Mountains alone, driven by a single desire.'

'What desire?' said Keir.

Daimon ignored him, then he placed the woman's hand on to Keir's forehead. The old woman frowned, then said something in Rahain. Bryce replied, using the same language.

'She says she cannot heal his teeth,' said Bryce, 'and his face will still look disfigured. I told her to proceed regardless.'

Keir tried to sit up, then he felt a powerful wave of healing ripple through him. He clenched his eyes shut and convulsed on the stretcher, as the bones in his leg, arm, hand and chest knitted themselves back together. The pain in his jaw evaporated and he groaned in relief as the woman's powers reached every part of his body. He panted, and opened his eyes.

Daimon was leering down at him. 'Feel better, Keir?'

Keir raised a hand to his face, and felt the gaps in his mouth. All pain had gone, but his teeth were still missing. He then felt his nose and realised that it was misshapen.

He turned to the old woman. 'Thank you,' he said in Rahain.

Daimon laughed. 'Can I tell him who she is, your Majesty?'

'What's the point if you're going to wipe his memories anyway?'

'I want to see the look on his face.'

Bryce sighed. 'Very well.'

Daimon turned back to Keir. 'A few thirds ago, Keir, you were related to this woman.'

'What?' said Keir. 'How?'

Daimon grinned. 'She was your mother-in-law. Keir, meet Ivy, Thorn's mother.'

'She can't be,' said Keir. 'Thorn's mother was captured by Sable almost ten years ago.'

'That's right,' said Daimon. 'And Sable took her to Rahain.'

'But we searched Rahain. There was no sign of her mother anywhere.'

'Did Thorn actually travel to Rahain to look for herself?'

'Well, no; but she had vision mages look all over Rahain. I looked. I searched for thirds.'

'Clearly you didn't search everywhere. Poor old Ivy has been passed around from one warlord to the other for years. After the Rahain government collapsed, she must have become a valuable asset to whoever owned her. Only her desire to be reunited with her family kept her going all those years. Tell me, Keir – how do you think Thorn will react, when we put a knife to her mother's throat?'

A horror gripped Keir at the thought. Thorn would break down. She had given up on ever seeing her mother again years before, and the sight of her in Bryce's grip would destroy her. With the pain from his body gone, Keir's savage hatred towards his former wife had faded, and he felt an unexpected pang of sympathy for her.

'Her death would grieve Thorn deeply,' Keir said.

Daimon cackled with glee.

'Take her back to her cage,' said Bryce.

'Aye, your Majesty.'

Daimon gripped the old woman's chain and led her away.

The Emperor smiled. 'Do you see, Keir? With Thorn's mother in our possession, the false Empress will despair, and her cause will crumble into dust. However, the next time you see Thorn's mother, you won't remember any of this. I will not take the risk that Karalyn will read your mind and discover the truth before we are ready to unveil our little surprise.'

Daimon returned to the main area of the tent, and approached the table.

'Remain lying down,' he said to Keir. 'This will just take a moment. When you awaken, you will believe that you have been given a dose of salve to heal your wounds, but you won't ask any questions about where it came from. You will feel happy, and grateful to be in the service of your Emperor; and you will thirst for revenge against your sister and the false Empress. Then, you shall return to your post in the expeditionary force, and resume your command of your ten thousand soldiers.'

Keir almost panicked at the thought of what the dream mage was about to do to his memories, then he felt Daimon's powers in his mind, and all recollection of what had occurred in the tent dissolved into nothing.

Salve, he thought. It was lucky that Daimon had managed to obtain some salve. Keir stretched his arms, and remembered how much he was looking forward to killing Karalyn and his ex-wife. He smiled, swung his legs off the table, and stood.

'Permission to rejoin my unit, your Majesty?' he said, saluting the Emperor.

Bryce smiled. 'Permission granted.'

CHAPTER 18
YOUNG AND IMMORTAL

Colsbury Castle, Republic of the Holdings – 7th Day, First Third Winter 534

Belinda crouched by the entrance to the tunnel that went under the Lesser Keep, and remained still. A few feet away, the cat was watching her from the shadows, ready to flee at any moment.

'I won't hurt you,' Belinda said.

The cat turned, and began to lick its paws, as if completely uninterested in the god's presence. Belinda edged forward, getting a little closer to the tabby, then she reached out with a hand, and her fingers touched the creature's soft fur. The cat bolted, racing off into the shadows of the tunnel. Belinda smiled. After several days of trying, that was the closest the tabby cat had allowed her to get; if she persevered, then she was sure they could become friends. The tabby was one of dozens of strays that dwelled on the isle. They were scrawny beasts, unloved by the human inhabitants of Colsbury, but tolerated for their rodent-hunting abilities.

Belinda stood. 'You can come out.'

Silva emerged from the passageway next to the tunnel, a frown on her lips.

'Any success, your Majesty?' the demigod said.

'She ran away again,' said Belinda, 'but she let me touch her for a moment. I will start carrying food around with me. I just need to be patient.'

Silva said nothing, a look of irritation clouding her features.

'There were no cats living on Colsbury when I last stayed here,' Belinda said. 'They must have spread from the mainland.'

'They are vermin, your Majesty.'

'They are not. They are beautiful and clever, and I like them. The next time you pass the kitchens, pick up a small bag of leftovers and scraps from the bins, and I shall see if I can entice the tabby into my quarters.'

Silva sighed. 'Yes, your Majesty.'

'I know you don't approve, but I think I prefer cats to people. You always know where you stand with a cat; they never try to conceal their feelings, or lie to you. Didn't I like cats before Karalyn scoured my mind?'

'No, your Majesty; you were indifferent to them. Only young gods tend to feel any affection towards animals whose lives are so fleeting.'

Belinda smiled. 'I am a young god. Sometimes, you forget that.'

'Things will change in a century or two, your Majesty. You will see.'

'I don't think I want to see, not if immortality means I become indifferent to the things I love. I don't want to become jaded and cynical, and I can't think in terms of centuries.'

'I couldn't agree more,' said a voice from the tunnel.

Silva frowned as a young man emerged from the shadows.

'Who are you,' Silva said, 'and why were you eavesdropping on her Majesty's private conversation?'

'My name is Austin,' the man said, 'and I didn't mean to eavesdrop. I was walking to the Great Keep to meet Sable, and I happened to overhear what you were saying.'

Belinda kept her eyes on the young man. 'Why do you agree with what I said?'

'I am a demigod,' he said, 'a young demigod, and I struggle with the idea of immortality. I can't quite imagine what it will feel like to be hundreds of years old. I have mortal friends and family, and I dread watching them age. Other gods don't understand; they've forgotten what it feels like.'

'How old are you?' said Belinda.

'Twenty-three. I have never taken salve. I look my age because I am my age.'

'My name is Belinda.'

He smiled. 'Yes. I know who you are. You are the second Ascendant I've met. The first tried to kill me.'

'If you are aware of her Majesty's identity,' said Silva, 'then you should address her correctly. You are talking to a Queen, boy.'

'Wait,' said Belinda. 'I remember you. You were in Ulna when I returned from Implacatus. You helped remove the crown from my head.'

'I did. A most unpleasant business. I'm glad you have recovered.'

'Have I? My body is healed, but my mind feels broken. At night, I still dream of being in the restrainer mask. Compared to that, the crown was nothing.'

'I have also been imprisoned and tortured,' said Austin. 'Older gods never seem to understand. I spent two years locked up on my own, and then months in a cage with my flesh peeling off. Like you, my body has healed, but my memories are still raw. Older gods say that in a few centuries the nightmares will fade, but I don't want to become – how did you put it? Jaded and cynical. It sounds stupid, but I cherish my memories, even the bad ones. They make me feel human, and I don't want to lose that.'

'I would like to spend more time with you, Austin,' Belinda said.

The demigod's eyes widened a fraction. 'I would like that, too. Are you going upstairs to meet Sable?'

'I'm here to meet Daphne, but her rooms are adjacent to Sable's. Let's walk there together.'

They turned for the passageway that led up to the entrance to the Great Keep, while Silva trailed along behind them.

'You came with the new dragon, didn't you?' said Belinda.

'Yes. Ashfall. She wanted to visit Frostback, and I wanted to visit Sable; so it worked out well.'

'Are you close to Sable?'

'Well, uh... you could say that. I helped her when she... when she...'

'You helped her slaughter the occupying forces on Dragon Eyre?'

His features flushed. 'Yes. It was a... grim experience. I guess I tried to restrain her, but I wasn't very successful. I watched her kill the Fifth Ascendant, among other things. Do you, uh, want me to call you "your Majesty"?'

'I would rather you didn't. Belinda will do. It is true that I was a Queen, but my realm was on Lostwell, and Lostwell is gone. After helping Sable, you are still her friend?'

'Yes. She's a good friend. She's calmed down a bit since the craziest days on Dragon Eyre. She was in a bad way after her dragon died, but then she rescued my mother and aunt from Implacatus. I will always be grateful for that. Are you also Sable's friend?'

'I don't know. I used to detest her with all of my heart. She did some terrible things, Austin. Cruel things. I want to believe that she's changed, because I like her now. I can't help it. It amazes me that Karalyn and Thorn appear to have forgiven her. Sable is responsible for ruining their lives, and yet they have welcomed her back with open arms.'

'I don't know what she was like before Dragon Eyre,' Austin said, 'but she's told me some of the things that she did. She used to say that she wanted the forgiveness of her family more than she wanted anything else. The guilt was eating her up.'

They entered the Great Keep, and began to climb the stairs. The building was busier than it had been in many years, and staff working for Shella and Daphne passed them on the steps. Each bowed their head towards Belinda, but she ignored them, her thoughts on Sable.

'Kelsey isn't here, your Majesty,' said Silva. 'I can still feel my powers.'

'She's with the dragons in their cavern,' said Austin. 'Ashfall offered to take me, but I wanted to stay here to get to know Colsbury a bit better. It's a beautiful island.'

'It's a castle,' said Belinda.

'And a palace,' said Austin, 'and the gardens are wonderful. I'm also appreciating the cooler weather, after years of nothing but heat on Dragon Eyre. It might snow soon, and I'm looking forward to that. I've never seen snow before.'

They reached the floor where the Holdfasts had their rooms, and Belinda knocked on Daphne's door. A moment later, Sable answered it, looking bleary-eyed and ill. She gazed out at the three immortals standing in the hallway.

Austin laughed. 'Hungover, Sable?'

'A little,' she said. 'Daphne and I had a late night.'

Austin reached out and touched Sable's hand. The woman closed her eyes for a moment and shuddered, then her complexion cleared, and she smiled.

'Thanks, Austin,' she said. 'Come in. You might have to do the same thing to my sister; she's throwing up in the bathroom.'

They entered Daphne's quarters, and Belinda grimaced from the reek of stale tobacco and weed smoke. Empty bottles of wine sat upon a low table, while a blanket lay tangled on a couch.

'Were you getting drunk with Daphne last night?' said Belinda.

'Yes,' said Sable. 'We were sharing our misery. I cried about Lara; she cried about Keir. It was quite the party.'

'Which way is the bathroom?' said Austin.

Sable pointed towards a door, then lit a cigarette and sat. Austin strode to the door, knocked, then entered.

Sable turned to Belinda. 'So, you've met Austin? Be nice to him, please – he's one of my favourite people.'

'He told me he helped you slaughter all those soldiers and gods on Dragon Eyre.'

'That's right. I put him through a lot, but he didn't break. He was the sole reason I kept my sanity after Badblood was killed. He's not like other gods.'

'He's young. That's why he's not like the others. I'm young, too.'

Sable nodded, but said nothing, then Austin and Daphne emerged from the bathroom.

'You're looking a little better, sister,' Sable said.

'There's nothing like a healing in the morning to cheer you up,' said Daphne. 'I feel great. Are you sharing those cigarettes?'

Sable passed one to Daphne, then lit it with her metal lighter.

'I want one of those,' said Daphne, pointing at the lighter. 'I watched you use it all evening, and I'm quite jealous. Matches are so annoying in comparison. Where can I get one?'

'Austin's brother bought it from a travelling merchant on Haurn,' said Sable.

'They're made on Implacatus,' said Austin. 'I've seen some gods and senior Banner officers carry them about. Someone in the new Banner might have one.'

'I shall have to make enquiries,' said Daphne. She glanced at Belinda. 'Thank you for coming to see me. Have you spoken to the Empress about your new position?'

'I talked to Thorn yesterday evening, Holder Fast,' Belinda said. 'She asked me if I was prepared to work for you in the command staff of the new Banner. I told her that I would think about it. I thought I would come along this morning to ask you what I would be doing.'

'Queens do not work for mortals,' hissed Silva.

Daphne glanced at the demigod. 'Silva, do you take decisions for Belinda?'

'Of course not,' Silva spat. 'Her Majesty is free to do...'

'Then please be quiet,' said Daphne. 'This does not concern you. If you have nothing constructive to add, then I would be obliged if you kept your mouth closed.'

Silva stared at Daphne with contempt, and folded her arms across her chest.

Daphne turned back to Belinda. 'As you know, the Empress has appointed me as Commander of the Banner of the Sapphire Throne. She suggested that I find you a position within my staff. To be frank, I am not altogether sure what position to offer you. You are the most powerful being upon this world, and it would seem almost insulting to offer you the rank of major or colonel. The Empress has told me all about your involvement in the wars with Agatha; about how you helped her lead her army from Rainsby to Amatskouri. She said you were a born leader, but I can't ignore the fact that you are also, most likely, the best warrior in Colsbury. So, should we keep you behind the lines, as an advisor and strategist, or should we place you at the tip of the spear, to lead the Banner into battle? Tell me what you want, Belinda. What do you see yourself doing in the coming struggle?'

Belinda hesitated for a moment. 'What are our aims?'

'Our aims?' said Daphne, raising an eyebrow. 'Well, Bryce's army was spotted yesterday. He is marching the imperial forces north, in the direction of Colsbury. Our immediate aim is to defeat them. If we could kill or capture Bryce and Daimon, then the war would be over. However, it would be unwise, as well as callous, to annihilate Bryce's army. The men and women serving under Bryce are mistaken, not evil. They are our fellow citizens of the Empire. Therefore, we shall take up a defensive position, and hold our lines.'

'An overwhelming display of power might persuade them to break and flee,' said Belinda. 'Casualties will be unavoidable, but they can be contained. If I were to destroy an entire regiment of imperial soldiers, in full sight of the others, there would be no need to hunt down and slaughter the rest of them.'

Daphne nodded. 'You are forgetting the presence of Daimon. He is accompanying Bryce on the march north. His powers might block yours. Karalyn's will also block his, though – the two dream mages will cancel each other out.'

'He cannot block my battle-vision.'

Daphne glanced at Sable. 'What do you think, sister?'

'I think Belinda should be the tip of the spear,' Sable said. 'The Banner forces are aware of who she is, and will follow her into battle. It's the role I wanted. There are only three of us who could do it – me, Corthie, and Belinda. Without me and Corthie, the position has to fall to Belinda. She also has the advantage that a stray crossbow bolt won't end her life.'

Daphne nodded, then she walked to a cabinet and withdrew a rolled-up map. She placed it on to the surface of a table, and laid it out flat.

'Come here, Belinda, if you would,' she said.

Belinda and the others walked over to the table.

'This is a map of the area to the south of Colsbury,' said Daphne. 'The island is just off the edge here, where this road is leading, while the defensive position that the Empress has identified runs along this ridge, overlooking the plains of the northern Plateau.'

Belinda pointed. 'Is that a farm?'

'It's a vineyard,' said Daphne. 'Quite extensive. These lines mark the terraces that have been carved into the slopes of the hills. Any attacking force will have to climb terrace after terrace, while our army will be dug in at the top of the ridge. The First Division will be arriving there this evening, and the Second should be joining them tomorrow. Karalyn shall remain in Colsbury, and block Daimon from there, while Thorn has asked Kelsey to oversee dragon operations.' She glanced at Austin. 'Will Ashfall be prepared to lend her assistance?'

'I think so,' said the demigod, 'though she has yet to confirm it. I would also like to offer my services in the coming battle.'

'Why?' said Daphne. 'This is not your cause. You are under no oblig-ation to help us.'

'It's Sable's cause, and Sable is my friend. I have powers that might be useful.'

'I know. Sable has told me much about you, Austin. However, as every squad in the Banner is being issued with salve, it is hoped that we shall have no need for healers, and Daimon will be able to block your flow powers.'

'I could use Austin's help,' said Sable.

The two Holdfast women glanced at each other for a moment, then Daphne nodded.

'Very well,' Daphne said. 'Austin, thank you for your offer. If you wish to help us, then please place yourself at Sable's disposal.'

Austin smiled. 'Should I be alarmed at that prospect?'

'Quite possibly,' said Sable. 'I'll give you the details later.'

Belinda gazed down at the map. 'Where would I be based?'

Daphne narrowed her eyes as she scanned the features on the map, then she pointed. 'Perhaps here, where the road goes north through the vineyards. It shall probably see the heaviest fighting, as Bryce's forces try to breach our defensive lines. Do you have armour and a weapon?'

'No. I lost everything on Implacatus.'

'Not everything, my Queen,' said Silva. 'The Weathervane remains here, ready for you to take into battle, if that is what you wish to do.'

'The Weathervane is required to keep the Sextant operational,' said Daphne. 'Karalyn needs it kept in place.'

'Why?' said Silva. 'Is she going to use the Sextant during the battle? She could transfer the enemy army to Dragon Eyre, or somewhere worse. She could send them to the bottom of the ocean.'

'We need to preserve the lives of the soldiers in the imperial army,' Daphne said. 'We shall not be obliterating them.'

'Find me armour and a decent sword,' said Belinda; 'and I will occupy the road through the vineyards. None shall pass.'

'Then I think we are decided,' said Daphne. 'I shall command the battle from the rear, and Belinda will lead from the front. We should travel to the tented city in Colsbrookdale, and I will find you some suitable equipment, and introduce you to a few of the major-generals.'

'I can take you all,' said Sable, 'and then I'll return here. The Empress wants me to transport the Banner soldiers over from Gyle today. Shella will already be in the valley, preparing to receive the new arrivals.'

'Let's get some coffee first,' said Daphne. 'Austin may have cured my hangover, but I still need a coffee in the morning to wake me up.' She smiled. 'I must be getting old.'

An hour later, Sable used her Quadrant to transport the small group to the banks of the river that ran through Colsbrookdale; then she vanished again, leaving them by the edge of the tented city. Dozens of small kitchens were distributing food, and Banner soldiers were eating breakfast by their tents in the pale morning sunshine.

Austin shuddered as he glanced at the thousands of soldiers.

'It's strange to see so many Banner here,' he said. 'Just a short time ago, Sable and I were trying to kill them all.'

'Try not to mention my sister's name too loudly,' Daphne said. 'It would be better if her involvement was kept quiet from the rank and file. Quite understandably, many of the soldiers here hate her.'

'They probably hate me, too,' said Austin.

'I will watch over you,' said Belinda. 'You will come to no harm.' She turned to Daphne. 'Why don't you hate Sable any more? You used to.'

'So did you, Belinda,' said Daphne.

'Is forgiveness so easy?'

'Perhaps it helps that my sister did nothing to hurt me or you personally,' said Daphne. 'We saw what she did to others, especially to Karalyn and the Empress, but we were never on the receiving end of her more notorious actions. I know what she did, and yet she is my sister and I love her.'

They walked between two long rows of tents, and approached an area vacated by the recently-departed First Division. Shella was there, organising wagons of food and salve, and she waved to Daphne and the others.

'My sister is in position,' Daphne said. 'We should expect the arrivals from Gyle to appear soon.'

Shella nodded. 'Okay. Now, the last batches knew they were coming, but this lot won't. There might be panic, maybe even a little hysteria. All of the other Banner units have been forewarned, and we have volunteers ready to go in to spread reassurance as soon as the enslaved soldiers arrive. Most will have been slaves for several thirds, and they might be in a rough condition; some might even die before we can reach them with food, water and salve.'

'How many are coming?' said Austin.

'My sister will have the precise figure,' said Daphne, 'but the Banner leadership on Ectus estimated about sixty thousand.'

'What about the settlers?' said Austin. 'Are they being left on Dragon Eyre?'

'Yes,' said Daphne. 'We are only extracting the Banner forces.'

'But the natives will have enslaved the settlers as well. Is that fair?'

'The settlers moved to Dragon Eyre to occupy another's world, Austin,' said Daphne. 'I'm afraid I have little sympathy for their plight. Did they not enslave the natives for several decades?'

Austin lowered his gaze. 'Not all of the settlers were bad people.'

'I'm sure you are correct,' said Daphne, 'but it is not our responsibility to save them from their mistakes. They made their choice, and now they shall have to live with it.' She paused, then nodded. 'My sister has just informed me that she is ready to proceed.'

Shella gestured to a large group of Banner soldiers. 'Get ready!' she yelled. 'Any moment now.'

The air crackled over the valley, then the entire area filled with people. Belinda gasped, her eyes wide.

'Get those wagons moving!' Shella cried.

Wild shouts and wails came from the tightly-pressed masses of new arrivals, as they stared around in confusion. Most were dressed in filthy rags, and some had already collapsed to the ground, overcome by wounds or hunger and exhaustion. All around them, soldiers from the first batches were moving into the crowds, telling their enslaved colleagues that everything would be alright, and handing out food, salve and blankets.

'I ordered several hundred pounds of chocolate for this occasion,' said Shella, as she and the others watched from the edge of the crowd. 'Along with cigarettes. I figured that a few comforts might help them come to terms with what's just happened to them.'

'Come with me, Austin,' Belinda said.

'Where?' said the demigod.

'Into the crowd. We are both healers – let us heal.'

She strode towards the masses of arrivals, and Austin hurried to catch up. Belinda raised her hand as she entered the crowds, and Austin did the same.

'Issue a wide-ranging burst of your powers,' Belinda said. 'Cover as many people as possible, even if some only get a little.'

Austin nodded, then they both released a great swathe of healing over the crowd. Belinda sensed Austin's powers leave his hand, and knew in an instant that she was many times stronger than him, but that didn't matter. All that mattered was that the injured and mistreated soldiers were recovering around them. Wounds vanished, and broken limbs were repaired in a chaotic intensity. Soldiers began weeping in relief, and many got to their knees in front of the two gods.

'I have given all I can,' said Austin, his hand lowering.

'I have more,' said Belinda, keeping her arm raised. She increased the tempo of her powers to make up for Austin, and dozens convulsed on the ground around her. They walked further into the crowd, and Belinda saw her first corpse. She glanced down at the emaciated body of the soldier.

'Shella was right,' said Austin; 'we can't reach everyone. Some of these poor bastards would have been dying before they were brought here. We can't save them all.'

'No, but we can try.'

Belinda carried on, sending out her powers as she walked through the tight crowds. Austin helped by keeping some of the more enthusiastic soldiers back from the Third Ascendant, then a clear voice sounded out over the valley.

'You are free! Eat, drink and rest.'

Belinda turned, and saw a high-ranking officer standing up on the back of a wagon. Next to him, two sergeants were holding up the silver and blue standard of the new Banner, which had been unfurled above the wagon, while on the ground below them, more soldiers were distributing salve to the new arrivals.

Belinda lowered her arm. Men and women were sipping from the large brown ale bottles that contained the healing substance, then passing them on to their comrades. Belinda glanced at Austin, and saw that the demigod was shaking his head at her.

'That was amazing,' he said. 'I healed hundreds, but you healed thousands. I've never witnessed anything like it.'

'It always feels better to heal, rather than kill.'

'Yes!' he said. 'I hate killing, and we did far too much of that on Dragon Eyre.'

She glanced at him. 'What do you think of cats?'

'Cats?' he said. He shrugged. 'I like them, I guess. It's been a while since I had a pet, but I had cats when I was a boy in Cumulus. They were always hanging around my father's harem.'

'Good answer,' she said. 'Let's go back to Colsbury, and I'll show you the tabby I'm trying to befriend, and then, if you like, we could eat lunch together.'

'That sounds good. How will we get back?'

'We can walk. It's only a few miles.'

'Alright.'

Austin smiled, and Belinda felt something she hadn't felt since the Falls of Iron. She frowned, and cautioned herself, remembering how she had been taken in by Naxor's smile. She had promised herself then that she would never get involved with another man, not without first understanding his true motives and feelings. She told herself not to be so stupid; she had only just met Austin, and barely knew him.

'I would like to get to know you better,' she said, as they strode back through the crowd towards Daphne and Shella.

He swallowed. 'I think I would like that, too. You know, I thought you would be intimidating. After all, you are the Third Ascendant, which means you're the second most powerful being in existence; but you're nothing like Bastion or Kolai.'

'Karalyn scoured my mind ten years ago,' she said, 'and I lost four years in an instant when we travelled to Lostwell. In reality, I have only been awake for six years, and two of those were spent in a restrainer mask.'

Austin puffed out his cheeks. 'That's rough; and I thought I had it bad. So, as far as you can remember, you have only been free, and awake, for four years?'

'Yes. Does that put you off?'

'No. It's good to finally meet another god who isn't hundreds of years old. Obviously, I know that you are really thirty millennia old, but if you can't remember any of it, it's like it never happened. Everything must still seem new to you.'

'Thank you, Austin. You might be the first person who actually understands what I'm going through. I am not a very good friend, you should know that; and people look at me as though they think I am strange. I say stupid things, because I still struggle with language, and the hidden meanings people put into their words. If you want to be my friend, then please, never speak to me in riddles.'

'I understand,' he said.

'Yes,' she said. 'I think you do.'

They arrived at the wagons where Daphne and Shella were organising the steady stream of supplies being sent into the crowd of new arrivals.

Shella laughed at them. 'Show offs,' she said. 'Still, good work; thank you, both. You just saved us a quarter ton of salve.'

'You're welcome,' said Belinda. 'Now, if you would excuse us, Austin and I are going to walk back to Colsbury.'

'I shall accompany you, my Queen,' said Silva.

'I would prefer that you didn't,' said Belinda.

Belinda turned, then she and Austin began to stride towards the road that led south to Colsbury, as Daphne raised an eyebrow. Belinda and Austin glanced at each other, then they walked down the road, leaving the tented city behind.

CHAPTER 19
DEPENDABLE

Marchside, Kell – 12th Day, First Third Winter 534

The wheels of the cart crunched over the thick layer of frost covering the track. The rain had stopped the previous evening, but the temperature had fallen, and a freezing cold wind was scouring the hillside. Aila pulled her hat down over her ears and tightened her scarf, while, next to her on the driver's bench, Corthie sat in silence, his eyes narrow with anger.

Aila wondered if she had done the right thing by telling Corthie what his brother Keir had done. Corthie had barely spoken since, his fury like a low, smouldering fire. She glanced at him.

'I can't wait to get back to the house,' she said. 'I'm going to sit down with a hot cup of tea, and wrap myself in blankets.'

Corthie said nothing, his gaze fixed on the track ahead.

'And then,' she said, 'I'm going to poke out my eye with a fork.'

He turned to her. 'What?'

'Ah, so you are listening to me. I thought you were too absorbed in thinking up ways to murder your brother.'

'I can do that and listen to you at the same time.'

'Do you wish you were in Colsbury?'

'I don't know. If I'd been there, then I would have... you know what I would have done. I would have killed Keir. I would have killed my own brother. It would have been easy. Too easy. One swing of the Clawhammer. I was always scared of him when I was a young boy, but that was before I had battle-vision.'

'You don't seem surprised by what he did. Kelsey was surprised.'

'Was she? I should be surprised, but I'm not. Keir's always had a vicious streak. The biggest surprise is how long it's taken everyone to realise it. I mean, Thorn was married to him for years before she came to her senses.'

'Maybe we should talk about something else.'

'Alright. When's Naxor leaving?'

'You know I can't answer that.'

'Are you really intending to break the promise you made to Queen Emily?'

'Of course I am, Corthie. I can't hand Naxor over to Jade – she'd rip him limb from limb. I only told her that so she would start mining salve again. I know Jade is a hero of the City and everything, but... well... she's... well, she's insane.'

'But I'm so sick of him sitting in our house every day, smirking and eating all of our food. There must be somewhere else he can go.'

'Where? Kelsey told me that the Empress likes the salve being refined down here in Kell. It's too remote for the imperial soldiers to reach. Look, after the next supply of raw salve arrives from the City, Naxor will be busy again, and then he can leave, once he's finished. You could see it as your contribution to helping Thorn and your mother.'

Corthie laughed and shook his head. 'Fine. I'll try, but he tests my patience.'

'I wish you got on better, I truly do,' she said. 'Naxor has been one of my closest friends for centuries. He's not as bad as most people think.'

'You sound like my mother talking about Keir. Next you'll tell me that he's just misunderstood.'

'I like having him around. I can't help it, but I'm not going to apologise for it, either. He's my only link to a past that goes back nearly eight hundred years. He reminds me of who I am.'

Corthie steered the cart on to the main road through the farm, and they began climbing the slope towards the farmhouse. They passed a few of their tenants, who were bringing hay to the sheep in their winter enclosure. They waved up at the cart, and Aila and Corthie waved back. The roof of the farmhouse was glistening with frost in the fading light of the afternoon, and Aila wondered when she would next feel the warmth of the sun on her skin. The dark days and cold nights seemed endless. Just three more months to spring, she told herself. The ponies pulled the cart into the courtyard in front of the farmhouse, and Corthie jumped down to the cobbles, his breath misting in the chill air. He reached up, and helped Aila get down, then he unhitched the ponies, while Aila unloaded the coal sacks from the back of the cart. She had done more physical labour since arriving in Kell than she had done in centuries, and her self-healing powers had reacted by making her fitter and stronger. She picked up the sacks with ease, and carried them over to the house, as Corthie placed the ponies back into their stables; then she emptied the sacks into the coal bin that sat close to the front door. A cloud of black dust rose up, and she closed the bin, then wiped her hands on her apron. They went into the house, and Naxor appeared in the hallway, wearing a dressing gown and holding a glass of wine.

'Ah,' he said, smiling; 'the peasants have returned from their toil on the farm. Did you work hard?'

Aila knelt, and began unlacing her winter boots, as Corthie pulled off his thick coat.

'Why are you drinking?' said Corthie. 'You're supposed to be looking after the children.'

'I saw your little cart appear through the window, and immediately poured myself a glass. Now that you are back, I intend to get roaring drunk.'

'It would be nice to spend an evening with you sober,' said Aila.

'Oh Aila, my dear cousin. While you and Corthie may have chosen to live in this dark and rainy land, it was forced upon me. I am an exile, unable to return to my home; banished from the comforts of Port

Sanders, lest the charming Lady Jade removes the head from my shoulders. If you were in my situation, you would also be reaching for the solace of wine.'

Aila walked into the living room. Konna was lying in her cot, her eyes closed, while Killop was sitting on a blanket spread over the floor, surrounded by little wooden toys.

'Did you do everything on the list?' she said.

'Of course,' said Naxor. 'All the chores have been completed. I nearly expired from the tedium, but I did it, rather than face your wrath.'

'What about dinner?' said Corthie, as he entered the room, his eyes narrow as he glanced around.

Naxor sighed. 'Yes, dinner has been cooked. The bathroom has been scrubbed, the floors swept, the washing put away, the children fed, the hearth prepared, the clothes tidied, and the windows cleaned. And yes, I even changed the nappies of your tiny offspring. Now, may I get drunk in peace?'

Aila laughed. 'You really don't want to get sent back to the City, do you?'

'Can you blame me?' said Naxor. 'If the price of my stay here is to reduce myself to the status of a lowly housekeeper, then it is a price I am most willing to pay. It's blackmail, of course; I realise that. If I do not make myself indispensible to you, then you might be tempted to fulfil the promise you made to Lady Jade, and, believe me – I would rather be your slave than Jade's plaything.'

'Pyre's arse,' said Corthie. 'It pains me to say it, but you are actually quite useful. Drink your wine, Naxor; you deserve it.'

'High praise indeed,' said Naxor. 'You must remember, however, that I will cease to be your servant as soon as the next batch of raw salve arrives. I hope that the new Empress will be so impressed with my diligence that she will rescue me from this oblivion and allow me to live in the salubrious surroundings of Colsbury. I could be very useful to Empress Thorn; very useful indeed. Alas, until then, I am at your service.'

Corthie laughed and shook his head as he picked Killop up from the blanket, and Aila smiled. If only Corthie could learn to like Naxor, she thought, then he might see how hard her cousin was trying. Naxor might be full of bravado, but Aila knew how desperate he was. The news of his exile from the City had hit him hard, as if he had never really expected his wicked acts to catch up with him, and he was clinging on to Aila's friendship like a drowning man adrift in the ocean.

'You're doing a good job, cousin,' she said. 'Sit down, and I'll serve dinner.'

Naxor was on his third glass of wine by the time they were finishing dinner. Killop was in his highchair, while Corthie was rocking Konna back and forth in his arms. To Aila's surprise, Corthie had continued to abstain from alcohol since his release from jail, and he was watching as Naxor got ever more drunk at the dining table.

When the wine bottle had been emptied, Naxor staggered over to a cupboard.

'Oh dear,' he said, as he crouched by the cupboard, 'that was the last of the wine. It wasn't a bad vintage, all things considered, although nothing beats the fine wines from the vineyards of Roser territory. It was far superior to the wine on Lostwell, however; that stuff was vile. I presume no wine is made down here in the dark depths of damp and dreary Kell?'

'The wine you were drinking was made in a place called Anamind-hari,' said Corthie.

'Yes?' said Naxor. 'I shall have to visit at some point.' He plucked another bottle from the cupboard. 'It looks as though Severton gin shall be my companion for the rest of the evening. Are you sure you don't wish to join me in a glass or two?'

'I'm sure,' said Corthie.

Naxor stood, and swayed slightly. 'How times change. I recall you in Kin Dai, Corthie. You drank more in a few months than most mortals manage in a lifetime.' He laughed. 'You terrified poor old Vana out of her wits.' His laughter ceased, and he glanced down. 'Poor old Vana. Oh Aila, my dear cousin, how our family has suffered; yet, here you are, with a new generation of demigods. Amalia would be so proud of you.'

'I seriously doubt that, cousin,' said Aila.

'You know,' Naxor said, as he retook his seat, 'our old grandmother wasn't as bad as you might think.'

'She opened the gates of the Middle Walls,' said Corthie, 'and married off Aila to Marcus.'

'Yes, that is quite correct,' Naxor went on, 'but her time on Lostwell softened her, I think. She was never quite the same upon her return to the City. Having a baby with that mortal changed her. She had no desire for power; she just wanted to live a quiet and peaceful life. Of course, that was never going to happen. She tried to hide her identity, but as soon as word got out, there was no chance she was going to be allowed to live in peace. And now she's dead. I miss her. I miss them all. Vana, Mona, Yvona.' He sighed as he filled his glass with gin. 'And my brother Salvor. Why did he have to resist Simon? Why? He knew what would happen, and yet he refused to submit. What a waste.'

The air shimmered, and Kelsey appeared in the midst of the dining-room. She dropped six inches to the floor, placed her Quadrant into her shoulder bag, and smiled.

'Evening, all,' she said. 'At least I didn't break any plates this time.'

Aila glanced at Naxor, and saw him immediately sober up.

Corthie stood. 'Sister. How is everything in the north?'

Kelsey shrugged. 'Fine, I guess.'

'Has Keir tried anything else?'

'Have you forgotten the part about him getting beaten to a pulp?' she said. 'He won't be walking for quite a while yet. But, Bryce is on his way to Colsbury with the imperial army, so things will liven up soon.'

'Do you have any wine?' said Naxor.

Kelsey nodded, and reached into her shoulder bag. She withdrew three bottles of wine and a dozen packets of cigarettes, and dumped them onto the table.

Naxor rubbed his hands together. 'Excellent work, Miss Holdfast.'

'I require something in return,' she said.

'Oh, yes?' said Naxor. 'And what might that be?'

Kelsey sat. 'Your eye-guards.'

'Eh, my what?'

'Don't bullshit me, Naxor,' said Kelsey. 'I need the eye-guards you were wearing when we spoke to Bridget and Daimon. You have no need of them. Corthie and Aila's minds are blocked to you, and no one has vision powers down here. The Empress needs them.'

'They are for the Empress?' Naxor said. 'I see. If, hypothetically speaking, I did happen to have these artefacts in my possession, and I handed them over to you willingly, would the Empress learn how cooperative and helpful I had been?'

'I'd be sure to tell her,' said Kelsey.

'And would that help my chances of being summoned to Colsbury, once the rest of the salve has been refined?'

'It wouldn't hurt your chances.'

Naxor stood. 'Then, please wait here. I won't be a moment.'

The demigod left the room, and Aila turned to Kelsey.

'What did the Empress say about the promise I made to Jade?' she said in a low voice.

Kelsey leaned in. 'She said that she hadn't made any promises herself, and that you had no right to make promises on her behalf.'

Aila nodded. 'Does that mean there's no possibility that the Empress might send him back to the City?'

'Not exactly,' whispered Kelsey. 'She implied that she might be open to a deal – specifically, a deal that would hand over Naxor, in exchange for the cancellation of Van's contract.'

Aila's eyes widened. 'Would she do that?'

Kelsey shrugged. 'Maybe. I don't know. The Empress has no emotional attachment to Naxor. I don't think she cares if he stays or goes. I think she views him as a bargaining chip.'

Naxor walked back into the room, but betrayed no sign that he had heard any of the hushed conversation. He sat, and held out a small box in front of Kelsey. He opened it, revealing two clear, circular disks lying on a bed of soft black velvet.

'Here they are, Miss Holdfast. Be careful – they are extremely old and quite delicate. They should be cleaned in a salted solution after each use, and then rinsed with pure water. They can be uncomfortable to wear, especially for long periods, but they will prevent any god or mage, even those with dream powers, from entering the wearer's mind.'

Kelsey took the box, and peered at the small disks. 'What are they made of?'

'I'm not sure,' said Naxor. 'As far as I know, Malik and Amalia brought several pairs with them to the world of the City. These are most likely the last. I know of no others. They are utterly priceless, and irreplaceable. By giving them to you, I hope you can begin to trust me again.'

Kelsey laughed. 'Don't push your luck, Naxor.'

'Come now,' said Naxor. 'Can I lie to you? You were there when Cael and Kyra placed those blocks in my mind. If I say you can trust me, then it must be so.'

'Do you want a cup of tea before you go?' said Corthie.

'Why not?' said Kelsey.

'I'll have one, too,' said Aila.

Corthie got up, and placed Konna in her cot.

'Naxor?'

The demigod blinked. 'Yes?'

'Tea?'

'No, thank you. I shall resume my progress towards drunken oblivion, if it's all the same to you.'

Kelsey stuffed the small box into a pocket as Corthie strode towards the kitchen. Naxor picked up a bottle of wine, and began to study the label.

'How's the farm?' said Kelsey.

'Cold, dark, damp and windy,' said Aila. 'I'm counting the days to spring. Just this morning, we had to...'

Naxor moved like lightning. He flung the bottle of wine at Kelsey, and it struck her on the head, then he lunged out, ripping the shoulder bag from over her arm. Kelsey cried out as she flew backwards, then Naxor was on top of her. He emptied the shoulder bag by turning it upside down, and the contents spilled out onto the floor. Aila jumped to her feet, as his hands reached for the Quadrant.

'No, Naxor!' Aila cried.

Corthie appeared in the doorway as Aila leapt at her cousin. She knocked Naxor off balance and they rolled on the floor together, then the air shimmered, and Aila and Naxor fell through the air, her hands grabbing his arms. They landed onto a rough patch of ground, and Naxor lashed out, pushing Aila away with his right hand. He scrambled free of her and pulled himself to his feet.

Aila groaned, then glanced up. The sky was a mixture of reds and purples. She was in the City, but she didn't recognise the half-ruined buildings around them.

Naxor shook his head at her. 'There was really no need to accompany me, my dearest cousin.'

'What have you done, Naxor? You stole Kelsey's Quadrant.'

'Nonsense,' he said, glancing down at the copper-coloured device clutched in his left hand. 'I merely retook what was mine. This Quadrant was given to me by the God-King himself; and I used it for centuries to trade salve on Lostwell. Yendra took it from me, then she gave it to Blackrose. Karalyn stole it from her, and only then did it come into Kelsey's possession. This Quadrant is mine, and it shall always be mine.'

'But why?' Aila said. 'I trusted you; Kelsey trusted you. Why would you do it, and why would you come back to the City?'

Naxor's eyes hardened. 'Do you think I am deaf, cousin? I heard you and the Holdfast girl gossip about me the moment my back was turned. The Empress intends to sell me out, so that Kelsey can have Van live with her in Colsbury. Is that all I am worth?'

'I wouldn't have let them take you,' Aila said.

'You would have been unable to stop them, my dear cousin. I do not blame you for this. I know that you didn't mean your promise to Jade;

but I am not a bargaining chip. Now, you may come with me for a little longer, if you wish; otherwise I will leave you here.'

He extended a hand, and Aila took it. Naxor pulled her up.

'Where are we?' she said.

'In the back streets of Ooste,' he said; 'in an area damaged by Dawn-flame's attack on the Royal Palace. I am going to raid the basement of the Royal Academy, to pick up some emergency supplies I left there some years ago. Don't worry; I won't be in the City long enough for Jade to discover that I have returned.'

He set off along the street, and Aila ran after him in her bare feet. Her mind was spinning over what had happened, and her heart sank as she tried to picture the reaction of Corthie and Kelsey in the farmhouse.

Naxor laughed as he walked. 'I thought you would have learned your lesson by now.'

'What lesson?'

'Never get too close to someone who is about to trigger a Quadrant. Isn't that how our dear grandmother ensnared you in the cavern of Fordamere on Lostwell?'

Aila frowned. 'Are you going to hold me hostage like she did?'

'Of course not, cousin. You are the only friend I have. I will do nothing to hurt you. Once I have retrieved my supplies and changed out of this dressing gown, I will be on my way.'

'Will you take me back to Kell?'

'Eh, no. I won't be returning to Kell any time soon.'

'But my children are there.'

'Your children will be fine. Corthie is there to care for them.' He smirked. 'And Kelsey, too.'

They went through an archway overgrown with weeds and shrubs, and entered the grounds of the Royal Academy. Its buildings were lying in silence, and seemed deserted. Naxor strode towards a tower, and ripped the ivy from an old doorway. He gripped the handle and pulled the door open, its hinges squealing in protest.

Aila leaned against the wall of the tower as Naxor disappeared into the dim interior. She thought about running to get help, but where could she go? The government of the City had moved to Tara, and the centre of Ooste was lying empty. She lowered herself to the ground, her back against the cold stones of the tower, and closed her eyes.

Naxor was finished. After what he had just done, no one in the Star Continent would ever trust him again, just as no one in the City believed a word he said. The Empress had been his last chance of redemption, and he had blown it. So, where would he go? A dark suspicion formed in the back of her mind, but she suppressed it. No. Naxor would never betray them to Implacatus.

She heard a noise and glanced up to see Naxor emerge from the tower wearing a set of travelling clothes, and with a large bag slung over his shoulder.

'This is where I leave you, cousin,' he said. 'It's been fun. Good luck with, you know, everything.'

'Don't do it, Naxor.'

He smiled. 'Don't do what?'

'Whatever scheme you're dreaming up in that mind of yours.'

'But, Aila, who am I without my little schemes and plans?'

She glared at him. 'You betrayed me; you betrayed my trust in you.'

'Not at all,' he said. 'If you hadn't tried to intervene, you would be sitting comfortably in your home with your husband and children.'

'What about the blocks Karalyn's twins placed in your mind? Weren't they supposed to stop you doing something like this?'

Naxor laughed. 'My dear, those blocks wore off some time ago. I felt it better not to mention it; and look how wise that decision turned out to be. Do you think Kelsey would have been so careless if she had known the truth?'

'Where will you go?'

'I think I shall keep that information to myself.'

He withdrew the Quadrant from the folds of his clothes.

'Wait,' said Aila. 'You can't just leave me here, stranded in the City. What am I supposed to do?'

'You lived here for nearly eight hundred years, cousin,' Naxor said. 'I'm sure you'll manage just fine.'

The air shimmered and Naxor vanished.

Aila rubbed her face, then she began to make her way through the grounds of the Academy. She passed the ancient hall where she had received lessons in her youth, her bare feet aching on the rough gravel of the path. Corthie and Kelsey would be beside themselves with anger at Naxor's actions, but what could they do? Without a Quadrant, Kelsey was stuck in Kell, just as Aila was stuck in the City. She tried to imagine the situation from Naxor's point of view. He had appeared calm, but perhaps that had been a front. Maybe he had been anxious about his future, and the words he had heard Kelsey say in the farmhouse had been enough to convince him that he had no choice but to act. From that perspective, Aila considered his actions almost rational, but would anyone else come to the same conclusion? Everyone would nod and smile knowingly when they heard what he had done. He was Naxor, after all, and most people expected him to be duplicitous.

She emerged from the grounds of the Royal Academy, and saw the burnt-out shell of the Royal Palace a hundred yards to her right. Across from it was a plaza, and then a row of harbourside buildings that led to the docks of Ooste. She shivered in the chill air, and made her way to the long quayside, but not a single boat was tied up by any of the piers that thrust out into the waters of the bay. Aila sat on the deserted quay. It was an eight-mile walk along the coast from Ooste to the centre of Tara, and she had left her boots in Kell. Worse, when she finally reached Princeps Row, she would have to tell King Daniel and Queen Emily what had occurred. Would they inform Jade and, if so, would the demigod go back to her previous stance of refusing to extract any more salve from the mountains?

'Damn you, Naxor,' she muttered, then she got to her feet and started walking.

CHAPTER 20
EVE OF BATTLE

Colsbrookdale, Republic of the Holdings – 13th Day, First Third Winter 534

The air crackled over the valley as though a thunderstorm were about to start. Fields that had recently been vacated by the Second, Third and Fourth Divisions of the Banner of the Sapphire Throne were filled with the latest, and final, batch of soldiers from Dragon Eyre. Unlike those who had arrived from Gyle, the last batch had been well briefed in Na Sun Ka before departure, and there was no panic on their faces as they gazed around. Volunteers from the earlier arrivals moved into the thick crowd, distributing food and water from the back of wagons, along with plentiful supplies of blankets and winter clothing.

'That's it,' said Shella; 'that's the lot.'

Thorn nodded, her hands gripping the railing that ran along the front of the wooden veranda.

'One hundred and sixty thousand men and women,' Shella went on; 'the remnants of eleven separate Banners. And now they are here.'

'You have done an incredible job, Shella,' Thorn said. 'A logistical miracle.'

The old Rakanese woman shrugged. 'It was easier than feeding six hundred thousand refugees crossing the Basalt Desert during the Migration. Now, *that* was a challenge.'

'Thank you for coming out of retirement,' Thorn said.

'I gave Bridget ten years of service,' Shella said. 'Ten long years. But she never asked me to do anything like this. All Bridget wanted me to do was kill people, or, at least, intimidate them.' She glanced at the Empress. 'I can't promise that I'll give you ten years. I might not have ten years left in me. But, if you want me to carry out work like this – organising things and spending your money – then I'll do it.'

'We are all in your debt,' said Thorn.

The Empress's thoughts went to the coming conflict, and she wondered how many of her new Banner would die in the next few days. It was tragic that they were being thrown into battle so soon after arriving, but that was Bryce's fault, not hers.

Your Majesty.

Thorn smiled. *Sable. Good work. The units from Na Sun Ka have arrived in one piece. Are you ready to transfer the Seventh Division directly to the vineyards?*

I am, your Majesty. Afterwards, should I proceed with the original plan, or should I look for Kelsey first? She should have returned yesterday.

Follow the original plan for now, and then travel to Kell to see if Kelsey is at her brother's house. We cannot move on to the other operation until she has returned. I shall join Daphne by the Seventh; give me a few moments to get there.

I'll be watching, your Majesty.

Thorn felt Sable leave her mind, and she turned back to Shella.

'Time to go,' she said.

Shella nodded. 'Good luck, your Majesty.'

Thorn stepped down from the veranda, and her personal guard of armoured Sanang warriors moved into position around her. Agang was also waiting for her, and he squeezed between the soldiers to walk by the Empress's side.

'It's a beautiful crisp day, your Majesty,' he said. 'If the weather holds until tomorrow, we shall have perfect conditions for a battle.'

'I suppose that depends upon your perspective,' Thorn said. 'The weather will also help our adversary. Rainstorms and thick mud would aid our defence of the vineyards.'

'That is so, your Majesty; but clear weather will allow our three dragons to operate unhindered.'

They passed between rows of tents, where thousands of former slaves from Gyle were recovering from their ordeal. Those fit enough to fight were being hastily drilled by the banks of the river, their new armour shining in the winter sunlight. The tops of the nearby mountains had received their first snow the previous night, and the air was cold, though still. They reached the Seventh Division, which was lined up in long columns by the side of the road, and made for the rear, where the Commander of the Banner was waiting for the Empress to arrive. Thorn glanced at the lines of Banner soldiers, and felt a surge of pride. True, they were paid mercenaries and had previously fought for the Ascendants, but they were a vision of what Thorn considered to be the ideal army – well-trained, disciplined, and loyal. She had watched them over the days since they had arrived, and had seen the tears of relief turn into a gritty determination, their subdued spirits rekindled. Did any of them understand the cause for which they had enlisted? Did it matter?

Thorn strode into the small group of senior officers clustered round Daphne. Belinda was there, wearing a set of steel armour, a Holdings cavalry sword strapped to her waist, and so too were Lucius Cardova and Caelius Logos. Both had been appointed to Daphne's staff, Lucius as the senior liaison to the officers of the Banner, and Caelius as the delegate of a council of sergeants that had been brought together to represent the lower ranks. Next to Daphne stood the major-general of the Seventh Division, and they bowed as the Empress approached.

'Your Majesty,' said Daphne; 'are we ready to leave?'

'Yes,' said Thorn. 'The final batch of twenty-five thousand soldiers from Na Sun Ka has arrived.'

Daphne nodded. 'Will seven divisions be enough to hold the ridges above the vineyards, your Majesty?'

'It shall have to suffice,' said Thorn. 'This battle is being forced upon us, Commander. If we had but a few more days, then a further three divisions might have been ready; but we cannot control our enemy's timing. Our army will be outnumbered, it is true, but we shall be fighting upon ground of our choosing. All told, I would rather have that, than a few more days.'

Are you ready, your Majesty?

Yes, Sable; we are ready.

The air crackled and felt heavy, then the entire Seventh Division appeared on the green slopes of a low hill. Daphne nodded to the major-general. The officer saluted, then gave the order for his division to start moving off to the west, to join the right flank of the Banner army positioned above them on the ridge. The columns of the Seventh Division wheeled about and strode off; row after row of soldiers marching over the trampled grass.

Thorn and Daphne climbed the slope directly ahead of them, the Sanang guardsmen flanking them, and they reached a line of deep trenches, where supplies had been gathered. Soldiers from the support battalions were unloading wagons filled with crate after crate of crossbow bolts and barrels of fresh water. The tracks leading north down the slope towards Colsbury had been churned into mud, which had frozen during the night, and dozens of thin tendrils of smoke were rising, as soldiers warmed themselves by small camp fires.

Daphne led the small party over a series of plank bridges and up on to the summit of the ridge. Forty yards to the left, the main road from Plateau City to Colsbury ran up the terraced hillside, dividing the vineyard in two, and the ridge above was bustling with activity. Earthen ramparts and ditches criss-crossed the terraces beneath where Thorn and the others stood, and hundreds of soldiers were digging, fashioning sharpened stakes, or erecting rudimentary palisade walls. Piles of pick-axes and timber lay dotted every twenty yards or so, and the accumulated sounds were creating a din of background noise.

'This is the centre of our lines, your Majesty,' said Daphne. 'This section is held by the First Division, who arrived here five days ago. To our left sits the Fourth, Fifth and Sixth Divisions, while the Second and Third are on our right, soon to be joined by the Seventh. To get up here, the imperial forces will have to climb six separate levels of terraced ground.'

Thorn nodded as she surveyed the landscape. 'Where are the vines?'

'They were burnt and cleared three days ago, your Majesty, to prevent Bryce's army from seeking cover on each terrace. The owners have been compensated.'

'What a bleak sight,' said Agang. 'All I can see are charred stumps, where once this entire hillside flourished.'

'Vines can grow back, Lord Agang,' said Daphne; 'whereas we have a finite number of soldiers. The imperials must be forced into taking each terrace one at a time, without the respite of cover.'

'And there they are,' said Cardova, pointing into the distance.

Thorn pulled her gaze away from the denuded terraces of the vineyard. At the bottom of the slope, the advance units of Bryce's army were arriving. Small squadrons of cavalry were clustered at the base of the hill, while endless columns of infantry were slowing and drawing to a halt.

'Might they attack now?' said Thorn.

'Not if they have any sense, your Majesty,' said Cardova. 'They will have to concentrate their forces first to have any chance of making it up this slope. I imagine they will try to soften us up before that happens.' He pointed again. 'I see several large artillery devices being assembled over there. Once they are ready, they will be moved up into range of the ridge, and the pounding of our lines will begin.'

Thorn watched as a small detachment of imperial cavalry charged up the road. The First Division had blocked the thoroughfare, ripping up the flagstones to create a ditch that sliced the road in two. The advancing cavalry rode into bow range, then quickly turned as the defenders unleashed a barrage of bolts at them from behind the barrier they had erected.

'They should have left their horses in their stables,' said Daphne. 'Cavalry will be useless in this battle.'

Thorn watched as the cavalry retreated to the east of the road, pulling away from the blockade; then she blinked as a powerful surge of mage powers tried to invade her mind. She flinched, then the feeling dissipated.

Daphne grimaced. 'Daimon is trying to reach us, your Majesty.'

'Yes. I felt it,' Thorn said.

'I think we all did, your Majesty,' said Cardova. 'Karalyn is shielding us from Colsbury.'

The air shimmered, and Sable appeared on the ridge next to them. With an arm, she was supporting a young woman, who seemed too weak to stand on her own. Caelius stepped forward to assist Sable, placing an arm around the young woman's shoulders.

'Here she is, your Majesty,' said Sable; 'Tilda Holdwain.'

'Thank you,' said Thorn.

'Did anyone notice your presence within the Great Fortress?' said Daphne.

'No,' said Sable. 'I was in and out in under two minutes.'

Daphne frowned. 'She looks ill. Has she said anything?'

'She didn't want to be separated from her supply of dullweed,' Sable said. 'I had to persuade her to come along.'

'Take her to Colsbury, and ensure she is well-guarded,' Thorn said. 'We can summon her parents from the Holdings after the battle.'

Sable nodded. 'And then Kelsey, your Majesty?'

'Yes.'

'She probably got drunk with Corthie last night,' said Daphne, 'and forgot what day it was.'

Thorn resisted the temptation to openly disagree with her Herald, then Sable vanished, taking Tilda Holdwain with her.

'That poor girl looked half dead,' said Caelius.

Thorn nodded, her attention drifting back to the huge numbers of imperial soldiers forming up by the bottom of the hill. The outlines of a vast camp were being staked out, and hundreds of soldiers were digging a ditch to protect the northern edge of the army. A trebuchet was being pulled forwards by a double line of oxen, and a long column of wagons was being parked to the rear. All the while, more imperial soldiers were arriving, and the sound of so many rose up the slopes to the ridge.

'Thoughts, Captain Cardova?' Thorn said.

The tall officer rubbed his chin. 'There are a lot of Kellach Brig-domin down there,' he said. 'No offence to the Holdings, but it's the Kellach who will be our primary foe tomorrow. If we break them, we win the battle. As far as I can tell, they'll deploy along a wide front, covering the entire ridge, probing for weaknesses. If they have tactical awareness, they'll keep several units in reserve to exploit any break-throughs in our defensive lines; but I think they are likely to focus most of their effort on the road. That represents our weakest point, where the slope is at its most gentle, and there are no terraces to climb. One other thing – we should consider holding our own force in reserve to launch a counter-attack down the hill if an opportunity arises.'

'I can lead a counter-attack,' said Belinda; 'but its success will depend upon the dragons providing cover from the air. I cannot kill a hundred thousand soldiers on my own, not if Daimon is blocking my death powers.'

'I shall not risk the dragons in any offensive operation,' said Thorn, 'not unless the threat from Keir has been neutralised. He will be down there, somewhere, no doubt cursing my name and thirsting for revenge. A few broken limbs won't stop him from unleashing lightning upon our forces.' She paused. She had almost added, 'I should have killed him', but with Daphne standing close by, it would have sounded callous. An awkward silence descended over the Empress's military advisors, as everyone avoided eye contact with Holder Fast.

'A command headquarters is being put together, your Majesty,' said Cardova, breaking into the quiet. 'It is located on the brow of the hill behind us, next to the main supply depots. Should we check on its progress?'

'Wait a moment,' said Daphne. 'Look at the road. A lone horseman is approaching our lines.'

They all turned, and Thorn saw the solitary cavalry officer walk his mount towards the barrier blocking the road. He halted out of bow range, and lifted his arms into the air.

'Perhaps Lord Bryce wishes to sue for peace,' said Cardova, a half-smile on his lips.

The cavalry officer dismounted, and strode towards the roadblock, leading his horse by the reins. The Banner soldiers on the road allowed him to pass, and he disappeared into their ranks.

'Send a scout to the road,' Thorn said, 'and have the cavalry officer brought to the new headquarters. We shall meet him there.'

'We should be cautious, your Majesty,' said Agang. 'Daimon might be in control of this officer. It could be an assassination attempt.'

'I will make sure we have plenty of my Sanang guardsmen protecting us, Chamberlain,' Thorn said. 'Please take us to the head-quarters, Commander.'

A scout was dispatched from the thick lines of the First Division, and Daphne led Thorn and her party back down the northern flank of the hill. They passed the supply trenches, and climbed a further slope that rose high above the vineyard. Tree stumps littered the ground, and timber was being hauled towards the front lines on carts. They came to a muddy track, and followed it to the top of the hill, where a series of tents had been erected.

'This is well out of the range of even the largest catapults and trebuchets, your Majesty,' said Daphne. 'From here, scouts can carry orders to each of the seven divisions dug in along the ridge; and we have flag-bearers who can send quick signals if redeployments are required. Each division can also signal this location if they need rein-forcements or supplies.'

'Excellent work,' said Thorn.

Daphne smiled. 'It helps that the Banners have all been trained in the same procedures, your Majesty. Every soldier in the army knows their job. In terms of training, only the Imperial Marines have anything like the same experience. Most of the infantry under Bryce's control will have been restricted to garrison duties for the past few years.'

'I am well aware of how professional the marines are,' said Thorn. 'If my judgement is sound, they will be the last to be sent against our lines come dawn tomorrow. I imagine Lord Bryce will not wish to waste them in his initial attacks.'

A small group of Banner soldiers appeared on the track leading to the road. In their midst was the imperial cavalry officer who had approached the defences. Cardova gestured to the soldiers, and they brought the imperial officer to where Thorn and Daphne were standing.

The cavalry officer gave a brief nod. 'I bear word from his Imperial Majesty Emperor Bryce, Holder of the World.'

'The usurper is not called that here, Major,' said Daphne. 'There is one Holder of the World, and you are standing in front of her.'

The officer smiled. 'Is there any way to conduct this conversation without either party losing face, Commander?'

'You shall address me,' said Daphne. 'What is Lord Bryce's message? Does he wish to negotiate?'

'His Majesty calls upon you to surrender,' said the officer, 'to save lives, and to bring this futile conflict to an end before these hills are drenched in blood.'

'If I am not mistaken, Major, it is Lord Bryce who has marched an army two hundred miles from the imperial capital. If he wished to save lives, he should have remained in the Great Fortress.'

'His Majesty will still require an answer, Commander. Do you surrender?'

'We do not,' said Daphne. 'We shall hold our lines. If we are attacked, then we shall defend ourselves with the utmost vigour. It must be plain, even to a rank amateur such as Lord Bryce, that we command the better position. There is but one route to Colsbury, and to get there, you will have to climb the terraces of the vineyard and break our lines. Every soldier in the imperial army will know this by now.'

The officer nodded. 'Emperor Bryce anticipated this response. Therefore, his Majesty has instructed me to inform you that, if you do not surrender by dawn tomorrow, the false Empress's mother shall be put to death in full view of both armies.'

Thorn narrowed her eyes, but her Herald chuckled.

'You are lying,' Daphne said. 'The Empress's mother perished in Rahain years ago.'

The major smiled. 'The Emperor also anticipated this response. To prove that he speaks the truth, High Mage Daimon shall allow you to use your vision powers, Commander, to check the veracity of our claim. Madam Ivy, mother of the soulwitch, can be found in a small tent to the east of his Majesty's command post, one half-mile south of this location. Furthermore, High Mage Daimon shall allow you to enter her mind briefly, so that there can be no room for any doubt.'

'Have you no shame?' said Caelius. 'What manner of tyrant threatens to murder an old woman?'

'You call his Majesty a tyrant?' said the major. 'What then, foreign mercenary, does that make your leader – someone who ordered the abduction of Tilda Holdwain from Plateau City under an hour ago? Did you think that High Mage Daimon was unaware of your underhanded plots?'

'There is a difference, Major,' said Thorn. 'For one, I do not intend to harm Tilda Holdwain, but to return her to her family. Commander, please use your powers to reveal the crooked lies of this emissary.'

The group silenced as Daphne's eyes glazed over. Thorn kept her face expressionless, but her heart was in turmoil. Could it be true? No, of course not. It was utter nonsense. Keir, Daphne and others had searched Rahain for years on her behalf, hunting for any sign of her missing mother; and they had found no trace of her. At some point, though Thorn couldn't tell when, she had begun to assume the worst. Her mother was dead.

Daphne coughed, then she glanced at Thorn, her eyes troubled. 'Your Majesty; it's true. Ivy is alive.'

Thorn staggered back a step as though she had been punched in the stomach.

'Bryce and Daimon have your mother in custody,' Daphne went on. 'She is chained up inside a cage.'

'And she will die at dawn tomorrow,' said the major; 'unless you surrender yourselves to his Imperial Majesty.'

Thorn turned, and stumbled away, as tears rolled down her cheeks. Daphne and Cardova started to follow her, but she brushed them aside. She walked on until she was alone, her back to the officers and the emissary, and wept.

How could this have happened? Not only was her mother alive, after Thorn had given up all hope, but that day would be her last, unless her sole surviving daughter gave up everything. She wondered if her mother knew that her other daughters had died – Clove in Stretton Sands, and Acorn in Colsbury. It was too much to bear, and Thorn sank to her knees on the hillside, her hands covering her face.

What would she do? What could she do? If she surrendered, then Bryce would probably parade her around the Empire in chains, and then have her executed. Every Holdfast, except Keir, would die. Daimon would take the Sextant, and then his power would be complete. Surely Bryce didn't expect her to actually surrender? Then she realised the truth. He didn't want her to surrender, he wanted her to be overcome with guilt and grief; he wanted her off-balance, and more likely to make a mistake. Daimon was probably watching her weep alone on the summit of the hill, thrilled at how their plan was working. Bryce and Keir would also be watching. They were laughing at her – a weak-willed woman brought down by pity, guilt and despair.

She had one choice. At dawn, she would witness her mother's death, and then she would order the Banner to crush the imperial army. She would unleash Sable, Belinda, the dragons, and every soldier under her authority, to kill her enemies and bring her the heads of Bryce and Daimon. There was no alternative.

She rose to her feet, and set her features. She had wept, but the time for weeping was over. She smoothed down the front of her blue dress, and turned back to face the others. The major had the slightest trace of a frown on his lips, while her own followers were wearing expressions that betrayed their anxiety.

Thorn walked back into their midst.

'There shall be no surrender,' she said to the major. 'Tell your wicked master to do his worst. Let him debase himself in front of the world; let all witness the barbarity of the usurper. Let every soldier see him murder my mother, an old woman who has never wronged him, an old woman who has spent her life healing, not killing. I will mourn her, but everyone will know which side in this conflict fights for what is right, and which side fights for all that is evil. I shall not be cowed by his threats, nor shall I turn away from his crimes. If my mother's blood flows tomorrow, then I shall know that I have won, even before the battle has begun. Then, when my victorious army sweeps you aside, I shall do unto Bryce what he has done to my mother. Good day, Major.'

The imperial officer gave a slight bow, then he turned and walked away, flanked by the same soldiers who had escorted him up the hill.

Agang opened his mouth to speak, but Thorn raised her hand. 'I need a moment to quell the bitterness in my heart,' she said; 'and my anger. Lord Bryce is trying to break my spirit, but this I will not allow. Walk with me, my Herald.'

She strode away, sensing Daphne's presence to her left.

'Have I made a mistake?' she said, once they were out of earshot of the others.

'No, your Majesty,' said Daphne. 'You gave the only response that was possible under the circumstances. A brave response; one that does you credit. I shall have Cardova relay your words to the seven divisions for distribution among the soldiers. They should know what kind of leader they are fighting for; and the kind of enemy we are facing.'

'Please do so; thank you,' she said. 'My mother. I can't believe it. We searched for her for years.'

Daphne nodded. 'Perhaps Daimon used his dream powers to locate her, your Majesty. His range is far greater than Karalyn's. He could have sensed her healing powers all the way from Plateau City.'

'That must be it,' she said. 'I feel so stupid. Stupid to have given up looking for her; and stupid that I did not foresee this.'

'I don't see how you could have foreseen it, your Majesty,' said Daphne.

They stopped, and glanced down the slope towards the top of the vineyard ridge. Beyond, yet more imperial soldiers were arriving at the bottom of the terraced hillside.

'Our strategy does not change,' said Thorn. 'As much as I yearn for vengeance, I know my duty. If I weaken over the course of the next day, I want you to remind me of these words. My heart must be as hard as stone, and my mind clear. I must not waver, nor bow to the savage instincts that burn within me. Do you understand?'

'I do, your Majesty.'

The air shimmered, and Sable appeared on the hillside next to them, with Kelsey by her side.

'Sorry!' Kelsey cried. 'I fucked it up. Naxor overpowered me and stole my Quadrant, then he grabbed Aila and they disappeared.'

Thorn composed herself. 'That demigod stole your Quadrant? How could you let this happen?'

'Cael and Kyra's powers have worn off,' Kelsey said, 'and Naxor pounced on me when I wasn't expecting it. I'm so sorry.'

'What's done is done,' said Thorn. 'Thank you, Sable, for bringing her back.'

'I do have one piece of good news,' Kelsey said. She rummaged in a pocket, then produced a small box. 'I have his eye-guards.'

'Well done,' said Thorn. 'All is not lost. Sable, come with me for a moment.'

Sable took the small box from Kelsey, slipped it into a pocket, then followed Thorn to the top of the hill.

'Do you see the approaching armies?' said Thorn.

Sable nodded. 'Is it time? The eye-guards mean I will be invulnerable to Daimon's powers, your Majesty.'

'There is a new complication,' said Thorn. 'Before I go over it, tell me – is Naxor a threat? Should we be concerned that he is on the loose with a Quadrant?'

'I doubt he will want to get involved, your Majesty. Remember that Bryce wishes to kill him, to avenge the death of Bridget. He is also exiled from Salve City. Naxor has very few options open to him. Corthie, for one, would beat him senseless if he ever shows up in Kell again.'

'And Aila? I presume she was an unwilling companion to the rogue demigod?'

'Most unwilling, your Majesty. According to Corthie, she was attempting to prevent Naxor's escape. Should I look for her? Corthie is anxious to have her home again.'

'One thing at a time, Sable. Wherever she is, Aila shall have to wait for a while. Now, that complication I mentioned. It appears that Daimon and Bryce are holding my mother hostage; the same mother that you handed over to the Rahain government.'

Sable's mouth opened, but she said nothing.

'For years,' Thorn went on, 'I have assumed that my mother was dead; killed by Lord Ghorley, or at the hands of Agatha and the other archmages. I was wrong. Would you like the opportunity to make amends for your earlier actions against my family?'

'Yes, your Majesty,' said Sable. 'I would very much like that opportunity.'

'Good, because Bryce and Daimon are planning to execute my mother at dawn.'

'Not if I kill them first.'

Thorn nodded. 'That's right. Not if you kill them first. Be my avenging sword, Sable. Show no mercy.'

'I will show them none, your Majesty.'

'Strike before dawn. Kill them all, and bring my mother to me.'

Sable bowed her head. For a long moment, she didn't respond, then she raised her eyes.

'It shall be done, your Majesty.'

CHAPTER 21
BATTLE OF THE VINEYARDS

Northern Plateau – 14th Day, First Third Winter 534

A hand shook Keir's shoulder, and he opened his eyes to darkness. He turned his head, and saw the silhouette of a Kellach Brigdomin soldier by his camp bed.

'Excuse me, sir,' said the soldier; 'the Emperor has requested that you attend the command post.'

Keir groaned, and rubbed his eyes. 'How long is it until dawn?'

'Sunrise is about three hours away, sir.'

'Tell his Majesty that I'll be there in a moment.'

The soldier nodded, then left the small tent. Keir swung his legs off the camp bed, and found his boots in the darkness. He pulled them on, then grabbed his winter coat. He yawned. It had been late the previous evening by the time he had retired to his tent, and he felt as though he needed a few more hours of sleep. He rifled in his pockets and withdrew a packet of cigarettes, then he crawled out of the tent and into the chill air of night. Frost was sparkling on the frozen ground, while a multitude of torches were lighting up the vast camp that had sprouted up at the bottom of the terraced slopes. Keir lit a cigarette and stared up at the hillside. No lights were visible from the rebel positions on top of the ridge, and he wondered for a moment if the Banner had fled during the night. Perhaps that was why he had been summoned. Maybe Thorn had fallen completely into despair at the news her mother was to be executed at dawn, and her hired soldiers were deserting, their cause hopeless.

Keir strode between the lines of tents, clinging on to the slim hope that there would be no battle. He still thirsted for revenge against Thorn and Karalyn, but he had no desire to fight his way up the long series of defended terraces against dug-in and determined opposition. He reached the armoured marines guarding the large command tent, and was allowed to pass through. A dozen senior officers were standing or sitting within the main area of the tent, their fingers clutching cigarettes and mugs of steaming coffee. A few nodded to him, though none looked him in the eye. Despite the healing he had received, his face had remained broken and he knew he had gained a frightening appearance. The knowledge hurt him to his core, but he wasn't going to show that in front of a bunch of officers. He would keep his head held high; and damn what anyone thought.

'Does anyone know what's going on?' said a colonel of the infantry.

'We're all hoping that the false Empress has decided to surrender after all,' said a lieutenant-general in the marines. 'She would do anything to save her mother.'

'Who wouldn't, sir?' said a cavalry major.

Keir moved to the rear of the tent, and poured himself a mug of hot coffee from a pot. There was no sugar available, thanks to the trade blockade of Sanang, but he added a splash of milk, and took it to a seat.

'Have you heard anything, my lord?' a staff officer from the artillery asked him.

'Nothing,' said Keir. 'The revealing of Thorn's mother was as much of a surprise to me as it was to anyone else.'

'You had no idea she was alive, my lord?' said the major.

'None whatsoever. The last I knew of the business, Ivy was dead in Rahain.'

'Were you watching the false Empress's reaction with your powers, my lord?' said the lieutenant-general.

Keir nodded.

'And? What did she do, my lord?'

'She burst into tears.'

Several of the officers laughed. Keir didn't join them. He had found Thorn's dilemma hilarious when Daimon had first informed him of it the previous morning, but for some reason he no longer thought it was funny. Besides, he was conscious that whenever he laughed, the gaps in his mouth were all too apparent. He had practised smiling with his mouth closed in the mirror, but it had made him appear smug and condescending, as if he were faking it.

One of the more junior officers, Keir noticed, was scowling while the others laughed. The major nodded to the sullen-looking Kellach captain.

'No sense of humour, old chap?'

The frowning officer shrugged. 'Am I the only one here who thinks that threatening innocent old women might not be the most honourable course of action?'

'Not if it shortens the war,' said the lieutenant-general. 'Besides, the Sanang have proved how treacherous they can be. Once this is over, we should march into Broadwater, remove the Matriarch from power, and raze the town to the ground as a punishment for supporting Thorn.'

'Hear, hear,' said the colonel.

'That doesn't make any sense,' said the dissenting captain. 'The Holdings also support Thorn, and yet six out of every ten soldiers in our army are from the Holdings. Should we punish them, too? Are you advocating the destruction of Holdings City, sir?'

The lieutenant-general scowled at the young Kellach officer. 'That's quite enough of your insolence, Captain. Perhaps you should keep your views to yourself from now on.'

The young officer saluted. 'Aye, sir.'

There was a swish of canvas, and the Emperor strode into the main area of the command tent, Daimon by his side. The officers who were sitting jumped to their feet, and they all stood to attention.

'Thank you for coming at this hour of the night,' said Bryce. 'There has been a change of plan. We have information that points to a night attack by the rebels, and so, to counter that, we shall attack first. The artillery shall commence action immediately. Mage Daimon shall guide the accuracy of the catapults and trebuchets. While the rebels are pinned down on the ridge, the first waves of infantry shall begin their advance up the slope. The central battalions shall strike directly along the road, and deal with the enemy there, while the left and right flanks attack the vineyards.'

The lieutenant-general frowned. 'A night assault, your Majesty? Our scouts are still out on the terraces at this precise moment, gathering intelligence about the various ways to the summit. They are due back in an hour or so. Should we wait until then, to learn what they have discovered about the enemy's defences?'

'What's to learn?' said Bryce. 'There are six terraces to climb, and then there is the ridge. With the vines destroyed, what better cover could our soldiers have than the cover of darkness?'

A few of the officers shared nervous glances.

'But, your Majesty,' said the cavalry major, 'the enemy shall hear us coming, while they will be invisible to our soldiers.'

'The rebels will not hear our soldiers,' said the Emperor, 'because they will be coming under heavy and sustained artillery attack. Their lines will be ripped apart by the combined weight of our throwing machines, and any rebel who raises his head will have it blown off.'

The major's cheeks flushed, and he glanced down at the floor of the tent.

'Your Majesty,' said the lieutenant-general; 'isn't there a risk that the artillery will come under attack from the dragons? If our machines are rendered inoperable, then our infantry will be horribly exposed.'

Bryce clenched his fists. 'I am growing tired of my orders being questioned. I commanded that the artillery commence operations immediately, and yet here you all stand, staring at me like stupid children. Keir will protect the artillery from dragon assault, and Daimon will protect Keir from Karalyn Holdfast. Despite the powers of the mages at this battle, it shall be decided by soldiers on the ground. Break the lines of the foreign mercenaries; grind them into the dirt. Take no prisoners among them – mercy shall not be shown to those who have taken the pay of the false Empress. Go.'

The officers saluted, and hurried from the tent.

'Not you, Keir,' said Daimon.

Keir halted by the entrance to the tent, and turned. 'Yes, High Mage?'

'Come closer.'

Keir strode over to where the Emperor and Daimon were standing.

'We need you for a little task,' Daimon said. 'The information the Emperor mentioned about a possible rebel attack this night – it will be a rescue attempt, aimed at freeing Thorn's mother from captivity.'

Keir nodded. 'Will Sable be involved?'

'Aye,' said Daimon. 'The same Sable who abducted your Tilda from the Great Fortress; she will be coming here, before dawn. We must be ready. Sable is clever, but she has made a mistake – she confided her plan to a demigod by the name of Austin, and I was able to penetrate his mind. Both Sable and Austin shall be making the attempt, and they intend to kill us as well as free Madam Ivy. We shall lay a trap for them. We have already assembled an elite force of veteran marines, who will lie in wait around Ivy's tent. Sable will have to waste a few moments getting the old woman out of the cage, and that will give us time to strike. You shall lead the operation. If possible, capture the witch alive.'

'Alive?' said Keir. 'Do you intend to bend Sable to your will, High Mage?'

'I do,' said Daimon.

'Then, perhaps,' said Keir, 'it would be better if you led the operation, High Mage. Sable's vision powers are stronger than mine.'

'Your aunt has secured a pair of eye-guards,' said Daimon, 'and while she is wearing them, her mind will be impenetrable to me. That's where you come in, Keir. As soon as Sable and Austin arrive, you will bring your powers to bear. You can slay the demigod, but use only enough lightning to stun Sable. Do not kill her, and do not damage her Quadrant.'

'It matters not if Ivy dies,' said Bryce. 'The old woman is expendable, next to claiming Sable and the Quadrant as our first prizes of the day.'

'What if we are Sable's first target?' said Keir. 'She might decide to leave Ivy until after she has attacked us.'

'I have already seen her plan, Keir,' said Daimon. 'We know what she is going to do. Her heart is wracked with guilt, as it was she who took Thorn's mother to Rahain in the first place. She desires nothing more than to return Ivy to her daughter. Her desperation to redeem herself shall be her undoing.'

Keir nodded. 'And the Quadrant? I should try to ensure its survival?'

Daimon and Bryce glanced at each other.

'You must ensure its survival,' said the Emperor. 'If you do this, I will be well pleased with you. Watch the skies for dragons, but make sure you are positioned next to Ivy's tent, and be ready.'

A whoosh came from outside, followed by the sound of straining ropes.

Daimon smiled. 'It sounds as though our artillery has opened hostilities. Please excuse me, your Majesty; I shall help guide their range and direction.'

'I shall not leave your side, Daimon,' said the Emperor; 'not this night, not when so much is at stake. Keir – go to your post and report to the marines guarding Ivy. Do not fail me.'

Keir saluted, then strode out of the tent and into the cold night air. Ahead of him, the massive throwing machines were bursting into life, hurling gigantic boulders through the sky and into the darkness of the terraced slopes. The fourteen enormous trebuchets were loosing at will, their crews competing against each other to see who was the fastest, while long lines of wagons loaded with large rocks were positioned behind them. Keir scanned the sky, but it was too dark to see anything. A dragon could be fifty yards away, and he wouldn't know it. He turned, and hurried to the far side of the command area. He saw the small tent that held Ivy's cage. Standing outside were the usual two soldiers on guard duty.

'I'm looking for the marines,' Keir said to them.

'Marines, sir?' said one of the soldiers. 'There are no marines in this part of the camp.'

A low laugh echoed across to them, and Keir and the two soldiers turned to see over two dozen well-armed marines emerge from the shadows around Ivy's tent.

A marine captain walked up to Keir. 'My lord,' he said, 'we were informed that you would be coming along to lend assistance.' He snapped his fingers, and the other marines slipped back into the thick shadows. 'We estimate that we shall have less than two minutes in which to respond to any rescue attempt.' He pointed at a nearby tent. 'We have positioned a ballista there.' He turned, and pointed at two other tents. 'And also there, and there. Where would you like to be based, my lord?'

Keir glanced at the small tent. 'I want to take a quick look at the prisoner.'

The captain nodded.

'What's going on, sir?' said one of the two soldiers outside Ivy's tent.

'Nothing for you army lads to worry about,' said the captain. 'All we require from you is that you remain at your posts. Open the tent.'

The soldier nodded, and pulled the side flap of the tent open. Keir crouched down, and gazed inside. Ivy was lying on the floor of a cage that was barely tall enough to sit up in, with a blanket over her body. Her eyes opened as Keir stared at her, and she gripped the bars by the entrance.

'I remember you,' she said in Rahain. 'I healed you a few days ago.'

'Don't lie to me,' said Keir.

'You owe me, boy,' said the old woman.

'I owe you nothing.'

'What's going to happen to me? If you think my daughter will surrender to save my life, then you know nothing about Thorn.'

'I know a lot about Thorn. She was my wife for seven years.'

The old woman gasped. 'Your wife? Thorn was married? Did you have children with her? Am I a grandmother?'

Keir shook his head. 'Sanang and Holdings can't have children.'

She peered at him. 'But you are not Holdings, boy. What are you?'

'None of your damn business.'

Keir stood, and the soldier re-closed the tent flap.

'Well, my lord?' said the marine captain. 'Your position?'

'What would you recommend?'

'You should stay with me, my lord, next to one of the three ballistae. That way, we can coordinate our attack.'

Keir nodded. He glanced back down at the small tent, and remembered the words of the dissenting officer from the command tent. Was it honourable to use an innocent old woman as bait? Probably not, he thought, but if it won them the battle, then did it matter? A flicker of shame went through his mind, and he struggled to suppress it.

He followed the marine captain to another tent, and they entered through a concealed entrance. A large ballista was stationed by the side of the tent, its yard-long steel bolt pointing in the direction of Ivy's cage. Several small slits had been cut in the fabric of the canvas – one for the ballista, and others so that the marines inside could keep a watch on events. Three marines were crouching by the cut openings, and more were standing by the ballista, ready to prime and loose the machine at a moment's notice.

'I need access to the sky,' said Keir.

The captain nodded, then he carried a chair over to Keir's location. The officer climbed up onto the chair, raised a knife in his right hand, and cut another slit in the fabric.

He glanced down. 'How's that, my lord?'

Keir nodded. 'It'll do.'

The marine captain stepped down from the chair. 'Are you aware of our orders, my lord? We are to endeavour to capture the Holdfast witch alive.'

'I know,' said Keir. 'I will use lightning, but I intend to stun her, not kill her. You marines will need to be careful with the ballistae.'

'The bolts will be used to keep the rebel witch pinned down, my lord, while a snatch team charges her position.'

Keir sat on the chair, and gazed up through the slit at the tiny patch of sky that was visible to him. He sent his powers out into the night air. To the north, he could see movement along the entire base of the hill, as thousands of imperial soldiers began climbing the first terrace. No response was coming from the rebels at the top of the ridge, and Keir strained his vision towards their defensive lines to see if any damage was being caused by the army's throwing machines. The fourteen trebuchets looked impressive, and were loosing load after load up onto the summit of the hill; but the Banner's position stretched for over two miles, and Keir frowned at the futility of the artillery operations. At the rate they were loosing, it would take several days of continuous bombardment for the imperial machines to destroy the Banner's defences. Keir moved his vision closer to the rebels' lines. Banner soldiers were huddling down in their trenches, keeping their heads low and biding their time. Buckets full of crossbow bolts sat every few paces, while a handful of scouts were lying exposed on the edge of the ridge, keeping a wary eye on the slowly-advancing imperial forces scaling the first terrace. None of the Banner soldiers looked frightened by the huge boulders being flung up the hillside. Even with Daimon's guidance, in the darkness most of the boulders were missing their targets, either falling short or flying too high, with only a handful striking the trenches.

Keir turned away from the hillside before despair could wither his spirits away. He needed to be searching for clouds, and gathering them in preparation for a lightning strike. He felt for his fire powers, and found them. He would need to work quickly when the time came, in case Karalyn detected what he was doing. Bryce had promised that Daimon would shield him, but with the high mage's attention on the trebuchets, Keir was taking nothing for granted. He drew in the closest clouds, and the air pressure increased above the imperial camp, then he blinked, and glanced around at the interior of the tent.

'I'm ready,' he said to the captain. 'I can have lightning strike the target within a few seconds.'

'Did you see the advance, my lord? How is it going?'

'Slowly. The first units have made it onto the lowest terrace, while the trebuchets and catapults are loosing as quickly as they can.'

'The army lads have a hard morning ahead of them, my lord.'

Keir fell into silence, and the captain went back to gazing through one of the slits in the side of the tent. An hour passed without the marines saying a word, as they sat and waited for Sable to appear. Keir checked the skies every few minutes, while the marines watched the tent where Ivy was being kept. Just when Keir was starting to believe that he would be unneeded, he noticed movement in the dark skies over the camp, and he shot to his feet.

'Dragons,' he cried. 'The damn dragons are coming.'

He powered his vision through the hole cut in the roof of the tent. For a moment he saw nothing, just the dark clouds that he had gathered overhead. Had he been mistaken? But no, he saw it again, a flicker of a dragon's wing reflecting the light from the camp fires below. Something was soaring down the hillside towards the artillery batteries. Without hesitating, Keir flooded the clouds with energy. A flash lit up the sky for a brief second, silhouetting three dragons. Keir unleashed a bolt of lightning, but the dragons were ready. They scattered above the camp, racing back out of range of the clouds, and the flash of lightning hit a barren patch of hillside, illuminating the companies of imperial soldiers scrambling up onto the third and fourth terraces.

'Damn it!' Keir cried, his vision trying to spot where the dragons had gone; the bright flash having ruined his ability to see anything in the night sky. He felt a presence find his mind, a presence that he recognised from his childhood. Daimon's defences rebuffed the presence, but it returned, stronger, and Keir fell to his knees as pain exploded behind his temples. He clutched the sides of his head, as Karalyn battered the barriers Daimon had erected in his mind. She was rebuffed again, but his sister's powers broke through on the third attempt, and Keir felt his vision and fire abilities blasted from his mind. He collapsed to the floor of the tent, the marines staring at him open-mouthed.

'My lord!' cried the captain.

Keir groaned. The pain was lifting, but his powers had gone, removed by his sister. The captain crouched by him, then helped him into a seat.

'It was a trick,' Keir mumbled; 'to lure me out.'

One of the other marines lifted a hand. 'She's here! Sable's here.'

Keir staggered to the side of the tent and peered through one of the slits, as the marines primed the ballista. Outside, Sable had appeared next to Ivy's small tent, a man next to her. Within seconds, the two army soldiers who had been guarding Ivy were cut down by Sable's sword, their bodies falling to the ground.

'Use your powers to stun her, my lord,' said the captain.

Keir stared at him. 'I have no powers. Karalyn's taken them from me.'

The captain blinked, then turned to the marines. 'Loose the ballistae, and send out the snatch squads!'

The ballista recoiled, and a yard-long bolt of steel ripped through the side of the tent, followed by another bolt from a different tent. Sable and the demigod dodged them both, keeping low as the bolts flew over their heads.

'Charge them!' called the marine captain, and one of his team blew on a whistle, sending a harsh note shrieking through the air. Dozens of marines emerged from the shadows around Ivy's tent. They loosed crossbow bolts at Sable, and then launched themselves forwards, wielding battle axes and swords. Sable swung her sword in the midst of the chaos and confusion, and two marines fell. Keir stared at his aunt through the slit in the tent, as another marine dropped to the ground, his neck cleaved. A crossbow bolt whistled past Sable's face, but she was moving at speed, and the black blade of her sword sliced off the arm of a charging marine.

'Get us out of here!' cried the demigod, as he crouched by Ivy's tent.

Sable plunged a hand into a pocket. The air shimmered, and both Sable and her companion vanished. The last of the marines rushed out from the tents, and Keir joined them. Two soldiers and four marines were lying dead, their blood pooling on the ground beneath their bodies. The captain raced to the small tent, and opened the flap. He cursed aloud.

The cage had gone, and with it, Thorn's mother. Keir ran forwards, and stared into the empty tent.

'Shit,' Keir muttered.

'That witch has made us look like fools,' the captain said.

'She had battle-vision, sir,' said one of the marines. 'She was too quick.'

'I don't want to hear any excuses,' the captain said. 'My commanding officer is going to chew our balls off for this.'

'We need nets, sir,' said another marine. 'She's too fast for crossbow bolts.'

'I will inform the Emperor,' said Keir.

The captain glanced at him, a flash of sympathy in his eyes, then Keir turned and strode away.

He walked towards the rear of the artillery batteries, keeping out of the way of the swinging trebuchet arms, as soldiers kept up the bombardment of the vineyard ridge. He noticed Daimon talking to an artillery officer, then Keir saw the Emperor close by, his hands clutched behind his back as he watched more boulders being hurled towards the summit of the hill.

Keir swallowed, then approached the Emperor.

'Your Majesty,' he said, his gaze lowered.

Bryce turned to him. At first, the Emperor was smiling, then he perceived the expression on Keir's face, and his eyes narrowed.

'The operation to capture Sable did not succeed, your Majesty,' Keir said. 'She was too fast for the marines, and she took Ivy.'

The Emperor's face transformed into a mask of rage.

'And you?' Bryce spat. 'Did your powers also miss Sable?'

'Keir's powers have been neutralised, your Majesty,' said Daimon, appearing out of the shadows by the rear of the trebuchets.

'How is that possible?' cried Bryce. 'I thought you were protecting his mind?'

'Karalyn distracted him with dragons, and drew out his position,' Daimon said. 'She was too strong for the barriers I had erected, and my entire focus was on guiding the artillery, as you had commanded, your Majesty. There was nothing I could do.'

Bryce pulled the battle axe from his belt. With his left hand, he gripped Keir's throat, and squeezed, pushing Keir down to his knees as the axe hovered over his head.

'You stupid bastard,' Bryce cried. 'I will split your skull open for this failure.'

Keir choked as Bryce tightened his grip on his throat. He raised his hands to try to prise the Emperor's fingers from his neck, his eyes never leaving the blade of the battle axe held inches from his face. Around them, dozens of soldiers were watching in silence as the trebuchets continued to loose.

'Your Majesty,' said Daimon. 'Please. Not in front of the soldiers.'

Bryce removed his hand from Keir's throat, and spat on the ground in front of him.

'Restore his powers,' said Bryce. 'At once.'

Keir rubbed his throat as he knelt before the Emperor, then Daimon stared into his eyes. The humiliation that had been burning through Keir like a wild fire evaporated, replaced by a deep desire to gain revenge over Karalyn, Sable and the accursed dragons who had conspired to make him look like a fool.

Daimon broke off eye contact with him. 'I have done what I can, your Majesty,' he said, 'but it will be hours before his powers will return. His sister did a thorough job. Keir will be of no further use to us for the rest of the battle.'

'He has been no use to us so far!' the Emperor cried. 'Get out of my sight, Keir. Go and cower in your tent while the rest of us do what needs to be done.'

Keir struggled to his feet, his eyes lowered, then he turned from the Emperor, and began trudging away in the direction of his tent.

A cry from the soldiers around the nearest trebuchet made him stop. He turned again, and glanced around. In the light coming from dozens of camp fires, three shadows were flickering in the sky above them.

'Dragons!' a soldier screamed. 'The dragons are coming!'

CHAPTER 22
GOD OF FIRE AND DEATH

Northern Plateau – 14th Day, First Third Winter 534

'Here they come again!' a Banner lieutenant cried. 'Eyes on the road.'

Belinda peered through a hole in the huge roadblock that had been constructed. It spanned thirty yards, bridging the shallow gap that ran through the middle of the ridge. Along the road ahead of them, imperial soldiers were moving at speed, their shields held up. They stepped over the bodies of those slain in previous charges, and formed up into thick lines.

'Wait until they close!' the Banner lieutenant shouted.

Belinda tested her powers, but they were being blocked by Daimon, and all she could feel was her self-healing and battle-vision. She crouched behind the thick beams of the barricade, watching as the imperial troops prepared to charge. At that moment, a flash of light illuminated the sky above them, and all eyes gazed up. Three dragons were flying overhead, wheeling and circling. A lightning bolt lashed out, but the dragons were already scattering, and the blast impacted against the side of the hill to Belinda's right. The stumps of several vines burst into flames, and the masses of imperial soldiers swarming over the terraces were lit up. Some groups seemed to have stopped, while others were wandering across the second terrace, looking for a way up. Other units had already reached the fourth level of terraces, and had become isolated from the rest of the imperial army.

'Look at them,' cried a Banner soldier. 'They don't know what they're doing. One hard counter-attack, and we could push them off the hill, sir.'

'Keep your damn eyes on the road, Private,' the lieutenant shouted.

All along the line of the barricade, rows of Banner soldiers were aiming their crossbows at the wall of shields marching up the road towards them.

'Loose!' yelled the lieutenant, and dozens of bolts whipped out from the barricade, slamming into the advancing imperial troops. Most bolts thudded into shields, but a few troopers were hit, their cries echoing up into the dark sky as they fell. More bolts spat out from the barricade, picking off exposed troops as gaps appeared in their lines, but the line of shields was getting ever closer to the Banner positions. A Banner soldier went down, a crossbow bolt embedded into his right eye, but the others continued loosing their bows into the approaching shieldwall.

'Ma'am,' said the lieutenant.

Belinda glanced at him. 'Yes?'

'Those imperials are going to reach the barricade in under a minute, ma'am. It might be time.'

'Time for what?'

'Time for you to make a difference in this battle, ma'am.'

Belinda stared at him for a long moment, then nodded. She glanced down at the sword buckled to her waist, drew it from its scabbard, then took a few paces back from the barricade.

'The Ascendant's going in,' the lieutenant shouted. 'Watch where you aim.'

Belinda sprang forward at a sprint, her sword gripped in her right hand. Her heavy steel armour was weighing her down, so she powered her battle-vision, and her pace exploded. She vaulted the barricade, her boots briefly touching the top of the wooden beams, then landed on the road. A crossbow bolt loosed by the imperials deflected off her breastplate, then she charged into the shieldwall. She kicked down a shield in her way, and lashed out with her sword, slicing through the neck of an imperial soldier. Most were Kellach Brigdomin, but she knew they were no faster or stronger than the countless greenhides she had slain in the City of Pella. Her battle-vision sang, her strength and speed unmatched by any mortal who had ever lived. It was like a dance, she thought, as another soldier fell to her sword. A dance of death. Part of her conscious mind retreated as her powers took over. The soldiers were surrounding her, but that only made them easier to reach, and every one that came into her range was cut down in a flash of steel. She felt a crossbow bolt slam into her left side, but she ignored the pain; it was nothing to an Ascendant. A huge Kellach soldier wrapped his arms round her from behind, and she touched his exposed skin with a finger. He screamed in agony, then his head disintegrated, spattering Belinda and the closest soldiers in blood and gore. A sword blade nicked off her helmet, and she drove her own weapon into the face of the soldier opposing her. She remembered back to the Banner soldiers that she and Corthie had slaughtered on the streets of the Falls of Iron. She had always been slightly in awe of Corthie's powers, but now, at last, she knew she was his equal – no, she knew she was better. She was the Third Ascendant, the Goddess of Fire and Death. Unstoppable.

She pulled her sword from the chest of a Kellach soldier, then glanced around for more to kill. She blinked. Aside from the several dozen bodies littering the ground, the road was empty. She gazed into the distance, and saw that the imperial soldiers had retreated from her, and she laughed, feeling more alive than she had done for a long while. Behind her, she became aware of cheers. The Banner soldiers guarding the barricade were shouting her name, calling out in praise and awe at what she had done.

She wondered why they were cheering. She had barely begun. She strode back to the barricade, and squeezed between the thick beams to rejoin the Banner soldiers of the First Division.

'How was that?' she said to the lieutenant.

'That'll do nicely, ma'am.'

One of the other soldiers pointed into the sky. 'The dragons are back!'

Belinda looked up, and saw three shadows in the darkness above them, their wings lit up by the glow of the fires all over the imperial camp. She felt a pressure in her mind.

Karalyn? Is that you?

Aye. Listen. Ivy has been rescued, and Keir's powers have been blocked. In a few moments, the dragons will destroy the imperial artillery. As soon as the machines are alight, Thorn is going to order a massive counter-attack down the hillside with all seven divisions.

I thought the Empress wanted us to remain on the defence?

Things have changed. The imperials are disorganised and struggling to climb the slopes in the dark. The sun will be rising soon, but the fires from the artillery will light your way until then. Head straight for Bryce's command tent. Stop for nothing.

Belinda grew annoyed. *Why are you helping us, Karalyn? I thought you didn't care about this conflict?*

I don't, but I cannot allow Bryce's army to reach Colsbury. For my children, I would do anything. If we win today, then the war will be over after a single battle. As far as I can see, that would be the best possible outcome. Will you do it, Belinda? Will you lead the Banner down the hill?

Belinda turned to gaze at the masses of imperial soldiers scrambling along the terraces.

I will.

Karalyn severed the connection to her mind. Belinda turned to the soldiers guarding the barricade.

'Send word to the companies behind us; we're going on the offensive. Start clearing the barricade from the road.'

'Yes, ma'am,' said the lieutenant.

The soldiers cheered again, then got to work. A runner set off towards the reserve lines of Banner soldiers stationed a hundred yards to their rear, while others began pulling beams from the barricade. A huge explosion rose up from the imperial camp as the gap was being created in the barricade, and Belinda turned. Three of the huge trebuchets were on fire, and Belinda watched as a dragon swooped down over the artillery battery, unleashing flames onto the lines of catapults. Another dragon opened its jaws, and two more trebuchets were enveloped in thick flames, lighting up the night sky. At that moment, the reserve columns of Banner soldiers from the First Division appeared on the road behind the barricade. Belinda heard whistles and cries come from the ridges to either side of the road, and a surging wave of Banner soldiers began charging down the uppermost terrace. Isolated pockets of imperial troops had managed to climb that far, and they were cut down in seconds. The Banner soldiers poured like a flood down into the next terrace, sweeping all before them as they picked off disorientated pockets of resistance. The imperial soldiers on the lower terraces could see what was coming. Some held their ground, while others started to retreat. A dragon soared overhead, and sent down a long blast of flames into the imperial troops on the lower terraces. Panic gripped them, and the retreat became a chaotic rout as the troops ran from the slopes to escape the dragons and the charging Banner soldiers.

'The barricade has been cleared, ma'am,' said the lieutenant. 'We are ready to join the counter-attack.'

Belinda turned back to face the enemy ahead of them. Imperial troops were holding their lines a hundred yards from the barricade, sheltering behind their shields as mayhem broke out on the terraces on either side of the road.

Belinda felt for her powers. Daimon was still trying to block them, but his attention was being pulled in a hundred different directions, and his focus had been lost. Belinda slowed her breathing. Daimon could not enter her mind, and he needed all of his strength to prevent Karalyn from blocking his own abilities. Belinda concentrated, then smiled as she felt herself take control of her powers again. She raised her right hand.

'Should we charge, ma'am?' said the lieutenant.

'Wait for my signal,' said Belinda, then she unleashed all that she had upon the imperial troops blocking the road. Death powers surged from her fingertips like the swell of the ocean, and a thousand voices rose up in agony, their screams rippling across the valley between the two slopes. The imperial soldiers on the road fell like cut wheat, blood dripping from their ears, nostrils and eye sockets.

Belinda lowered her hand amid an awed hush from the Banner soldiers.

'Praise the Ascendant!' cried the lieutenant, and the hush turned into another roaring cheer.

Belinda raised her hand again, but this time she was clutching her sword. 'Charge!'

The soldiers of the First Division streamed through the gap in the barricade, with Belinda at their head. They leapt over the heaped bodies of those slain by Belinda's powers, and rushed into the backs of the retreating imperial units, cutting the troops down until every imperial soldier left on the road was fleeing for their lives. Belinda's blade sang again, her right arm rising and falling until her sword was notched and useless. She picked up a heavy mace from a slain Kellach soldier, and battered her way towards the massive command tent.

'To Bryce!' Belinda cried.

She reached the ditch marking the edge of the camp and vaulted over it, as the Banner soldiers scrambled to keep up with her.

The sun appeared on the eastern horizon, flooding the terraced slopes with light, and making clear the scale of the catastrophe that had overtaken Bryce's army. Everywhere Belinda looked, imperial soldiers were either lying dead, or were in headlong retreat, their shields and weapons cast to the blood-soaked ground. Columns of them were streaming away from the camp towards the south, where the fertile fields of the northern Plateau lay, while Banner forces were in control of the entire hillside, and were rushing down from the terraces. Belinda noticed an area of the camp where resistance was stronger. It was the Imperial Marines, she realised. They had formed together into thick, close ranks, and were still fighting as they staged a disciplined retreat from the battlefield. Somewhere in their midst, Belinda guessed, the false Emperor would be taking shelter, hoping that his elite forces would be able to extricate him from the disaster that had befallen his army.

The lead units of the First Division ran into the baggage and wagons of the huge supply train, and hundreds of imperial soldiers threw down their weapons and raised their hands into the air.

'Secure the baggage,' Belinda cried.

'Shouldn't we leave it and pursue the retreating enemy, ma'am?' asked the closest officer.

'No. Let them go,' said Belinda. 'The Empress sees no worth in massacring them. Let them run.'

Belinda paused for a moment as the Banner soldiers carried out her orders. Hundreds of surrendering imperial troops were herded together, a number that soon became thousands, as Banner soldiers sealed off the camp. Belinda took an offered water skin and drank deep, then she glanced at the location of the marines, some three hundred yards to her right. They were maintaining their discipline, while under severe pressure from the Banner soldiers of the Second and Third Divisions; and were edging their way south one step at a time. The false Emperor was going to get away, and there was nothing Belinda could do about it.

The air shimmered, and Sable appeared by her side, a dark-bladed sword in her right hand.

'Where's Austin?' Belinda said. 'I thought he was with you?'

'I left him in Colsbury,' Sable said. 'He's not much use in a straight fight without his flow powers, and I would rather he didn't get his head chopped off on my account. No, what I need right now is a powerful warrior with battle-vision to match my own.' She smiled. 'Any suggestions?'

'I assume you are referring to me?'

'You assume correctly.' Sable pointed towards the mass of marines retreating from the camp. They had passed the burning trebuchets and catapults, and were close to the main road that led back to Plateau City.

'Bryce and Daimon are in there,' Sable said. 'Shall we put an end to this war, you and I?'

'Do you have a plan?'

'Well, it's not much of a plan. We'll use the Quadrant to appear right in the middle of the marines, then you can hold them off while I kill Bryce and his pet dream mage. Or, we could do it the other way round. I'm flexible.'

'We'll try your first suggestion,' Belinda said. 'You can have the glory of slaying Bryce and Daimon.'

'Alright, although the glory will be shared between us. Are you ready? Are you going to use that mace?'

Belinda nodded. 'All weapons are inferior to the Weathervane. The mace will suffice.'

Sable held out her hand. 'Try this – it's a Fated Blade.'

Belinda smiled. 'Are you sure?'

'Yes. You'll need it if you're going to carve up the marines. I'll take the mace.'

They swapped weapons, then Sable nodded, and placed a hand into her pocket. The air shimmered, and chaos erupted around them as they appeared in the midst of the thick ranks of marines. Belinda swung her arm, and the black metal of the Fated Blade sliced through the steel armour of the marine in front of her as if it were paper. Within seconds, Belinda and Sable had carved out a space for themselves amid the marines.

'I see Bryce!' Sable cried. 'Follow me.'

The noise was deafening as Belinda cut her way through the marines, remaining alongside Sable as they charged towards the false Emperor. Sable's movements were fluid, almost perfect, and Belinda felt her respect for the Holdfast woman grow with every step they took. She was much smaller than Corthie, and her reach was less than Belinda's; but she moved with a grace unparalleled by either. It was beautiful to watch, and some of the marines seemed bewitched by her, their eyes wide as she delivered death to all in her path. Sable burst through a ring of marines, and came face to face with Bryce, Daimon and Keir. The dream mage screamed in terror as Sable launched herself at them. From out of nowhere, a large net was hurled out from the ranks of marines, and it enmeshed Sable as she was leaping towards Bryce. Someone pulled on a rope, and Sable came crashing to the ground, her limbs tangled in the thick cords of the net. Marines were on her in a flash, their fists striking down, and their boots kicking.

'The Quadrant!' cried Bryce. 'Bring me her Quadrant!'

Belinda ratcheted up her battle-vision and let her instincts take over as she cut her way towards Sable, the Fated Blade feeling like an extension of her arm. On the other side of the formation of marines, Banner soldiers from the Third Division had broken through, and their weight of numbers was causing the marines' lines to buckle and bend. Belinda ignored what was going on around her, her sole thought on saving Sable. She reached the press of marines around the Holdfast woman, and lashed out with the black-bladed sword. Blood was drenching her face and armour, and sweat was getting into her eyes, but she pushed herself to new limits, killing all that stood between her and Sable. A marine lifted something into the air, and threw it towards Daimon, just before Belinda sliced through his arm.

Daimon caught the object, swept his fingers over its surface, then he, Bryce and Keir vanished. The moment Bryce had gone, there was a hushed silence, then the marines threw down their weapons and raised their hands into the air.

'It's over!' cried a marine officer, tossing his sword to the bloody earth. 'The Emperor has abandoned us.'

Belinda pushed her way through the surrendering marines, and crouched by Sable's body. She pulled the net from her and threw it to the side. Blood was covering Sable's face, but she was still breathing. Belinda clasped her hands on to Sable's head, and flooded the woman with healing powers. Sable choked, and blood spilled from her mouth, as the gathered marines watched. Banner soldiers from the Third Division were approaching, shoving the surrendered marines into groups, and a squad reached Belinda's position. They formed up around Belinda and Sable and cleared the area, as more Banner soldiers poured in from the north.

'The battle's over,' Belinda said.

Sable opened her eyes. 'Did we win?'

'Bryce and Daimon got away,' Belinda said. 'They took Keir with them.'

Sable reached for her pocket, but it was ripped, and her eyes closed again.

'My Quadrant – it's gone.'

'I know,' said Belinda.

'The bastards got me with a net,' Sable mumbled. 'They could have killed me. Why didn't they?'

Belinda glanced up. She saw a Banner sergeant, and gestured for him to approach.

'Bring me one of the marines who was here,' she said. 'I want to question him.'

'Yes, ma'am,' said the sergeant, then he disappeared into the crowds that were surrounding them.

Sable sat up, and glanced down at her torn clothes. A few moments later, the sergeant emerged from the crowd, a tall Kellach marine following him.

'This one says he was here, ma'am,' said the sergeant.

Belinda and Sable glanced up at the marine.

'What were your orders regarding Sable?' Belinda said.

'We were to restrain her, ma'am,' said the marine; 'then remove her eye-guards and hand her and the Quadrant over to Daimon.'

Sable lifted her fingers to her eyes, and cursed. 'The eye-guards have gone, too.'

'Why did Daimon want her alive?' said Belinda.

'I don't know, ma'am.'

Belinda nodded to the Banner sergeant. 'Take this marine back to where the other prisoners are being held.'

The sergeant saluted, then escorted the marine back through the crowd.

A shadow flickered overhead, then Belinda noticed that a large space in the imperial camp was being cleared of soldiers. She glanced up, and saw the three dragons. Frostback landed first, followed by Halfclaw, then Ashfall descended to the ground, the three dragons forming a large triangle, with Belinda and Sable at its centre. Belinda extended a hand, and pulled Sable to her feet.

'I saw what you did, god,' said Frostback, her eyes glowing as she stared at Belinda. 'You were able to use your death powers, even though Daimon was here. My rider was very impressed.'

'I wasn't *that* impressed,' said Kelsey, from the silver dragon's shoulders. She unbuckled the harness straps and clambered down to the ground. 'We thought you were dead, Sable. You disappeared beneath a dozen Kellach marines.'

'They wanted me, my eye-guards, and the Quadrant,' said Sable; 'and they got two out of three. Bryce has gone.'

'We saw,' said Frostback. 'Was the battle fought in vain?'

'That depends,' said Belinda. 'We don't know where Bryce and Daimon went. I didn't know that Daimon knew how to use a Quadrant.'

'He was in my head when I went to Plateau City after Bridget died,' said Sable, 'and he read my thoughts.'

Kelsey gave her a crooked smile. 'I feel a little bit better knowing that I wasn't the only numpty who lost her Quadrant.'

Belinda turned back to the silver dragon. 'If Daimon returns, then the war might not yet be over. But, he now has no army; therefore today's battle was not in vain.'

Frostback brought her head closer to Belinda. 'You reek of blood and death, god. Great is the number of mortals who died at your hand this day.'

'Every death was regrettable,' said Belinda, 'but there was no other way to defeat Bryce.'

Sable groaned. 'I've just realised that we're going to have to walk back to Colsbury. I haven't walked that far in many years.'

'Is that your way of asking if I will carry you, witch?' said Frostback.

Sable raised an eyebrow. 'You would carry me? The last time you carried me, you dropped me over a pool of lava.'

The silver dragon's eyes gleamed. 'That was a long time ago, witch. My heart has softened towards you since those days. You are my rider's kin, and she would be upset were I to bite your head off for past misdeeds. There is one more thing we share – you and I have both slain Ascendants. You took the life of Kolai, and I slew Leksandr and Simon.'

Sable raised an eyebrow. 'I thought Kelsey was claiming the credit for those two? That's what she told me.'

'I only claimed half a point for each,' said Kelsey, laughing.

Belinda frowned. 'Is it right to make jokes when so many have just died?'

Frostback, Sable and Kelsey turned to her.

'Sometimes,' Sable said, 'laughing is the only thing you can do in the face of so much destruction. Would you rather we wept?'

'You and I differ from these mortal humans, Belinda,' said Frostback; 'but let me turn to the reason we have landed in the camp of our defeated foes. The Empress is coming to greet her champions.'

'When?' said Belinda.

Frostback gazed at her. 'Now.'

The air shimmered, and Karalyn appeared by the forelimbs of Ashfall. Empress Thorn, Daphne Holdfast and Agang Garo were by her side, along with several Sanang guardsmen wearing enamelled armour of dark blue. Thorn was clad in a dress of the same shade of blue, and her slender crown of white gold was upon her brow. A great cheer went up from the masses of Banner soldiers in control of the imperial camp as the Empress's blue and silver standard was unfurled by two of her guardsmen. Thorn smiled at the cheering soldiers, then strode into the centre of the triangle.

'The day is won,' she said, to another roar of noise, 'but the false Emperor has escaped. So, too, has his mage Daimon, and the traitor Keir. Before I speak about that, however, I wish to thank the brave dragons for their help. Without the destruction of the enemy artillery, our forces would have been unable to launch the counter-attack that swept the imperial forces from the vineyards.' She bowed her head towards each dragon in turn. 'Thank you, Frostback, Halfclaw and Ashfall.'

'You are most welcome, Empress,' said Ashfall.

'I also want to thank Lady Belinda and Sable Holdfast. Belinda, for leading the charge that broke into the enemy camp, and Sable for saving my mother from a shameful execution. Daphne, the Commander of the Banner, planned this victory to the last detail, and Kelsey, as always, provided loyal service. I thank you all. An Empress is nothing without the hard work, courage and inspiration of her closest friends.' She turned to the Banner forces. 'Most of all, I want to thank the Banner of the Sapphire Throne. A few days ago, many of you were still on Dragon Eyre, and today you have won a resounding victory over superior numbers. I cannot find the words to describe how I felt when I watched you charge down the hillside towards the enemy; it was a moment that will live with me forever.'

Thorn lowered her gaze. 'However, as I said – the false Emperor and two of his mages have escaped, and our situation is more perilous than many here might imagine. Karalyn, to whom I also owe my thanks, was watching as Daimon triggered the Quadrant. She has informed me of their destination.'

Thorn glanced at Karalyn. 'Please tell them where Bryce, Daimon and Keir have gone.'

Karalyn raised her eyes. 'They have gone to Implacatus.'

An awful silence fell over the imperial camp.

'Why?' said Belinda. 'Do you know why they went there?'

Karalyn nodded. 'They mean to betray us all to Edmond. Not just this world, but the world of the City of Salve. Daimon knows the locations of both, and how to reach them with a Quadrant. I looked into Bryce's mind while Daimon was distracted. Bridget's son is not the same man we used to know and respect. His thoughts have been twisted beyond recognition by Daimon, and he would do anything to become the sole ruler of this world, even sell himself to the Ascendants.'

'We have to warn Emily,' said Kelsey. 'The City will be in danger.'

'I will take care of that,' said Karalyn.

Belinda frowned. 'Do you mean to fight this time, Karalyn, or will you remain secluded within Colsbury, hiding from the troubles of the world?'

'I did not wish to become involved in a civil war between the peoples of the Star Continent,' Karalyn said. 'I have never claimed otherwise; but this is different. The Ascendants have the means to destroy us all, and I will not stand by and allow that to happen. I saw their power on Cumulus. Edmond is the mightiest god to have ever lived, but he can be beaten, even if Daimon decides to serve him.'

Karalyn locked gazes with the Third Ascendant. 'Aye, Belinda; I will fight.'

CHAPTER 23
HARD DONE BY

Tara, Auldan, The City – 6th Darian 3423

Aila walked into the small dining room, and bowed her head in front of the King and Queen of the City.

Emily glanced up at her. 'Good evening, Lady Aila; thank you for joining us.'

'Thank you for the invitation,' said Aila.

'You are our guest here,' said Daniel. 'Please, take a seat.'

A courtier pulled out a chair for Aila at the dining table, and she sat down, with Emily to her left and Daniel to her right. A waiter entered the room and began to pour white wine from a bottle, filling three tall glasses.

'Thank you,' said Emily, and the waiter bowed low.

'Our food should be arriving soon,' said Daniel, as the courtier and waiter left the room. He picked up his glass and took a sip. 'Lovely. The City may be suffering from untold shortages, but at least the supply of wine remains excellent.'

Emily sighed. 'Must we discuss shortages, darling? It's all I think about during the day, and I need a moment to relax.'

Aila tried to smile. She quite liked the Aurelian monarchs of the City, but she didn't know them very well, and felt a little awkward in their presence. For four days, she had been lingering around Princeps Row, unsure of what to do except wait for someone to arrive from the Star Continent to take her home.

'The supplies that Kelsey brought must have helped,' she said.

'The forty per cent?' said Emily. 'That sufficed to repair a few of the boats in the fishing fleet, and has postponed the date upon which the City will start to starve, but it was hardly enough to calm my anxieties. And now that Kelsey's Quadrant has been stolen, the future of the salve deal we agreed is in serious doubt. Jade will not be happy when she learns that Naxor has absconded. I'm not happy, for that matter. The challenges we are facing seem insurmountable.'

'I thought you didn't wish to discuss the shortages,' said Daniel.

'I don't,' said Emily. 'Let's change the subject before I lose my appetite completely. I wanted to talk about Kagan and Maxwell. I was thinking of asking them to come and live with us on Princeps Row. I worry about that man, stuck out there in the countryside with a baby demigod to care for on his own.'

'I have no objections to asking him,' said Daniel, 'but I doubt he will agree. To be frank, I don't think he likes us very much.'

'But he should have people around him who can help,' said Emily. 'If not here, then perhaps he could live in Tonetti Palace with Lydia and Doria? Maxwell has a long future ahead of him, and poor Kagan needs support.' She glanced at Aila. 'What do you think? Your situation has parallels with Kagan's. At the moment, Corthie will also be on his own in a remote location, looking after two young demigods.'

Aila swallowed. 'Yes. In his case, I hope that I will be back with him soon. If, for some reason, I was stuck here forever, I would want him to move back to Colsbury to be around his family; but he's stubborn. We also have two families of tenants living on the farm who can help him. I think he'd want to stay where he is. Kell is also a little more remote than the Roser countryside. It takes months to travel there from Colsbury, not hours.'

'Quite true,' said Emily. 'Having lived in the City all my life, I can forget how big other worlds can be. Months? I can barely imagine such distances. The Circuit seems far away, never mind the Eastern Mountains.' She sighed again. 'The City is so small; a tiny beacon of civilisation amid an ocean of sun, ice and greenhides.'

'I remember being overwhelmed by the size of Khatanax on Lostwell,' said Aila, 'and that was small compared to the Star Continent. The distance between Tara and the salve mine is the same as the distance between Colsbury and the Imperial Capital, and they appear next to each other on a map of the Star Continent. Even Kell seems huge to me. Our hundred-and-eighty-acre farm is tiny there, but in the City it would make us major landowners to rank alongside any Roser aristocrat.'

Emily nodded. 'In my darkest moments, when I feel that the City has no future, I start to imagine what it would be like to transfer the entire population to the Star Continent. Kelsey told me that the power of the Sextant could do this. She also said that there are large areas of the Star Continent that are under-populated. At a stroke, most of the problems associated with living here would disappear. Of course, we would have new challenges, but there would be no more greenhides sitting at our walls, and no more agonising over the lack of space. Every inch of the City has to be accounted for; every tree, every cistern. It's a constant struggle to survive.'

Daniel frowned. 'You have never talked about this idea before.'

'It is a counsel of despair, darling,' said Emily; 'not a serious proposition. Please don't mention it to your mother. She would advise removing the Evaders to Kell immediately, and many would support her.'

'How many people live in Kell?' said Daniel.

Aila shrugged. 'Um, about twenty thousand, or thereabouts.'

'Is that all?' said Emily.

'Yes. There are a lot more in Domm; but if the people of the City had to flee in a hurry, then I would suggest the Plateau rather than Kell. Under a million people live on the Plateau, and it's an enormous area. The weather is also better than Kell. The people wouldn't thank you for sending them to a place where it rains nearly every day. You could build a new city by the shores of the Inner Sea, and the rest of the Star Continent would barely notice.'

Aila watched as Emily and Daniel shared a glance, and wondered if she should have kept her mouth shut.

The door to the dining room opened, and a waiter walked in, pushing a trolley.

'Ah, dinner,' said Daniel.

The waiter placed plates and covered dishes on to the table in front of the King, Queen and Aila, then bowed and departed, taking the trolley with him. Emily lifted the lid from a dish, and a slight grimace crossed her features. Aila gazed at the food laid out before her. The bread was a greenish colour, having been padded out with seaweed, and there was no meat on offer. A thin soup sat in a deep bowl, it too flavoured by seaweed.

'This is what we used to eat in the Circuit,' Aila said.

'Everyone eats it now,' said Daniel. 'The land of the Scythes is barely able to feed the population of the Bulwark, leaving little for Medio and Auldan; and we still have to send food to Jezra. Our gravest danger will be getting through this coming Freshmist. Once summer comes, every spare piece of ground in the City will be used to grow food, but there are still many months before that can happen.'

'We shall be lucky if only a few thousand die of starvation by then,' said Emily. 'Families are already going without, and we're only halfway through winter.'

'Are things really so desperate?' said Aila.

'Simon disrupted everything,' Daniel said; 'and we were still suffering from the effects of the greenhide invasion when he arrived. The salve trade was our biggest hope.'

'I will speak to Empress Thorn when I return,' Aila said. 'If she knew this, then I'm sure she would be willing to send more assistance.'

'Would she?' said Emily. 'She is in the middle of a war, and she showed no sympathy for our plight when she reduced the amount of supplies that Kelsey brought us. At the moment, I am none too impressed with Empress Thorn. So far, we appear to have lost more than we have gained from our agreement with the Star Continent. Frostback and Halfclaw have gone, which has ended our hopes of safely developing Jezra. Kelsey has also gone, along with Captain Cardova, Caelius Logos and, yes, even Naxor. Amalia, too, was enticed away, and she paid for her decision with her life. Next, they'll be wanting Van.'

Aila said nothing, remembering the potential deal that Kelsey had mentioned about swapping Van for Naxor. Seen from Emily's position, Aila could understand how unfair the situation seemed. She would have to intervene when she returned to the Star Continent. She still considered the City as her true home, and she had vague plans to settle there again with her children after... after Corthie's time was over. She couldn't do nothing if the City was dying; she had to help.

'I will do what I can,' she said. 'The Holdfasts are reasonable people – well, most of them are. I will make them help you.'

'And what would they demand in return?' said Emily. 'Our obeisance? Would we have to bow before them as our new overlords; or send our youngest and best to fill the ranks of their army?' She shook her head, her eyes dark. 'You know, if it came to the very survival of the City, I would do it. I would kneel before the Empress to save the people of this world.'

'Let us hope it never comes to that,' said Daniel.

Two hours later, Aila was sitting by the sunward-facing window of her room in the Aurelian mansion. She had looked over the books in the small library, but she had read every one, some several times over. She had been hoping to find something to distract her from thinking about Corthie, Killop and Konna. Her family was never far from her thoughts, and it felt longer than four days since she had last seen them. She gazed out of the window at the ruins of Maeladh Palace. Would it ever be rebuilt? How could the City justify the cost when so many were going hungry? Under the old regime of Prince Michael, Aila imagined that work would have already begun to repair the enormous building, but the Aurelian monarchy did things differently. The stone and timber brought over by Kelsey had been distributed to those who needed it the most, rather than expended on ostentatious building projects that benefitted no one but the gods. It was what Yendra would have wanted, and even though the princess was dead, her legacy lived on.

Aila thought she noticed a crackle of lightning in the sky, which was a strange thing to see in winter, then she heard shouts coming from the street outside. She glanced down, but the thick hedgerows and lines of trees were blocking her view of Princeps Row. It was probably nothing, she thought, and turned back to gaze at the purple swirls in the sky.

A few minutes later, there was a knock at her door. Aila got up from her chair and walked to the entrance. She opened the door, and saw a palace courtier in the hallway outside.

'Lady Aila,' he said, bowing; 'their Royal Majesties request that you please come downstairs. It appears that someone has arrived from the Star Continent.'

Aila grinned before she could stop herself, and hurried from her room. She bounded down the stairs to the ground floor, and almost ran into King Daniel as he emerged from a doorway.

'Ah, there you are, Lady Aila,' he said. 'Have you seen who has just arrived?'

'I heard a noise from the window,' she said, 'but couldn't see anyone. Is it Sable?'

'Come and see for yourself; I am about to go out to greet them.'

Them? Aila thought, her eyes narrowing. She followed the King towards the front of the mansion, where two burly Banner soldiers opened the main doors. The air was cold outside, and a light frost was developing across the driveway leading to Princeps Row. More soldiers had gathered by the roadside, while Van and a few officers were approaching from the Banner headquarters a few buildings along.

Aila and the King stepped on to the road, flanked by courtiers. In the middle of the street was a small mountain of sacks and crates that reached as high as the level of the upper floors of the Aurelian mansion, and, at its base, stood Karalyn and her two eight-year-old children. The twins looked tired, and Cael was yawning.

'Miss Holdfast,' said the King; 'welcome back to the City.'

Karalyn nodded, then she glanced at Aila. 'I thought I might see you here.'

'I presume you have come to return Lady Aila to her family?' said King Daniel.

'No,' Karalyn said. 'We need to speak. Where is the Queen? She needs to hear what I have to say.'

'Wait,' said Aila. 'You mean you're not here to transport me to Kell?'

Karalyn shook her head. 'You also need to hear what's happened.'

'We can go inside and find a quiet room where we can sit and talk,' said King Daniel. 'Before we do so, might I ask about these sacks and crates? Are they part of the salve deal?'

'They're a gift from Thorn,' said Karalyn. 'Food and weapons.'

The King blinked. 'I am grateful for the gift of food, but the mention of weapons concerns me. Why would we need weapons, Miss Holdfast?'

Karalyn seemed irritated. 'That's what I want to tell you about.'

'I shall remain out here, your Majesty,' said Van, 'and start moving everything over to the Banner headquarters.'

King Daniel nodded. 'Very well.' He eyed Karalyn. 'Come with me, Miss Holdfast. We shall summon the Queen from her bed, and find that quiet room I was talking about.'

He turned and strode back towards the mansion.

'How's Corthie?' Aila said, as she, Karalyn and the twins followed the King.

'I don't know,' said Karalyn. 'I haven't been down to Kell recently.'

'You didn't come here for me, did you?'

'No, although I had a feeling that Naxor might have brought you to the City. Kelsey told me what happened to her Quadrant.'

'Before you ask, I have no idea where Naxor went.'

'I don't care about Naxor,' Karalyn said.

'Are you not concerned that he might have gone to Implacatus?'

Karalyn gave her a wry smile, but said nothing. They entered the mansion, and a courtier rushed away to find the Queen. The King led Aila and Karalyn to a small study, and the Holdfast woman sat down on a couch with her two children.

'I'll need somewhere for the twins to sleep,' she said.

'Are you staying?' said the King, still standing.

'Aye.'

'For how long?'

'I don't know; as long as it takes.'

'I would quite like to see my children,' said Aila.

'Sorry,' said Karalyn, 'but you'll have to wait.'

'Why? It would only take you a few minutes to deliver me to Kell.'

'I can't afford to leave the City for that long. Besides, you have powers that might prove useful.'

'But...'

'Please keep your questions for when the Queen gets here,' Karalyn said, 'so I can avoid repeating myself.'

Aila folded her arms across her chest, growing more annoyed with Karalyn's attitude with every passing moment. The King walked to the door and opened it, then he spoke to one of the courtiers stationed outside. He glanced back at Karalyn.

'A bedroom is available for the twins, Miss Holdfast,' the King said. 'Do you wish them to go now?'

'Aye,' said Karalyn. She stood, then took each twin by the hand. 'Go with the courtier, children, and I will come and see you soon. Sweet dreams.'

The twins went to the door, and the courtier led them away. A moment later, the door opened again, and Emily appeared, wearing a long dressing gown.

She glanced at Karalyn. 'I presume this is urgent?'

'Aye,' said Karalyn. 'You should all sit for this.'

The King and Queen shared a glance, then they sat on the couch. Aila joined them, her eyes narrow as she waited to hear what the Holdfast woman was going to say.

'Two days ago,' Karalyn said, 'there was a battle on the Star Continent, twenty miles south of Colsbury. Bryce brought almost a hundred thousand imperial soldiers, while Thorn had seventy thousand from the new Banner army fighting for her. Despite his superior numbers, Bryce was heavily defeated.'

'Is the war over already?' said Aila.

'The first part of the war is over; the second is about to begin. At the end of the battle, Sable and Belinda attempted to kill Bryce and his dream mage Daimon. They failed. Daimon took Sable's Quadrant and fled with Bryce and Keir. They have left the Star Continent.'

'How did Daimon know how to use a Quadrant?' said Emily.

'He read Sable's mind,' said Karalyn. 'Sable, as you know, had knowledge of how to get to several worlds – this one, the Star Continent, and Implacatus. Daimon now shares that knowledge. In the moments before they fled, I was able to penetrate Bryce's mind. I was unable to incapacitate him, as Daimon has wound many layers of protection over his consciousness, but I was able to see his plans. He and Daimon had devised a scheme – one that they would use only in the direst emergency. They decided that, if all else failed, they would travel to Implacatus and, once there, they would betray our worlds to the Ascendants. In return for help in regaining the throne of the Star Continent, Bryce is prepared to sell the Sextant and the location of this City to Edmond.'

Emily gasped. 'No.'

'I am here to warn you; to warn the City that the Ascendants are coming.'

'Are we absolutely sure about this?' said Daniel. 'Do we know for a fact that they went to Implacatus? Regardless of their previous plans, they might have decided to hide in a remote corner of the Star Continent.'

'What you say is true,' Karalyn said. 'We don't know for certain that they are on Implacatus. I was only in Bryce's mind for a brief moment. They also took Keir with them, but they hadn't told him of their plan. This was a secret kept between Bryce and Daimon alone. Perhaps their courage failed them at the last moment, and they decided not to go to Implacatus. Perhaps they are hiding in a cave in the southern regions of Rahain. I don't have all the answers. However, I judge it likely that they will betray us. Bryce was terrified when I read his thoughts, as Sable was inches away from ending his life. At that precise moment in time, all Bryce wanted to do was flee, and his plan flashed before his eyes. You can ignore my warning if you wish, but I believe you need to take it seriously. As a gesture of unity, the Empress has sent thirty tons of grain and hundreds of weapons – crossbows, bolts, swords, and so on. It is a gift.'

'Thirty tons of grain?' said Emily.

'Aye.'

'That's very generous, but how is it supposed to protect the City from the Ascendants?'

'It's not. I am.'

'I'm sorry?' said Daniel.

'What's so difficult to understand?' said Karalyn. 'I promised you that I would come here in person to defend the City if it was ever threatened by Implacatus. Did you think I would forget my own words?'

The King and Queen stared at her.

'If the Ascendants come, then I will be waiting for them,' said Karalyn. 'The Star Continent has Sable, Belinda, Kelsey and the dragons; not to mention Corthie – the greatest mortal warrior of all time. Who do you have? I'll be honest with you; my mother didn't want me to come here. She felt it would be better if I stayed in Colsbury, to defend my own world. But, I gave you my word. There have been moments over the last two days when I have regretted making my promise to you, but that doesn't change the fact that I did.'

'I don't know what to say,' said Emily. 'Thank you.'

'We shall summon the commanders of the Blades, Banner and Brigades here tomorrow morning for a grand council,' said Daniel. 'We must start our preparations in earnest. Whatever you need, Miss Holdfast, will be put at your disposal.'

Karalyn nodded. 'The grand council is a good idea, but right now, I need to go to the Eastern Mountains to fetch Jade and Dawnflame.'

'I'll come with you,' said Aila, as she got to her feet. 'Jade can be... difficult, and you have never met her. She can be especially awkward around strangers.'

'Alright.' Karalyn glanced at Daniel and Emily. 'We'll be back soon. You should try to get a good night's sleep.'

Aila blinked, and found herself standing in the little valley where the salve mine was located, Karalyn a yard to her right. The valley was in darkness, with only the purple glow from the skies providing any illumination.

'There are no dragons here,' said Karalyn.

'Dawnflame must be at the colony with the infant dragons,' said Aila. 'She has a young son called Firestone, and she is also looking after Darksky's three children.'

'Do any other dragons live in the colony?'

'Yes – two older dragons. There's Bittersea, who is Dawnflame's mother, and Burntskull.'

'Can either of them fight?'

'They're very old for dragons, so I would guess no.'

Karalyn nodded, and they started walking towards the waterfall and the caves by the narrow end of the valley.

'Come no closer!' shrieked a voice from the shadows. 'If you do, I will rot your brains.'

Aila came to a halt on the grass. 'It's me, Jade. It's your cousin Aila.'

'Oh. Have you brought Naxor for me? That doesn't look like Naxor.'

Jade emerged from the shadows of the trees by the base of the waterfall. She peered through the gloom at Karalyn.

'Who are you, and what are you doing in my valley?'

'I'm Kelsey's sister,' said Karalyn. 'You know Kelsey, don't you?'

'Yes, unfortunately. Hmm, so you are another one of the Holdfasts, eh? What do you want?'

'Your powers, Jade.'

Jade narrowed her eyes.

'The City is under threat,' said Aila. 'Something terrible has happened, and the Ascendants might be coming.'

'So? I managed to defeat one of them. I can do it again.'

'We need you back in the City,' said Karalyn. 'You are the only immortal on this world with the power to resist any invaders.'

'What about the salve?' Jade said. 'I'm supposed to be mining salve out of the side of the mountain.'

'That will have to wait,' said Karalyn. 'Picture the location of the dragon colony in your mind.'

Jade frowned, then shook her head. 'No.'

Karalyn smiled, then Aila jumped as she realised they had moved again. Surrounding them were high cliffs, and a stream was running through the centre of the gorge. In the side of the cliffs to their right were several large cave entrances. From one, an old yellow dragon was watching them.

'How did you do that?' cried Jade. 'Where is your Quadrant?'

'I don't need a Quadrant,' said Karalyn. She turned to the dragon. 'Greetings, Burntskull. Go inside and tell Dawnflame that we are here.'

The yellow dragon's eyes widened, then he disappeared into the darkness of the cavern.

Jade sighed. 'Another mortal witch. I might have guessed. Why are you here? Why do you care about what happens to this world?'

'I made a promise to defend the City from attack,' Karalyn said.

'Do you have death powers?'

'No.'

'Battle-vision?'

'No.'

Jade laughed. 'Then what use could you be against the Ascendants? Can you breathe fire?'

Karalyn smiled.

A noise came from the caves, and three dragons appeared through the gloom.

'Who has disturbed my sleep?' said Dawnflame.

Jade pointed at Karalyn. 'It was her idea. She says more Ascendants are coming.'

'Is that true?' said Dawnflame. She moved her head closer to Karalyn. 'You look like a taller version of that Kelsey insect. Am I to assume that a Holdfast stands before me?'

'I have heard great things about you, Dawnflame,' Karalyn said. 'While most submitted to Simon, you resisted. There is a strong possibility that the Ascendants of Implacatus shall be coming here in force, to finish what Simon started. Are you prepared to fight again?'

'Why should I?' said Dawnflame.

Karalyn stared into the dragon's eyes. 'Because you are brave, strong, and you know it's the right thing to do.'

The dragon said nothing for a moment, then she tilted her head. 'You are correct. I am brave and strong. Yes, I will fight.'

'She has bewitched you, daughter,' cried Bittersea.

'Impossible, mother,' said Dawnflame. 'I am too powerful for any mortal to overcome. You did not answer my other question, stranger. Are you Kelsey's kin?'

'My name is Karalyn Holdfast,' she said. 'Sable is my aunt, and Kelsey is my sister.'

'Can you block the powers of the gods, as Kelsey can?'

'Aye.'

'She can do a lot more than that,' said Aila. 'She can…'

Karalyn glanced at her, and Aila decided it would be better to say nothing else.

'I need you in the City by sunrise tomorrow, Dawnflame,' said Karalyn. 'You can fly, or I can take you there now.'

'Show me your Quadrant, Holdfast.'

'She says she doesn't need one,' said Jade.

'More lies,' said Bittersea. 'This insect is a witch. Do you recall Sable in the Catacombs, daughter? Frostback was right all along. The Holdfasts are unnatural.'

'We've been called worse things,' said Karalyn.

Dawnflame stared at her. 'I shall fly to the City, and meet you in

Tara at sunrise, Holdfast.'

Karalyn nodded. 'Bring Jade.'

Dawnflame tilted her head. 'It shall be so.'

The air wavered, then Aila found herself standing outside the Aurelian mansion on Princeps Row. Karalyn started walking towards the side door, and Aila hurried to keep up.

'That was all you, wasn't it?' Aila said. 'You were in my mind, and Jade's, and you made the dragons do whatever you asked of them.'

'I didn't have the time or patience for a long debate,' Karalyn said.

'What are we going to do now?'

'Now? I'm going to say goodnight to my children.'

They entered the mansion, and walked into the kitchen. Emily was there, still in her dressing gown, and she was filling a glass with water for Cael, who was standing next to her.

'What are you doing out of bed, Cael?' said Karalyn, crouching down next to him.

'He had a nightmare,' said Emily.

'It was about the greenhides,' Cael said. 'I woke up, but you weren't there, mama.'

'You had another dream about the greenhides?'

'Aye,' said the boy. 'I was trying to control them, like I did in the desert; but this time, they weren't listening to me.'

Karalyn brushed a strand of hair from the boy's face. 'It was just a dream.'

'Wait a minute,' said Aila. 'What happened in the desert?'

'Didn't you hear?' said Emily. 'Cael managed to command some greenhides, down by an oasis far to sunward. They were going to attack, but somehow Cael was able to stop them.'

Aila gasped. 'He can control greenhides?'

'Sable can do it, too,' said Karalyn.

'Can she?'

'Aye. She used her powers to terrible effect on Dragon Eyre.'

'And what about you? Can you do it?'

Karalyn smiled. 'I guess we'll find out soon enough.'

CHAPTER 24
THE GREATEST GIFT

Colsbury Castle, Republic of the Holdings – 17th Day, First Third Winter 534

'This is all like a dream,' the old woman said, her eyes gazing at the trees. 'Or as if I have woken up from a long nightmare.' She smiled. 'Woken up to discover that my little girl is the ruler of the world.'

Thorn said nothing as they walked along the path through the gardens of Colsbury castle. It was a beautiful morning, and she felt as though she could listen to her mother speak for hours.

'I have so many questions,' Ivy said. 'Some are about happy things, like how you have managed to rise so high; and some are about sad things – things I can barely believe. The last time I saw you, I had three daughters, and now I have one.' She shook her head, her eyes welling again. 'I had always feared for your life, and Clove's, when I saw you both taken by the Sons of Sanang. I knew that I might have only one daughter left, but I thought it would be Acorn. The Rahain, of course, told me nothing.'

'Were you treated well by Lord Ghorley?'

'Lord Ghorley was dead by the time I reached the great capital city of the Rahain; it was all they talked about. I didn't understand what they were saying at first, but I quickly learned to speak their language.

The words "Lord Protector" and "Ghorley" were among the first I mastered. He had been murdered by one of his own staff, and a woman called Agatha was in charge. She had no need of a healer; she could heal herself. I only saw her once, for a few minutes, and then I was separated from Bluebell. I never saw her again; nor did I ever see the Holdings woman who abducted us all from Rainsby – not until she appeared in front of my little tent a few days ago. I was held by a rich Rahain family, who used me to heal them and their friends. It reminded me of what life had been like when I was a young woman in Sanang. I wasn't allowed to go outside on my own, and I wasn't to speak unless spoken to. But, I wasn't mistreated; at least, not until things fell apart. No one gave me any news of the war, but it was obvious that Rahain was losing. More and more young men and women were being drafted into the army, and even the rich family's two sons were forced to join. Without those boys around to earn money, the rich family quickly became poorer, and they started to charge for my healings. In the end, I was stolen from them, and taken to another underground city, where I healed a thug and his gang of thieves. They weren't as kind as the rich family had been, and I saw them do many terrible things, but they were careful not to kill me. They kept me locked in a small room, and would bring me out whenever the gang had returned from a raid, so that I could fix their broken limbs and close up their crossbow wounds. And so it went on, for years. Rahain is a desolate place now, full of ruined buildings and dark, empty caverns, where the people kill each other for a scrap of food.'

'How did you escape?'

'One day, not very long ago, the thug and his gang were slaughtered by a rival group. They broke into the caverns under Tahrana City where I was being held, and killed everyone. I was stabbed several times, but none of them realised that I was a hedgewitch, and I played dead until they had gone. Then I searched the bodies, and found the key to my shackles. After that, I wandered the underground city, looking for a way out. I wore a long hood, and pretended to be an old Rahain woman, and no one paid me any attention. When I found a gate that led to the open air, I glanced upon the sunlight for the first time in years. I cannot describe the feeling to you; it was beyond anything I could put into words. I began to make my way north, and it was there, on the road to the Great Tunnel, that I heard a man mention your name. He had travelled down from the Plateau, smuggling stolen goods into Rahain, and one night he told me that the Empire was on the verge of a civil war, with the late Empress's son on one side, and a young Sanang pretender to the throne on the other. A pretender by the name of Thorn of Greyfalls Deepen.'

Ivy smiled. 'After that, I hurried towards the Plateau. I had not realised that imperial soldiers were occupying the Great Tunnel, and I was detained by the garrison on the Rahain side, where I was questioned by a mage with vision powers. I have to assume that the mage learned my identity, for I was then escorted to Rainsby and placed on board a ship bound for the imperial capital.'

Thorn nodded. 'Did you speak to Daimon?'

'No. Daimon does not speak Sanangka, nor does he understand the language of Rahain; but I learned who he was, for I spoke to the Emperor himself.' She smiled. 'Sorry; the false Emperor. He seemed nice at first, but then I was put inside a cage and brought along with his army. Did you know that I healed a man who claimed to have been your husband?'

'His name is Keir, and we were married for seven years,' said Thorn. 'We were divorced a few thirds ago. He was unfaithful to me.'

They came to the graveyard in the centre of the gardens, and Thorn led Ivy to where Acorn had been buried. Ivy knelt by the graveside, and laid down the flowers she had brought with her.

'My poor little Acorn,' she said, as tears rolled silently down her face. 'How did she die?'

'She...' Thorn hesitated as her own eyes welled up. 'She died to save me, mother.'

Ivy said nothing.

'We were fighting a battle against Agatha, and she gave her life so that I could live.'

'Acorn was like that,' Ivy said in a low voice. 'She always put others first.'

'I'm sorry, mother.'

'You have nothing to apologise for. Acorn would be very proud of you, my girl. I am very proud of you. Do you remember when we used to make fun of your ambitions? Greyfalls Deepen was always too small to contain your spirit. You saw the Matriarch, and you wanted to be like her. And then you saw Empress Bridget, and I knew at the time what you were thinking. We all did. I am sorry we laughed at you.'

'Don't say that. I left you to suffer. We hunted for you. For four years, I cared for Karalyn's young twins, while vision mages searched the cities of Rahain for any sign of you or Bluebell, but they found nothing. In the end, I gave up all hope. People kept telling me that you had to be dead, and I came to believe it.'

'Empress Thorn,' Ivy said, as if trying out the words. 'Should I be calling you "your Majesty"? What a silly question – of course I should.'

'No,' said Thorn. 'You are my mother. You never have to call me that.' She smiled, despite the tears that she was holding back. 'If Acorn were here, I would insist that she used my correct title. She would have hated that.'

'She would have pretended to have hated it, Thorn, but she loved you deeply. Did you make your peace with Clove before she died?'

Thorn thought back to her last moments with her eldest sister. She pictured the small room where they had been held by the Sons of Sanang, and recalled the smoke as Clove had set fire to the books they had found. Her sister had been determined to end her life before the Sanang warriors could touch her, and she had wanted Thorn to join her in her act of self-immolation. They had done nothing to mend their marred relationship, and Clove had died in the flames.

'Yes.'

'You hesitated for too long, my girl,' Ivy said. 'It's all right. Clove was never as strong as you or Acorn. The hospital in Rainsby nearly drove her mad. She was too gentle to be taken into a place of suffering and death. It was my fault for bringing her along with us. I was so proud of my three hedgewitch girls that I didn't stop to think about how it would affect you. About how it would affect Clove. Lichen was right all along. She remembered what it was like to live through a terrible war, and she tried to warn me.' She glanced at her daughter. 'Do you know if Lichen still lives?'

'I sent word to her after the war,' Thorn said, 'to tell her that Bracken had died, and that you had been taken to Rahain; but I didn't get a response.'

'Haven't you been back to Greyfalls Deepen in all this time?'

'I couldn't, mother. I promised Karalyn that I would look after her two children. She was my sister-in-law; I couldn't refuse. We thought she would only be gone for a few thirds, but four years had passed before she returned. By that time, I had almost convinced myself that the twins were really mine. A letter to Lichen was all I could manage.'

'It was cruel of Sable to have killed her daughter.'

'I know. Murdered for speaking too loudly.'

Ivy frowned. 'That's not what happened. It was Clove who was crying out, not Bracken. Sable killed Bracken because she was the only one among us who wasn't a hedgewitch. She had no use for her.'

Thorn narrowed her eyes. Is that how it had occurred? Her memories of that terrible time had become confused over the years, but the image of Bracken lying dead on a back street of Stretton Sands was imprinted into her mind.

'Tell me,' Ivy went on; 'how did you find yourself forgiving Sable? She killed your best friend, and her actions led to the death of Clove, as well as my long confinement in Rahain. And all those people that the fire mage soldier murdered in Rainsby? She was giving him the orders. How could anyone be forgiven such things?'

'I believe that Sable has changed.'

'She couldn't look me in the eye when she rescued me from Bryce. Her young friend Austin was polite and friendly, but Sable couldn't bring herself to utter a single word to me. She took me here, to Colsbury, and left without saying anything. It was Austin who made sure that I was comfortable, and that I was given food and something to drink. He's a nice boy. Do you know him?'

'A little.'

'And what happened to the beast of Rainsby? The fire mage? Is he dead?'

'Yes.'

'Are you sure?'

'I'm sure. His name was Lennox and he fathered Karalyn's twins.'

Ivy's face darkened. 'You cared for that murderer's children?'

'None of what happened was his fault. Sable forced him to burn down the hospital.'

'Oh, my girl. If such a thing as evil exists in this world, then it has Sable's face. Her pretty smile masks a thousand crimes.'

'She risked her life to save you from Bryce. He was going to have you executed at dawn, in order to hurt me.'

'Does one good deed overturn a hundred bad?'

'I am the Empress. I cannot let my own feelings get in the way of what needs to be done.'

'So, you do have feelings about this?'

'Of course I do, mother. What Sable did fills me with bitterness and disgust. When Karalyn rescued her from Dragon Eyre, I was asked to heal her injuries. Me! I wanted to kill her as soon as I saw her. And yet, the first thing Sable did was apologise for Bracken, and then she apologised for what she did to you. Did I do the right thing by healing her instead of killing her? I don't know, mother. But, I do know that Sable is one of the mightiest warriors on this world, and I need her.'

Ivy glanced back at Acorn's gravestone, her lips sealed.

'Halfclaw will soon be coming to carry me to the vineyards,' Thorn said. 'Do you want to come?'

'You are returning to the battlefield?'

'Yes. The imperial army is due to formally surrender to me this afternoon.'

'I should be surprised that you have grand armies kneeling before you, Thorn; but, somehow, I am not. I think I will remain here. Soon, though, I would like to go back to Greyfalls Deepen, to see if Lichen is still alive.'

'I would like you to stay here with me.'

'Are you commanding me to stay?'

'No.'

'Then I shall go. I promised Lichen I would be back in a year, and I have been gone for ten. I am too old for ceremonies and the splendour of an imperial court. I want my old life back; a simple life. Will you help me return to Greyfalls Deepen?'

'If that is what you want.'

'Thank you, my girl. For now, please leave me in this beautiful garden with Acorn. I wish to sit by her grave.'

Thorn nodded, then turned away, her steps quickening as she struggled to hold back her tears. Pechtang was waiting for her by the edge of the garden, a squad of guardsmen next to him.

'Your Majesty,' he said, bowing his head; 'the blue and green dragon is waiting for you in the forecourt by the Summer Palace.'

Thorn nodded, knowing that any words might set off her tears. The warriors flanked her as they went through the tunnel that ran under the damaged Lesser Keep, then they emerged in the vast forecourt between the palace and the Great Keep. Halfclaw was there, with a harness strapped to his shoulders.

'Empress,' he said, his head tilting to the side.

One of her guardsmen helped Thorn reach for the dangling straps, and she climbed up onto the harness. The dragon extended his wings, and ascended into the air.

'Shall we make straight for the field of battle?' said Halfclaw.

'Yes.'

'Very well. It is a beautiful day for flying, and the air is clean, if a little cold. Tell me; what is upsetting you?'

'How do you know I am upset?'

'It is as clear to me as the sun in the sky, Empress.'

'My mother wants to go back to Sanang,' she said, not sure why she was unburdening herself to the dragon. 'And, she didn't say it, but she hates me for forgiving Sable. She was in chains in Rahain for ten years, while I rose to Empress. She thinks I'm selfish, and she's right. I didn't do enough to search for her. I gave up too soon, and left her to suffer at the hands of savages.'

'You are being too hard on yourself,' said the dragon, as they soared over the still lake. 'You should realise that it is impossible to rule and please everyone at the same time.'

'I don't want to please everyone, but she's my mother.'

'Daphne Holdfast is your mother now; is that not correct? I was told that you had been formally adopted into the Holdfast tribe. We dragons are familiar with such concepts. You have left your old mother behind, and taken a new one.'

Thorn burst into tears. 'What have I done?'

'I remember a situation like yours in the Catacombs,' the dragon said. 'A young dragon lost his father, and was adopted by another. Then, some time later, the young dragon's father re-appeared unexpectedly. He had been wounded, not killed. It made no difference. The young dragon was part of his new kin. He still loved his old father, but his duties were to his new family. There was pain, but there was also joy. You, Empress, are a Holdfast, and yet your old mother has returned. I can feel your pain, but you must not forget to be happy. You have two mothers now, and are loved by both.'

'And what about Sable?'

'The Holdfast witch is a complicated woman. She was your enemy, and now she is not only your friend – she is also your kin. I also despised Sable once. She was responsible for Frostback being exiled from the Catacombs, and I hated her for that.'

'But you don't hate her any more?'

'Life is too short to carry such hatred with you. Other dragons would disagree. Our kin often hold grudges until their dying breath; but I have seen where that leads. The dragons of the Catacombs tore themselves apart over grudges and petty squabbles, and then the dragons that went to the City did the same thing. Deathfang against Frostback; Burntskull against Dawnflame. Darksky alone carried more grudges than any dragon should bear. I want to be different. So, Empress, my answer is no. I do not hate Sable any longer. Let those whose spirits are mired in bitterness carry their grudges. You should free yourself, Empress. Forgiveness is a gift; perhaps the greatest gift of all.'

Thorn glanced down. Through her tears, she saw the terraced slopes of the vineyard appear. Beyond stood the massed ranks of the Banner, and the lines of the defeated imperial forces.

'I will circle for a while,' Halfclaw said, 'so that you have time to compose yourself before we land.'

'Thank you.'

'You are most welcome, Empress.'

Thorn closed her eyes, and the air rushed past her face, drying her tears. She thought about what the dragon had said, and resolved that she would try to be more forgiving. She didn't care if others perceived it as a weakness. She was the mother of the world, and mothers forgave their children.

She took a slow breath, and calmed her features. 'I am ready.'

The dragon tilted his head, then began to descend. Thorn looked at the vast array of soldiers below her. The other two dragons were also there, standing side by side behind a platform that had been erected. The Banner of the Sapphire Throne was arranged by both flanks of the dragons, their armour gleaming in the pale winter sunshine. In front of the platform, the unarmed soldiers of the vanquished imperial army had been formed up into long lines, their officers at the head of each column. They had been separated into their different components, with the cavalry to the left, the army in the centre, and the marines on the right. Thousands upon thousands were gathered on the site of the imperial camp, but Thorn knew how many had died. Over twenty thousand imperial soldiers had lost their lives in the chaotic night battle, and their bodies had been buried under huge mounds of earth that dotted the landscape to the south. Compared to those losses, the casualties sustained by the Banner seemed almost negligible, with under a thousand dying in action along the terraced slopes. Thorn mourned each death. If they were to prevail against the Ascendants, then she needed every soldier that remained on the Star Continent. None could be spared.

Halfclaw circled once more, his altitude lowering as he came down between Frostback and Ashfall. A great roar came up from the ranks of the Banner as they caught sight of their Empress on Halfclaw's shoulders, and she raised an arm in greeting. Opposite the platform, the soldiers and marines of the defeated army were also watching, but they remained silent.

The blue and green dragon landed, and a dozen Sanang guardsmen rushed to his side. Thorn unbuckled the straps of the harness, and climbed down to the ground, as warriors assisted her. Sable pushed through the Sanang, and held out a brush in her hand.

Thorn glanced at it.

Sable smiled. 'Do you want to address two hundred thousand people with your hair looking like that, your Majesty? You should tie it up before riding on a dragon's shoulders.'

Thorn took the brush and began to pull it through her tangled hair.

'I forgive you, Sable,' she said.

The Holdfast woman's eyes narrowed.

'I have had a long talk with my mother,' Thorn went on, 'and I want you to know that I forgive you for what you did to my family.'

'You do?'

'Yes. Halfclaw helped me see the truth. I needed you, but I still harboured many ill feelings towards you. I know how hard you are trying to redeem yourself, and it must be difficult to face those you have grievously wounded. It took courage to apologise, and I want to recognise that.'

'Thank you, your Majesty. I will try to live up to your expectations.'

'You deserve a fresh start, Sable, and I count myself lucky to call you my friend.'

Sable's gaze lowered. 'Even after all the crimes I have committed?'

'What's done is done. You have a reckless streak, Sable, one that might get you killed one day, but no one else came close to killing Bryce and Daimon. More than that, though, you saved my mother, and that more than balances the loss of the Quadrant.' Thorn handed her the brush. 'You should stay here.'

'I know, your Majesty,' said Sable. 'The Banner are not as forgiving as you.'

Thorn walked towards the platform, where Daphne, Belinda and Agang were waiting for her, along with the senior officers from the Banner.

'Your Majesty,' said Agang, bowing low as Thorn stepped up onto the platform. 'The imperial army is ready to submit to your authority. The cavalry shall be first to approach.'

Thorn sat on the throne in the centre of the platform and gazed out at the huge number of soldiers standing on the other side of the camp. On the right, where the cavalry was located, almost every soldier was from the Holdings. In the immediate aftermath of the battle, most of the cavalry had fled south, but they had started to return as soon as word had reached them that Bryce had abandoned the Empire. Their horses and weapons had been confiscated by the Banner forces upon arrival, but most seemed happy that the war was over.

'How many?' Thorn said.

Agang glanced at Daphne.

'Around nine thousand of the imperial cavalry have handed themselves in so far, your Majesty,' Daphne said. 'We estimate that three thousand are still at large on the Plateau. They experienced no losses in the battle barring a few accidents, and remain in good shape.'

'Have them approach.'

Daphne gestured to a Banner officer, and the senior commanders of the cavalry marched forward. They stood in a line before the platform, then each descended to one knee, their heads bowed.

'Your gracious Majesty,' one called out, her voice ringing clear; 'we bid you accept the surrender of the imperial cavalry, and beg that you readmit us into your service. You are the rightful Empress, the true Holder of the World, and it is to you that we pledge our allegiance.'

'Please stand,' Thorn said.

The cavalry officers rose to their feet.

'I accept your surrender, and your pledge of loyalty. The past shall be forgiven. The Banner shall return your mounts and your weapons to you, and you shall remain here, ready to face the next challenge. There shall be no courts martial and no punishments for the service you gave the false Emperor. Return to your positions.'

The cavalry officers bowed low, then strode back to their troopers.

'Summon the army commanders next,' said Thorn.

Daphne nodded. 'Yes, your Majesty.'

A few minutes later, over fifty of the senior officers of the imperial army were kneeling before the Empress. She repeated her words of forgiveness to them, and many stared at her in stunned amazement, as if they could not believe that their lives were to be spared. When they returned to their lines, Thorn asked for the marines. She watched as the commanders of the elite force strode towards her. The overwhelming majority of the marines were from Kellach Brigdomin, and she guessed that many still felt loyalty towards Bryce. Bridget had been a hero to them, their own Empress from Brig, and some saw Thorn as the real usurper. From the looks on their faces it was clear that they expected to be severely punished for their role as Bryce's most loyal force, but they glanced at Thorn with defiance rather than fear.

The Empress remained still as each marine officer fell to one knee before the platform, and a hush descended over the camp.

'Imperial Marines,' she said, after a long moment; 'you know who I am. In the war against Agatha, it was the marines who fought, bled and died alongside me. You spilled your blood in the streets of Rainsby and Stretton Sands, and you will always occupy a place in my deepest affections, regardless of your loyalty towards Lord Bryce. Time may erode all things, but it will never diminish the pride I feel when I look at you. I loved you then, and I love you still. Nothing will ever change that. I bear you no grudge, and there is nothing to forgive. Therefore, I do not command you to pledge your loyalty towards me. If you truly believe Lord Bryce to be the Emperor, then I shall allow you to walk out of this camp unscathed. However, if any of you wish to return to my service, then I will accept you with open arms, as a mother accepts a child who has returned home. Take your time to consider my words. Go back to your companies and squads and talk it over with them; then do as you will.'

The officers continued to kneel for a few more moments, as if unsure what to do. Then one stood, bowed his head towards the Empress, and walked back towards the large mass of marines. The others glanced at each other, then did the same, until the area in front of the platform was empty.

Thorn raised an arm. 'The civil war is over. The war against the Ascendants is about to begin. Only if we stand united shall we be able to save this world from those who wish to destroy us. The Banner of the Sapphire Throne and the Imperial Army are now under my authority. Together, you are the greatest military force this world has ever seen. Tomorrow, all senior officers shall assemble in Colsbury, and we shall decide how to save the things we love.'

'A cheer for the Empress!' cried a Banner major-general from the platform.

The Banner soldiers raised their voices in noisy acclaim then, slowly, the Holdings cavalry troopers did the same, followed by the majority of those from the imperial army, and then, finally, a large portion of the marines joined in. Thorn smiled as the sound echoed off the terraced slopes of the vineyard. She basked in it for a moment, then she arose from the throne, stepped down from the platform and strode towards the dragons.

'Those were gracious words, your Majesty,' said Agang, as he hurried to keep up.

'Perhaps too gracious,' said Daphne. 'I predict that half of the marines will have fled by nightfall.'

'Then we shall let them go,' said Thorn. 'I would rather have one loyal marine than ten half-hearted ones. My Herald, please make arrangements for all senior officers to travel to Colsbury for tomorrow's council of war. It shall take place in the castle forecourt, so that the dragons can attend.'

'My thanks,' said Frostback, her eyes on Thorn. 'I think you were right, my beloved Halfclaw; this woman has the makings of a fine ruler.'

Daphne gave a slight frown, then she bowed before Thorn, and turned back towards the platform. Thorn strode to Halfclaw's side, where she found Sable standing in the same place where she had left her, the brush still in her hand.

'Will you tie my hair back, Sable?' Thorn said.

Sable blinked. 'What? Yes, your Majesty; of course.'

Thorn turned. She felt Sable brush and pull her hair into a ponytail, then she looped a ribbon round to secure it in place.

'I have worked for many rulers,' Sable said, as she tied the ribbon. 'Some good, some bad, some downright awful. You are the first that I would die for. That's all I wanted to say.'

Thorn faced the Holdfast woman. 'Thank you, Sable; but I don't want you to die for me. I want you to kill those who threaten this world; I want you to kill them all.'

Sable nodded. 'I can do that, too.'

CHAPTER 25
A GOOD DAY

Keir stared out of the window at the filthy back street. There was no glass in the opening, and he could smell the rank odours emanating from the piles of refuse that littered the stained cobbles. Every now and again, he also heard a rustling coming from the thick shadows. He suspected the sound was being made by rats, but he had yet to see one.

'Get away from there, you idiot,' snapped Bryce. 'What if someone sees you?'

'There's no one out on the street, your Majesty,' said Keir.

'Are you speaking back to me? How dare you?'

Keir sighed, and moved away from the window. The interior of the shabby apartment was almost as filthy as the back street, and what furniture was there was broken and falling apart. Keir sat on the wooden floorboards, his back to a wall, the bare bricks showing through the crumbling plasterwork.

'We should have left you on the Plateau,' Bryce muttered. 'I don't know why Daimon thought it would be a good idea to bring you along. You've been nothing but a hindrance, Keir. Worse than useless.'

Keir lit a cigarette, his eyes lowered.

'And who said you could smoke?' barked the Emperor. 'It's a disgusting habit. Put it out at once.'

Keir moved his arm to stub out the cigarette, then he stopped. For three days, the Emperor had been berating him for his stupidity, in between mocking him for his disfigured face, and Keir was sick of it.

'Did you hear what I said, you misshapen piece of shit?'

'I heard, your Majesty.'

'And yet you are still smoking. Do I have to come over there and strike you? Don't make me strike you, Keir.'

Keir's eyes tightened. 'What happened to you, your Majesty?'

Bryce stared at him.

'You never used to be like this,' Keir went on. 'People used to respect you; they even admired and loved you.'

'What would you know about respect, admiration or love?' said Bryce. 'You have never earned any of these things.'

'Maybe; but you did, your Majesty. Even the Holdfasts held you in high esteem.' He shook his head. 'Half of them voted for you at the high mages' convention. I doubt any would vote for you now.'

'Are you trying to mock me?'

'I am just trying to understand, your Majesty. Has power done this to you? Or was it Daimon?'

A flicker of doubt passed over Bryce's features, then it turned into a sneer.

'You are weak, Keir – that's your problem. You wanted to pick the winning side; that's the only reason you swore loyalty to me.'

'It doesn't feel as though we are on the winning side, your Majesty. We have been trapped on this world for three days, living in filthy squalor. We have no army, no money, and no friends.'

'We are not trapped; we have a Quadrant.'

'Then why don't we use it, your Majesty? Why did Daimon bring us to Implacatus? What could we possibly hope to achieve here?'

The same doubt troubled Bryce's features again, and Keir wondered for a moment if Daimon's absence had loosened his control over the Emperor.

Bryce swallowed. 'We have a plan.'

'We do, your Majesty? What plan?'

'Never you mind. Daimon shall explain it all when he returns.'

'What if he doesn't return, your Majesty? He's been gone for over a day. He might have triggered the Quadrant already.'

'Daimon would never abandon me. You think you are being clever, but all you are doing is proving your ignorance.'

Keir took a draw of his cigarette, and noticed that Bryce failed to reprimand him.

'Can I ask you about Lady Brogan, your Majesty? What do you think she will do?'

'My sister will remain loyal to me, of course. She will gather my armies, and...'

'Your armies? What armies? Our soldiers were defeated, your Majesty; you were there. Even the marines cracked in the end. You have no army.'

'Nonsense. There are still forces garrisoning the Great Tunnel and the fortresses along the frontier of Rakana. Even without an army, if that bitch Thorn tries to enter Plateau City, my loyal subjects will rise up against her, and slaughter her paid mercenaries. We are going to win this war, Keir.'

'Are you trying to convince me, or yourself, your Majesty?'

Bryce jumped to his feet and charged towards Keir, his fists clenched. Keir stared up at him, saying nothing, and Bryce lashed out, a fist clipping the side of Keir's head.

'What would your mother think if she could see you now?' Keir said.

Bryce struck out with a boot, and kicked Keir in the stomach. Bryce started laughing as he kicked Keir again.

'Your Majesty,' came a voice from the doorway; 'is that necessary?'

Keir glanced up from the floor, and saw Daimon standing a few yards away, a large bag of groceries in his hand.

'He insulted the memory of my mother,' Bryce said.

'Perhaps you should calm down, your Majesty,' said Daimon.

Bryce's enraged expression changed in an instant, and he smiled like a child, then went and sat down again.

'Thank you,' said Daimon, walking forward. 'I have food.'

Keir pushed himself back up, leaned against the wall, and clutched his stomach. 'Where have you been?' he said to Daimon. 'You were gone for a whole day. Shopping doesn't take that long.'

'I have been exploring Serene,' Daimon said, as he crouched on the floorboard and reached into the bag. 'I have been learning many things, and reaching out to those who may provide the help we need.'

Keir frowned. 'Reaching out to whom?'

Daimon glanced at Bryce. 'I thought you would have informed Keir of our plan by now, your Majesty.'

'I was waiting for you to return,' said Bryce. 'You can tell him.'

Daimon nodded, then he passed some bread and cheese out to Keir and the Emperor.

'Alright,' he said. He glanced into Keir's eyes. 'His Majesty and I came up with a plan some time ago. We hoped it would never be needed. We hoped we would be able to defeat Thorn and her mercenaries on our own; but the odds were always stacked against us. Thorn has Sable, Belinda, and three dragons to defend her. I was able to cancel out the usefulness of Karalyn and Kelsey, but what could I do against the Third Ascendant? Then an idea came to us. Who has the power to defeat the Third Ascendant?'

Keir waited for the answer.

'Well?' said Daimon.

Keir frowned. 'I don't know.'

Bryce laughed. 'He really is as stupid as he looks, Daimon.'

'The answer, Keir,' said Daimon, 'is the Second Ascendant.'

'You can't be serious,' Keir said.

'Oh, but we are,' said Daimon. 'As I mentioned, it was a plan that we hoped we would never have to use. But think it through. The Second Ascendant wants three things, all of which we have the power to grant him.'

'What three things?'

'Why don't you try to guess?'

'Belinda?'

'Aye. Well done. He wants Belinda. What else?'

Keir narrowed his eyes. 'Salve?'

'Correct again. And the third thing?'

'I don't know.'

'The Sextant, Keir. He wants the Sextant. Now, what if we were to offer him these three things, and in exchange, he could lend us his assistance? With the might of Implacatus behind us, we could utterly destroy our enemies, and lose nothing of any worth to us. What does it matter if the Ascendants conquer the salve world? They are welcome to it. And, would we miss either Belinda or the Sextant? Let Edmond have them both. All we require in return is his aid.'

Keir stared at Daimon in disbelief. A hundred doubts and questions rattled through his thoughts, then Daimon smiled at him, and Keir smiled back. Everything would be fine. It was a clever plan. How could it fail?

'Let's eat,' said Daimon, 'and then we can leave this apartment. The Ascendants are waiting for us at the border of Cumulus.'

Keir shoved a chunk of bread into his mouth and chewed. It tasted great, and he wondered why he had ever doubted Daimon's judgement.

***

Keir gazed up at the enormous stairwell. It was like nothing he had ever seen before, a palatial expanse of glass, marble and gold. The stairs ran round the edge of the circular walls in a tight spiral, with landings on every level, but it wasn't the stairs that impressed him the most. In the centre of the floor, three gargantuan statues rose into the air, the tops of their heads almost brushing the glass dome that covered the open space.

'Who are they?' he said.

Daimon raised an arm. 'The old woman on the left is Theodora, the First Ascendant; the old man is Edmond, and the other old woman is someone you know, though she looks a little younger these days.'

'Belinda?'

'Aye.'

'How do you know all this?'

'There's a god standing on the fourth floor above us. I have just read his mind. They are expecting us.'

'Is this Cumulus?' said Keir.

Daimon laughed. 'No. We are still in Serene. To get to Cumulus, we shall need a god to build a bridge to span the chasm that lies between the two cities.'

'Why don't we use the Quadrant to get there?' said Bryce.

'Because I don't know how, your Majesty.'

Bryce glared at his high mage. 'You told me you read the information from Sable's mind.'

'I did, your Majesty, but there is a lot to learn about the use of a Quadrant, and I had little time in which to act. I took from Sable only what I thought might prove useful. I know how to travel between worlds, but I don't know how to make the Quadrant move us anywhere within the same world. For now, I'm afraid we shall have to walk.'

They set off again, and left the squalid lower levels of the city behind as they climbed the steps that wound round the stairwell. They passed several squads of heavily-armoured soldiers, along with their robed gods. Several gods eyed them as they went by, and Keir overhead a few muttered comments, but no one attempted to stop them. They reached as high as the shoulders of the three massive marble Ascendants, and then Daimon led them along a wide passageway, passing another set of soldiers and gods.

'Do they know who we are?' Keir whispered.

'Aye, they do,' said Daimon. 'They have been ordered to let us pass. Lord Edmond is eager to meet us.'

Keir frowned as he started thinking about the plan. It had seemed sensible when they had discussed it earlier, but some doubts were starting to emerge, and he had a sickly feeling that Daimon had been manipulating his thoughts again. It seemed obvious to Keir whenever Daimon used his powers on Bryce, but he had never caught Daimon doing it to him. Could any of his thoughts or feelings be trusted? Were any his own?

They emerged from the passageway into the open air, where trees and a garden had been planted. To their left, the tall peaks of the mountain range stretched away into the distance, while the garden was so high that some clouds were below them to their right. A few men and women were resting in the shade of the trees. They were wearing expensive robes, and all of them appeared young. Keir wondered if they were gods. Apart from Belinda, he had never really known any gods, and Belinda acted more like a child than an immortal, so she was clearly atypical. He had briefly seen Agatha and a few of her companions during the wars, but he hadn't known that they were gods. At the time, they had been referred to as archmages by the ignorant inhabitants of the Star Continent; a mysterious and powerful band of strangers whose origin was unknown. Now, years later, Keir was in the home of the gods. He wished he could tell Karalyn – to brag to her that he had also been to Implacatus; then he remembered that he wanted to kill her.

Daimon led them along a path between the trees, until they reached the edge of a precipice. Keir glanced down, but the bottom of the chasm was wreathed in clouds.

'Here comes our escort,' said Daimon, pointing to their left.

Keir turned. A man in black robes was striding towards them, accompanied by at least a dozen massive soldiers in brightly-coloured armour. The god looked about twenty-one, but he had silver-grey streaks in his hair. He halted a few yards in front of Bryce and the others, and examined each one in turn. He stopped when he reached Daimon.

'You must be the dream mage,' he said, his voice sounding older than his features.

'I am,' said Daimon.

'The Blessed and Beloved Second Ascendant wishes to talk with you and your companions,' the god said. 'However, we have been the victims of unprovoked aggression by people from your world before, so you will understand if we are cautious.' He nodded to a soldier. 'Search them for weapons.'

The huge soldiers approached Daimon and the others, checking the belts and clothes they were wearing. One plucked a Quadrant from the folds of Daimon's tunic. He handed it to the god.

'I shall keep a hold of this for now,' the black-robed god said.

'You will give it back to me,' said Daimon, smiling, 'or I shall kill every one of your guards.'

The god laughed.

'This is your last chance,' said Daimon. 'I presume that Edmond is watching this little conversation. Give me the Quadrant, or I shall show him exactly what I can do.'

The god shook his head. 'It appears that you are labouring under a delusion, mortal. You are not our guests, you are our prisoners.'

Daimon clicked his fingers, and the heavily-armoured soldiers started running towards the precipice. They reached the edge and hurled themselves into the abyss, as the god's eyes widened.

'You were saying?' said Daimon. 'The Quadrant. Now, if you please.'

He held his hand out, and the god placed the Quadrant on to Daimon's palm.

'Excellent,' said Daimon. 'Take us to Edmond.'

The black-robed god narrowed his eyes, then he turned towards the chasm and raised his arms. A grinding noise echoed out, then a sinewy bridge of rock began to rise up from the edge of the precipice. It shot across the gap, its far end disappearing into a thick bank of cloud.

'Follow me,' the god said, then he stepped on to the bridge.

Keir resisted the urge to look down as they crossed. They entered the cloud, and Keir could see nothing beyond Bryce's back a yard in front of him. The clouds thinned after a while, and a huge forbidding wall loomed up before them. The god stepped down onto the far side of the bridge, then waited for Keir and the others to join him.

'This is Cumulus,' the god said. 'The City of the Gods.'

Cut into the huge wall was an imposing steel gate, with towers and turrets rising above it into the cloud-flecked sky.

'Is that the Second Ascendant's palace?' said Bryce.

The god laughed. 'No, you foolish mortal, this is merely the gatehouse of Cumulus. Your friend may have considerable power, but it is clear that you are lacking in knowledge. Come with me, and I will take you to the Palace of the Almighty.'

It was an hour-long walk to reach the home of the Second Ascendant, but Keir barely noticed the minutes pass. Everywhere he looked, he saw splendour, wealth and power on a scale he had never imagined possible. Towers stretched so far into the sky that their tops were lost in the clouds, while palaces glittered with gold. There were no paved roads in Cumulus, and the god led them by a series of high walkways and bridges that spanned ravines and chasms. They seemed to be the only ones outside, and the city was still and quiet. When they finally came face to face with the Palace of the Almighty, there was no mistaking it. A sheer, smooth wall of windowless granite rose up from the depths of a deep ravine. It stretched out for hundreds of yards to either side, while its many towers and spires pierced the sky.

The god came to a halt by the edge of the ravine, and pointed towards a single, small opening in the wall of the palace, then he moved his fingers and formed another bridge before their eyes.

'There's a body up there,' said Bryce; 'nailed to the wall.'

'There is,' said the god. 'It is Nathaniel, the Fourth Ascendant. The Blessed and Mighty Second Ascendant placed his withered corpse above his doorway as a warning to the gods of Cumulus not to betray him.'

'The Creator?' said Keir.

'He was known by that name sometimes,' said the god. 'Nathaniel was a renowned world-builder before he became a traitor. He made the world that birthed you all. You are his sub-created beings; his idea made flesh. Were it not for him, none of you would exist. Follow me.'

The god led them over the bridge and they entered the Palace of the Almighty. The doors swung shut behind them with a dull clang, and the god hardened his glance.

'Your Quadrant is now useless,' he said. 'Nothing can penetrate the walls of this palace. Do you understand? It matters not what powers you have, you shall leave with your lives only if the Blessed Second Ascendant allows it.'

He took them down a long, featureless corridor and into a large chamber, where a tall, handsome man was sitting upon a throne. Huge gods with battle-vision stood guard by the walls, their stone armour shimmering in the bright lamp light.

'Bow your heads before the Sacred Second Ascendant, mortals!' cried the black-robed god who had brought them from Serene.

Daimon laughed at the figure on the throne. 'We are immune to your powers, Ascendant. We are not intimidated by you, and I bow to no one.'

Edmond said nothing for a moment, then he glanced down at the god in black robes. 'Thank you for bringing them here, Bastion. Which one is the Holdfast?'

Bastion gestured to Keir. 'He has the same eyes as Sable, my lord.'

'And who is the third visitor?'

Bryce took a step forward. 'I am the Emperor of the Star Continent. My name is Bryce ae Brannig ae Brig. My throne has been taken from me by the Holdfasts and their allies. Give me aid, and we shall reward you.'

'But you have a Holdfast with you,' said Bastion.

'Keir is the only one of that family who has remained loyal to me,' said Bryce. 'We have three things to offer you in return for your assistance. First...'

'I know what you have to offer, mortal,' said Edmond. 'Daimon has already communicated with the gods of Cumulus. I believe that we can come to an agreement, but I also have conditions. The first is that you will kneel before me and pledge your loyalty to my rule. You are not my equal, Bryce of Brig; you are a mere mortal; a speck in the fabric of time. Your life means nothing to those of us who cannot die. Kneel, Bryce, and then we can talk further.'

The same flicker of doubt from before passed over Bryce's face.

'No,' he said. 'Emperors do not bow.'

Daimon glared at Bryce. 'Your Majesty, do not imperil our position here. You must kneel if we wish to return to rule the Star Continent.'

'But...'

'Kneel, your Majesty.'

Bryce's features altered in an instant. He smiled, and fell to his knees.

'What is this?' said Bastion. 'Are you controlling this man, Daimon? Are you using your powers to make him do as you command?'

'Of course not,' said Daimon.

Bastion shook his head. 'You may be powerful, but you are a bad liar. Are you also controlling the Holdfast boy?'

'He is not controlling me,' said Keir.

'But he is controlling Bryce?'

Keir hesitated.

Edmond chuckled from his throne. 'How amusing. I have often pondered how to defeat the Holdfasts. I came to the conclusion some time ago that the best way would be to ally myself with a rival dream mage, one who could balance out the powers of that unholy family. But how could I ever do such a thing, I wondered. Well, Bastion, here is our answer. With Daimon as our ally, we would be able to destroy every Holdfast who opposes us.' He smiled. 'Daimon, look at me. I am wearing eye-guards, and cannot be touched by your powers.' He gestured to the armoured gods in the chamber. 'They are also wearing eye-guards, as is Lord Bastion. If I wished it, I could order them to cut you down, and there would be nothing you could do to stop them.'

Daimon edged back, and swallowed.

'You thought to use me, didn't you, Daimon; and yet you are now in my power. Release Bryce from your control. I wish to see the extent to which you can manipulate someone's true feelings.'

Daimon hesitated. Bastion nodded to one of the armoured gods, and the enormous man raised his sword and took a step forward.

'Wait!' cried Daimon. 'I will do it, but it shall be my only concession. If you want the salve and the Sextant, you will make me your ally, not your slave. Swear it now.'

'I can agree to this trifling condition,' said Edmond. 'After all, you would be of no use to me if you were unwilling to use your powers on my behalf. Yes, an ally, rather than a slave; I swear it. Now, you must swear the same.'

Daimon nodded. 'Allies. I swear it.'

The dream mage pointed a finger at Bryce. The Emperor screamed in agony and rolled on to the floor, then he panted, sweat forming on his face, and looked up.

'Keir?' he said. He looked confused, then the terrible realisation of what was happening seemed to strike him. He turned to Daimon, his eyes lit with rage. 'You filthy little traitor! What have you made me do?'

Bastion frowned. 'Does he remember everything that has occurred?'

'Aye,' said Daimon. 'He sees it all as clear as day. I have also removed the protections from his mind. You will be able to read his thoughts and memories, if you wish.'

'You bastard!' Bryce cried, then he launched himself at Daimon, his hands reaching for the dream mage's throat.

Bastion raised a finger, and Bryce's head exploded.

Keir stumbled backwards, the front of his clothes dripping with blood, and an armoured god gripped his arm.

Daimon stared at the headless body of Bryce lying on the granite floor. 'This wasn't part of the deal. Bryce was my puppet. I have been grooming his mind for a long time, preparing him for power. All that work – gone!'

Edmond laughed. 'What a fuss over a weak mortal. You can be the Emperor of the Star Continent, Daimon. I care not.'

'I don't want to be Emperor,' Daimon said. 'I am the power behind the throne, not on the throne.' He pointed at Keir. 'He can be the new Emperor. Aye – a Holdfast for an Emperor. We can get rid of the rest of his family, and leave him to sit on the throne.'

'Me?' said Keir.

'Yes, you,' said Edmond. 'This idea amuses me. I can hardly be accused of having a grudge against the Holdfasts if I appoint one to rule the Star Continent in my name. Keir Holdfast, kneel before me, or die as Bryce did.'

The armoured god released Keir's arm, and he almost fell over.

Kneel, you fool! Daimon shouted in his mind.

Keir dropped to his knees in front of Edmond, his guts churning with terror. He closed his eyes, ready for his own head to disintegrate, but heard only mocking laughter.

'Now pledge your loyalty to me,' said Edmond. 'Swear that you will serve me always, and obey my commands, from now until the moment of your death. Do this, and I shall do everything in my power to make you the Emperor of your world. You shall have palaces, and great riches, and the most beautiful women to serve you. You shall eat only the finest foods, and drink nothing but the best wines. All that you desire shall be yours, Keir Holdfast. Serve me, and become the mightiest mortal on the Star Continent. All will worship you; all will fear you.'

Keir shuddered. His thoughts flashed to his mother and the rest of his family. They would despise him more than they already did if he acquiesced to Edmond's wishes, but what was the alternative? If he refused, his brains would be coating the floor and walls just as Bryce's were. He hated himself, but there was nothing else he could do.

'I swear to serve you, my lord,' Keir said.

'Good boy,' said Edmond. 'Daimon, it is time for you to give me what I need. I want the location of the salve world, and the location of the Star Continent, and I want them now.'

Daimon smiled. 'Tell Bastion to remove his eye-guards, and I'll do it.'

'Do as he says, Bastion,' said Edmond. 'If it is a trick, then Daimon will die.'

Bastion frowned, then he raised his hands to his face. He pulled back an eyelid, and plucked something from his left eye. He gazed at Daimon, and the dream mage gazed back.

'I have the locations, my lord,' said Bastion.

'Summon my armies,' said Edmond. 'We shall strike both worlds at once. Every Ascendant must take part, with no exceptions. We shall open portals and flood the two worlds with every god and soldier at our disposal.'

Bastion bowed. 'Yes, my lord.'

'The Ninth Ascendant Lord Esher shall command the forces that will invade the salve world,' Edmond went on. 'His objective is clear - he must secure the supply of salve for all time, and obliterate any resistance.'

'Yes, my lord.'

'You and I shall go to the Star Continent, Bastion. We shall accompany Daimon and Emperor Keir Holdfast; and we shall find both the Sextant and my errant bride.'

'It shall be so, my lord.'

Edmond smiled, and his face seemed to radiate its own light. 'This is a good day. After our recent troubles I had concerns for the future, but those concerns have been scattered to the winds. Rise, Emperor Keir of the Star Continent; it is time to plan your accession to the throne of your world.'

Keir slowly got to his feet. Daimon slapped him on the back, and looked him in the eye. Keir smiled.

Edmond was right. It was a good day.

CHAPTER 26
A FEW AWKWARD WORDS

Colsbury Castle, Republic of the Holdings – 18th Day, First Third Winter 534

'Home?' said Austin. He looked thoughtful as he gazed down from the hillside at the island of Colsbury. 'I would have to say Dragon Eyre. It's the place I most consider to be my home now. My mother and aunt live on Ulna, and we have rooms in the bridge palace in Udall. Did you know that Blackrose has promised to feed and house my mother and aunt for the rest of their lives? They love it there. What about you?'

Belinda watched as Banner soldiers swarmed over the bridge leading to the island. Teams of them were working all over Colsbury – repairing and extending the defences, and renovating old barracks and turrets. The large gatehouse that guarded the entrance to the isle was covered in wooden scaffolding, and the sound of saws and hammers was drifting up to where Belinda and Austin were sitting on the grassy slope of the hill.

'I don't know,' she said. 'Here, I suppose.'

'Do you mean this world in general, or Colsbury in particular?'

'I have more affinity with Plateau City than with Colsbury. The imperial capital was where I first awakened after Karalyn scoured my mind, and I lived there for longer than I have lived anywhere else. I like

Colsbury, though. Well, I did when it was quiet. I remember when only two dozen people stayed on the island. Now, it's more like two thousand.'

'If Plateau City is the capital, why has Empress Thorn decided to stay here? I had imagined that, after the battle, we would have pushed on and re-occupied Plateau City.'

'We shall probably find out the reasons today, once the council starts.' She glanced at him. 'You will be attending, won't you?'

Austin nodded. 'Yes, as Ashfall's rider. She wants me to be there.'

'Have you considered that Ashfall might not want to move back to Dragon Eyre?'

'I've talked about it with her. She's happy to remain here for now but, in the long run, she wants to settle down with a mate and have children; and she won't find any available male dragons on this world. But, she's in no hurry.'

'Dragons live for five or six centuries,' Belinda said. 'She has plenty of time. Does that mean that you might be on this world for a few years to come?'

Austin glanced away. 'I have my mother and aunt to think about. They're mortal, as you know, and their lives are brief.' He shook his head. 'I can't bear thinking about it. I can't quite grasp the fact that I will be a young god when my mother and aunt die. I will still be considered young when Ashfall grows old. Sometimes, I wish I was mortal.'

'So do I,' said Belinda. 'In a hundred years, every single person who is now on Colsbury will be dead. In a thousand, no mortal will remember what happened here, or who was involved; but we will remember everything.'

'It helps having someone else who understands,' he said.

'If Aila decides to stay here, then her children will soon be in the same position. We can help them.'

'I hadn't thought of that,' he said. 'I wonder how many demigod children they will have.'

'That depends on whether Aila and Corthie both survive what is coming. If they do, then Corthie told me that they wanted a large family. Ideally, a dozen, he said.'

Austin laughed. 'A dozen demigods?'

'That's what he told me. He might have been joking. I find it hard to tell, sometimes.'

'And you?'

'Me?'

'Yes. Do you see yourself having children? Any child of yours would be immortal, even if the father wasn't a god. You're an Ascendant.'

'I have already given birth to many children. I saw some of their tombs on Lostwell. Silva said that I probably have several direct descendants still living on Implacatus. You might have met some without even knowing it.'

'I have never heard of any children of yours. You would have had them with Nathaniel, I presume?'

'I assume so.'

'Well, with both you and Nathaniel having been branded as traitors for the past few millennia, maybe any children you had have kept quiet about the identity of their parents.'

'You mean they might have disowned me?'

'If they wanted to live in Cumulus, they may have had to. I guess the other Ascendants would know. Certainly, I have never met anyone who claims to be your descendant. If your wedding to Edmond had gone as he had planned, perhaps some would have emerged from the shadows.'

Belinda grimaced. 'Please don't bring that up. I was seconds away from being married to the Second Ascendant, although I can remember none of it. I was in the spiked crown at the time. Maybe I would still be wearing it as Edmond's wife. The thought makes me sick.'

'I won't mention it again.'

'Maybe we can talk about it when some time has passed.' She smiled. 'Let's give it a century or two.'

'Alright. What about having more children in the future?'

'Who would be the father? You?'

Austin's face flushed, and he glanced down. 'That's not what I meant. I was just... wondering, you know... I didn't mean to suggest anything untoward.'

Belinda frowned. What had been untoward about what he had said? And why was he acting as if he were embarrassed? She had been speaking hypothetically when she had suggested him as a father, but he seemed to have derived a more personal meaning. She glanced down at the island of Colsbury, wondering if she would ever understand other people.

'Well,' he said, after a while; 'this is a little awkward.'

'Why?' she said.

He lowered his voice. 'Are you serious?'

'Yes. Explain what just happened.'

'Alright; I'll try. We have known each other for a very short time, yes? And, well, we're at the stage of getting to know each other. Nothing romantic has occurred between us, but...'

'But what?'

He took a breath. 'But, well... I don't know how to say this. Alright. Let me think. What I'm saying is that, right now, there is potential. Damn it, that sounds like such a presumptive thing to say. Things are... possible. And, well, talking about having children at this stage is awkward, because it implies a level of intimacy that we haven't reached; that we might never reach.'

Belinda frowned again. 'I still don't understand. If what you say is true, and there's the possibility of something developing between us, then shouldn't we discuss things like having children? I think you would make a fine father, and a loving husband. Is it wrong of me to say that? It's not the same as saying that I'm in love with you. I am not in love with you, just so that is clear. But, I like you. You make me happy.' She sighed. 'The rules confuse me. I end up saying too much, or I don't say anything at all. Either way, I seem to put people off. When I was infatuated with Naxor, I completely lost my senses for a while. I made a fool of myself. I won't make that mistake again.'

Austin nodded.

She turned to him. 'Ask me that question again; the one about having children, and I will try to think of a different answer.'

'Alright. Do you think you might like to have more children in the future?'

'Maybe,' she said. 'Having children sounds nice. How was that?'

'That was a more socially acceptable response. Was it true?'

She shrugged. 'I think so. I used to pester Naxor about having children, so I might have an innate need to feel like a mother; or perhaps I just wanted something that we had made together. I'm glad we didn't, though. I wouldn't want to look at a child and be reminded of Naxor.'

'Now, it would be polite to ask me the same question.'

'Alright. Would you like to have children, Austin?'

He smiled. 'Maybe. Having children sounds nice.'

She laughed, then, for some reason, she imagined what it would be like to kiss Austin. Her face flushed.

'What is it?' he said.

'I don't think I'll say. If I did, it might make you feel awkward again.'

Belinda and Austin strode into the vast forecourt that lay between the Great Keep and the Summer Palace. Workers had been busy, and the throne had been relocated from the battlefield, and was sitting on a high platform in front of dozens of chairs. Several seats had also been placed to either side of the throne for the most senior members of Thorn's court, and wide areas of the forecourt had been kept clear for the three dragons. The Empress had yet to appear, but there was a low hubbub of noise coming from the dozens of officers who had already arrived. They were mostly sticking to their own groups, with Banner talking to Banner, and imperial army officers mixing with their own colleagues; but Belinda noticed that Lucius Cardova was speaking to a group that included Kellach marines as well as a few Banner personnel.

Belinda saw Kelsey and caught her attention.

'Morning, Bee,' Kelsey said, as she walked over. She nodded in

Austin's direction. 'Nice walk?'

'We sat rather than walked,' Belinda said. 'We were up on the hill that overlooks Colsbury.'

'We had an interesting discussion,' said Austin.

Kelsey smiled again, as if she knew something secret that she found hilarious. It annoyed Belinda when people made that expression, but it was even more irritating when Kelsey did it.

'Do you know where we are to be seated?' said Belinda.

'Aye.' Kelsey pointed to the throne. 'You're up there with the high and mighty; while Austin will be wherever Ashfall chooses to land. The dragons should be along any moment, or so I hear. Once they arrive, the Empress will join us and the council can begin.'

'Have you heard from Karalyn?'

'Nope, but I suppose that can only be good. Sable would tell us if something was happening in the City. She's been using the Sextant to keep an eye on what's going on over there, and to transport more supplies. Oh, did you hear? I'm an imperial legate.'

'What does that mean?' said Austin.

Kelsey grinned. 'It means that if the Empress isn't present, then I can speak for her. You know, for meetings or negotiations; that sort of thing. Of course, it's not quite as useful now that I've lost the damn Quadrant, but it's my first official job for a long time.'

'Congratulations,' said Belinda.

'Thanks, Bee.'

Belinda frowned. 'Don't call me that.'

Daphne emerged from the crowd of officers and approached them.

'The dragons are a mile to the north-west,' she said. 'We should take our places.'

Belinda nodded, then she turned to Austin. 'Will I see you later?'

'It depends what Ashfall wants to do,' the demigod said.

Belinda felt a twinge of jealousy.

'I could ask her to take us both for a flight,' Austin went on. 'How does that sound?'

'It sounds like the socially acceptable thing to do.'

Austin laughed, while Kelsey and Daphne narrowed their eyes at the Third Ascendant.

'I'll do that,' said Austin. 'See you later.'

Daphne led Belinda through the crowd of officers towards the throne.

'Getting along well with Austin, are you?' said Daphne.

Belinda tried to discern the tone of Daphne's question. Was she asking to be polite, or was she fishing for information? Perhaps she was being sarcastic; who knew?

'I think so,' she said.

'Excellent.'

Belinda said nothing. They were about to step up onto the platform when three shadows passed overhead.

'Here come the dragons,' said Daphne, stating the obvious.

Frostback swooped down, and alighted by the throne.

'Where is my rider?' she said, her eyes scanning the crowd.

'We left Kelsey in the crowd,' said Daphne. 'She was watching the skies for you.'

'Is something wrong?' said Belinda.

'Perhaps,' said Frostback. 'Four of those creatures you call winged gaien are approaching, and they are carrying a wooden vessel beneath them.'

'From which direction are they coming?' said Daphne.

'From the south-east, Holder Fast. They are about ten miles from Colsbury.'

Kelsey appeared again, pushing her way through the crowd.

'We should investigate,' said Daphne. 'It's unlikely, but it might be an assassination attempt.'

'Why does your mind always turn to things like that?' said Kelsey.

'When one has been an assassin, daughter,' said Daphne; 'one tends to think like an assassin. It's what I would do if I were Bryce. I would fill a flying carriage with flammable material and drop it on to the forecourt; thereby eliminating the senior commanders of my enemy in a single stroke.'

Kelsey narrowed her eyes at her mother.

'Climb up, my rider,' said Frostback, 'and we shall force this wooden vessel to land.'

'I should also come,' said Daphne.

'Why? So you can take over?' said Kelsey.

'There might be important dignitaries on board the carriage.'

'I'm the Empress's legate; I can deal with whoever it might be.'

'And I am the Empress's Herald, daughter. Legate or not, I still outrank you.'

Belinda watched as mother and daughter glared at each other.

'I will take you both,' said Frostback. 'Legate and Herald. Belinda, would you also like to come? Perhaps you could sit between my rider and her mother?'

'Is Ashfall going, too?'

'She is, once she has collected her rider.'

'Then I shall come.'

Kelsey and Daphne shared a glance, their bickering forgotten as they rolled their eyes at Belinda. Daphne then turned to Shella.

'We shall be leaving for a short while, to investigate a flying carriage approaching from the south-east. Please let the Empress know if she comes down.'

'Sure, Daffers,' said Shella.

Kelsey and Daphne clambered up the straps that hung down Frostback's flank, then Belinda ascended. Kelsey had already taken the middle seat, with Daphne to her right, so Belinda climbed over them and took the place to Kelsey's left. As soon as they were buckled into the harness, the silver dragon beat her wings and rose up over the isle of Colsbury. Halfclaw had remained airborne, circling over the upper reaches of the Summer Palace, while Ashfall was soaring up into the sky with Austin on her back.

'I have told the Empress what we are doing,' said Halfclaw, as the dragon sisters joined him. 'She was with Sable and Agang on the highest balcony of the palace. We are to report to her once we have discovered who is coming.'

'Then we must fly quickly,' said Ashfall, 'before the four gaien creatures reach Colsbury.'

The three dragons banked, then sped off to the south-east. Belinda gripped the handle that ran along the front of the harness, as the wind rushed past her face. They crossed the shoreline, and raced over the foothills and the road that led down to the Plateau. Soldiers and wagons were moving along the road in both directions, performing part of the complicated manoeuvres worked out by Daphne, Shella and Cardova in the aftermath of the battle. Entire divisions of the Banner and the imperial army were being shuffled around like pieces on a gaming board, creating a ring of steel surrounding Colsbury. The dragons flew on, leaving the road behind, and Belinda saw the flying carriage in the sky ahead of them, its four winged gaien connected to it by thick cables.

'Those brutes give me a queasy feeling,' said Frostback.

'They wouldn't last a day on Dragon Eyre,' said Ashfall. 'They are mindless abominations.'

'That's a little harsh,' said Kelsey. 'It's not their fault they're stupid.'

'No?' said Frostback. 'Imagine if there were a human equivalent – a creature that looked almost identical to a human, but one that could not think or speak; one that made noises like a cow.'

Kelsey shrugged. 'That sounds like a few people I know.'

'We should surround them,' said Halfclaw, 'and force them to land.'

The three dragons split up, and began circling in front of the four winged gaien, who ignored them.

'They don't understand what we are doing,' said Frostback. 'Dreadful creatures.'

A hatch on the top of the flying carriage opened, and a Holdings man climbed out, his waist secured to the vessel by a rope. Daphne leaned over the flank of Frostback and jabbed her finger towards the ground in full view of the man, who saw what she was doing and raised an arm in acknowledgement. The man descended back into the carriage, and the hatch was closed.

'Is that human guiding the vessel?' said Frostback.

'Yes,' said Daphne. 'The gaien are controlled by pulling on the cables that connect them to the carriage. Pull left to go left; and right to go right; that sort of thing.'

Belinda watched as the winged gaien began to descend. They lowered the carriage over a flat piece of hillside, until its underside was resting on the ground, then all four gaien were released. They flew off together, ignoring the three dragons, and set off towards the east.

'They are fleeing!' cried Frostback.

'They will return when the pilot whistles for them,' said Daphne. 'This is standard practice. Take us down, please.'

Frostback and the other two dragons circled once over the wooden carriage, then landed around it. Daphne, Kelsey and Belinda unbuckled themselves from the harness, and climbed down to the ground. Austin joined them, and they turned to face the side of the carriage, where a large hatch was starting to open.

'Draw your sword, Belinda,' said Daphne.

'I didn't bring one,' Belinda said.

'But you can't use your powers when Kelsey is here.'

'Worry not,' said Ashfall. 'You have three dragons with you, Holder Fast. You are not defenceless.'

The side hatch fell open, its lip banging off the ground, then a squad of imperial soldiers emerged from the interior. They were armed with crossbows, and Belinda prepared her battle-vision. Once the soldiers had left the carriage, another figure appeared.

'Brogan?' said Daphne, her eyes widening.

The young woman looked ill, her features drawn, and she hobbled down from the carriage as though she were in pain.

'She looks like she drank five bottles of Severton's finest last night,' said Kelsey.

Brogan halted when she saw the three dragons, then her eyes went over the four humans who were waiting for her. She gestured to the imperial soldiers, and each of them placed their weapons onto the ground and raised their arms into the air.

Brogan shuffled forwards, then she stopped again, and started to cry.

'Lady Brogan,' said Daphne, her eyes like steel. 'How can we help you? Are you here to surrender?'

Brogan nodded, then she put a hand to her face. 'I... I have... realised what has been happening.'

Belinda frowned. 'What do you mean?'

'I don't know,' said Brogan. 'It is as though a cloud has lifted from my mind. Before the battle, I was certain about things. Aye, certain. I was sure what we were doing was right. But... now, I... I don't know any more. Has my brother really gone?'

'He fled the field of battle with Daimon and Keir,' said Daphne.

'They went to Implacatus,' said Kelsey, 'to betray us.'

Brogan took a step back. 'My brother would never do that.'

'Tell me, Lady Brogan,' said Daphne, 'was your brother as certain about things as you were?'

'Aye. He was.'

'And did your doubts emerge once Daimon had left the imperial capital?'

Brogan nodded.

Daphne smiled. 'Then you have your answer. You were under the spell of Daimon's dream powers. That is why you thought you were doing the right thing. Daimon bewitched you both. He bewitches Bryce still. Your brother will do whatever Daimon commands him to do.'

'That is what I have started to suspect,' Brogan said. 'The triplets feel the same. Bethal has been almost hysterical for days, weeping over what has happened. She thinks Thorn will put our entire family to death. I have come to beg you to spare them. Take me, if you must, but please spare the triplets. They were too young to understand. The blame lies with Bryce, and with me, for trusting Daimon.'

The rage in Daphne's eyes started to fade. 'It's not your fault, Brogan. I know what it's like to have my mind turned inside out by a dream mage. There was nothing you could have done to prevent Daimon from twisting your thoughts. However, I am still going to take you into custody. It is for the Empress to decide what shall be done with you.'

'It is the Empress I wish to see,' said Brogan.

Kelsey raised an eyebrow. 'Are you acknowledging that Thorn is the real Empress?'

'What choice do I have?' said Brogan. 'I would do anything to save my sisters and my little brother. I still believe that my mother had every right to appoint her successor, but it seems that very few now agree, and I must bow to necessity; just as I will bow before Empress Thorn.'

Daphne turned to Belinda. 'Would you mind flying back on Ashfall, if she will take you? I would prefer to stay close to Brogan as we return to Colsbury.'

'I don't mind,' said Belinda.

'I will carry the Ascendant,' said Ashfall.

'What about the soldiers who accompanied me here?' said Brogan.

'They can walk the last few miles to Colsbury,' said Daphne, 'and hand themselves in there. If they are prepared to swear allegiance to Empress Thorn, they will be assigned to a unit of the imperial army.'

'What is the imperial army doing in Colsbury?' said Brogan.

'Working for the Empress,' said Daphne. 'Her Majesty was very forgiving. Even the marines have pledged their loyalty to her. As we speak, the Banner of the Sapphire Throne is working side by side with the imperial army to prepare this world for imminent invasion by the gods of Implacatus; and a council of war is about to get underway. Your presence there could be useful.'

Brogan lowered her gaze. 'Will Thorn humiliate me in public? Will she force me to grovel, and shame me before the soldiers I used to command?'

Kelsey smiled. 'I think you might be in for a surprise, Brogan.'

Brogan walked forward, and Daphne escorted her to Frostback's flank. Belinda turned, then she and Austin started striding towards Ashfall.

Belinda smiled. 'It looks as though I shall be getting that flight with Ashfall, just like you said.'

'Yes,' he said. 'It's a pity it will only take two minutes; I had hoped for longer.'

***

The three dragons circled over the Summer Palace, then descended into the packed forecourt. The Empress was sitting upon the throne in the centre of the platform, and every seat was taken, with many officers having to stand to the sides and rear. A large space was quickly cleared for the dragons, and they landed behind the throne. Belinda unfastened the straps, and climbed down to the ground. Austin was going to stay with his dragon, so Belinda walked up onto the platform, and waited for Daphne to bring the prisoner.

None of the Banner knew Brogan's face, but many of the officers from the imperial army gasped as she stepped up onto the platform, her head bowed. Daphne led her to the front of the throne.

'Your Majesty,' she said, 'may I present Lady Brogan? She has flown from Plateau City to seek an audience with you.'

'Thank you, my Herald,' said Thorn. She glanced down at Brogan. 'Speak.'

Brogan lowered herself to her knees as a hush descended over the forecourt.

'Your Majesty,' Brogan said, her voice faltering. 'I surrender. I am here to beg for the lives of my family, and to apologise for the acts I committed as Bryce's Herald. I...'

'Enough,' said Thorn. 'I have heard enough.'

Brogan swallowed, as if she expected a sword to strike her neck at any moment. Thorn stepped down from the throne, and placed a hand on to Brogan's shoulder.

'Stand,' she said.

Brogan got to her feet, and Thorn embraced her. Someone from the Banner let out a cheer, and within seconds every officer in the forecourt was on their feet, applauding and roaring out their support. Thorn pulled back from Brogan, and raised a hand for silence. The forecourt calmed, and quietened.

'The quarrels of the past are over,' the Empress said. 'I shall not harm Lord Bedig, Lady Berra or Lady Bethal. They are the children of the greatest ruler this world has ever known. Let all witness the following – Lady Brogan, by her words today, has absolved herself of any mistakes she may have made in the past. Lord Bryce, too, I would forgive, if he were to say the same words to me as she has done. Unfortunately, as we know, that is unlikely to happen; but I do not hold Lady Brogan responsible for the actions of her elder brother. We face some hard choices; choices that will decide the future of this world.' She turned to Bridget's eldest daughter. 'Lady Brogan, I will now ask you to take your place at this council. You are part of this world, and deserve a say in its future as much as anyone else.'

Brogan stared at the Empress, her eyes wide, then Daphne led her to a seat on the high platform. Belinda followed her, and sat down between Shella and Agang.

The Empress resumed her place upon the throne. 'To open the proceedings, I would like to call our first speaker. She has experience of dealing with Ascendants, and I have asked her to provide some insights into their motivations.'

Sable rose from her seat and strode forwards. She glanced over the large crowd, and placed a hand on her hip.

'Good morning, everyone,' she said, her voice sharp and clear. 'Before I get started – to all of the Banner officers standing or sitting in front of me – my name is Sable Holdfast. Yes; you heard me correctly. It was I who ravaged your occupation of Dragon Eyre, and I who forced the gods to flee from that world in terror. Many of you may loathe me, but as the Empress has said – the quarrels of the past are over. All I ask of you now is that you listen to what I have to say. You may think me a heartless, ruthless, murdering witch, but I don't care, as long as you listen to my words for a few minutes.'

She took a breath.

'Some of you may be wondering – what do the Ascendants want with this world? Why would they invade? Well, I am here to add my own thoughts on the matter. We all know the Ascendants are after salve, that is no great mystery, but that does not affect this world. So, what *do* they want?' Sable pointed at Belinda. 'First, they want Lady Belinda. The Third Ascendant was supposed to marry Lord Edmond, but she proved to be an unwilling bride, and was rescued from his clutches by the Hold-fasts. The Second Ascendant wants her back. For that reason alone, I would fight the Ascendants until my dying breath, as Belinda is my friend; but I understand if not everyone here would be prepared to do the same. Second, they want the Sextant. Many of you may have never heard of this device, and might wonder if it is worth going to war over. I can understand that, too. However, there is a third thing that you should all know.' She paused, her eyes scanning the crowd. 'Implacatus is dying.'

A few of the Banner soldiers gasped, their faces darkening in shock or disbelief.

'Yes,' Sable said. 'Once again, you Banner officers heard me correctly. Implacatus is a dying world, just as Lostwell was. The lowlands below Serene and Cumulus are poisoned wastelands where nothing can live; a great toxic desert that is growing and spreading. This is the reason the Ascendants wished to conquer Dragon Eyre. They are in need of a new home. In desperate need. Having been driven out of Dragon Eyre, they are now casting their eyes around for another world to take; and guess what? This world suits their needs perfectly. It is clean, and unspoiled, with enough resources to last for thousands of years. With the Sextant under their control, they could transfer the entire population of Cumulus to our shores. As far as they are concerned, there is only one problem with this world – the people who already live here. If the Ascendants come, they will be embarking upon a war of annihilation, aimed at wiping out every mortal mage line that exists. The gods of Implacatus fear and hate nothing more than the concept of mortals with powers. To them, the only good mortal is a slave. To oppose them, we shall need to be as ruthless as the gods.' She paused again. 'As ruthless, in fact, as I was on Dragon Eyre. If those bastards want a war of annihilation, then we shall give them one, only it will be the gods of Cumulus who shall be annihilated!'

Many officers from the imperial army cheered, but Belinda noticed that the majority of those from the Banner were looking uncomfortable with the content of Sable's speech. Some were glaring at the Holdfast woman, while a few looked close to despair.

To Belinda's left, Shella let out a long sigh.

'I don't understand,' whispered Belinda. 'Why do the Banner officers look unhappy?'

Shella glanced at her as if she were mad.

'Belinda,' whispered Agang; 'they are unhappy because they have just discovered that not only is their home world dying, but that they are now expected to fight the gods whom they have served for thousands of years. Worse, the woman who has just told them this is the same woman who slaughtered countless numbers of their colleagues on Dragon Eyre.'

'Oh,' said Belinda.

'Quite,' said Agang. 'Let us all hope that their contracts are binding.'

'They are,' said Shella; 'and I should know, because I helped write the damn things.'

Sable strode from the platform, and the Empress lifted her hand.

'Now,' Thorn said, 'I would like to hear from the officers assembled before me. We shall start with the Banner of the Sapphire Throne. I want to hear the thoughts of any who wish to speak.'

A dozen arms shot up.

The Empress glanced at a man in the front row. 'Yes, Major-General?'

The officer stood. 'Your Majesty,' he said, 'Sable Holdfast is a war criminal who should be tried and executed. I am appalled that she was permitted to speak, and I am disgusted by the lies that came from her mouth. What proof can you show us that Implacatus is dying? The families of the soldiers who serve in the Banner dwell in the city of Serene – are they destined to die? Is there a plan to save them?'

Shella sighed again. 'This is going to be a long day.'

CHAPTER 27
A DECEPTIVE APPEARANCE

Pella, Auldan, The City – 15th Darian 3423

'You know,' said Aila, as she sat next to Karalyn on the cold sandy beach, 'what you told me was untrue. You could have taken me back to Kell. I could be with my children right now. You've been here nine days – nine days!'

Karalyn kept her eyes on the twins, who were running by the lapping waves of the bay.

'Maybe the Ascendants aren't coming,' Aila went on. 'Maybe Daimon only thought he knew how to use a Quadrant, and they appeared in the middle of an ocean.'

'Maybe,' said Karalyn.

Aila glared at her. 'Is that all you have to say?'

'Do you imagine that I want to be here?' said Karalyn. 'That I would choose to bring my children to the City?'

'It would have taken you five minutes to transport me to Kell.'

'And what if the Ascendants had appeared in that time?'

'It was a risk worth taking.'

Karalyn smiled, but her eyes remained cold. Aila turned her face away from the Holdfast woman, worried that she might say something she would regret. At times, she could barely believe that Karalyn and

Corthie were related to each other.

'What if you go back to Kell, and bring Corthie and my children here?' Aila said. 'Then Corthie could defend the City, and you could go home. We would all benefit.'

'Corthie's good, but he wouldn't be able to save the City on his own.'

'Are you implying that you can?'

'Aye.'

Aila laughed. 'How are you going to do that without killing anyone?'

Karalyn said nothing.

'Are you going to abandon your principles?' Aila went on. 'Are you going to pick up a sword? No offence, but I'm a better fighter than you. I'm pretty handy with a sword, even without battle-vision. I trained for decades, then, as soon as I get together with Corthie, everyone forgets, and sees me only as a wife and a mother. You don't have death powers, or flow, fire, or even stone. How do you think you are going to defeat an army? Even my powers might turn out to be more useful than yours.'

'Your powers will be useful. If an Ascendant arrives, and you catch a glimpse of him or her, then you'll be able to mimic their appearance, and sow confusion among the enemy.'

'Yes. I know. Wait. Is that the real reason you haven't taken me home? You want to use me as a distraction?'

'Partly.'

Aila sighed. 'Why didn't you tell me that? Really, Karalyn, you don't do yourself any favours. If you want me to help you, then help me.'

'How?'

'Well, for a start, you could place an image of the Second Ascendant into my mind. You've seen him. If I knew what he looked like, then I could copy his appearance.'

Karalyn frowned.

'This hasn't occurred to you, has it?' said Aila. 'You're supposed to be the mightiest mage alive, and yet you don't seem to have thought things through.'

Karalyn turned to her, and the image of a man appeared in her mind.

'Is that Edmond?' Aila said.

'No. It's Bastion.'

'Who's Bastion?'

'Edmond's son, and his chief lieutenant. His arrival in the City would be more believable than Edmond turning up. If the Second Ascendant wished to send reinforcements here, he would send Bastion. The other gods are terrified of him.'

Aila smiled. 'At last; we're getting somewhere. Was that so difficult? What else can you do to help me?'

'To be honest, I hadn't thought about it.'

'No kidding. Well, think about it now.'

Karalyn lit a cigarette. 'Alright.'

Aila glanced away as Karalyn sat in silence. The woman infuriated her at times. Karalyn was clearly intelligent about some topics, but utterly ignorant about other things, including simple human interactions. Was she so wrapped up in her own thoughts that she barely noticed how other people were feeling? She remembered Kelsey telling her that her big sister could be inconsiderate, and now Aila knew the truth of it. She peered up at the red sky over the bay, and saw Dawnflame circling over Pella, keeping watch, and remaining ready for any attack. It was true that Karalyn had used her powers to persuade the dragon to protect the City, but Sable could have done that; and Sable could also fight.

'Right,' said Karalyn; 'I've thought of something. Look into my eyes.'

Aila frowned, but did as she was told. She felt something pulse within her mind.

'I've adjusted your powers,' Karalyn said.

Aila stared at her. 'You've done what?'

'Your powers are fairly simple, Aila,' Karalyn said. 'You can manipulate the sight of others to appear as someone else. Well, now you can make people not see you at all.'

'Eh, what?'

Karalyn sighed. 'Do I have to explain it to you as though you were a child, Aila? You can now make yourself invisible. You're welcome.'

'But... how do I... what do I have to do? I...'

Karalyn pointed towards a family of Reapers sitting on the beach to their left. 'Go and practise on them, and leave me in peace to think.'

Aila got to her feet, her boots digging into the soft sand. She wondered if Karalyn had arrived at her idea because she wanted Aila to leave her alone; but it didn't matter. If she could make herself invisible, then a whole realm of possibilities had opened up for her. She glanced at the Reaper family. There were several adults and children on the beach. In summer, every inch of sand would be covered with Reapers, but a cold wind was coming from iceward, and only the hardiest were braving the beach in such weather.

You see me as...

No, she thought. That wouldn't work.

You cannot see me.

She walked towards the family. No one paid her any attention, but that didn't prove anything. She got closer to them, and stood by the edge of the group, and still no one glanced in her direction. She stepped into the centre of the group. Nothing. Aila smiled, than began to wave her arms around as if she were as crazy as Jade. She shouted, and jumped up and down, but the Reapers completely ignored her.

You can see me.

The Reapers cried out at the stranger in their midst. Two children screamed, and their father raised his arms to shield them.

You cannot see me.

A stunned silence fell over the family. The father's eyes glanced around, passing over where Aila was standing.

'Malik's crotch, where did she go?' someone yelled.

Aila retreated from the group, backing away until she had left them behind, then she laughed to herself and walked back to where Karalyn was sitting.

'It worked!' she said.

'Of course it did,' said Karalyn. 'Use your new power responsibly.'

Aila sat. 'Could you make me appear like a tree?'

'Why would you want to look like a tree?'

'Well, what if I am being chased through a forest?'

'Then make yourself invisible.'

'Oh. Yes.'

Karalyn's eyes darkened. 'They're here.'

Karalyn stood without another word, and gestured for her children to come closer.

'What is it, mama?' said Cael.

'We're going back to Tara,' she said, 'and then you will hide, just like we talked about. I don't want you to see the things I will have to do. Stay close to Aila, and protect the King and Queen with your powers. The Queen has a Quadrant. Use it if you need to escape.'

Aila got to her feet. 'Who's here?'

'Who do you think, Aila?' said Karalyn. 'The gods of Implacatus have just opened a portal in Tara.'

The air shimmered, and they appeared on Princeps Row. Aila almost panicked. A large, wavering black circle was hovering over the surface of the road by the ruins of Maeladh Palace, and soldiers were pouring through it. Squads of armoured warriors were already fanning out towards the mansions on the street, heading for the home of the Aurelians, while several bodies of those loyal to the City were lying dead on the ground.

Karalyn raised her arm, and the god controlling the portal on Princeps Row cried out in agony. He dropped his Quadrant, then over a hundred enemy soldiers collapsed to the ground. Karalyn sprinted through the chaos, picked up the Quadrant, and the portal closed. A company of Banner soldiers aimed their weapons at Karalyn, and she raised her arm again, and they fell to the flagstones. Aila gasped. While she had remained frozen to the ground, Karalyn had dealt with a god and every enemy soldier who had come through the portal. And now she also had a Quadrant.

Van burst out onto the road, his armour on, and nearly collided with Aila.

'The enemy soldiers are sleeping,' Karalyn shouted, as she stood over the body of the writhing god. She hesitated for a moment, her eyes pained. 'Kill them all.'

Van swallowed, then he nodded. 'Do as she says.'

Banner soldiers loyal to the City drew their swords, and began slitting the throats of those who had crossed through. Aila shuddered at the sight, then walked towards Karalyn, the twins following her.

'I told you to hide in the mansion,' Karalyn said. 'What I have to do is not for the eyes of my children, Aila.'

'You... you...'

Karalyn sighed, then she glanced down at the god by her feet, who was clutching the sides of his head and groaning in agony.

'Who is it?' said Van, approaching.

Karalyn shrugged. 'I don't know, and I don't care. The Ascendants will be planning to open another portal soon. I guessed that the first one would be here, but the next one could be anywhere. Deal with him for me, Van. Aila – take the twins indoors.'

Van stepped forward, and pulled his sword from its sheath.

'Aila,' Karalyn repeated. 'Wake up. It's happening. Take the twins indoors.'

Dawnflame swooped low over Princeps Row, and Karalyn glanced up. Her eyes clouded over for a second, then the dragon banked, and sped off towards Medio. Aila took a breath, then tried to smile at the twins.

'Come with me,' she said. 'Let's find Emily and Daniel.'

She took their hands and turned the twins towards the Aurelian mansion, as Van raised his sword over the god. All over the street, the City Banner were carrying out Karalyn's command, and blood was staining the flagstones as the sleeping soldiers were butchered. The twins stared at the carnage, and Aila wished she had spared them the sight. She ushered them behind the hedgerows and away from the awful spectacle, and guards allowed them to enter the Aurelian mansion. She found the King and Queen in their audience chamber. Both were by the window, staring out at the scene.

'Did you see what happened?' Aila said.

Emily turned, her features pale. 'Yes.' She noticed the twins. 'Those poor children. What have they just witnessed?'

'Don't worry,' said Kyra. 'Mama will kill all of the bad people.'

Jade ran into the room. 'Did you see that?' she cried.

Daniel nodded. 'We saw it, Jade.'

'They'd better leave some for me,' Jade yelled. 'I'm going out there. I'm not staying in here if there's killing to be done. Aila, are you coming?'

'Karalyn told me to protect the twins.'

Kyra frowned. 'We can look after ourselves.' She glanced at the Queen. 'Give me your Quadrant.'

Emily blinked, then she walked to a large cupboard. She unlocked it, opened the door, then withdrew a leather pouch and handed it to the child.

Kyra grinned. 'Thank you.'

Daniel stared at his wife. 'You cannot hand over the Quadrant to a child, Emily.'

Emily blinked again. 'What?' She seemed confused, and stared at Kyra as the girl pulled the device from the pouch.

'Who wants to come?' said Kyra. 'Let's kill some gods.'

'Me!' said Cael.

Kyra frowned at her brother. 'I wasn't going to leave you here, Cael. Who else wants to come? Mama needs our help.'

'No,' said Daniel. 'You must not leave the mansion. It's far too dangerous for children. I forbid...'

Kyra raised a finger, and the King's mouth clamped shut, and he sat down.

'I'll come, little mortal child,' said Jade, a wild grin on her face.

Aila stared at the twins. If she said nothing, then they were liable to vanish in an instant. She rushed to the wall, where several swords were hanging, and lifted one from the hooks that were keeping it in place.

'Me too,' said Aila. 'Your mother asked me to watch over you, and I have to do as she says.'

'Alright,' said Kyra. 'Cael, you keep watch behind us, and I'll look ahead.'

The air shimmered, and they found themselves back out on Princeps Row. Van was directing the City soldiers, who were finishing off the last of those sleeping on the flagstones. By Van's feet lay the decapitated body of the god who had opened the portal, but there was no sign of Karalyn.

'Uncle Van,' Kyra cried; 'where is mama?'

Van glanced up, and saw the twins walking with Aila and Jade towards him.

'You shouldn't be out here,' he said. 'Go back indoors and...'

Kyra narrowed her eyes. 'Where is mama?'

Van's expression altered in an instant. 'Karalyn sensed another portal opening in the Bulwark, by Arrowhead Fortress. She's gone there.'

Kyra grinned. 'Thank you, uncle.'

The air shimmered again, and Aila found herself high up on the battlements of the Great Wall. To her left was the moat, and then the plains that led all the way to the Eastern Mountains. Masses of greenhides were congregating just beyond the range of the wall's artillery, the low temperature keeping them more docile than they were in summer. Aila turned away from them, her attention pulled by the sounds of violence coming from the interior of Arrowhead Fortress. There was no sign of any portal, but Blades were battling hundreds of Banner soldiers from Implacatus across the open courtyards of the castle. Dawnflame soared down, but the two forces were intertwined, and the dragon refrained from sending a burst of flames into them. By the base of the Wolfpack Tower was a cluster of robed gods, standing with their arms raised at the dragon, but no powers seemed to be coming from them. Aila scanned the chaos for Karalyn, but could see no sign of her.

'I'm going after those gods,' said Jade, pointing at the tower.

'You don't need to worry about their powers,' said Kyra. 'Mama has turned them off. They don't even have self-healing any more.'

Jade laughed, then ran towards the stairs.

'Where's mama?' said Cael.

'I don't know,' said Kyra. 'Give me a moment.'

Kyra's eyes glazed over, and Aila turned to stare at Jade, who was running down the stairs of the curtain wall. Halfway down, she stopped, raised her hand, and the gods by the base of the tower screamed out in agony, their flesh withering and peeling off their faces, until all that was left were bare skulls. Their robed bodies toppled over, and the Blades let out a cheer. Jade then started to pick off the Banner soldiers a dozen at a time, her finger flicking between the armoured men. Each time she pointed, more soldiers fell, and the Blades began to push the Banner soldiers back against the high curtain wall.

Another scream distracted Aila, and she turned back towards the greenhides. Aila stared in disbelief. Hundreds of Banner soldiers had appeared in the midst of the mass of creatures, who turned on them in an instant, their claws and teeth ripping through them. Aila was certain that she could see Karalyn down among them for a split second, then the Holdfast woman vanished. A second later, Karalyn appeared on the battlements next to Aila and the twins.

'Mama!' cried Cael.

Karalyn glared at Aila. 'What are my children doing here?'

Aila stared at her. 'I couldn't stop them.'

'It's not her fault,' said Cael. 'We wanted to help you.'

Karalyn gave the twins a sad smile and crouched down next to them. 'I'm going to be very busy for a while, and I don't want to have to worry about you. You should have stayed in the mansion.'

'Is the mansion safer than here, mama?' said Kyra.

'Maybe not, but who is protecting the King and Queen?'

Cael and Kyra glanced at each other.

'Did you take the Queen's Quadrant?' Karalyn said.

A guilty look flashed over Kyra's features.

'What did I tell you about taking things without permission?' Karalyn said.

'Did you close another portal?' Aila said.

Karalyn glanced up at her, as though she had forgotten Aila was there.

'No,' she said. 'This was just a diversion. They sent through a thousand soldiers and a few gods, then opened their main portal in the middle of Port Sanders. I need to return there – the gods are besieging Tonetti Palace. I've transported a few regiments of Blades there, but an Ascendant is leading the enemy – and he's wearing eye-guards. Where's Jade?'

Aila pointed towards the stairs. Jade was still there, whooping and laughing at the carnage she was causing to the Banner soldiers in the fortress courtyard.

'Jade!' Karalyn called. 'I need you.'

'We can help, too,' said Cael. 'Please let us help you, mama.'

Karalyn stood. 'No. I will take Dawnflame and Jade, and then you three shall make yourselves invisible and stay here. I will be angry if you disobey me, children. Look after Aila, and stay safe.'

Jade appeared at the top of the stairs, and then she and Karalyn vanished.

Kyra scowled. 'I don't care what mama said. We're going to help her.'

'Wait,' said Aila.

The twins glared at her, defiance shining in their eyes.

'We should make ourselves invisible first,' Aila said. 'That might be fun.'

Cael laughed. 'Alright. It's done. No one will see us now.'

Kyra touched the Quadrant, and they appeared in the streets of Port Sanders. Bodies were littering the ground – civilians, Blades, Sanders militia, and Banner soldiers from Implacatus, and blood was streaming down the open gutters. Aila recoiled in horror, and felt her stomach churn. The sun was still low above the horizon, and the red light from the sky was reflecting off the walls and tiled roofs of the town, making Port Sanders appear as though it was bathed in blood.

'You shouldn't be seeing things like this,' Aila said to the twins. 'You're too young for this.'

Cael swallowed. 'I don't like it here.'

'Be brave, brother,' said Kyra. 'I'm frightened, too. Remember how you saved us from the greenhides in the desert. You were brave then.'

Cael nodded, and they began walking through the slaughter, heading towards the noise of battle. The number of bodies increased as they hurried along the alleyways of Port Sanders, then they turned a corner and saw a full-scale battle taking place under the red skies. Thousands of Blades were confronting an equal number of Banner soldiers, and they were fighting through the streets around Tonetti Palace. Fires were raging in some quarters of the town, and thick coils of black smoke were rising into the blood red sky.

Aila wanted to turn and flee, but she couldn't, not while she had the twins with her. They were invisible, she remembered, but that wouldn't help if a stray crossbow bolt struck them.

'Stay behind me, children,' Aila said.

They edged forward a few paces, then four Blades in front of them had their heads blown off in an explosion of blood and brains. Aila cowered back for a moment, her arms shielding the twins, then she saw the Ascendant. He was standing on top of a great heap of the slain; his arms raised. He pointed, and more Blades lost their heads.

'I can't get inside his mind,' said Kyra, her clothes spattered in blood.

'Bow before the might of Implacatus, mortals!' the Ascendant cried, his face lit with power. He swept an arm from left to right, and dozens fell, their heads bursting open like ripe fruit. He then pointed at a burning building, and flames rose into the sky, spiralling away from the ground, and forming themselves into a mass of white hot fire. He brought his hand down, and the flames smashed into the front of Tonetti Palace. The façade of the ancient edifice erupted into an inferno, and stones cascaded down, crashing into the streets below.

At the base of the mound of corpses, Jade was racing towards the Ascendant, her hands raised as she screamed and yelled at the top of her voice. A dozen Banner soldiers fell before her, but the Ascendant remained immovable. He pointed at the demigod, and a blast of death powers sent her flying backwards through the air. Jade slammed into the side of a building, and disappeared among the chaos. The noise was deafening, as screams and cries ripped through the narrow streets.

'It is over!' cried the Ascendant. 'Submit! Kneel before me, and your lives shall be spared.'

A figure appeared on the mound behind him, a sword in her hand. The Ascendant seemed oblivious to her presence, and Karalyn drove the sword through his back, the point bursting out from his chest. The Ascendant turned, and raised his hands, but Karalyn remained where she was, his powers unable to reach her.

Kyra touched the Quadrant again, and they appeared on the mound. Aila swung her sword, and sliced through the Ascendant's left arm, severing it at the wrist, then she plunged the steel blade deep into his throat. The Ascendant fell to his knees, the sword lodged in his neck. Karalyn rammed her fingers into his eyes, then withdrew them a moment later.

The Ascendant stared at her, then his eyes closed and he fell to the side, one sword embedded in his back, and another in his neck. Karalyn placed a boot onto his side and heaved her sword from his body; then she swung it down, cutting off his right hand. She staggered back, swaying, as sweat ran down her forehead, then she crouched by the body of the Ascendant and removed the Quadrant from his robes.

'Is he dead?' said Cael.

'No,' said Karalyn. She glanced at Aila as if she were about to issue another reprimand, but shook her head instead, and sat down on the heap of corpses.

Kyra turned, lifted her right hand, and hundreds of Banner soldiers fell to the ground, their eyes closed. The Blades stared about in shock and disbelief. Karalyn surveyed the scene with tears in her eyes, then she got back to her feet.

'Kill them, Blades,' she cried from the heap of dead. 'Let none of the enemy survive this day. Esher, the Ninth Ascendant, is now my prisoner.'

The Blades roared in victory, then they surged among the sleeping Banner soldiers, their swords drawn. Karalyn took hold of the twins and turned their faces away from the street.

'I'm sorry you saw that, children,' Karalyn said. 'Let's take the Ascendant to the King and Queen.'

'What about Jade?' said Aila.

Karalyn glanced over the carnage in the streets. 'I don't see her.'

'I do,' said Kyra.

The girl disappeared without warning, then she returned a moment later with an unconscious Jade by her feet.

'Is it over?' said Aila.

'I want to say yes,' said Karalyn, 'but we know how much the gods desire salve.'

Aila stared at the burning palace. 'Are Doria and Lydia alright?'

'I can sense their self-healing powers down by the harbour,' said Karalyn; 'they're fine.'

The air shimmered, and they appeared on the gravel driveway outside the Aurelian mansion. Several City soldiers jumped at their arrival, their bows tensed in their hands, then they backed away from the sight of the wounded Ascendant. Jade opened her eyes, and coughed up some blood.

'What happened?' she groaned.

'The plan worked,' said Karalyn. 'Your distraction gave me the time I needed to get behind the Ascendant. Thank you, Jade.'

Van approached, flanked by Banner soldiers loyal to the City. He stared down at the body of Esher, then gestured to his men.

'Bring chains, and bind the Ascendant.'

A sergeant saluted, then raced off.

'I presume you meant to keep him alive?' Van said, his eyes on Karalyn.

'Aye. For now. He will be unconscious for another few minutes. Do you have a knife?'

Van nodded, then he held out a hand to one of the soldiers, who passed him a small blade. Karalyn took it, and drove it into the Ascendant's left eye. Cael jumped back, his face wide with shock.

'Should I take the twins inside?' said Aila.

Karalyn started to laugh, but it quickly turned into tears, and she wept, a hand covering her face.

'It's all right, mama,' said Kyra.

The King and Queen emerged from the mansion, along with dozens of City soldiers, and they surrounded the unconscious Ascendant. Daniel stared open-mouthed at the enormous body, his eyes going from the knife in his eye, to the sword in his throat, and then to his severed wrists.

'Amalia's sweet breath,' gasped Emily. 'You got him.'

Dawnflame circled overhead, then landed on Princeps Row. She pushed her head through the trees and glanced down at Karalyn.

'All Banner forces are in full retreat, Holdfast witch,' she said, 'and every god that came with them lies dead. No more portals have been opened. Should I bite the insect's head off?'

'Not yet,' said Karalyn, wiping the blood and tears from her face. 'I'm going to need the King and Queen to stand back. Aila, make yourself appear like Bastion. Van, you and your soldiers shall pretend to be working for the Ascendants. The children and I shall disappear from sight, along with Jade.'

Van saluted. 'Yes, ma'am.'

'What should I say to him?' said Aila.

'Find out if and when reinforcements will be coming,' said Karalyn. 'We need to know how much time we've got.' She handed the two Quadrants she had taken from the gods to Emily, and then the King and Queen moved back through the crowd of soldiers.

You see me as Bastion.

Van stifled a cry, and a few of the City's Banner soldiers paled in fear.

'I shall awaken our guest,' said Karalyn. She glanced down at the huge body of the god for a moment, then she, the twins and Jade vanished from sight.

The Ascendant roared out in agony, then opened his right eye.

'You have failed me, Lord Esher, and you have failed the Blessed Second Ascendant,' Aila cried.

The Ascendant's gaze turned to Aila, and panic flashed over his wounded face. He tried to lift his hands to remove the knife and the sword, then he stared at the stumps at the end of each arm, and cried out in anguish and pain.

'Lord Bastion,' he sobbed. 'I am sorry.'

'I should kill you for your incompetence, Esher,' Aila said. 'Why did you not call for reinforcements, if you were being defeated?'

Esher looked confused for a moment. 'But, my lord, I was told that no reinforcements from Implacatus would be coming, not unless I failed to report the capture of the City within six hours.' His features altered a little, as if he was starting to suspect that he was being tricked. 'Why are you here, my lord? I was informed that you would be leading the invasion of the Star Continent. You told me this yourself.'

A massive wave of vision power tried to penetrate Aila's mind, and her disguise slipped. The Ascendant forced her to her knees, then Karalyn made herself visible again. She pulled Esher's face towards her, and his right eye rolled up into his head.

'I have scoured his mind,' the Holdfast woman said. 'Nothing remains of his consciousness – no thoughts, no memories. He will not be troubling us again.'

'We should kill him,' said Emily, pushing her way back through the crowd. 'We killed Simon; why not Esher?'

Karalyn frowned. 'Put him somewhere safe for now.' She stood. 'You all heard what the Ninth Ascendant said. If he fails to report within six hours, then we can expect more forces to arrive in the City. Dawnflame, I would be obliged if you would help with the destruction of the last remaining enemy forces within the walls of the City. Take Jade with you; she has proved herself yet again.'

The dragon tilted her head, while Jade brushed the grime from the front of her dark green dress and strode toward Dawnflame's flank. The demigod climbed up onto the harness, and then the dragon beat its wings and ascended into the red skies. Soldiers approached the body of the Ascendant, and began securing him with chains, as the others watched.

'I will take the twins inside, and clean the blood from their faces,' said Karalyn, her features drawn and exhausted. 'I would also like something to eat, and maybe a glass of wine.'

'Take whatever you need,' said Daniel, 'and thank you.'

'Yes,' said Emily, 'thank you, Karalyn. You have achieved more in one hour than we achieved against Simon in months.'

Karalyn nodded, her eyes heavy with guilt, then she ushered her children towards the main doors of the Aurelian mansion.

The King and Queen turned back to watch the body of Esher be wrapped in chains by a squad of soldiers. Aila joined them.

'A short time ago,' Aila said, 'I was sitting on the beach in Pella with Karalyn, watching her children play on the sand. I asked her how she thought she could possibly defeat an invasion from Implacatus. Well, now I know.'

'She is the miracle we required,' said Emily, glancing at the two Quadrants in her hand. 'If she desired power, she could be a god.'

'Thank Malik she is on our side,' said Daniel.

Emily started to cry. 'And her children... I knew they were powerful, but...'

The last of the chains were fixed to the Ascendant's body, and Van nodded.

'Good work,' he said. 'Take him to the dungeons under the ruins of Maeladh Palace, and post guards. No one is to approach without Karalyn or their Majesty's permission.'

The soldiers saluted, then they began dragging the body down the gravel driveway towards Princeps Row.

'Set a timer for six hours, Major-General,' said Daniel. 'And inform us when there is one hour remaining.'

'Yes, your Majesty,' said Van.

'We should get some rest, darling,' the King said to Emily. 'This is not over yet.'

Emily wiped her eyes. 'Will it ever be over?'

'Before today,' said Aila, 'I would have doubted it, but now? After everything I have seen, nothing is impossible; and if anyone can end this, Karalyn can.'

CHAPTER 28
PUT TO THE TEST

Colsbury Castle, Republic of the Holdings – 25th Day, First Third Winter 534

'Thank you all for coming,' said Daphne to the sixteen major generals of the Banner. 'On behalf of her Majesty, I hope we have answered your questions regarding some of the matters you have raised.'

The most senior member of the Banner leadership stood. 'Thank you for inviting us, Commander. We shall speak to the personnel under our command, but I suspect that many will still feel aggrieved. We are grateful that Sable Holdfast will no longer be permitted to address the Banner, but this does not get to the heart of the problem. We were told on Dragon Eyre that we would be involved in a civil war upon this world, not that we would be expected to fight our fellow Banners from Implacatus. The bond that unites all Banners is strong, and some in the Sapphire Throne may flinch from being led into open conflict with our home world – a home world that you insist is about to die. I must warn you, Commander, that the soldiers' councils currently being formed might reject our authority. Some are of the opinion that the contracts they signed were agreed under false pretences, and are therefore invalid. I, and the other major generals gathered here today, cannot guarantee that discipline can be maintained under such circumstances.'

'I understand,' said Daphne. 'Please keep us informed of any decisions taken by the soldiers' councils, and know that we are always prepared to negotiate over any of the conditions laid out in the contracts.'

Thorn kept her expression neutral as she gazed at the senior officers of the Banner. She had felt it better to let Daphne lead the talks with them, in an attempt to distance herself from the bitter disputes that had broken out since Sable's speech at the council of war. Whether it had worked or not was still unclear, but her heart was heavy with doubts and apprehensions.

The sixteen commanders of the Banner divisions stood and bowed before the throne, then they filed out of the grand audience chamber in the Summer Palace. Sanang guardsmen closed the double doors behind them, and Thorn glanced at her advisors. Daphne, Shella and Agang were sitting on her left, while Kelsey, Cardova and Caelius were on her right. Thorn stepped down from the throne and turned to face them, so she could address them all at the same time.

'Your thoughts?' she said.

'This is a disaster,' said Shella. 'Half of the Banner are refusing to obey orders, and won't leave their barracks, while the others are only begrudgingly doing what they are told. If it wasn't for the imperial army, who were our enemies just a few days ago, Colsbury would be undefended.'

'I don't understand,' said Thorn. 'Isn't it the case that there is a Banner working for the King and Queen of Salve City? I was told that they are utterly loyal to their new employers.'

'That is true, your Majesty,' said Cardova, 'but the Banner of the Lostwell Exiles had a long time to come to terms with their new situation before they were put to the test against Lord Simon. Even so, their loyalty to the crown of the City was contingent upon a vote held by the soldiers' council there, and Major General Van Logos came close to losing his position. The soldiers from Dragon Eyre have only recently been torn from their old lives and placed upon this world. They still see their true home as Implacatus.'

'We should never have allowed Sable to speak at the council of war, your Majesty,' said Agang.

Kelsey groaned. 'Do we have to go over this again? It was impractical, not to mention dishonest, to keep Sable's presence here a secret. The Banner would have found out on their own, and then they would have accused us of lying to them.'

'I agree,' said Thorn. 'Caelius, what do the sergeants make of all this?'

The old veteran frowned. 'It doesn't look good, your Majesty,' he said. 'Most of the sergeants I have spoken to are reading their contracts very carefully, looking for any excuse to have them declared invalid. There are some, of course, who feel the same way about the gods as I do, but they are in the minority. Most just want to return to their homes in Serene, to be reunited with their families.'

'I want to turn to a question that no one has yet asked,' said Thorn. 'What will the Banner do if Implacatus invades this world?'

No one spoke for a moment, then Cardova raised his head.

'If Lord Edmond were to arrive today with gods and the remaining Banners from Implacatus,' he said, 'then many in the Sapphire Throne will refuse to take up arms against them. If the major generals try to assert their authority, they will be removed from their positions by the soldiers' councils, for recklessly endangering the lives of those under their command. They might even decide to form a rival Banner, and switch sides.'

'You mean,' said Thorn, 'that we might have inadvertently supplied Lord Edmond with a massive army that will oppose us?'

'That's the worst case,' said Cardova. 'You have to remember, your Majesty, that many in the Sapphire Throne still feel gratitude toward you for having rescued them from Dragon Eyre. They were abandoned by the gods of Implacatus, and left stranded and alone on a foreign world that despised them.' He paused. 'If I had to guess, and it's only a guess, then I think the most likely outcome is that the Banner will split. Some will stay loyal, some will prefer to remain neutral, while others will go over to Lord Edmond.'

'There will be chaos, in other words,' said Thorn. She glanced at Daphne. 'I want the imperial marines moved on to the island of Colsbury, and the Banner units sent to the mainland. If Edmond invades, I would rather rely on those who are prepared to fight to defend this world.'

'I will do so, your Majesty,' said Daphne. 'However, it is my duty to point out that this course of action may only serve to increase the sense of mistrust among the Banner soldiers. If we treat them all as potentially disloyal, it may push the undecided into the arms of those who wish to be openly disloyal.'

'Should we recall Belinda from the mainland?'

'In some ways, your Majesty,' Daphne said, 'Belinda is our greatest hope. Her presence among the Banner divisions defending the approaches to Colsbury has so far worked in our favour. The soldiers from the Sapphire Throne seem to prefer working for an Ascendant, and the three Banner divisions under her command have remained loyal. If we were to recall her to the island, then her forces may decide to refuse to obey any further orders.'

Thorn gave a wry smile. 'And to think that I was told that the Banners are the most loyal and professional forces in existence. Their loyalty to me appears to be as shallow as a puddle of rainwater. We have healed them, fed them, and armed them, and yet they would desert our cause at the first obstacle.' She sighed. 'Belay my orders for now, my Herald. Leave the Banner and Belinda where they are, and I shall give the matter more thought. This meeting is adjourned. I wish to speak to Sable regarding the practicalities of transporting several hundred thousand civilians from Serene to this world. Perhaps if the families of the soldiers were here, the Banner may be more likely to remain loyal. Kelsey, come with me.'

Thorn and Kelsey stepped down from the platform and strode to the door that led to the private stairs. A squad of Sanang guardsmen accompanied them as they passed out of the audience chamber and up the steps.

'May I speak, your Majesty?' said Pechtang, as they ascended the stairs.

Thorn nodded.

'We should be rooting out the traitors from the Banner, your Majesty. Every one of those ungrateful bastards should be questioned, and reminded of the oaths they swore. If they refuse to serve you, they should be executed.'

'The Banner outnumber my other forces two-to-one, Pechtang,' the Empress said. 'If they resisted such questioning, then open conflict would break out, and we shall have done Lord Edmond's work for him.' She turned her gaze to Kelsey. 'You remained fairly quiet during our discussion. I would like to hear more of your thoughts.'

'It's an impossible situation, your Majesty,' said the Holdfast woman. 'Whatever we do, there will be consequences. It sounds crazy, but our best chance of success might come from Edmond. If he arrives here, and decides to treat the Sapphire Throne as traitors, and then kills many of them, the others might conclude that their best chance of staying alive is to remain loyal to us. We have to hope that Edmond is as much of a bastard as we think he is.'

They reached the upper levels of the Summer Palace and entered Thorn's private quarters. The Sanang guardsmen remained outside, and Thorn walked with Kelsey into the large apartment. Ivy and Sable were already there, standing out on the highest balcony that overlooked the island.

Sable nodded as the Empress approached with Kelsey. 'How did it go, your Majesty?'

'Badly,' said Thorn. 'It looks as though we will soon have a mutiny on our hands.'

Sable lowered her gaze. 'Maybe Agang was right, and I shouldn't have spoken in front of the officers.'

'It wasn't so much your presence that irked them,' Thorn said, 'though they clearly weren't delighted to see you. No, it was more the content of your speech that has upset their sensibilities.'

'I only spoke the truth, your Majesty.'

'Yes, I know. However, the truth can hurt, and the truths you mentioned have wounded them deeply. Of course, they have a point. We recruited them to fight a civil war, not to take on their fellows from Implacatus. Lucius believes that the Banner will split into many fragments if Edmond arrives in force, and I tend to agree with his analysis. If only I could know in advance which units will remain loyal to us, then we could take some practical steps, but such knowledge is impossible to obtain. Not even you could read the minds of a hundred and sixty thousand soldiers, Sable.'

'The truth will arrive at the same time as Edmond,' said Kelsey.

'Indeed,' said Thorn, 'but by then it will be too late.'

'May I smoke, your Majesty?' said Sable.

'You don't need to ask permission when we are out on the balcony,' Thorn said.

Sable lit a cigarette. She offered one to Kelsey, but the younger woman shook her head. Thorn leaned her arms on the balcony railings, and glanced down into the forecourt. Work on renovating the defences had come to an abrupt halt in the aftermath of Sable's speech, and nothing had been done in the seven days since. Piles of building materials lay stacked up, while the Banner soldiers stationed in the Gatehouse were refusing to leave their barracks. Thorn glanced to her right, where the slender bridge joined the island to the mainland. The majority of the imperial army had been positioned far to the north and south of the road that ran from the Plateau through the mountains to the Holdings, and the little village was being occupied by Belinda and her three divisions of Banner soldiers. If there was a mutiny or rebellion, Colsbury would be a dangerous place to be, and only the Sanang guardsmen would stand between Thorn and the Banner.

She turned back to Sable. 'Have you begun investigating the removal of the Banner families from Serene?'

'Yes, your Majesty,' Sable said. 'I spent a few hours on the Sextant yesterday, looking into the possibilities. The main problem is knowing who to transport. The Sextant doesn't know which civilians are related to the soldiers in the Banner, and it would take far too long to pick out individual families. We would need a year, and a detailed list of names and addresses. The only other option would be to bring them all here – the entire mortal population of Serene. That means millions of people, dumped on to this world. None of them would feel any kind of allegiance to the Star Continent, and they would be more likely to help the gods.'

'Many of them hate the gods,' said Kelsey.

Sable nodded. 'But they also fear them.'

'Bringing millions of unwilling civilians to our lands would cause chaos, quickly followed by famine,' said Thorn. 'Is there no way to warn them about the impending death of their world?'

'None that I can think of,' said Sable.

Thorn turned her glance to the snow-capped mountains on the far side of the lake. She had been sole Empress of the world for eleven days, and already the problems she faced were threatening to overwhelm her. She was barely able to sleep at night, her thoughts whirling until each became another knot of anxiety and worry. If she had a year, she told herself, then she could work through each problem individually, but she doubted that Edmond would be so generous with his time. She wanted to weep, but couldn't do it in front of Sable, Kelsey and her mother. She noticed that Ivy had remained silent throughout the conversation, not comprehending the Holdings language spoken by the others.

'Can we talk in Rahain so that my mother can understand?' said Thorn.

'I do have one idea,' said Kelsey, switching to the Rahain language, 'but it's a little extreme.'

'Don't keep it to yourself,' said Thorn. 'I will listen to any suggestion.'

'Alright. Well, the Sextant is very powerful, aye? It can create worlds, and it can also… destroy them. What if we, uh, destroyed Implacatus? We could annihilate our enemies with one stroke.'

'Is this what it has come to?' said Thorn.

'I'm not saying I agree with my own idea,' said Kelsey, 'but it's an option.'

'I could ask the Sextant if it's possible,' said Sable, 'but I think I already know the answer. I believe it would work.'

Thorn shook her head, her nerves stretching to breaking point. 'You are talking about the slaughter of millions – children, innocents, slaves, the sick and the old. I will not deliver death to an entire people who have done nothing to hurt the Empire. Do you think me a monster?'

'The Ascendants would do it,' said Sable. 'Maybe we have to be as ruthless as them to win.'

Thorn glared at Sable. 'Are you in favour of this idea?'

Sable took a moment to respond, her eyes narrow. 'No,' she said eventually. 'It's too much. There is a point at which any victory would be hollow, if it meant that we had stooped so low to achieve it.'

'I am glad you think so,' said Thorn.

'Could you not use the Sextant to drop the gods of Cumulus into the middle of the ocean?' said Kelsey. 'Or into a volcano on a barren world?'

Sable shook her head. 'Do you remember what their palaces are like? They are designed to prevent vision powers and Quadrants from accessing their interiors. If I tried to remove everyone from Cumulus, I would only reach the servants and slaves who move around outside. The Ascendants might not even notice.'

'I do not envy you, daughter,' said Ivy. 'From all that I have heard, you are faced with troubles that would drive the wisest to despair. All you can do is remain true to yourself. If you carry out slaughters and massacres, then you will be no better than the gods you oppose.'

Thorn hung her head. 'Are we destined to be defeated?'

Ivy placed a hand on to Thorn's arm. 'No. Nothing is destined, daughter. There is always hope.'

'Shit,' Sable muttered.

The others turned, and saw Sable pointing into the forecourt below them. A dark, swirling mass had appeared in the area between the Great Keep and the Summer Palace. A few Banner soldiers by the doors of the gatehouse stared at it for a moment, then turned and ran.

'It has begun,' said Sable.

Thorn gazed in shock as huge figures started to pour through the black void, each as tall as any Kellach marine. They were wearing brightly-coloured armour, and bore long swords and axes.

'Who are they?' said Ivy.

'Ancients with battle-vision,' Sable cried. 'I'm going down there.'

'No,' said Thorn. 'Summon the dragons at once, and then go to the Great Keep. Protect the Sextant at all costs, Sable; that is my command to you.'

Sable frowned, then she glanced towards the village on the mainland. 'Another portal has been opened, about a mile away, south of the village.'

'The dragons, Sable.'

Sable's eyes glazed over for a second, then she nodded. 'They are on their way, your Majesty.'

The doors to the private apartment burst open, and Sanang guardsmen rushed inside.

'Your Majesty!' Pechtang cried. 'We are under attack!'

'Go, Sable,' said Thorn; 'and good luck.'

Sable nodded, then sprinted for the door, dodging between the Sanang warriors. Thorn gazed down at the armoured gods massing in the forecourt. Over a hundred had already raced through the portal, and more were entering Colsbury with every second that passed. In front of them, three gods stood apart from the others, and were gesturing up at the Summer Palace, and at the Great Keep.

A full battalion of a thousand Sanang guardsmen were emerging from the lower floors of the Summer Palace, and they charged into the ranks of the Ancients. The portal had closed, leaving some three hundred gods in the forecourt, but they were more than a match for the mortal warriors, and Thorn heard Pechtang cry out next to her as they watched the Sanang start to fall. The Sanang were fighting as well as any mortals without battle-vision could, their powerful arms wielding weapons that dealt injury after injury to the Ancients. But each wound closed as soon as it had been delivered, and the bright armour worn by the Ancients was deflecting most of the blows. By the time the first Ancient died, his head shorn from his shoulders, over a dozen Sanang had perished. Sable appeared in the forecourt, a Fated Blade in her hand. She rallied the Sanang warriors, and they charged back into the Ancients with Sable at their head. Her sword moved faster than Thorn's eyes could follow, and Ancients began to fall in numbers.

'Leave her!' cried the leader of the gods. 'Storm the keep – bring me the Sextant!'

Around half of the Ancients turned away from Sable and the Sanang, and charged through the open doors of the Great Keep. Sable broke off from the fight and went after them. She entered the keep and disappeared from sight. Without her powers to assist them, the remaining Sanang were pushed back towards the Summer Palace by the Ancients who had stayed in the forecourt.

'Here come the dragons!' yelled Kelsey.

Thorn glanced up, and saw Frostback, Halfclaw and Ashfall soaring down from the heavens towards the island. They formed a column, and descended over the forecourt. Frostback arrived first, and unleashed a ferocious blast of flames upon the Ancients; then Halfclaw followed. He opened his jaws, and the flames enveloped a dozen armoured gods, who fell to their knees amid the conflagration. Halfclaw swooped low and picked up an Ancient with both forelimbs, then he ripped the god's head from his shoulders and tossed the remains into the lake. Ashfall came last, and her mighty jaws added to the inferno. Smoke rose up from the burning forecourt, but Thorn could see Ancients still moving amid the flames and the heat.

The three dragons banked, readying themselves for another pass, then Ivy pointed towards the east.

'Look. More dragons are coming. Are they on our side?'

Thorn narrowed her eyes at the large cluster of black specks in the sky. Perhaps Blackrose had come in their hour of need, bringing a hundred of her kin, but then she heard Kelsey cry out in anguish.

'They're not on our side,' the young Holdfast woman said. 'They're the same bastards we ran into on Implacatus. Edmond must have brought them.' She raised her arms in the air. 'Frostback! Look out!'

The new dragons arrived in a rush of noise. Each was black, but their wings were torn, and their faces withered and gaunt. Thorn stared at them, and shuddered. They were dead. Risen monstrosities, reanimated by the gods. Too late did Frostback and the others see them. Kelsey's cries had been lost in the wind, and the three dragons were turning by the Spire when the undead creatures were upon them. Two charged into Halfclaw, their claws and fangs tearing into his flanks. Frostback went to his assistance, but three undead dragons were right behind her, and she had to swerve and dive to avoid them. Ashfall tried to gain altitude, but she was surrounded, and the slender grey dragon disappeared amid a dozen of the undead beasts. Frostback unleashed fire at those attacking Halfclaw, and he managed to wriggle free of their grasp as two fell burning into the lake, their tattered wings aflame. Frostback and Halfclaw tried to reach Ashfall, but were driven off by over twenty of the undead creatures, then the slender grey dragon came back into sight, as those who had surrounded her dispersed. Ashfall's wings were broken, and her head and throat ripped to shreds. For a moment, she seemed to hang in the air unsupported, then she fell. Her vast body struck the surface of the lake, and was gone.

Frostback let out an anguished roar of grief.

The undead beasts formed back into a group and flew at the silver dragon and her wounded mate. For one horrible moment, Thorn thought that Frostback and Halfclaw were going to stay and fight, that they would throw their lives away in grief and rage; but they turned, and soared away towards the mountains, their speed outmatching that of the undead creatures pursuing them.

Kelsey burst into tears, and Thorn embraced her.

'What shall we do, your Majesty?' said Pechtang, his features drawn.

'Look,' said Ivy. 'The Banner are surrendering.'

Thorn pulled her gaze away from Kelsey, and glanced down. Over a hundred Ancients were still in the forecourt. Their armoured plates were blistered and scorched, but very few had died from the flames of the dragons. Over by the gatehouse, a mass of Banner soldiers were emerging, their hands in the air. An officer ran out from their midst, and prostrated himself before the Ancients. One of the gods spoke to him for a few moments, then nodded. The officer rose to his feet, more words were exchanged, and then the Banner soldiers began to return to their posts in the gatehouse.

'They have changed sides,' said Thorn. 'I fear this battle will be over soon.'

'Treacherous fools!' cried Ivy. 'Is that all it takes for them to break their oaths? What shame this day has brought; what infamy!'

'Let us hope that the Banner divisions under Belinda's command do not turn so easily,' Thorn said. 'She is our last hope.'

'I can feel the Ascendants from here,' whispered Kelsey. 'Four have entered this world through the other portal Sable mentioned. Even Belinda cannot defeat four Ascendants.'

'We must escape this island,' said Pechtang. 'If the Banner are in control of the gatehouse, then they will let the Ascendants in without a fight. We have to leave, your Majesty.'

'The Ancients are entering the Summer Palace,' said Ivy. 'They are coming for us.'

Pechtang's eyes fell. 'It is too late to run. So be it.' He turned to the guardsmen under his command. 'We shall fight those bastards for every inch, every step. We will not be abandoning our Empress. Issue the command – no retreat, no surrender. We will show the gods that the Sanang can die with honour.'

A guardsman saluted, then ran for the doors.

'You should barricade yourselves in here, your Majesty,' Pechtang went on. 'My men and I shall defend the doors to our last breath.' He bowed before her. 'It has been the greatest honour of my life to serve you, Empress. If, somehow, you survive this day, do not forget me.'

The guardsmen left the apartment, and the doors were closed and locked. Thorn wiped the tears from her face, and walked into her sitting room. Ivy and Kelsey joined her, and the three women stood together in silence facing the doors, as the sound of battle grew nearer.

'Should we jump from the balcony?' said Kelsey.

'Out of the three of us,' said Thorn, 'only you would die, Kelsey.'

Kelsey cast her gaze downwards. 'Then maybe I should jump. If I died, then you would be free to use your powers.'

'No, Kelsey,' said Thorn. 'I will not have you sacrifice your life for me. Besides, I can think of no better reason to die than in the defence of our world. It is the ordinary people I feel sorry for. If the Ascendants prevail, then every mortal who lives here will suffer.'

'Sable might be in control of the Sextant, daughter,' said Ivy, 'and Belinda has the strength to match anyone. Do not despair. Even if we three die, this war is not over.'

'I'm never going to see Van again, am I?' said Kelsey. 'Or Frostback, or Karalyn. How I wish Karalyn was here.'

'Perhaps she will come for us,' said Ivy.

'Then she'd better be damn quick about it,' said Kelsey.

The sound of battle reached the doors of the apartment, and Thorn shuddered as she heard the Sanang warriors fall one by one. There was a roar of defiance, then it fell silent. Thorn took Kelsey's hand to her left, and Ivy's to her right, and raised her chin.

The doors of the apartment were smashed open, and armoured Ancients peered in over the bodies of the slain guardsmen. One of the Ancients stepped over the corpse of a Sanang warrior and entered the apartment.

'Who are you?' he said.

'I am Empress Thorn,' she said, 'the Holder of the World.'

The Ancient smiled. 'And the others?'

'To my right stands my mother, and on my left is Kelsey Holdfast.'

'One of the Holdfasts?' he said. 'Is anyone else in the apartment?'

'No.'

The Ancient nodded to the others behind him. 'Search the place, in case she's lying, then gag, hood and shackle all three. The Blessed Second Ascendant would like to meet them.'

CHAPTER 29
THE FALL

olsbury Castle, Republic of the Holdings – 25th Day, First Third Winter 534

Keir walked through the portal and stepped on to the grassy hillside. For a moment, he gazed around at his surroundings. The road from the Plateau to Colsbury ran from left to right in front of him, and the shore by the lake was filling rapidly, as soldiers from the Banners marched through the shimmering void from Cumulus.

He felt a hand touch his arm.

'Let's not stand in the way, your Majesty,' Daimon said. 'There are wagons and carriages behind us that also need to pass into the Star Continent.'

Keir smiled serenely, and allowed Daimon to escort him a few paces to the right. For seven days, he had been an honoured guest of the Blessed Second Ascendant, and had lived within the walls of the Palace of the Almighty, and he savoured the fresh air that was gusting along the valleys of the Barrier Mountains. On his right were two Ascendants – the Eighth, Lord Tamid, and the Twelfth, Lord Lloyd. They were wearing the finest armour Keir had ever seen; great plates of compressed granite that sparkled in the afternoon sunshine. Flanking them were over two hundred armoured Ancients. A further three hundred had been sent ahead to Colsbury as an advance force, but Keir was glad he had remained with the main army. He was an Emperor, and mere fighting was beneath him.

Keir surveyed the army that was being assembled between the lake and the hillside. Every Banner soldier in Serene had been called up for duty, and even though only a small fraction had so far passed through the portal, the ranks lined up by the shore looked impressive enough to defeat any enemy.

'What a glorious sight, your Majesty,' Daimon said. 'The combined might of Implacatus: Ascendants, Ancients and their loyal Banners. How lucky we are to have them on our side. With their aid, we shall brush the usurpers aside, that you may reclaim the throne that is your birthright.'

Keir smiled. His birthright. It was strange to imagine that, just a few days before, he had been unaware that he was the true Emperor, when now it seemed so obvious, so right. So natural. He was destined to rule the Star Continent. The Sacred Lord Edmond would remain his over-lord, of course, but the Star Continent would be Keir's.

Lady Albrada, the Eleventh Ascendant, strode through the portal, flanked by a hundred gods from her household. Dressed in a magnificent set of full battle-armour, the Eleventh Ascendant was a radiant vision of power and splendour, and Keir gasped at the sight. A tear trickled down his cheek at her beauty, and he knew he was the most fortunate mortal alive. To have such allies who were willing to help him take the throne of the Empire took his breath away.

'Make way for the most Blessed and Beloved Second Ascendant!' Albrada cried, her voice the most beautiful thing Keir had ever heard.

The Ancients, gods and mortal soldiers close to the portal bowed their heads. Keir did the same. He might be the Emperor of an entire world, but he was nothing compared to Lord Edmond, his protector, his patron. The crowd hushed as the Second Ascendant made his appearance, striding through the portal with Lord Bastion by his side, and Keir felt an urge to fall to his knees and weep with joy. Lord Edmond gazed at his gathering forces, a benign smile gracing his radiant lips, then he walked with Bastion towards the other Ascendants. Lloyd, Tamid and Albrada bowed low before him, then an Ancient in pink and green armour stepped forward, and fell to one knee.

'My Blessed Lord,' the Ancient said.

'Speak, Commander Atheron,' said Edmond.

'The advance force of three hundred Ancients are in the castle of Colsbury, my lord,' Atheron said. 'They are currently brushing aside all resistance. Some two hundred thousand mortal soldiers are based upon the mainland, but many are too far north or south to interfere with our plans. However, a large force is blocking the approach to the bridge that leads to Colsbury.'

At that moment, the air crackled overhead, and Keir glanced up. Over a hundred of the mighty dragons that served Lord Edmond had appeared in the sky above the shoreline. They swarmed together, wheeling and banking over the gentle slopes and still waters of the lake, then they turned as one, and soared away in the direction of Colsbury.

'Continue, Lord Atheron,' said Edmond. 'Where are the Holdfasts?'

'Something is blocking all vision powers from penetrating the palace upon the isle, my lord,' said the armoured Ancient; 'therefore, we suspect that Kelsey Holdfast is present. There is no sign of Corthie or Karalyn, but Sable and Daphne Holdfast have both been seen within the walls of the island.'

'Sable is here?' said Bastion.

'Calm yourself, my son,' said Edmond. 'You are wearing eye-guards, as am I. Sable cannot hurt us. Lord Atheron, tell me – where is the Third Ascendant? Where is my bride?'

'Lady Belinda has been seen two miles to the north of our position, my lord,' said the kneeling Ancient. 'She is close to the bridge that joins Colsbury to the mainland, rallying three divisions of the Banner forces extricated from Dragon Eyre, and is preparing to attack down the coastal road.'

Edmond laughed. 'My bride is going to attack us? What spirit she has; but then, you already know that, don't you, Atheron?'

The ancient kept his head bowed, and said nothing. Keir glanced back at the portal for a moment. Banner soldiers, gods, wheeled artillery devices, and wagons filled with supplies were still emerging from the black void, an unceasing procession of power and strength.

Edmond turned to the other Ascendants. 'Lord Lloyd and Lady Albrada shall accompany Lord Atheron and the army to the north, and there you shall defeat the Third Ascendant's forces and seize the bridge to the island. The Banner soldiers under Belinda's command shall be deemed traitors, and treated as such. Give them no quarter.'

The two Ascendants bowed their heads.

'My most noble lord,' said Albrada; 'if we come face to face with the Third Ascendant, are we permitted to slay her?'

Edmond said nothing for a moment, then a glistening tear rolled down his radiant cheek. He gave the briefest of nods to the Eleventh Ascendant. 'Yes,' he whispered.

'My lord?' said Bastion.

'I have given the Third Ascendant every opportunity to repent her evil ways,' said Edmond, his voice aching with sadness. 'There comes a time when justice must outweigh sympathy. I shall mourn her for a thousand years, but she will not make a fool of me again. A thousand gods witnessed her humiliate me upon our wedding day, and for that she must pay the ultimate price. Bring me her head, Eleventh Ascendant.'

Albrada bowed again. 'It shall be done, my lord.'

Edmond turned to Daimon. 'Do you detect the presence of Karalyn Holdfast on Colsbury, dream mage?'

'No, but that doesn't mean she isn't there,' said Daimon. 'She could be keeping her powers quiet, and remaining unseen.'

'I believe that the advance force would have flushed her out into the open by now,' said Bastion. 'She would have used her powers to destroy them if she were here.'

Daimon nodded. 'Aye. That's likely. She lacks the ruthlessness needed to bide her time and set a trap for us.'

Edmond glanced at the lake and the snow-capped mountains that lay beyond the still waters.

'Where is she, I wonder?' he said. 'Our mission upon this world cannot be deemed a success until Karalyn lies dead at my feet. Bastion, summon my guard. We shall move with haste to Colsbury and retrieve the Sextant, while Lord Lloyd and Lady Albrada crush the disloyal Banner forces led by the Third Ascendant. Lord Tamid, you shall accompany us.'

The Eighth Ascendant bowed his head. 'Yes, my lord.'

'Your task shall be to protect the new Emperor and my dream mage, Lord Tamid,' Edmond said. 'They are feeble mortals, all too easily killed by a loose arrow or an errant stroke of a sword.'

'It would be an honour, my lord.'

Edmond moved to a clear space on the hillside, away from the ranks of soldiers still marching through the portal. Lord Tamid joined him, escorting Keir and Daimon along the grassy slope, then Bastion gathered a force of sixty armoured Ancients, and they surrounded the two Ascendants.

'Take us to Colsbury, my son,' Edmond said.

Bastion took a Quadrant from his black robes, and swept his fingers over the surface. The air shimmered, then they appeared in the vast forecourt that lay between the Great Keep and the Summer Palace. Smouldering bodies of Sanang warriors littered the bloody and scorched flagstones, along with more than a score of Ancients, their armour blistered and burnt.

'I see that the Holdfasts' dragons have been here,' said Edmond.

'Our own force of dragons has defeated them, my lord,' said Bastion. 'One was slain, and the other two were driven off.'

Edmond glanced up at the Summer Palace. 'Is the Sextant in there?'

'No, my lord,' said Bastion. 'It is being kept within the keep behind you.'

Edmond smiled, then turned to face the keep. 'Damn these eye-guards. It makes one feel almost blind. However, if Sable is here, they will be essential to our success.'

'Sable had eye-guards the last time I saw her,' said Daimon. 'I instructed my soldiers to rip them from her face, but I don't know if they succeeded.'

Edmond frowned. 'Why would Sable don eye-guards? Surely she needs her eyes to use her powers?'

'She needs them to protect herself from me, my lord,' said Daimon.

A dozen armoured Ancients emerged from the ground floor of the Great Keep, their armour scorched and blackened. One approached, and bowed before Edmond, Bastion and Tamid.

'The advance force has achieved its objectives, my most noble lord,' the Ancient said. 'The Banner forces guarding the gatehouse have submitted to us, the palace has been cleared, and my forces are surrounding the Sextant chamber on the upper floor of the castle keep.'

'Why are they surrounding it?' said Bastion. 'Is the Sextant not yet in our possession?'

'It is being defended by Sable Holdfast, my lord,' said the Ancient, his gaze lowered, 'and she is resisting our attempts to seize it.'

'Sable Holdfast has the Sextant?' Edmond cried. 'You fools! Bastion, take us to this chamber immediately; we must prevent her from activating the device. She could take it anywhere she pleased.'

'But, my lord,' said Bastion, 'my eye-guards are preventing me from seeing into the interior of the keep.'

'Then remove them, my son. Now.'

A flicker of fear passed over Bastion's face, then he lifted his fingers to his eyes, and plucked out one of his eye-guards. He stared up at the Great Keep for a moment, then quickly slipped the eye-guard back into place. Keir frowned. Why would a mighty Ancient fear a mere mortal such as Sable?

'Ensure that we appear between Sable and the Sextant,' said Edmond.

Bastion nodded. 'Yes, my lord.'

Bastion glided his fingers over the Quadrant, and they appeared amid the chaos of the Sextant room. Decapitated Ancients lay sprawled across the floor, and the dozen armoured gods that Bastion had brought along were packing out the chamber, forming a line of steel in front of the Sextant. Tamid shoved Keir and Daimon behind him and drew his sword, as Sable glanced over, her Fated Blade dripping with blood. Next to the witch stood a young man, his right hand raised.

Edmond laughed. 'We meet again, Sable Holdfast. You should have fled when you had the chance. The Sextant is now mine.'

Sable locked eyes with the Second Ascendant, and sprang through the air. Her sword cut down the nearest Ancient, the dark blade slicing through his armour and cleaving his body in two, then she lunged towards Edmond.

Daimon raised his hand and Sable crashed to the floor, dropping the Fated Blade as her fingers gripped the sides of her head.

'Hold her down!' Daimon cried, as he ran towards her.

Two Ancients moved forward, knelt, then grasped Sable's shoulders and legs as she writhed on the floor. Daimon crouched over her, and forced one of her eyes open. He stared into her face.

'Don't resist,' Daimon laughed. 'This can only end one way.'

Sable cried out, emitting a scream of terror and helplessness, then her body stilled.

Daimon glanced up at Edmond. 'She is now under my control, my lord.'

'I don't want her under your control,' said Edmond; 'I want her dead.'

'But, my lord,' Daimon said, 'think how powerful we would be with someone like Sable fighting our battles for us. With her abilities, we could hunt down and kill every Holdfast on this world, at no risk to ourselves.'

Edmond smiled, then he glanced at Bastion. 'Well, my son; what do you say? You are the one whose mind was wounded by this mortal witch. Would you prefer to see her butchered, or would you like to see her kill our enemies?'

The young man who had been with Sable pushed his way forward, and pointed at Edmond.

'Look out!' Keir shouted.

Daimon turned. He lifted a hand towards the young man, who cried out, then fell to the floor unconscious.

'Who is he?' said Edmond, looking down at the body lying on the floor by his feet.

'He is a demigod by the name of Austin,' said Daimon. 'He assisted Sable on Dragon Eyre.'

Edmond nodded. 'Kill him.'

An Ancient raised his sword.

'Wait,' said Bastion. 'My lord, if Daimon speaks the truth, then have him command Sable to kill this demigod. Then we shall see how useful the witch might be to our cause.'

Keir blinked, as a strange feeling seeped into his mind. In some ways, he felt as though he was awakening from a deep sleep. He glanced around, then remembered that he was in the Sextant chamber within the Great Keep on Colsbury. Where had he been before that? Oh, yes – he had been imprisoned within the Palace of the Almighty in Cumulus. No, not imprisoned; he had been Edmond's honoured guest. A sickly sense of realisation grew. He had bowed before the Second Ascendant, after watching Bryce's head disintegrate in front of him, but everything was vague and cloudy after that. There was only one explanation – he had been under Daimon's control. Now that the dream mage was focussing all of his energies upon Sable, his grip on Keir had weakened. Fear gripped his heart. If anyone noticed that his own consciousness had resurfaced, what would they do? Keir kept his face expressionless as he glanced at the other people in the room. He recognised Lord Tamid, the Eleventh Ascendant, which proved that some of what had occurred had remained intact within his memory, and then he saw Sable lying on the floor next to a young man. Austin, Daimon had named him.

'Very well, Bastion,' said Edmond. 'Daimon, make your puppet dance for us. Have her slay the demigod.'

Daimon got to his feet. 'This will take a moment or two, my lord,' he said. 'Sable's mind is strong. To break it down completely will take a considerable amount of power.'

Edmond raised an eyebrow. 'Is that an excuse I hear? And I thought you were a mighty dream mage, Daimon. Surely the mind of a feeble mortal woman cannot be too great a challenge for you to overcome?'

'Oh, I will break her; have no doubt about that, my lord.'

Daimon raised a hand, and pointed it at Sable. Her body remained motionless, but Keir could see the terror in her eyes. She was fighting the dream mage with everything she had, but Keir knew her defeat was inevitable. A flicker of sympathy for his aunt flashed through his mind, but he did nothing, too afraid of Daimon and the Ascendants to act.

Sable got to her feet and stood with her back straight, the tears on her cheeks the only sign that a small part of her mind was free to know what was happening. She turned towards Austin.

'Butcher him,' said Daimon. 'Cut his head off, Sable. I command it.'

The Ancients and Ascendants in the chamber stilled, each gazing at Sable to see what she would do. The Holdfast witch crouched, and picked up the Fated Blade. She glanced down at Austin, and raised the weapon.

'She can't bring herself to do it,' said Tamid. 'Look; she hesitates.'

'The first kill is always the hardest,' said Daimon. 'Once she has slain her friend, she will become more pliable.'

Sable kept the dark-bladed sword steady over Austin's unconscious body, her eyes betraying the torture her mind was enduring; then her hand brought the weapon down. The blade sliced through Austin's neck, and his head rolled to the side. Edmond picked it up, and laughed, while Sable remained frozen, her tears unchecked.

'Well done, Daimon,' said Bastion. He turned to Edmond. 'May I strike the Holdfast witch, my lord? She has caused me much pain.'

'You may do so, my son; but do not kill her. Daimon has proved how useful she could be.'

Bastion reached forwards and gripped Sable's throat in his left hand. He lifted her off the ground, gave a look of utter hatred, and punched her in the face. Sable flew backwards, colliding with a wall and sinking to the floor, where she collapsed in a heap.

Daimon frowned. 'I will need to ensure that my controls are still in place,' he said, his voice tinged with anger. 'If you hurt her too much, her mind might rebel.'

'Do as you must, dream mage,' said Edmond. 'We should shackle her while she is not needed.'

'I will see to it, my lord,' said an Ancient, bowing.

'Is anyone else within the keep?' Bastion asked.

'Every mortal within these walls has been slaughtered, my lord,' said the Ancient.

Bastion's face lit with rage. 'You were ordered to spare the Holdfasts and their closest allies,' he cried. 'They are ours to kill.'

'My lord,' said the Ancient, 'the only Holdfast in the keep was Sable. Some others were arrested within the palace, and are now in our custody.'

'I see,' said Bastion, his anger fading. 'Who, exactly?'

'We have the false Empress, my lord. She was taken with her mother and Kelsey Holdfast. We also found two mortal mages upon the lower floors of the palace – a woman with flow powers called Shellakanawara, and a man with limited death powers named Agang Garo. We are holding them within a secure location in the palace basement.'

'We have Kelsey?' said Edmond. 'Excellent. Perhaps we could watch Daimon's puppet slay the Holdfast girl. Have the captives brought here while you fetch the shackles for Sable.'

The Ancient bowed his head again, then hurried from the chamber.

Bastion turned to Keir. 'Where are the other Holdfasts?'

Keir jumped, then remembered that he was supposed to be under Daimon's control. He tried to smile.

'My mother...' he said; 'I don't know where my mother is. She might be with the army. My younger brother Corthie is thousands of miles away, in a southern land called Kell, while my... son will be on the Holdfast estate.'

'Your son?' laughed Edmond. 'Why didn't I know you had a son and heir? We shall have him brought here, but before he looks upon his father, we shall have to do something about your appearance. At present, your broken face would scare any child.'

Edmond extended a hand and touched Keir's cheek. A wave of intense healing powers burst into Keir, and he felt his features reform. His nose cracked back into place, and new teeth sprouted up from his jaws, replacing those that had been lost. Keir cried out in pain, then panted. He touched his face. It was whole again.

'There,' said Edmond. 'Now you are presentable.'

'What about Karalyn?' Bastion said. 'Keir has neglected to mention the location of his other sister.'

'I... I don't know where she is,' Keir said.

'I can answer that,' said Daimon, as he crouched by Sable's unconscious body. 'Karalyn went to the City of Salve to assist in its defence.'

Edmond's face darkened. 'Then I fear for the success of Lord Esher's mission.'

The Second Ascendant strode towards the Sextant, and the armoured Ancients parted to let him through. Edmond placed his hand on to the glass surface of the device, and a broad smile broke across his majestic face.

'Ah, the Sextant. It has been a very long time since I heard its voice ask me what I desire. Show me the world of salve, Sextant, that I may see what occurs there.'

Edmond's eyes glazed over as the others watched.

Keir edged away a step. No one was paying him any attention, and he wondered if he would be able to flee before...

'Stay where you are, Keir,' said Daimon in a low voice. 'If you try to run your mind will be crippled with agony; and we don't want that now, do we?'

Keir froze, his spirits withering. He had betrayed his own world, and for what? His looks? Would he stand and do nothing if Daimon ordered Sable to murder Kelsey? He swallowed. And why had he mentioned Cole?

Edmond turned from the Sextant, his features burning with a savage rage. 'That vile witch!' he cried. 'Karalyn has ruined our plans for the salve world.'

'What did you see, my lord?' said Bastion.

'Piles of dead Banner soldiers,' Edmond spat, 'along with the headless bodies and burnt remains of over a dozen Ancients. Esher has gone, where I know not, but his mission has failed.'

'Did you see Karalyn, my lord?'

'Of course I didn't see her, you fool! She is a dream mage, and can hide from anyone she chooses. But, she is there; I know it. She has elected to protect that world, and has deserted her own.'

Bastion bowed his head. 'Should we organise another portal, my lord; to send reinforcements?'

'Why – so that they can also be destroyed?' Edmond took a breath. 'No. The salve world will have to wait until we can bring a far larger force; one that includes Daimon. Only a dream mage can defeat another dream mage. This lesson I have learned well. Karalyn can have the salve world for now. We shall deal with her once this world has been subjected.'

'Shall we proceed with our plan, my lord?'

'Yes, my son. It will soon be time to bid farewell to Implacatus forever.'

Edmond turned back to the Sextant.

'My lord?' said Tamid. 'Why would we be bidding farewell to Implacatus? It still has several decades of life left in it before it becomes uninhabitable.'

'We must seize this opportunity while it still exists, Eighth Ascendant,' said Edmond. 'We cannot wait mere decades for catastrophe to overtake us.'

'But I have many friends in Cumulus, my lord,' Tamid said.

'And they shall all be saved,' said Edmond. 'Fear not, Eighth Ascendant, for I shall not be destroying Implacatus this day. We must subdue this world first, and transport every Ancient, god and demigod to our new home upon the Star Continent. Why do you think I summoned so many of the inhabitants of Cumulus out into the open before we departed? Did you think it was just so they could wave us on our way? They are outside for a reason.'

The Second Ascendant placed his hand back on to the device.

'Sextant,' he said, 'locate the immortal beings in Cumulus. How many are visible?' He paused, as the Sextant spoke in his mind. 'Transfer them here, to this world. Bring them to the same valley where the soldiers from Dragon Eyre arrived, six miles north of Colsbury. Do it now.' He paused again. 'Excellent; they are here. The process has begun. As soon as this world is in our possession, I shall command the Sextant to destroy Implacatus in its entirety. Nothing of our home world will remain but dust and the eternal void of darkness.'

Tamid sobbed, but Edmond was too absorbed in the Sextant to notice. Keir glanced at Bastion, but the Ancient's face was unreadable, and if he felt anything about the cataclysm threatening his home world, he didn't show it. Keir thought back to Serene, and the millions of mortals who dwelt there, but he was too stunned to feel any pity.

Edmond turned, and gazed at the silent gods in the chamber. 'This world is now our home, for evermore. Tamid, you shall return to Cumulus in my stead, for I wish never to set foot on Implacatus again. Gather the remaining immortals from their palaces, and begin moving them and the last Banner forces to this world.'

Tamid bowed. 'Yes, my lord.'

'Bastion,' Edmond went on, 'you shall transport yourself to our army on the mainland opposite Colsbury. There, select a hundred gods, and travel to the valley in the mountains to greet the first batch of arrivals from Cumulus. Send them far and wide, to conquer every corner of this world. Corthie Holdfast and his mother must be hunted down and slain, and every mortal family with even the slightest trace of mage powers must be put to the sword.'

'It shall be done, my blessed lord and father,' said Bastion, bowing. He removed his eye-guards, touched the Quadrant, then he and Tamid vanished from the chamber.

Daimon got to his feet. 'So, you're staying, eh? I suspected you might.'

'And yet,' said Edmond, 'I have not heard any objections come from your lips, dream mage.'

Daimon shrugged. 'I don't care if you decide to live here. I think we work well together. Leave me in peace for now, though, so that I can continue to set controls into Sable's mind. Oh. One more thing. If you would rather that Karalyn didn't turn up here unexpectedly, then you should remove the Weathervane from the side of the Sextant when you aren't using it. Karalyn relies upon that to travel between worlds. With no active Sextant to communicate with, she will be stranded on the salve world until we are ready to deal with her.'

Edmond raised an eyebrow. 'Is that so? Thank you, Daimon; you have proved a most useful ally.'

The Second Ascendant crouched by the right-hand flank of the huge device, and pulled the Weathervane out. The low hum from the Sextant ceased, and it seemed to lower a few inches, the floorboards creaking beneath it.

Edmond strapped the sword to his belt. 'We shall leave you now, Daimon. Ensure Sable does not slip from your grasp before the shackles get here.'

Daimon nodded, then turned back to the Holdfast woman.

Edmond gestured to Keir and the Ancients in the chamber. 'Let us leave this charnel house. The Holdfasts must have a more pleasant room in which to sit. Keir, lead the way.'

Keir swallowed, then strode from the room. The armoured Ancients followed, flanking Edmond as they moved through the upper floor of the Great Keep. Keir stopped at the door of the sitting room, where he had often seen his family gather to eat, drink and talk, and he felt a surge of pity and grief pass through him. He might not be able to flee, but with Daimon channelling his powers into Sable, the dream mage's control over him was fading with every moment that passed.

Keir opened the door, and a bloody scene stretched out in front of him. Servants lay dead on the floor, their bodies cleaved by the weapons of the Ancients. Keir suppressed his nausea, then his eyes fell on the body of Tilda Holdwain. She was slumped over an armchair, her skull split open. Keir put a hand to his mouth, but his cry pierced the air.

'Tilda,' he cried, and ran to the chair. He knelt by the body and wept, no longer caring if the gods were watching him.

'Oh dear,' said Edmond. 'It appears that you may have been a little hasty when you massacred every mortal in this keep, Commander. It seems that this woman was dear to the new Emperor.'

'Apologies, my lord,' said an Ancient.

'It matters not,' said Edmond. 'We shall find him another mate. He can have a whole harem, for all I care. Clear the bodies from the room, and have them burned in the forecourt.'

'Yes, my lord.'

The Ancients strode into the sitting room, and began picking up the corpses. Edmond glanced around, then walked to a cabinet and withdrew some bottles, which he laid out on a table in front of him.

'Brandy from Rahain,' Edmond said, 'wine from… Anamindhari, if that is how one pronounces it. Whisky from Severton. Which do you recommend, Keir?'

Keir glanced up from the side of the armchair. 'My lord?'

'Never mind,' said Edmond. 'There is plenty of time to try all of the delights that this world has to offer.' He sat in an empty chair. 'I wonder if this is where Daphne Holdfast used to sit. For too long we lived in fear of the Holdfasts, and here we are. To be honest, I was expecting a harder fight.'

The door opened, and an Ancient entered. 'My lord,' he said. 'Shackles have been delivered to the Sextant chamber, and Sable Holdfast has been bound. We have also brought the prisoners, as you requested.'

Edmond nodded. 'Send them in.'

The Ancient bowed his head, then led in the captives. Each had chains attached to their wrists and ankles, and they clanked as they shuffled across the carpet. Keir raised his eyes. Thorn was the first to enter, followed by Ivy and Kelsey, then Shella and Agang.

Edmond smiled. 'Well, well; how the strong have become weak. A Holdfast, a usurper, and three… others.'

Kelsey spat on the floor in front of Edmond. 'We aren't scared of you.' She glanced at Keir. 'Get up, brother. Stand on your feet and stop weeping like a child. If you're working for these arseholes, then at least have some dignity about it.'

Edmond laughed.

'Aye, laugh, ya prick,' Kelsey said, 'but one day a Holdfast will be laughing over your cold, decapitated body. Go back to Implacatus, while you still have the chance.'

'I had no idea this would be so amusing,' said Edmond. 'Unfortunately for you, my delightful Holdfast, I shall not be returning to Implacatus.' He smiled. 'I shall be staying here from now on. This world is now my home.'

'I am the rightful ruler of the Star Continent,' Thorn said; 'and you are not welcome here.'

'Nonsense,' said Edmond. He pointed at Keir. 'This mortal is my appointed ruler, not you. Behold your new Emperor, his glorious Majesty Keir Holdfast.'

'You're out of your mind if you think we're ever going to bow in front of him,' said Kelsey.

Edmond stared at the young Holdfast woman. 'Where is your mother? Where is the head of this noxious family?'

Kelsey stared back at him. 'Fuck you.'

Edmond raised a hand to strike her, then Daimon coughed from the doorway.

'Is your pet securely bound?' said Edmond, lowering his hand.

'She is, my lord,' the dream mage said, as he strode into the sitting room. 'You should probably know that I sensed Daphne Holdfast's battle-vision when we arrived. She was fighting in the depths of the Summer Palace.'

'And now?' said Edmond.

'I haven't sensed anything from her for a while,' Daimon said. 'She's probably dead.'

'We shall have Colsbury searched,' Edmond said; 'in case she yet lives. If you sense her again, inform me immediately.'

Daimon nodded. 'Aye, my lord.'

'Where is Sable?' said Thorn.

'Wrapped in chains and under Daimon's control,' said Edmond. 'Now, which one of you should I kill first?'

'How about yourself?' said Kelsey.

The door opened again, and another armoured Ancient entered.

'My lord,' he said, 'I bear news from the mainland.'

'Then speak,' said Edmond. 'Are the Eleventh and Twelfth Ascendants bringing me the head of the Third?'

The Ancient lowered his gaze. 'No, my lord. The Third Ascendant is pushing our forces back towards the bridge. If she reaches it, we might not be able to prevent her from getting on to the island.'

Edmond's eyes darkened. 'Have the dragons recalled at once, and direct them against the Third Ascendant. Bring everything we have to bear upon the bridge. If necessary, destroy it. Belinda must not be allowed to set foot on the island. Go, now.'

The Ancient bowed and rushed away.

Thorn's eyes kindled with hope. 'The Third Ascendant is still fighting?'

'You've had it now, Edmond, ya bawbag,' Kelsey laughed. 'Belinda's coming, and no power on this world can stop her.'

Edmond stared at the prisoners, as fear flickered across his face. 'Gag them.'

CHAPTER 30
NO VICTORY

Colsbury Castle, Republic of the Holdings – 25th Day, First Third Winter 534

Belinda swung her sword, her right arm pulsing with battle-vision. The steel blade carved through the shield of an Ancient, but then shattered against the stone armour protecting his neck. She released her grip on the hilt, turned and grabbed the head of another Ancient, who was charging towards her. Belinda heaved upwards, and ripped the god's head from his shoulders. To her right, ten Banner soldiers under her command disintegrated into a cloud of red mist, and she pushed her death powers out in an arc, using them to shield the others fighting alongside her. Over a hundred enemy soldiers withered and died from her powers, and the area before them cleared, excepting the dozen armoured Ancients still rushing towards them. Two fire bolts whooshed overhead, slamming into the lines of Belinda's three divisions, and the earth trembled from the explosions as flames and smoke rose into the sky. Belinda picked up a long halberd, its axe blade stained red, and rammed it into the face of the closest Ancient. The spike tore through his mouth and nose, leaving half of his head hanging loose, then Belinda dropped the weapon and rolled as a ballista bolt sped past her.

She ripped the stone breastplate from a dead Ancient and held it in front of her as she got back to her feet.

'Fight!' she screamed, and the Banner soldiers behind her charged into the carnage, following the Third Ascendant into almost certain death. Thousands of dead littered the battlefield, heaped up along the lanes and streets of the little village opposite the bridge that led to Colsbury. Thousands, she thought, in little over an hour of fighting. The two Ascendants, the Eleventh and Twelfth, had attacked her force from the south while Belinda had been trying to organise her own offensive, and the army from Implacatus had occupied the bridge before Belinda's soldiers could reach it. The village was in smoking ruins, pulverised by enemy artillery, and set ablaze by fire bolts sent by the gods and Ascendants, and every road was blocked by mounds of the fallen.

Belinda picked up another sword and charged forward, climbing one of the mounds, as her loyal Banner forces followed like a wave behind her. A hailstorm of arrows and bolts rained down upon them, killing dozens as they clambered up the hill of corpses, but not a single Banner soldier under her command faltered or fled. Moments before the battle had begun, Belinda had wondered if they would fight for her, but that had been before Albrada and Lloyd had unleashed their death powers upon them, slaughtering hundreds in seconds. As soon as Belinda's three divisions of the Banner of the Sapphire Throne had seen that, their loyalty had no longer been in question.

Two Ancients leapt down from the summit of the mound and crashed into Belinda, knocking her off balance. Her fingertips grazed the bare skin of one, and his head exploded, then she gripped the other by the throat and drained his life force, feeling his power enter her. She cast the withered corpse to the side, then lifted her right arm, and a wide column of fire rose from the burning village. She flicked her hand, and the flames tore through the lines of enemy Banner soldiers between her and the bridge, incinerating dozens. Amid the screams and smoke, Belinda clambered to the top of the mound, and stood.

'I am the Third Ascendant!' she cried. 'Surrender or die.'

She saw Albrada, the Eleventh Ascendant, standing a few yards from the bridge. The woman had her hands raised, and Belinda felt a powerful wave of flow and death powers pound at her defences. The Third Ascendant gritted her teeth and stood her ground, then she sent her own powers back into Albrada. The Eleventh Ascendant screamed, then was flung back through the air as blood burst from her face. She crashed into the still waters of the lake; no doubt still alive, Belinda knew, but out of action for a while. The Banner soldiers behind her cheered, and surged down the far side of the mound, and into a ferocious barrage of crossbow bolts loosed by the thick lines of enemy combatants remaining between Belinda and the bridge. Another fire ball smashed into the ranks of the Sapphire Throne, but the others kept going, charging down the mound. The two armies met by the water's edge, shields pushing against shields, and Belinda charged into the mayhem. The lines of the enemy bent and buckled under the onslaught of Belinda's sword, her death powers flashing out from side to side in an orgy of destruction. Two columns of armoured Ancients attacked Belinda's force from the south, carving their way through the tight press of soldiers. Belinda turned to face the new threat, but Lloyd, the Twelfth Ascendant, split the ground under her with a surge of rock powers. Belinda stumbled backwards, falling to the ground among the dead and injured. Her soldiers were dying so quickly that she felt close to despair. What had begun as thirty thousand Banner soldiers had been reduced to a handful of battalions and companies, and more were falling with every second that passed.

A roar of noise came from her right, and the enemy forces by the northern flank of the bridge began to break. Belinda got back to her feet and turned. Thousands of soldiers from the imperial army had arrived, fanning out over the hillside as they waded into the enemy ranks. Holdings cavalry were charging the enemy Banner formations protecting their artillery, their lances lowered, while marines were advancing down the road, battering the enemy soldiers aside with their heavy shields and maces. Belinda stared at them for a moment, her spirits soaring with pride at the sight; but her heart was stained with pity, for she knew that many would die. She felt another surge of powers come from Lloyd, but she was ready, and she deflected them into the two columns of Ancients attacking from the south, blowing the heads off over a dozen. The marines reached her position, sweeping away the last of the enemy Banner soldiers from the edge of the bridge, and Belinda turned, not to face them, but to stare at the oncoming Ancients. She lifted a hand, gathered her strength, and the crack in the ground next to her widened, and opened up beneath the charging gods. The ragged chasm split the earth, and the waters from the lake poured in, flooding the Ancients in their heavy armour and pulling them down into the swirling darkness of the abyss. As the Ancients tried to scramble clear, she sent down her death powers, and the scream that arose tore through the heavens.

'Ma'am?' said a panting marine officer, the front of his armour spattered with blood. 'Shall we charge the bridge?'

'No,' Belinda said. 'Leave the bridge to me. If you charge, the Twelfth Ascendant will kill you all. I need the imperials to contain the army from Implacatus. Close the portal, if you can.'

'Aye, ma'am,' said the marine officer. 'You heard Lady Belinda,' he cried. 'To the portal!'

Several sergeants and officers began to guide the marines towards the foothills where the invading army had arrived, leaving Belinda and her sorely-depleted companies of loyal Banner soldiers alone on the broken shoreline. Belinda turned back to the bridge, and gazed at Lloyd.

'It's just you and me, Twelfth Ascendant,' she said, as she strode forwards.

Lloyd remained on the bridge. Over a dozen armoured Ancients had gathered around him, but panic was in his eyes.

A tall, broad figure in pink and green armour pushed his way to the front of the Ancients guarding the Twelfth Ascendant, then he walked forward a few paces, a long, steel sword held in both hands.

'To reach Colsbury, you will have to get past me first,' the figure said. 'Dearest mother.'

Belinda stared at the figure opposing her. He was wearing a helmet that covered his face, but she knew she wouldn't have recognised him even if his head had been bare. Was he lying? Was this a trick?

'Who are you?' she said.

'Have you forgotten me, mother?' the man said. 'I am Lord Atheron, one of the most powerful Ancients alive, and I am your son. For millennia, I have lived in shame and disgrace, thanks to the actions of you and my father. Today, by your death I shall be redeemed. Come, mother. Embrace your son.'

Belinda sent out her vision powers, but Atheron's helmet visor had a thick grille protecting his eyes, and her powers were rebuffed.

Atheron laughed. 'Are you frightened, mother? Lord Edmond chose me especially for this battle, for he knew I longed to spill your blood. Grant your son a gift, and place your life into his hands.'

He charged at her, crossing the last few yards of the bridge in seconds, the huge sword raised in both arms. Crossbow bolts spat out from the loyal Banner soldiers to her rear, but they were turned away by the stone armour. Belinda dodged Atheron's first blow, then ducked under the second.

'Wait,' she cried. 'Must I kill you? Can we not talk? I could never...'

Atheron charged again, his sword sweeping against her breastplate and sending her spinning through the air. She somersaulted, and crashed into a ditch by the edge of the chasm she had opened. A squad of Banner soldiers ran at Atheron, but he cut them down in moments. Belinda pulled herself up, and realised that she was crying. How stupid, she thought. Crying over a son whose existence she hadn't even guessed. She remembered what Silva had once told her in the basement under the palace of Dun Khatar on Lostwell, when they had been inspecting the sarcophagi of her dead descendants, but she could scarcely believe that a living, breathing son was walking towards her, ready to end her life.

'Why are you doing this?' she cried.

'Because I hate you, mother. You abandoned me on Implacatus when you betrayed the Second Ascendant to run off with Nathaniel. Do you have any idea what the Ascendants did to me? How much I suffered, before they would believe that I was loyal to them, and not to you? Where were you, mother? Why did you leave me?'

'If you know anything about me,' she said, 'then you will know that I can't remember any of that.'

He raised a hand, and his death powers surged around her defences, and she knew at once that she was stronger than her son. She shielded herself, but sent no powers back into him.

'Don't make me kill you,' she said.

Atheron laughed. 'Kill me? You are too weak-minded to kill me, mother. I saw you in Cumulus, when you were wearing the crown of spikes. Lord Edmond invited me into the Palace of the Almighty so that I could see you with my own eyes. He forbade me from ending your life that day, but the Blessed Second Ascendant has changed his mind. He wants your head, and I will be only to happy to oblige him.'

He raised the sword again, and she dodged to the right, but he had anticipated her movement, and the blade swerved, cutting through Belinda's left arm and severing it halfway between her wrist and her elbow. Belinda cried out in agony, and fell to her knees, her blood soaking the ground.

'Look at me, mother,' Atheron said. 'I want to gaze into your eyes when I take your life.'

Belinda wept.

Atheron laughed. 'Sobbing, mother? Does the prospect of your death pain you so much?'

'I weep for you, my son,' she said, 'and for what I must do.'

Her right hand gripped her sword, and she threw it at her son. The tip rammed through the visor of his helmet, and he toppled backwards, the great weight of his armour driving him to the ground. Belinda pulled the sword free, whipped off her son's helmet, and severed his head with a savage blow. She crouched by his body, and looked at his face. The face of the son she had just killed. She screamed, not from the pain rippling through her left arm, but for the sadness that had marred her life. The pain in her bloody limb seemed as nothing compared to what she had endured in a few short years. Her loyal Banner soldiers gathered round her as she surrendered to her tears, forming a wall of shields as bolts and flames tore through the air around them.

'My lady,' said a soldier; 'you are badly wounded. Should we retreat?'

Belinda said nothing. Her world was collapsing around her, and she wondered if death would be preferable to living with the knowledge that she had slain her son.

'Look!' another cried. 'The undead dragons are returning. My lady, we have to leave!'

'Then go,' said Belinda, her voice barely audible above the cacophony. 'You have done enough; more than I could have ever asked of you. Save your lives. If you must fight, then help the imperial army drive the invaders from our world. What I must do, I shall do alone.'

'No, my lady. We swore to defend you...'

'Go!' she cried. 'I release you from your vows.'

The soldiers scattered. Belinda glanced up. The bridge was empty, but the gates of Colsbury were closed to her. Crossbow bolts were flying out from the battlements, and one skittered off the ground next to her feet. She gazed at her left arm. Her self-healing powers had stopped the bleeding, but the wound was ragged and torn. She thought about placing a makeshift bandage over the stump, but what was the point? She was an Ascendant; she wasn't going to die from the loss of a single hand. She got to her feet, and noticed the swarm of black specks in the sky grow larger. Bolts whistled past her, and one deflected off her armour; but she ignored everything and stepped on to the empty bridge, her sword in her right hand.

A gaunt black dragon swooped overhead, but she knew they couldn't kill her. She raised her right hand and sent out a wide-ranging wave of flow powers. Death powers had no effect on the risen, but flow didn't care if the subject was alive or dead. The moisture in the dragon's head exploded in a crescendo of noise above her, and pieces of skull rained down onto the bridge. A second later, the headless monstrosity crashed into the lake, and Belinda was sprayed with water.

A second dragon approached, then a third and fourth, and still

Belinda walked across the bridge. A crossbow bolt glanced off the side of her neck, and her head flinched back, but she didn't stop. She ended the half-life of another undead dragon, and it smashed into the curtain wall surrounding the island, demolishing a turret. She took another step, heard a click, then too late she noticed the explosive devices that had been planted by the retreating enemy. The bridge erupted in an explosion of white light and smoke, sending tons of rubble hundreds of feet into the air. Belinda was blown back and to the side, the flesh on her face shredded, and her armour ripped to tattered shards of steel. She crashed into the waters of the lake, stunned, blinded and deafened.

For a while, Belinda drifted under the surface of the cold water, passing in and out of consciousness. She felt safe, and insulated from harm, but knew it couldn't last. To stop herself thinking of the son she had slain, she had tried to picture Austin's smile. Maybe, one day, she would kiss him. Maybe, one day, they might even have children of their own. Maybe.

She surfaced by the tall cliffs that ran by the outer wall of the Summer Palace, and used her right hand to pull herself from the water. There were no battlements on that stretch of Colsbury's perimeter, and she sat huddled on a rock for a few minutes. The sounds of battle were still coming from the direction of the portal. That was a good sign, she supposed. It meant that the invaders were still facing resistance; that they hadn't yet won. She glanced up at the cliffside, steeled herself, and began to climb.

It took thirty minutes of painful effort to ascend the cliff. Her right hand was aching, and she could feel her self-healing powers straining at their limits. Weaponless, and with her armour full of holes, she finally pulled herself up onto the ledge that ran next to the ground floor of the Summer Palace, where she lay on her back for a moment, as exhaustion gripped her. She sent out her vision powers. She knew it would alert Daimon and the Ascendants to her presence, but she no longer cared. She needed to know what was happening. Her vision scanned the palace, but she found nothing except for the bodies of Thorn's Sanang guardsmen. She turned to the Great Keep, and discovered that her powers were being rebuffed from the upper floors. She got to her feet. She didn't know if it had been Kelsey or Daimon who had blocked her vision, but it didn't matter. She could rescue one, or kill the other. She followed the ledge round to the western flank of the Summer Palace, climbed over the low wall, and dropped into the vast forecourt. She glanced around, and saw a large funeral pyre in the centre of the yard. Banner soldiers were throwing bodies on to the flames, and thin tendrils of oily black smoke were rising to pollute the air.

'There she is!' cried an armoured Ancient.

Twenty hulking warriors with battle-vision charged at her across the open flagstones of the forecourt. Belinda walked towards them. She waited until they were a few feet away, raised her right hand, and killed them all with flow powers, their bodies exploding within the stone armour each wore. The Ancients toppled to the ground, their armour intact, as blood and liquefied body tissue leaked out from every gap; and the Banner soldiers by the pyre scattered.

Edmond would know where she was. They all would. She wondered if they were scared of her. They should be.

She entered the ground floor of the Great Keep, and killed another two Ancients by the stairs. She picked up one of their swords, then powered her battle-vision and ran up the steps. She reached the upper floor, and ran into another two Ancients. Unable to use her powers any longer due to whomever was blocking them, she charged into the gods. Her sword flashed out, beheading one, then the other struck her side with a war-axe, finding a gap in her torn armour. Belinda grunted, and drove her sword into the Ancient's face. She twisted it and his nose disappeared; then she pulled it out and sliced through his neck.

Belinda staggered, then collided with a wall of the corridor, her legs weakening. Her self-healing was attempting to focus all of her energy on to the stump at the end of her left arm, and it took discipline and concentration to divert some power to the injury in her side. She waited for the wound to close, then carried on. She passed the Sextant chamber, and looked inside. It was empty, and the huge device had been deactivated. She scanned the room for the Weathervane, but saw nothing except for the pools of blood that were staining the floor.

She reached the sitting-room, and listened by the door. Silence. She frowned, moved to the side of the entrance, and swung the door open with a boot. A yard-long ballista bolt whipped past her from inside the room, embedding itself into the opposite wall. Belinda charged into the room before the device could be reloaded, then skidded to a halt. In front of her, five gagged prisoners were on their knees, their wrists and ankles bound by chains. Each prisoner had an armoured Ancient standing behind them, a sword held to their throats.

'Here you are at last, my errant bride,' said Edmond, sitting in an armchair with a glass of something in his hand. 'I thought you would never come.'

Belinda moved out of the path of the large ballista that had been placed inside the room, and edged round the wall, keeping her sword out in front of her. She glanced at the prisoners – Thorn, Kelsey, Agang, Ivy and Shella. For a moment, Belinda wondered where Sable and Daphne were, then she flicked her eyes back to Edmond. Standing behind the Second Ascendant were several of his allies. Keir was there, his face healed and his eyes wild with terror; so too was Daimon, who was leering at her; while next to the two mortal men stood Albrada and Lloyd, the Eleventh and Twelfth Ascendants.

'Did you meet Lord Atheron?' Edmond said. 'Family reunions can be so bittersweet.'

'I am the god of fire and death,' Belinda said. 'Fight me.'

Edmond laughed. 'I don't fight people, Belinda; I have others to do that for me. You should know that I have changed my mind about marrying you. After what occurred on our wedding day, I have lost all desire for you. You are not the same woman that I once knew.'

'No, I am not. I am someone better than that.'

'That is a matter of opinion. Do you wish to surrender?'

Belinda glanced at the five prisoners. 'Will you spare their lives if I do?'

'No.'

'There is nothing good in your heart, Edmond; no love, no pity, no compassion. Others serve you because they fear you, not because they respect you.'

'And you are weak,' spat Edmond, 'your mind befuddled by childish notions. Yes, you are a child, a child in a woman's body. Rebellion I could forgive, but not this... this foolishness. Pity? Compassion? Do you hear how stupid you sound?'

Belinda launched herself through the air. The Second Ascendant shrieked as Belinda decapitated two of the Ancients guarding the prisoners with a single stroke of her sword. She landed, her sword out again, and the other Ancients hesitated as they waited for orders.

'Enough,' said Edmond. 'Daimon, you know what to do.'

'Aye, my lord,' said the dream mage. His eyes glazed over for a moment. 'It's done. She's on her way.'

Another figure appeared at the door, and Belinda felt hope rise within her.

'Sable!' she cried. 'You attack the Ascendants, and I'll...' Her voice trailed off. Sable was standing still, a Fated Blade in her right hand. Her face was expressionless, but her eyes were burning with fear and pain. 'Sable?'

'Kill her,' said Daimon.

Sable raised her Fated Blade, and strode towards Belinda.

'No!' cried Belinda. 'Sable, it's me.'

Tears rolled down Sable's cheeks, but she continued to advance. It must be a trick, Belinda thought. Yes, it was one of Sable's tricks. At any moment, she would turn on the Ascendants, and the dance would begin. Together, they would kill their enemies, and they would win.

Sable sprang at Belinda, her sword flashing out, and the tip grazed the front of Belinda's armour as she stepped back. Belinda edged along the wall of the room, leading Sable away from the ballista and the prisoners.

'Please, Sable,' she said. 'Listen to me. Look into my eyes.'

Sable did so. Her gaze pierced Belinda. Belinda stared back, and what she saw broke the Third Ascendant's heart. Sable was still in there, aware of what was happening, but she was no longer in control of her actions.

'No,' Belinda sobbed. 'Don't do this, Sable; don't make me fight you again.'

Sable seemed to pause, and Daimon raised his arm, his eyes clouding over. Sable sprang back into life, and unleashed a whirlwind attack on Belinda, the Fated Blade whistling through the air. Belinda swerved and dodged, unwilling to cut her friend down. She had been reluctant to fight Sable in Yoneath, and that had been at a time when she had loathed the Holdfast woman. How could she fight her now that she loved her as a friend? At that moment, Belinda understood what the outcome would be. There would be no escape, no redemption, and no victory. If she would not kill her friend, then she would die. Sable pushed Belinda back, her sword moving so fast that Belinda had to strain every ounce of her battle-vision to keep her head on her shoulders. She felt her self-healing start to flag, and the stump at the end of her left arm began to bleed again. She parried a blow with her own sword, but the Fated Blade sliced straight through the steel. Sable kicked her in the stomach, and Belinda slammed against a wall; then Sable rammed her sword into Belinda's chest, and dragged it down, ripping the black blade through the Third Ascendant's flesh. Belinda coughed up blood, and sank to her knees.

Belinda's sight began to blur, and she heard Kelsey cry out, but it seemed to be coming from far away. More blood came up from Belinda's mouth, and she slumped back against the wall, as Sable raised the Fated Blade.

Belinda's looked into her friend's eyes for the last time, then Sable's arm swung the Fated Blade.

EPILOGUE

Colsbury Castle, Republic of the Holdings – 25th Day, First Third Winter 534

Kelsey screamed as Belinda's headless body slid to the floor. Next to her, Agang was weeping uncontrollably, and Shella and Ivy were sobbing through their gags. Only Thorn was quiet, her features closed, and her eyes never leaving Sable.

'So ends the Third Ascendant,' said Edmond, rising from his armchair. He walked over to where Belinda's body lay, and glanced down. 'Such a terrible tragedy. Daimon, remove your puppet from my presence; she repulses me.'

'Sable,' said Daimon; 'return to your room.'

Sable sheathed the Fated Blade, then she turned from the scene of her bloody handiwork and strode from the sitting room without a word. Kelsey bit down on her gag, but it was immovable. She wanted to unleash her anger upon the Second Ascendant; no, she wanted to kill him. Kelsey had never taken another's life; but at that moment, she would have happily plunged a knife into Edmond's heart.

The Second Ascendant turned away from Belinda, and gestured to one of the three Ancients guarding the prisoners.

'Get Belinda's body out of here,' Edmond said, 'and remove the two

Ancients that she killed. Throw their corpses on to the pyres in the castle forecourt.'

The Ancient bowed, then walked over to Belinda and crouched down. He lifted the Third Ascendant's head, then dragged her body from the room by an ankle, leaving a smear of blood across the carpet.

The Second Ascendant turned back to the prisoners. 'No tears, Thorn?'

The Empress did not respond.

Edmond pulled Thorn's gag from her mouth. 'Speak, usurper.'

The Empress kept her face serene, and turned away from him.

Edmond shrugged, then he removed Kelsey's gag. She spat on him.

'The Holdfasts are animals,' the Second Ascendant said, as he wiped the spittle from his stone breastplate. 'Uncouth and vulgar.'

The air shimmered in the middle of the room next to the ballista, and two figures appeared. One was holding a Quadrant, while the other was a massive warrior in full battle armour, who was wielding a fearsome weapon with three greenhides claws protruding from its end.

'Kill them, brother!' Kelsey screamed. 'Kill them all!'

Corthie tore into the Ancients standing next to the prisoners, swinging the Clawhammer with both hands, the talons ripping through their armour and tearing the two gods to pieces. Edmond stepped behind Daimon and the other Ascendants, while Keir stared at the sight of Corthie and his Clawhammer. Lloyd withdrew a Quadrant and vanished, then he re-appeared a moment later with twenty more armoured Ancients.

'Where are the others?' Corthie yelled.

'They're not here, brother,' Kelsey shouted. 'Naxor; now!'

Naxor slid his fingers over the surface of the device, as the massed Ancients in the room charged. The air shimmered again, and Kelsey found herself on a rugged hillside, with rain falling from the dark clouds above. The other four prisoners were kneeling on the wet grass next to her, their shackles weighing them down.

Corthie stepped behind his sister and slashed through the steel links with the Clawhammer's talons. Kelsey jumped to her feet. She hugged Corthie, then turned and slapped Naxor across the face.

'Ow!' he cried. 'Is that what I get for rescuing you all?'

'You bastard!' Kelsey yelled. 'That was for whacking me on the head with a damn wine bottle. If you hadn't stolen my Quadrant in the first place, then... then...' She started to weep, falling back to her knees on the sodden grass as the rain cascaded down her face.

Corthie stared at her, then he went from prisoner to prisoner, freeing them from the shackles. Thorn stood as her chains fell away, her eyes grim and unyielding. As soon as Agang was released, the old soul-witch sat down on the wet grass, his head in his hands. Shella tried to comfort him, but the Sanang man was lost in grief.

'Are you all well?' said Corthie, as he gazed at them. 'Where's my mother, and where are Sable and Belinda? And Cardova, and the others? Do you know? Do we need to go back for any of them?'

No one answered him.

Corthie removed his helmet and slung the Clawhammer over his shoulder. He looked as though he wanted to ask more questions, but said nothing, his eyes narrow.

'To be frank,' Naxor said, 'I was expecting a little more gratitude. That was a daring rescue mission, and no one has even given me the courtesy of a quick "thank you". Sometimes, I wonder why I bother.'

'Shut up, Naxor,' said Corthie. 'If I hadn't caught you sneaking around the farm trying to steal the salve you hid, you wouldn't have rescued them.'

'A mere technicality,' said the demigod.

Shella looked up from where she was sitting with an arm over Agang's broad shoulders. 'Why did you return to Kell?'

'I had been flitting about from place to place,' said Naxor, 'trying to discern where upon this world I could live unmolested. I had settled on the Holdings, but while I was taking a look around, I happened to witness the arrival of an exceedingly large number of gods from Implacatus. I rushed back to Clackenbaird to retrieve my, uh, hidden supply of salve; but I was ambushed by Corthie.'

Corthie nodded. 'He told me what was happening, and I forced him to help.'

'Forced?' said Naxor. 'Come now; I was only too delighted to offer my assistance. Can we go back to Corthie's original question? If anyone here happens to know the locations of others we need to save from the clutches of the Ascendants, then speak up. Daphne Holdfast, for example?'

Thorn rubbed her wrists, then she turned away to stare out at the view of the green hills, as the rain washed down her face.

'Are we in Kell?' said Shella.

'Aye,' said Corthie. 'The farmhouse is at the top of the hill behind us. Will someone please tell me what is happening? Did we interrupt some clever plan that you had concocted to escape? Have we ruined things?'

'No,' said Kelsey. 'You saved us. Thank you.'

'At last,' Naxor said.

'Shut up, Naxor,' Kelsey cried. 'Just shut up. Don't you get it? Belinda is dead.'

Corthie's shoulders sagged. 'What?'

Kelsey tried to stop crying, but her heart was wracked with despair.

'You saved us, brother,' she said, 'and I'm grateful; but you were ten minutes too late.'

'Sable did it,' said Shella. 'She killed Belinda.'

'No,' said Corthie. 'Sable and Belinda had become friends.'

'Sable is under Daimon's control, Corthie,' Kelsey sobbed. 'It wasn't her fault. But, aye; she did it, right in front of us.'

Corthie fell to his knees next to his sister and wept, his hands covering his face. Thorn walked over to them. She placed one hand on Corthie's shoulder, and the other on Kelsey's.

'You must try to remain strong,' the Empress said. 'If we despair, we are finished.'

'We've just lost Belinda,' said Kelsey; 'let us weep.'

'I cannot allow myself to weep,' said Thorn; 'for if I did, my tears would never cease. The full might of Implacatus has invaded our world, and our armies are scattered and defeated. It would be wise to assume that no one who was in Colsbury when the Ascendants arrived still lives.'

A stunned silence fell over the figures huddling on the windswept hillside, as the cold rain continued to fall.

'What about Karalyn?' said Naxor.

'Edmond took the Weathervane out of the Sextant,' said Thorn. 'Karalyn is stranded in the City of Salve.'

'We must keep Kelsey close,' said the demigod. 'With her blocking powers, the Ascendants would never find us. We would be safe; we can hide.'

'Hide?' said Thorn, her eyes hardening. 'What makes you think I wish to hide?'

Naxor shivered. 'Then, your Majesty, what do you intend to do?'

Thorn raised her chin, as the rain soaked her blue dress. 'I intend to fight.'

AUTHOR'S NOTES
JANUARY 2023

Thank you for reading Holdfast Imperium – just one more book to go to complete the Magelands arc!

Drafting Holdfast Imperium was straightforward, as I knew in advance the story I wished to tell; editing it, however, was a long, hard struggle – perhaps one of the toughest tasks I have undertaken throughout the entire series. I found myself compelled to come back to the manuscript again and again, unable to leave it alone. The final few chapters in particular caused me considerable trouble. They were revised and rewritten several times, not so much to change the story, but to ensure that I delivered the best version I was capable of writing. It was painful, like picking at an open wound, but I owed it to Belinda.

RECEIVE A FREE MAGELANDS ETERNAL SIEGE BOOK

Building a relationship with my readers is very important to me.

Join my newsletter for information on new books and deals and you will also receive a Magelands Eternal Siege prequel novella that is currently EXCLUSIVE to my Reader's Group for FREE.

www.ChristopherMitchellBooks.com/join

ABOUT THE AUTHOR

Christopher Mitchell is the author of the Magelands epic fantasy series.

For more information:
www.christophermitchellbooks.com
info@christophermitchellbooks.com